Sincerely, Mildred

Ashley Hayden

To Brian—
Thanks for the support
and feedback! I'm glad
you enjoyed it!

Ashley Hayden

poppy
+
duncan

Published by Poppy + Duncan Publishing, an imprint of CreateSpace.
4900 LaCross Road, North Charleston, South Carolina 29406, USA

CreateSpace trade paperback ISBN: 978-1-983-90071-6
Subjects: LCSH: Pacific Northwest—Fiction. | Women cannery workers—Fiction.
Aviation, recreational—Fiction. | Great Depression, 1929—Fiction.
Leukemia in children—Fiction. | Prohibition—Fiction. | Coming of age—Fiction.

PRINTED IN THE UNITED STATES OF AMERICA

To my mother, Michelle,
the novel you never got to read
that was written especially for you...

ACKNOWLEDGEMENTS

First of all, I have to thank my husband, Ben, for pushing me to pick up *Sincerely, Mildred* after I let it sit for over six years. I had been writing this book for my mother and when she suddenly passed away in 2010, I couldn't continue. My husband didn't want me to stop and after much crying on my part, I realized he was absolutely right. I had to write the book for her. It took only eighteen months to finish but without his support, I don't know if you'd be reading this right now. I love you, Ben.

I'd like to thank my beta readers: Jim Cram, Josh Dankovchik, Dina Kalmbach, Kristen Karns, Kirsten Lane, Katy Pietsch, Melissa Potts, Renee Reed, Kim Rinard, Mari Ripp, Alexia Rostow, Margaret Scott, Kathi St. Pierre and Heather Whitlock.

Thank you to Hannah Taylor-Anderson for granting me the use of the beautiful cover art. The photo is actually Hannah modeling one of the many beautiful vintage dresses she sews, which are available on her Etsy shop, Let's Backtrack.

CHAPTER ONE

DIAMONDS, LOTS AND LOTS of diamonds. They dangle from my ears like clusters of stars, glistening around my neck and wrist. All eyes are on me as I perch at the bar in a stunning dress sipping my champagne and trying not to get my lipstick on the glass. While the band warms up, a handsome gentleman winks at me and I get the feeling he may want to dance...

It was early in the month of April 1932 and Mildred Anne Westrick, nineteen-years-old and unmarried, loved to picture herself dancing in clubs she'd probably never visit, wearing expensive jewelry she'd definitely never own. The glitz of her daydreams made her reality that much more disgusting. For Mildred, reality involved gutting salmon and hosing blood down the drain at Pacific Bounty Cannery in Bresford.

Bresford was a sleepy town nestled along the Columbia

River in Washington State, the sort of town that is cozy and familiar, where the townsfolk are like family and knew almost everything there was to know about everyone else. Mildred liked the townsfolk well enough, but she loved the nature surrounding Bresford most. One of her favorite sounds was the whistle of a train making its way to Ridgefield or Kalama on tracks that paralleled the river. There was something about the lonesome whistle that resonated within her.

As much as she loved the riverside town she was born and raised in, some days she yearned to escape without telling anyone, no chance of being tracked down. She'd dream about packing a bag and climbing into a boxcar, just to see where she would end up. Perhaps she'd begin a new life in Canada or Oregon. It didn't matter, just as long as nobody knew her. Whenever she had this particular fantasy, it remained just that, a shy girl's dream.

When she wasn't on hosing duty at the cannery, Mildred would stand at the conveyor belt and slit fish bellies for hours or pull guts until her fingers cramped. By the end of the day, her knuckles were pink and swollen. She would've given anything to be one of the pretty girls working the front counter at Dominic's or even wearing a silly hat and serving root beer floats at Dream Fountain. Hattie Kilpatrick, the one who happily called herself Mildred's best friend, happened to be gifted with captivating eyes that turned upward and blonde hair that the movie stars used peroxide to get. It wasn't a surprise that she found work behind the perfume and glove counters at Dominic's. Not Mildred Westrick. Awkward girls like Mildred Westrick didn't work the counters or turn heads in town. They worked in the sorting room at the post office or at Pacific Bounty Cannery.

"Mildred, don't forget the corners! Stop being lazy and hose them down!" The manager of the cannery, Albert Murray, liked to pretend he owned the place. He analyzed every move from over the railing, catching mistakes the second they were made. Every morning, piles of fish came in for processing with Albert barking intermittently before disappearing into his office.

"Sorry!" With her thickly gloved hand, Mildred grabbed the swivel hose attached to the ceiling and pointed the spray at the glossy fish intestines, pushing them back into a pile to go into the guts bin later. This was followed by more endless hosing. Once more, she slipped into her daydream in an attempt to shut out the cannery around her. The room turned into the club and the assortment of noises became the jazz and voices of patrons.

The comb in my waved hair has gobs of diamonds and emeralds on it. Other girls would ask where I found my dress and we'd become friends and smoke cigarettes. The bartender notices that my flute is almost empty, so I say...

"I'll have more champagne, please." With the rushing water from the hose, nobody could hear Mildred. In her mind, she was wearing a green velvet dress with a droopy back that revealed her shoulder blades and came daringly close to her bottom. Little did she care that she was actually wearing brown waders with an ugly coat and a thick knit cap.

The man who winked at me is in an expensive tuxedo. He walks closer and closer through a cloud of cigarette smoke. When he is right next to me, he asks me to dance, but not just any dance. He wants to do the Charleston! In no time, he is impressed with my mastery of the steps and we fall in love on the dance floor...

"Stop! Damn it, Mildred! Stop, stop, *stop!*"

Mildred opened her eyes and fumbled to shut off the hose. Three people working along the conveyor belt glared at her, their coats dripping with water. They weren't as upset about their coats as they were about the salmon on the floor. The man who yelled at her was Fred, an old veteran at the job. He shook his head and grabbed the wayward fish by their tails. Fred dipped their shiny bodies in a bucket filled with solution meant to kill any contaminants. Once they were done soaking, he tossed them back on the belt. The only sympathy she got was from Winnie, who gave her a tiny wink, as if she knew about the Charleston that took over Mildred's body.

Albert appeared from his office upstairs. "Mildred, would you come up here, please?" A familiar feeling came to her. It didn't happen often to her as a child, but the times she had to be disciplined by the headmistress in front of the classroom, she felt low and worthless for the rest of the day. She hated the staring eyes glued to the back of her head and hearing her classmates whisper about her. Sighing, she scraped fish scales off the toe of her boot and took her time getting upstairs. While everything else in the building smelled of old fish blood and the ocean, Albert's office smelled like vanilla tobacco with a hint of Palmolive shaving cream. Mildred wasn't a fan of either smell, but she was pleasantly reminded of her grandfather. Her rain gear squeaked as she sat in a chair with a cracked leather seat.

Before Albert could speak, he smoothed his mustache out of habit. "Now, Mildred, you seem to keep making these mistakes that otherwise shouldn't happen. Last week, you hit Fred in the back of the head with the sweeper and two weeks ago, you bruised your rump after you slipped. You tell me the same story each time, but it is starting to sound ridiculous. What is it this time that caused you to spray everyone down the line?"

It *was* starting to sound ridiculous, even to Mildred, but Albert would never understand why she made those stupid mistakes. He was content managing Pacific Bounty Cannery and didn't need to create another world in his head to escape.

"Mr. Murray, I was daydreaming and I...well, I was doing the...the Charleston."

His frown grew under his mustache. "The Charleston, Miss Westrick? You're not a flapper or a showgirl, the last time I checked. Do your job instead of dancing around. You're lucky to have a job at all and that's pointing out the obvious. If you want to get paid, get yourself downstairs and finish cleaning up the floor. Next time, I won't be this nice. I can bring in someone who will hose down equipment and not their coworkers. You understand?"

"Yes, Mr. Murray." Mildred scurried out of his office and resumed hosing the fish guts into a pile for scooping. She was sorry for making the mistakes, but she wasn't sorry for dreaming. When she smacked Fred in the head with the sweeper, she'd just been asked by a handsome stranger to do a little swing dance...

JUST BEFORE DINNERTIME, Mildred raced into the driveway on her bicycle. Her father's baby blue Ford coupe was already home, which normally didn't show up until seven in the evening. Next to it was her stepmother's car, a 1931 Ford Model A convertible roadster. Darnella had it enrobed in a coat of custom emerald paint and inside was creamy, white leather interior that still smelled new. It smelled new because it *was* new. Every time Mildred saw Darnella's flashy car, she gritted her teeth.

Mom never begged Dad for a new car. She was happy driving around the old truck she shared with him, Mildred said bitterly in her head. Her stepmother was the queen of Juniper Street and she was only in the family because Mildred's mother was dead. Not only did Darnella come swooping in without even letting Mrs. Grace Westrick be mourned properly, she dragged along her daughter, Opal. At the time, Opal was just a baby, but now she was a spoiled six-year-old.

"Momma, Mildred parked her bike on the *graaaaass!*" Opal screeched from the front porch.

Darnella rushed to the door dressed as if she was going to a fancy club but wore an apron without any stains. "Mildred, move your bicycle! How many times must I ask you not to do that? I take pride in keeping a beautiful lawn and I won't let tire marks ruin it. Now get washed up for dinner."

Mildred barely had a chance to breathe in the time it took between being tattled on and scolded. With a grumble, she moved her bike and rested it against the garage. This was her life until she could find a way out. At nineteen, she should've been married by now, possibly even pregnant. It was obvious neither would be happening anytime soon.

On the living room rug, Opal surrounded herself with her frilly dolls and stuffed animals. Mildred's father, Harvey, was reading a book in his relaxing chair. She envisioned her mother sitting in the chair opposite the side table, sketching on a large pad of paper, something that Mildred seemed to inherit from her. Grace would sketch Harvey, landscapes of Mount Saint Helens from postcards, Mildred napping, or anything that caught her eye. Over the years, her collection of sketch pads grew to over three dozen. At five, Mildred also began drawing and filled up sketch pads of her own.

"How was work, Dad?" Harvey put his book on his lap and rubbed his tired face. While Mildred knew that her father was generally considered a handsome man, she couldn't help but notice that he looked more weary than handsome these days. Or rather, these last five years. His wavy hair, once glossy and completely dark, now boasted streaks of gray and creases dashed his brow. Down at Farnsworth Farm & Feed, her father managed the store seven days a week, working long hours during the spring and summer to accommodate local farmers. When Grace was still alive, Harvey was a skilled mechanic at the shop downtown and often came home covered in grease that took several rounds of hard scrubbing to remove, but his cuticles and fingernails were permanently stained. However, as soon as he remarried, Mildred watched as Mrs. Darnella Riley-Westrick pushed her father into applying for the manager's position at the feed store and shortly after that, he stopped bringing sputtering engines back to life.

Harvey sighed deeply. "Work was good and it's only going to get busier with farmers getting their orders in. I can't complain, especially in this economy. I'm grateful that we get to have food on the table." By that, Mildred felt he truly meant, *I'm killing myself to keep Darnella happy.*

"Daddy Harvey, look at this! My bear is pouring tea!" Opal cried. "They need cookies!" She ran into the kitchen to pester her mother for some. As soon as Opal left the room, Mildred noticed something that happened every time his new wife and her child weren't around. His face relaxed and he spoke freely. Quiet were his words, but still candid.

"I'm glad you were never like Opal," Harvey whispered as he read. "Darnella lets her do whatever she wants, but your mother, she disciplined you and that's why you turned out so well."

Mildred smiled. "Thank you, Dad. You helped with that, too, you know." She picked up one of the dolls and looked at its finely painted face, its empty eyes looking as forlorn as she felt inside. She never had dolls this beautiful.

"*Those are my dolls!*" Opal had a handful of cookies and dropped them all over the rug to swipe her toy out of Mildred's grasp. If Mildred had done this as a child, her father would've yanked her by the arm and swatted her bottom at least a dozen times. He didn't even flinch. Instead, he calmly turned to the next page in his book.

"I was just looking at it, Opal. You don't need to have a fit." She sucked on her throbbing pinky that had gotten caught in the crook of the doll's armpit.

"Mildred, don't get after her," her father said, a hint of sharpness in his voice.

She was flabbergasted. "Didn't you just say…"

"It's time for my famous meatloaf!" Darnella announced from the kitchen. Harvey put on his fake smile just in time for Darnella to see. He set his book down and patted Opal's back.

"Hey, kiddo, let's go eat, huh? It smells delicious!" Mildred had a slight urge to scoff. Not only was his smile entirely artificial, but his behavior was over the top. Opal scurried into the dining room with Harvey play-chasing after her. Mildred took that moment to snatch the fine porcelain doll and tucked it into her sweater.

There was nothing famous about the meatloaf except that it was dense and flavored with copious amounts of salt. Nothing tasted like her mother's food, not that she expected anyone to even come near replicating her mother's wonderful recipes. For one, Grace Westrick incorporated vegetables into every dinner from her modest garden. Darnella despised vegetables, so nothing green, orange or red ever graced their plates. The only exception was potatoes. They were the perennial favorite served mashed, scalloped and baked. The garden had since been filled in and turned into a patio for Darnella's parties, the dirt suffocated by unfeeling concrete and topped with yard furniture.

Darnella swallowed her mouthful and said, "I got a new dress today from Dominic's. He has such an eye for style and I couldn't say no to him when he said it was a limited run from France."

"Another imported dress, my darling? I thought you were only going to get one every month. This is the third one in two weeks." With Grace, Harvey would've never needed to have this conversation.

Her stepmother made an odd, guilty sound. "Well, yes, but you surely don't expect me to wear the same outfits like some pauper, do you? What would people say?"

"Fine," he sighed. "Mildred, are you sure you're putting all of your wages into the family pot?"

This wasn't the first time Mildred heard her father ask this question. It was fairly common for working family members to throw their money together to buy items like groceries, pay for utilities, practical things. In the Westrick household, Darnella was given a stipend to spend on cosmetics and outfits. If it came between paying the milkman and getting a new tube of lipstick, she was certain that Darnella would choose the lipstick.

"Yes, I've been contributing ever since I started earning," Mildred answered. Tears welled up in her eyes at being accused of not sharing her wages, of being dishonest.

"You know, Mildred, if you curled your hair a bit and borrowed some of my lipstick, you would be surprised who would notice you, even at that cannery. It wouldn't hurt you to spruce up once in a while. All of the other girls do it and they have beaus or are in the middle of planning their wedding. It might be high time that you think about doing the same." Darnella nodded as if turning heads and getting engaged could be so simple.

That was all it took. Mildred bubbled over beyond the point of stopping herself and the pounding in her head drowned out the soft voice of her mother's cautioning.

"Is that how you caught my father, with just a little lipstick and fancy hair?" She set her fork down and looked at her father, who appeared even more exhausted than normal under the electric lights. "Was that the trick? If I recall, Mom never wore makeup and you loved her for it. She never complained that we didn't have lots of money and she certainly never begged for new dresses!"

Stunned, Darnella let her mouth hang open. "I did not catch your father that way! What has gotten into you?"

"You're right, Darnella, my mistake. You invited yourself in one day from selling hats door-to-door because your husband was unfaithful and you needed somebody new. Then you tell your story to my widowed father and then suddenly I have a new mother a month later!"

Darnella narrowed her eyes and raised her thin brows. "It was not a month! We got married *two* months later. There is a difference. And I don't beg for dresses; I deserve them."

Harvey didn't expect his meek daughter to speak in such a manner, had never seen fire in her eyes like this before. He cleared his throat and said calmly, "Stop talking, Mildred. You're being ridiculous."

Opal swallowed her mouthful of mashed potatoes and sneered, "Yeah!"

By now, a scarlet flush glowed from Mildred's cheeks. "What do you mean by that, Dad? Don't you understand how I feel, how this looks?"

He took a few purposeful moments before speaking. "It's been five years and people change. I married Darnella and that's enough on the subject. I think it's about time you change and grew up."

The words, albeit spoken gently, forced Mildred to sit back in her chair. She felt drained from the outburst, too. Softly, she said, "You replaced Mom so fast and I was still a child. I just miss her and I don't think that will ever change." Her eyes searched her father's face for some shred of the man she remembered, as the happy man who loved Grace more than life.

"I'm done with this discussion." Just like that, Harvey resumed eating the salty meatloaf and without another word, Mildred made her exit from the table.

In her room upstairs towards the back of the house, Mildred found comfort in her childhood bedding and cried into her pillow. She couldn't count how many times her pillow caught her tears over the years: for not getting a part in the school play, for not being invited to a party, for wishing her mother was alive.

Something finger-like poked her in the ribs. Mildred rolled over and fished out the elegant doll from her sweater pocket. It was a shame that something so nice should belong to such a horrible child. Mildred would've been over the moon had she received a doll like this as a girl. Her dolls, however, were made by her mother out of flour sack towels, buttons and a bit of leftover yarn sewn into the crown for hair. The finishing touch was mother's red nail polish to paint the doll's flower bud of a pout. Those rough dolls meant more to her than a porcelain doll ever would have. Mildred could never get her childhood playmates back, though. While Harvey's grief was still fresh, he donated everything that reminded him of Grace the week after she passed: aprons that her mother practically lived in, cookbooks with Grace's beautiful handwriting in the margins with life-changing recipe alterations, her everyday jewelry and special occasion hats. What Mildred wanted most was her mother's copy of *The Complete Home*, gifted to Grace when she was Mildred's age. But it all went to charity. The only thing that Mildred was able to save was a stack of Grace's sketchbooks.

Rage curdled inside her, the unfairness in her life fueling her as she raised the doll above her head and poised to smash it against the floor. But a little voice inside told her it wouldn't be right. She wondered if it was her conscious or a whisper from Grace. Reluctantly, Mildred set the doll on the bed.

"Sorry," she whispered, as if the doll could hear her. Mildred realized that none of what happened over the last five years was Opal's fault, even if she was annoying and spoiled.

She moved to sit at her vanity mirror and admired how much she looked like her mother. While admittedly quite plain, she had gentle brown eyes with long lashes that made her look shy. Somewhat wavy hair of the same color came to her shoulders. She could never do anything with her hair like her best friend Hattie could. Fancy curls, creams, sprays and jeweled pins were outside of Mildred's basic styling skills. The most she could manage was a bobby pin on either side at her temples to hold back a little bit of her hair. Her clothing choices even mimicked Grace's with a small array of practical sweaters, reserved blouses and skirts, and T-strap shoes in black and brown. Perhaps that was why Darnella seemed like a great option for a new spouse in her father's eyes. He wanted a vain peacock to waddle around his home, to make him look better somehow.

"She's a peacock on the outside, with the soul of a cranky, old hen on the inside," Mildred mumbled. She was happy being a sparrow, but even little, brown sparrows got lonely.

THE NEXT MORNING, MILDRED gathered up enough nerve to go to the breakfast table. She wasn't needed at work for another hour and since her routine required nothing more than a splash of water on her face and a quick brush through her hair, she had plenty of time to enjoy whatever breakfast there happened to be. Luckily, her father had already left to open the feed store and she wouldn't have to endure watching him kiss Darnella or Opal goodbye.

At the table, Darnella drank coffee and read her Redbook magazine. *The Bresford Daily* didn't interest her, even though she was president of the Bresford Ladies' Aid Society and should've cared more. The only time she whipped open a newspaper was when she knew her name or photo would be in it. She'd clip out the article and save it as a trophy of sorts. She was still in her loud Japanese silk robe that she had ordered special from Dominic's. The robe alone required an extra shift from Mildred to add enough money to the family pot to be able to afford it. Her brown bob was set with rows of candy pink curlers and her bare face would soon be covered with beige makeup, mascara and a healthy swipe of lipstick. She would then apply some unnatural color on her eyelids and pencil in her thin eyebrows to finish up the look. This was Darnella's everyday routine, even if she didn't have plans to see other people.

"There is no shame in making yourself up," Darnella said every now and then as if to excuse the amount of cosmetics she wore. Mildred knew that her mother would've mistaken Darnella for a harlot upon first sight.

"Breakfast is on the counter," her stepmother said coolly without looking up from her magazine. Breakfast consisted of toast, orange marmalade and coffee. Not that anything was essentially wrong with a good slab of bread with some sweet marmalade, but Mildred desperately wanted some of her mother's baking powder biscuits with fresh sausage gravy and piping hot eggs with runny yolks. The toast paled in comparison, but it was better than nothing at all. Mildred slathered a bit of marmalade onto her toast and poured a mug of coffee with cream.

Hoping to smooth over last night's outburst, she asked, "What are your plans for the day, Darnella?"

As if she was ready for the question, Darnella bounced in her seat and said, "Oh, let's see. I'm getting the ladies together to discuss upcoming events we'd like to help out with this summer and your father wants to take us out to dinner tonight at The Orchard!"

The Orchard was where families went when they had a little extra cash to play with, just down the highway about ten miles in Ridgefield. Mildred had only been to The Orchard once. She was twelve at the time. Her father had been paid well for all of the repairs he made that week at the shop and he wanted to treat his wife and daughter. Her memories of The Orchard were akin to a palace, with chairs painted gold, a cold marble floor, and the tables set with thick napkins folded into tents. Certain things she remembered and didn't know why, but she smiled at the memory of her mother's face lighting up over the most beautiful Cornish hen she'd ever seen, perfectly roasted and dressed. Mildred's favorite dish there wasn't exotic, but the spaghetti with fat, tender meatballs was the best. Her mouth started watering at the thought.

"What time do I need to be home? Maybe you could help me curl my hair and pick my outfit?" Mildred offered as an olive branch.

Darnella's face dropped. "I guess your father didn't tell you?"

Mildred felt her hope disintegrate like an old soap bubble. The first time she heard that line a year ago, it went like this: "Your father didn't tell you? He wanted to take me and Opal whale watching at the coast. Little Opal would love to see whales. He knew you'd understand since you've already done it before." Mildred went whale watching with her parents when she was two. Nobody remembers anything from when they were two-years-old.

"No, he hasn't talked to me about anything. Am I not included?"

"Well, he figured you'd be working late at the cannery, so he made four o'clock reservations for just the three of us. You can go to The Orchard with us next time. Alright, I must finish myself and get ready for the girls!"

The Bresford Ladies' Aid Society, including Vidalia York, usually met at the Westrick house on Friday afternoons and Darnella never wasted a chance to put on her upper-class act. Mildred would've bet good money that Darnella wanted something to brag about to the ladies *and* make reservations early enough to exclude her stepdaughter.

Outwardly, Mildred appeared to be her normal, quiet self, but deep down, she felt like a volcano that had been awakened from a long sleep, the rumblings of fury stirring her closer to eruption. The idea she entertained of wanting to leave the house, including the people inside it, formed roots stronger than ever.

I can't live like this anymore, she told herself. And she meant it. Despite the swirling frenzy inside her, she did her best to smile and be pleasant.

"So, you know where the food is to make yourself some dinner." Darnella paused by the refrigerator and said, as if it were an epiphany, "Won't it be nice having the whole house to yourself?"

Mildred nodded dumbly. As her stepmother floated off to finish painting her face, Mildred grabbed *The Bresford Daily* and opened it up randomly, something to take her focus off the urge to scream. When it came to newspapers, she had never been dedicated to one section or another, just read whatever her eyes found first. She glanced at the sports that bored her, a few twists on making preserves, and an article about a three-year-old girl in Lewis County that survived after her mother's car rolled over her. On the next page, the title of the article announced something entirely different.

Pilot Marty Townsend to come to Bresford for donations!

Her brown eyes glued themselves to the black and white photo of the striking pilot. Even with the fuzzy quality of the newsprint picture, Marty Townsend's soft eyes, strong smile and broad shoulders were enough to make her breathing quicken and heart thump harder. In fact, it hasn't beaten that hard since...

It's never beaten like this, she realized. The way it acted now could've been mistaken as heart trouble. It skipped beats and pleasantly ached. Anxiously, she scanned over the article for more information.

> *Martin 'Marty' Townsend is on a mission to bring donations from around Washington State and deliver them to the needy currently living in the Elliott Bay shantytown. While the Hooverville is seen as a blight to Seattle, Townsend sees it differently.*
>
> *"I happen to know a few people who needed to relocate to the [Elliott Bay] Hooverville. While they are struggling to make ends meet, I decided that I can help by relying on the good people in this state to make life a little easier for them. My friends aren't criminals, just people down on their luck. They can use those extra flannel shirts, books or hats lying around. I'm honored to do this for them."*

"When are you coming to Bresford? That's what I want to know," Mildred muttered. She took another long sip of coffee. It was already stone cold but she didn't care.

> *"Townsend told* The Bresford Daily *that he is flying to Bresford on Saturday, May 7th. Citizen of the Year, Mr. Dominic York, will lead the town in greeting Townsend at the Manchester Fairgrounds at noon. FREE DONUTS AND COFFEE PROVIDED. Details on where to bring your donations will be announced in a later edition."*

May seventh. That meant Marty Townsend would be coming to Bresford in exactly a month. Cobwebs in the corner of her soul suddenly loosened up their steel grip and blew away. A warming, silky light filled that once-empty corner, a light that she wanted to feel more of.

Mildred took one more bite of toast and went in search of her stationery.

CHAPTER TWO

Mildred wasn't expected at Pacific Bounty Cannery for another twenty minutes. This gave her enough time to build up the nerve to fashion her first letter. She smoothed her hair down before she read it aloud, as if her intended audience could see her.

> *Dear Marty Townsend,*
>
> *You probably get letters from other people all the time, but I wanted to tell you that I'm genuinely impressed by your selflessness. Helping the people in the shantytown is an honorable undertaking. If I am able to get time off from work, I'd love to assist you with gathering donations. I wish more*

people were as generous as you and perhaps this would be a better world.

Again, I think what you're doing is a wonderful act of giving and I hope we can meet someday so I that I may thank you in person.

Sincerely,
Mildred Westrick

Skimming over it once more, Mildred approved of her succinct letter and delicately folded it to fit into one of the pale pink envelopes she had in her stationery box. With her best penmanship, she wrote his address and affixed a two cent Lake Placid skier stamp in the corner. The second she looked at the complete envelope, Mildred couldn't even imagine mailing it.

"He'll think I'm crazy!" With a flick of her wrist, the letter floated to rest on tissues and torn hosiery in the flowery trash bin. For a few seconds, she stared at the letter, the waste of paper and a stamp. But it radiated something, telling her it didn't belong in the bin. She retrieved the letter and stuck it in her only hatbox on the highest shelf in the closet, then pulled on her stocking cap and left for work.

FRANK WAS THE FIRST to greet Mildred at the cannery, usually a sign she took as bad luck, especially if he chose to be a grumpy old man that day.

"Hey, kiddo! Any new dance moves planned for today? Make sure you hit someone *else* in the head this time!" His laugh bounced off the clean equipment like a tinny radio program. She giggled along but didn't think it was as funny as he thought. Gladys, one of the sweet older ladies at the cannery, tapped Mildred's shoulder.

"You're on belly slitting duty with me today!" Gladys found a disturbing joy in processing dead fish. If only Mildred could be as excited as Gladys.

"That's great!" Mildred did her best to fake enthusiasm. At least she could talk to Gladys if she wanted to.

"Here we go! Fish time, folks!" Albert hollered the same thing every morning, sounding more like a football coach than a cannery manager. He activated the conveyor belt and men began pouring fish onto it from big tubs brought in by the first boat. Gladys, Mildred and Winnie each grabbed a salmon and expertly cut a straight line from the anus to the head. Scarlet blood oozed out of the incision and bloodied the belt until it looked like a massacre just took place. Mildred couldn't watch when she first started working at the cannery last year. Over time, watching Frank and the others rip out the sloppy guts while preserving the egg sacs and seeing more blood than she ever imagined, the gore became acceptable. It was more the sound of it than the sight that got Mildred feeling woozy. Frank would tug on the guts until they gave, making a wet, snapping sound that made her stomach churn. It didn't help that everything at the cannery was constantly damp, stinky and loud. Every minute was punctuated by the *chop, chop, chop* from the fish guillotine. Buckets of fish heads and tails collected faster than could be emptied, often leading to an avalanche of silvery parts. Mildred had to clean it up most of the time.

After ten minutes into the day, Mildred slit fish bellies robotically, enough to dream herself away from the bloody mess before her. Her dreams didn't change and found herself back at the smoky club from yesterday.

I'm at the bar, dripping in diamonds. My hair is sleek and curled just so. Bessie Smith is crooning at the piano, wearing one of her feather boas. Her song makes my champagne taste even better and then I see...

"Marty," she said, just to hear his name leave her lips. She recalled his face from the paper, his tender eyes and good hair. If she guessed his age, she'd say he was no older than twenty-five.

Marty. His hair is also sleek, he's laughing with some pals. I'm drinking my champagne and minding my own business, enjoying Bessie's voice. I look up from my glass and Marty isn't with his friends anymore. He isn't at the bar getting another drink or going to Bessie to request a song. Then I feel a tap on my shoulder. I knew it would be him. Up close, his eyelashes are longer than mine. He puts out his hand to me and I take it, leaving my glass half drunk.

"Who's Marty?" Gladys asked. "Did you finally meet somebody? God bless him if he can stand the fish perfume." Her comment had an unintentional sting. Mildred knew that nobody wanted a girl who smelled like cannery for a wife. It just wasn't the fashionable thing to do.

The daydream lifted from Mildred's mind. Her diamond earrings and necklace disappeared and Marty's offering hand pulled back into darkness. "Uh, party, I said party. I'm going to a party."

Gladys raised an eyebrow, looking skeptical but mostly amused. "If a man invited to a party, then I'm Abraham Lincoln!" She laughed at her own wit.

"Why is that hard to believe?" Nothing needed to be said and Mildred understood the irony of her own question. "One of these days, I could meet someone." She knew that Gladys was only teasing, but then again, she didn't revel in the fact that people regarded her as an old maid before her time. The next fish that came before her was dead, luckily. Mildred ripped the guts out with a ferocity that scared Gladys and even herself.

AFTER SCRUBBING THE LAST bit of fish crud off her boots,

Mildred pedaled home as fast as she could. Darnella's Ford was gone and she remembered that the family was dining at The Orchard this very moment. Without her stepmother there, Mildred parked her bicycle on the grass next to the front step. No Opal whining, no Darnella primping and no father to ignore her. It wasn't as lonely as she expected and it was actually exciting to be the only one in the house. She flew upstairs, grabbed her stationery box and took it to the kitchen.

"Alright, what to have for dinner..." Inside the cupboard, there was a wild array of canned foods, none of which piqued her interest much. She grabbed a can of pork and beans. It plopped into her bowl, congealed as one blob until she smashed it apart with her spoon. It definitely didn't compare to The Orchard's glorious bowl of spaghetti and meatballs that she craved. After a few chilled bites, Mildred placed a fresh sheet of paper before her and began to write.

Dear Marty,

Hello, again. I hope you are in good health. This will sound very silly, but you came into my daydream at work today. You were just getting ready to ask me to dance when I got interrupted. I tried thinking about it again but once I stop daydreaming in the middle of it, it takes a while to start back up. I'd really like to go dancing someday and not just in a daydream. There isn't much chance around here in Bresford for dancing, except at the big summer dance in August. That's the best part of the year, better than the Fourth of July and Christmas combined. There is dancing, of course, but this incredible band plays all day and into the night and there is more food than we all know what to do with. Aside from the summer dance, Bresford is actually a very boring place, especially if you're from someplace big and exciting like Seattle.

I just want to get out of here and see what else is beyond here. Do you know what it feels like to have dreams and know you may never carry them out? Everyday feels like this void that can't be filled and I don't even know if I'll be lucky enough to get out. I pray you don't know what I'm talking about and I'm guessing you don't. With your plane, you can get as far away as you want. You're one of the lucky ones.

Sincerely,
Mildred Westrick

She took one last bite of her beans, saving the pork chunk for last. Her letter took a sad turn, not what she was expecting.

"Knock, knock!" The voice wasn't Darnella's, but Hattie Kilpatrick's. Mildred grabbed everything and shoved it into her stationery box before Hattie sashayed into the kitchen.

"What are you up to, Millie?" Hattie was the only one that called her that and she didn't mind. "Writing a letter or what?" She eyed the box.

"Just looking at my supply. I need to get more stamps and I'm running low on envelopes. Do you have all that at Dominic's?" Mildred knew the answer already because that's where she got her box.

"Sure! Stamps are at the post office but we have some gorgeous stationery that arrived last week. Come in when you're not working and I'll show you!" Hattie laughed, "If I didn't know you better, I'd say you were writing a love letter!"

Mildred felt herself instantly flush. "*Me?!* A love letter? You're very funny. You know how slim the options are in Bresford, honestly. Except that you have Leland, remember?"

"My Leland. He was so sweet today! I was at work when he hand-delivered the tastiest marshmallow malt to me. Luckily,

Mr. York wasn't there. He would've had a fit if he saw that sugary thing near the glove counter!" Hattie hung her hat on the kitchen chair and sat down, ready to divulge more of her romance to Mildred.

Jealousy wasn't something Mildred let live in her mind. If she did, she would be the unhappiest person in Bresford, Cowlitz County or maybe even all of Washington. Darnella and Opal occupied their own category in Mildred's mind nowhere near envy. However, she had *plenty* of reasons to be jealous of Hattie: she had golden hair, long curly lashes, the ability to wear red lipstick, plus she had the love of a man. Leland was nineteen, same as Hattie. He possessed the voice of a man but still had the gangly look of adolescence. While others might've commented on Leland's big ears and the fact that his pants were always too short, Hattie only saw the most perfect man for her and because of that, Mildred was happy for the both of them.

Hattie found the cookie jar, helped herself to a few gingersnaps from the store and offered one to Mildred. "Where's everyone else tonight?"

"The Orchard," she said with a hint of disgust as she took the gingersnap.

"Darnella's idea, I'm assuming?" Hattie shook her head in disapproval, sending her golden locks swinging.

"She made four o'clock reservations when she knew I'd be at work. Why can't I be like you and just find a man to fall in love with? Then I'd be able to get out of this house! Besides you, I'm alone. It's going to be me and those salmon until I'm an ugly, old maid." Hot tears slipped down Mildred's cheeks.

"Millie, honey, no!" Hattie soothed, wrapping her slender arms around her friend. "You're not alone! I'll help you find someone, okay? I won't let my best friend feel like this." She kissed Mildred's cheek. "Oops, I forgot the lipstick. Actually, you should go look at yourself!"

They both went to the hall mirror. Mildred laughed at her reflection, her face a puffy mess with a bright red lipstick print on her cheek. "Hattie, you have a lot of work ahead of you!" She laughed some more, but oddly, Hattie wasn't. She grabbed Mildred's shoulders and they locked eyes in the mirror.

"Do *not* talk about yourself that way. When you're not crying, you should really take a look at yourself, Millie. Everything about you is soft: your hair, eyes, little nose and cheeks. You're sweet and the right man will want your kind of sweet. Did you know that I hate my nose?"

"What? Your nose is lovely!" She wiped her eyes with the back of her sweater sleeve.

"This thing? I'm lucky that it's not any *more* bulbous than it already is! It starts out pretty, at the top here, but it ends like a knob!" She cupped her hand at arm's length from her nose, illustrating how big she felt her nose really was. It worked at making Mildred smile and laugh.

Hattie paused for a few moments. "Tell you what. I'm going to bring all of my makeup and hairstyling doodads and show you what you could do for fun. You always fight me but you're not going to win this time. You're getting a makeover next Saturday, like it or not!" Hattie folded her arms across her small chest. "I'd do it this Saturday, but Leland insisted I go to this dance at a friend's barn in Ridgefield. How am I even supposed to dress for that?"

Mildred leaked a few tears of gratitude. "Hattie, what would I do without you?" She hugged her petite blonde friend and sighed. "Okay, now tell me more about Leland and this dance. I'm sure you'll find *something* to wear, you always do."

"It's tricky because I want to look my best, even at a barn dance. What if he proposes there? I hope he doesn't, as much as I don't want to say that, because I want him to propose more than anything. But it *is* a barn, after all, with cow pies and hay.

Not a very romantic setting, in my opinion." On and on Hattie went. Mildred couldn't wait until the day she could go over every detail of her romance with Hattie. Even if they were mundane, at least she'd *have* details.

A WEEK LATER, MILDRED wrote three more letters to Marty. When she reread them, she noticed that she had a consistent theme. It was evident that she wanted to escape from Bresford, from her life. In the letters, Mildred didn't write about her mother or her job at the cannery, but kept to her habit of daydreaming and wishing she could start anew. It wasn't an unfamiliar desire, but it bewildered her how intense it came across on paper.

"What am I even doing with these?" she wondered, looking at the three pink envelopes on her desk. Nonetheless, she stashed them in her hatbox with the others, totaling five letters. She imagined what Marty was doing that exact moment. Maybe he was getting a shave? Or he was on a dinner date with his girlfriend? Or perhaps he was wondering if someone like Mildred was out there for him? She sighed at the last guess, knowing she wasn't the kind of girl that men typically dreamed of.

"Hattie is here!" Opal hollered from downstairs. Quickly, Mildred took down the picture of Marty on her vanity mirror and hid it in a drawer. Her stepsister's kid-sized thuds on the stairs and down the hall announced her arrival before she swung open the door to Mildred's room and shouted, "*Hattie's here!*"

"Beat it, rag-a-muffin," Hattie barked as she rushed by Opal. She toted a worn leather satchel that looked like it had been on the front lines of war.

"Mommy says slang is..."

"*I said beat it!*" Hattie repeated. Opal screamed and ran off, most likely to tattle on them. "It's glamour day! Are you ready,

Millie?"

All week, Mildred felt like she was truly ready to take the leap and let Hattie tackle her with cosmetics and brushes, but now that the moment was here, her heart sank to her stomach.

"I don't think I am. I'm not a fashionable kind of girl, you know this! No matter what you do to me, I'll still be nowhere near as pretty as you!"

"Fiddlesticks. I was a fast learner. You're probably just a late bloomer. What do you have to lose anyway?"

She couldn't argue that point. "Nothing."

"Okay, before we get started, why don't you get us something to drink? I'll lay the tools and makeup out on a little napkin, like a real salon! It'll be fun!"

"Good idea. I'll be right back," said Mildred, feeling a little less apprehensive about her makeover. She trudged downstairs and immediately got Darnella's wrath.

"How dare your friend have the audacity to yell at my little girl!" she snapped. Her freshly curled hair bounced with each word. Mildred would normally sink within herself and apologize, but knowing her sassy friend was upstairs, she felt braver.

"I'm sorry, Darnella, but she barged into my room and Hattie's not that patient. I'm sure Opal will be fine. If you'll excuse me, I need some Coca-Colas."

DOWNSTAIRS, HATTIE HEARD THE commotion between Mildred and her stepmother, most likely caused by Hattie yelling at the urchin who burst into the room. It didn't take her that long to set up the makeup station and hairbrushes, but she wondered how long Darnella would keep Mildred.

"Might as well get the finishing touch ready," she said. Mildred wasn't into accessories as much as Hattie, that was for sure, but Mildred had her one and only hat that she wore whenever the occasion required. Up in the closet sat the lone hatbox. With her red manicured fingers, she clutched the box and sat it on the bed. Inside was the trusty wide-brimmed burgundy wool hat with a bunch of sapphire blue silk flowers pinned on the side.

"What are these?" Under the hat were five letters, all in pink envelopes. Hattie grabbed them and studied the address. "Marty Townsend? Seattle? Millie, you devil! You *do* have a beau! I knew it!" The idea hit her like a bus. The letters were addressed, stamped...but obviously not mailed. She put the hatbox back in the closet.

"Oh, Millie, Millie, Millie. I'm going to help, just you wait." Her leather satchel became the perfect hiding place for the envelopes, right in between *Good Housekeeping* (because as soon as Leland proposed, she would have to be a good housekeeper) and *Redbook*. Mildred huffed back into her room, clearly irritated but bearing the chilled Coca-Colas.

"Now, sit down and prepare to become a whole new Mildred Anne Westrick!" It *was* like being at a salon, complete with a towel around her shoulders and radio tunes filling the room.

Mildred drank her cola. "Honestly, I'm excited about this now."

"What look do you think would great on you and help you catch a man's eye?" Hattie couldn't resist.

"What do you mean? To look like you?" Mildred started to panic. She didn't want to bleach her hair and wear red lipstick all day. Looking like Hattie would take too much work every morning.

"No, silly. Say, if we went to Seattle for a little shopping, dancing and were on a bit of a toot, how would you want to look in high society?"

"On a toot, drinking the night away during Prohibition? That's impossible. I've never..."

"Calm down, it's just a scenario, Millie."

"Besides, Seattle is a three hour drive from here! Who in their right mind would drive three hours for *shopping?*"

"That's not the point. Imagine, if we were dancing in the ritziest place in Seattle, what would you want to look like for that special guy? Come on, Mil, think!"

On cue, Mildred tuned in to her favorite daydream, the one she could depend upon to carry her away: *I'm wearing a velvet dress the color of moss. A comb with clusters of emeralds and diamonds adorns my glossy waved hair. I'm drinking champagne from a delicate flute between my bejeweled fingers.*

"I guess I want to look like Ingrid Bergman," Mildred finally answered.

Hattie smiled back at her in the vanity mirror. "I knew it! You'd be a ringer for her! A little curl here, a little eyeshadow there, finish up with a swipe of red on your lips. I'm sure any guy from Seattle would want you!" She combed and combed, relaxing Mildred's fine brown hair until it was velvety soft.

"Why do you keep mentioning Seattle?" Mildred asked. She instantly connected Marty with Seattle, but it was her secret. Nobody knew about the letters and they were stashed safely in her hatbox.

"Oh, you know, Seattle's a big place. I just named it, that's all. Now stop moving your head!" Hattie rooted in the satchel and fished out a spray bottle of sugar water and a glass container of bobby pins. Like a professional, she pressed her finger against Mildred's scalp and pinned back a wave with three pins. In five minutes, one side of Mildred's head was pinned to death and coated with the sugary water to aid in setting the waves. Hattie shifted over to the other side and started pinning away.

"Hattie, how strange would it be if I ever met someone?" Mildred asked. As soon as the words left her lips, she felt as if her dirty secret was spelled out on the biggest sign for all to see.

"What do you mean?" her friend asked playfully. "Do you have someone hiding in your closet?" Hattie went further. "Is this why you finally relented and let me work on you, to look nice for someone? Please tell me!"

Mildred was now flaming red in her face. "No! I don't have anybody yet. I just thought...well, I'm nineteen and it's time I should meet someone, but I don't know when that'll happen." The rush of her shortcomings reared up in her mind. She was too ashamed to tell her best friend about writing Marty.

How pathetic is that? Hattie tells me everything about Leland! She's not even engaged and isn't afraid to tell me every single, stupid wedding plan! I can't share with one human being this detail about my life...

"Millie, are you crying?"

She used her sleeve to mop up the tears forming at the corners of her unmade-up eyes. "I just want a change so badly that it hurts."

Mildred felt some relief when Hattie rubbed her shoulders. "Don't worry, honey. Let me doll you up some more, show you what you can do and I'm sure things will change. You have to be positive if you want anything to be different in your life. Leland didn't get me when I was sad! Now close your eyes, it's time for my favorite part!"

"To be correct, Leland got you after he spilled cherry malt all over the lap of your tweed dress, so you *were* a little sad, until he paid for the drink and asked to buy your next one."

"Oh, be quiet, you! Now close those peepers or I'll poke them out!" They giggled.

She did as she was told and felt the soft pressure of Hattie's eyeshadow brush on her naked eyelid, depositing frosty pink powder and then a plum shade in the crease. Hattie voted to skip the rouge since Mildred had a natural blush to begin with.

"Okay, open your eyes, but don't blink or look at the mirror!"

Hattie ordered. She had a large mascara brush that she raked over a black cake of Maybelline pigment and smudged it onto Mildred's fluttering eyelashes. Then, Hattie added definition to her brows with a pencil.

"Hold still, Millie! You're looking fabulous!" Those words alone elated Mildred's mood by several stories high. If just by a few cosmetics she could look "fabulous," then she couldn't be *that* helpless. By now, the sugar water dried and Hattie gingerly slid the dozens of pins out of Mildred's hair. The longest part she twisted and pinned into a chignon at her nape.

"Look at yourself!" Hattie squealed, clapping her hands together.

For the first time, Mildred actually liked her reflection instead of only acknowledging it.

That had *never* happened before.

"Now for the finishing touch..." Hattie handed Mildred a tarnished golden tube containing her precious Kissproof lipstick, worn down to a nub that only had a few more uses left. With untrained hands, Mildred smooshed the crimson wax onto her lips, making corrections as Hattie gave them, and ended up with an impressive pout.

"I don't even look like me at all!" Mildred gasped.

"That's the point, silly," said Hattie. The fish girl who didn't have a chance was gone and before her was a doe-eyed woman with looks to kill an eligible bachelor. She had commanding brows and deeper, seductive eyes, all things she never thought she'd possess. All of a sudden, her future looked much brighter and more glamorous. All she needed was the green velvet dress and jeweled comb from her dreams.

CHAPTER THREE

Later that week, the pin waves had long become loose, the mascara from her lashes wiped clean and the lipstick leaving nothing more than a faint cherry stain.

If only Marty could've seen me, maybe he would've loved me, if he knew I existed. Writing to him seemed like a fool's errand, the more she thought of it. Who in their right mind would fall in love with a cannery girl writing random letters to a man she saw in the paper? If she were Marty, she would've burned the letters and not spent another second thinking of the insane person who penned them.

Regardless, she reached for her stationery set.

"This time, just wish him luck with the donations. He doesn't need to know your every thought," Mildred muttered to herself. Her schoolgirl cursive formed the words she felt Marty would need to read. She wondered if perhaps he didn't get any support from anyone else and her letters brightened his day.

Maybe I am the only one writing to him, she let herself think hopefully. In her mind, she also believed hundreds of prettier girls wrote to Marty, just like she did, and even had the nerve to mail them. What if they enclosed glamour shots, the kind she saw in Hollywood magazines?

"Why didn't Hattie take my picture when I was done up?" she moaned. After all the work with the pin waves and Hollywood makeup, there wasn't any proof Mildred ever looked that spectacular. Little did it matter, as the glamour shot would never reach Marty's hand, had it been taken. This letter was much shorter than the others, offering him a few words of encouragement in his venture with donations for the Elliott Bay shantytown. She glanced up at his picture taped on her vanity mirror. When Hattie was expected, Mildred hid his picture in her desk, but the rest of the time, it hung there for Mildred to shamelessly admire. Marty's eyes pierced through the crude newspaper print the same way they did the first time Mildred found the article. For good measure, she wrote in the letter that she'd love to meet him when he came to Bresford.

"Wait, didn't I write something like that in the first letter?" She couldn't remember. They all seemed to run together, an endless cursive tome of her thoughts. From her squeaky wooden chair, she hopped up and went to her hatbox to reread the last letter. For her own reference, she numbered them on the backside in the lower left corner. Swiftly, she tossed the lid aside, removed the wool hat and fished around for the five letters. Her fingers only found a few loose petals that fell from the silk flowers on her hat.

The letters weren't there.

Like a bomb, her heart sank and exploded into her stomach,

cold sweat popping up on her brow. A gigantic wave of dizziness came over her.

"Where did they go? Where are they?"

Opal.

Mildred marched from her room to Opal's, where she was predictably playing with her numerous dolls, drinking pretend tea and eating real cookies. The little girl looked genuinely shocked to see her stepsister towering over her, radiating a fury she'd never seen before. Her mouth dropped open and her dolls fell over in their tiny chairs.

"Did you get into my hatbox and take out some letters, Opal?"

"Isn't your hatbox up real high in the closet?" Opal illustrated with outstretched arms pointing to the ceiling.

Mildred didn't think of that. "Well, yes, but did you climb a chair and get it down? I had letters in there that were private, for my eyes only. I know you go in my room."

Opal was on the brink of crying. "I only wore your shoes a couple of times, but I didn't wear your hat!" It was enough to convince Mildred to step back. Her next candidate was none other than Darnella.

"Mildred!" Darnella's voice trilled up the stairs and Mildred's nerve to ask her if she took the letters disappeared. If she asked, then Darnella would suddenly become interested and have to know everything. "There is some mail for you. It's from a Mr. Townsend. Is that someone we know? Sounds like a stuffy lawyer's name, if you ask me."

The same wave of wooziness rushed over her again as she raced down the hall, the blood pounding loud enough in her ears that she swore she misheard her stepmother. "Who is it from again?"

"It's from someone named Mr. Townsend." She took her manicured nail to the seal.

"Stop!" Mildred yelled. Darnella pulled her hand away in surprise. "I meant, he's in admissions and I asked him to send me information on...on...an art program I've been interested in attending." Meekly, she held out her hand.

"You're still interested in the art program? I thought you gave that ambition up a long time ago when your poor mother passed away."

Two barbs in one tiny sentence, something Darnella was good at. The blood rushed to Mildred's face and the memories to the forefront of her brain. After a week-long art program at the Longview Community Center a few towns away, fourteen-year-old Mildred knew she would someday become an artist, although she wasn't sure which medium she wanted to become proficient in just yet. Grace picked up Mildred from the front of the community center, beaming like a springtime sunrise from inside the cab of the truck. Memories of their discussion were hazy, but Mildred knew they talked about college and what a bachelor's degree was, how long it would take to get one. The only details that kept every shred of clarity were the ones Mildred wanted to forget forever.

Her proud mother with a smile that almost made her eyes disappear, her voluminous brown hair tucked back elegantly with a tortoise shell clip, the smell of the exhaust as they rumbled down the highway to Bresford in Harvey's Ford Model T truck. Warm sunlight came through the dirty windows, illuminating the natural blush of her mother's soft cheeks and glinting off the thin gold hoops in her ears.

An explosion shattered the driver's side window, tearing a tunnel through Grace's neck. Blood sprayed all over Mildred's blue dress, the entire length of the dashboard and the landscape sketch that she got honors for in class. Grace slumped down in the seat and her eyes appeared to be staring at the radio, but didn't blink. After a minute, the truck finally rolled to a stop on the highway. The whole time, Mildred knew she had been screaming but everything was silent. Her ears had a painful ring in them and she was covered in glass, some bits falling out of her hair as she looked around. The shooter had long disappeared. She vaguely remembered a younger couple helping her out of the truck and waiting for police. The woman wrapped her in a blanket from their car and Mildred, feeling numb all over, didn't fight as the woman held her close. When she glanced back at her mother sitting lifelessly in the driver's seat, still staring at the radio, Mildred began to wail again. It was several hours later that she made it home and Harvey was beside himself with worry when he yanked the front door open. Before any words were spoken, his eyes filled up with tears as he studied the young couple with his daughter. When Mildred mustered enough strength to tell her father what happened, his deep howls of agony were unlike anything she'd ever heard. Mildred and her father became shadows of themselves, both wishing they had died with Grace.

Nothing else mattered anymore.

Darnella clicked her tongue and raised her brows. "Well anyway, here's your letter. If you are thinking about school, your father and I can't help because of the economy being in such a terrible state. You know how it is, right?" Irony would have it that as Darnella turned her nose up to spending money on an education, she drove a new car and waved around a chunky sapphire ring that she picked up a few years ago from Dominic's. It wasn't fake and Darnella took pride that she owned such a bauble.

With the letter in her hand, the blood-stained memories went back to where they came from. There it was, presumably in Marty's handwriting, the letter containing his reply.

But how? Who mailed them? Clearly it wasn't Opal and Darnella had no idea…

"Hattie!" Mildred ran to her room and slammed the door, grabbing the back of her chair for support. *That's* why Hattie kept hinting at Seattle, thinking that Marty was her romantic pen pal. If only Hattie was aware that Marty had no inkling that someone named Mildred Westrick was in love with him.

But now he knew.

THE PILE OF MAIL on Helena's desk looked uninviting, boring, but she spied a flash of color, like a flower blooming from the snow. With cautious fingers, she plucked the envelope from the stack. It had a 3 on the back and came from someone named Mildred Westrick in Bresford.

Bresford...May seventh. That was the day of Marty's speaking engagement.

The pale pink envelope asked to be opened with a delicate hand or risk breaking the sender's heart for mishandling her stationery.

Dear Marty,

I can't stop myself from looking at your picture from the paper. What is it about you that does this to me? It must be your eyes because I'll catch myself staring for minutes on end. If I stare hard enough, I can almost see you blink and smile. Sometimes I think you can see me from your side, wondering about who I am.

There isn't much to me, but I know I could find out more about myself if I could leave Bresford someday. Other girls are prettier, which means that they can get away from here with a ring on their finger. I don't seem to have that type of luck.

Inside, I know I'd make a great wife. I'm a hard worker, I don't need fancy dresses or shoes and I can cook fairly well. Most importantly, I can listen better than anyone I know. Listening

*and being listened to is, I believe, worth more than anything
else. People can talk all day long and it doesn't mean anything if
nobody takes the time to listen. My only friend is a good listener,
but if I don't see her, I can go all day without talking. Something
tells me that you'd be a good listener.*

Sweet dreams and I hope you dream of me.

Sincerely,
Mildred Westrick

The letter was addressed correctly, even though it sounded
like it was addressed to a movie star's fan club. Helena dug in
the pile of mail addressed to Townsend Timber and found four
more pink envelopes, all from the same girl. What struck Helena
as odd was that Marty was the recipient of the letters. He had a
few female friends, but none of them were interested in his
recent charitable activities.

"Marty! There's mail for you!" Helena hollered from her
office. She'd been the secretary at Townsend Timber for over
fifteen years and felt more like a paid family member than an
employee. This far engrained in the Townsend history, she had
long known everything there was to know about Marty. He
received the usual mail: University of Washington looking for
donations from alumni, motor magazines, invites to social events
around Seattle. Most of the mail went unanswered, social events
passing by like clouds.

"Marty, honey! I think you may have an admirer."

A second later, Martin Samuel Townsend sauntered in,
clearly awakened from a nap and still in his less-than-
presentable clothes. A smear of grease sullied the leg of his
newest canvas trousers and his plaid shirt smelled of both sweat
and exhaust.

"Did you really have to use your new Carhartts as a rag? It will be impossible for your housekeeper to get that engine grease out." She held out the stack of envelopes and pointedly glared at the stain on his tan pants. "You know how your father hates that you fly. It's dangerous."

"What does he hate more about it? Is it the fact that I help the 'lazy hobos' or the actual act of flying?" To an outsider, it might have sounded like Helena was hounding him to the point of being rude, but he knew that if she didn't care, she wouldn't have stayed with the family for as long as she has to feel free to say the things she did.

"Both! You know what he wants you to do and you like to stir him up, go the other direction! Your poor mother is preoccupied with your little sister, so that just leaves me to deal with everything, including your father's tantrums when you refuse to get in a log truck and learn the business. It's a wonder I am still here running things." Marty slipped the letters from Helena's fingers and kissed her on the cheek, filling the air around her with the intoxicating sweat and exhaust perfume.

"The company would fall to pieces without you, I'm sure. Besides, you stay around because you love me so much, despite all those times I put frogs and earthworms in your desk as a boy." Marty winked at her.

"I do love you, just as long as I'm getting paid for it."

He lumbered over to a leather chair and hung his legs over the arm. "Are you sure these aren't addressed to Cary Grant or some other famous fellow?" He slipped off his ball cap and shook out his wavy, chestnut hair, but failed to get rid of the indent from his hat.

"Possibly. He is better-looking than you, you know." Helena smiled at Marty and continued tackling her mountain of correspondence. He took one envelope from the five and looked it over. All were from a girl named Mildred Westrick in Bresford, just a few hours south of Seattle.

"Why does Bresford sound familiar, Helena? Bresford, Bresford..." He knew the names of plenty of cities, but Bresford wasn't in his lexicon.

"Your father pays me to be his social secretary. I suggest you do the same."

With added sweetness, Marty beamed at her. "I love that blouse on you, very snappy. It makes you look more radiant than usual."

Helena sighed. "Alright, you win. Bresford is where you'll be collecting donations from. It is the only place you got a response from for that silly radio ad you put out a while back."

He felt stupid that he couldn't remember that detail. "Of course, thank you! Mr. Dominic York wouldn't let me off the damn phone, I remember that much. Going on about his daughter, the town, how he hopes to become mayor soon." He stopped rambling and shuffled the letters on his lap.

The numbering system on the back, he guessed, was to keep the letters in order. Gingerly, he peeled open the first envelope, nervous as to what he would find. He hoped that a lock of hair or a tissue with a lipstick kiss didn't fall out on his lap.

It started out with an apparent crush this Mildred girl developed after seeing him in *The Bresford Daily*, how she adored his "soft, kind eyes" and applauded his good deeds, and then turned into a wordy narrative about her sad life, that she'd basically give anything to get out of Bresford to begin a new life. It didn't come across through any of the letters that she knew about the money he was connected to, which is what truly caught his attention. She was just a simple, honest girl who had plenty to say but nobody to tell it all to.

"Too bad you didn't send a picture, Miss Mildred, since you've seen mine."

A picture! Of course! The obvious solution, he felt, would

be to write the odd Miss Westrick back. It would only be fair, considering she sent him five letters. On some blank Townsend Timber letterhead he swiped from Helena's desktop, Marty began to write.

HATTIE'S TELEPHONE LINE RANG for a few seconds before she answered. "This is Hattie Kilpatrick speaking."

"Hattie!"

"Millie? Is that you? What's going on?"

Mildred felt so many emotions at once that she couldn't put one before another. She was embarrassed, excited, in love, depressed, flattered, and all the while wanting to hide under her quilt.

Words escaped her, too. "I can't...why would...Hattie, you sent my letters!"

"Letters?"

"Yes, the letters that were hidden in my hatbox!"

Hattie drew out her confession. "Millie, I just thought I was doing you a favor. They were even addressed and stamped. Why? What's happened?"

"*He replied!*" Mildred breathed heavily into the receiver.

"That was fast. Wait, isn't that good?"

Mildred couldn't have this conversation effectively over the phone. "Meet me at Dream Fountain and you're going to buy me a shake!"

Fifteen minutes later and somewhat soothed by the cool marshmallow shake, Mildred laid the stiff white envelope on the table. It was slightly saturated from her sweaty palm and the top was torn where she hesitated to open it.

"First, tell me who Marty is." Hattie bounced in her seat and acted giddy as if it was her own romance.

Mildred rolled her eyes, feeling ill. "Did you read that article in *The Bresford Daily* last week about the pilot coming to

Bresford to get donations for the shantytown in Seattle?" A blank look overtook Hattie's face. "I'll take that as you haven't. Marty is the pilot and he's coming to Bresford. This is bad."

"No it isn't. Girls write celebrities all of the time. Why would writing to a pilot in our town's dumb paper be any different?"

Mildred wiped her damp hands on her skirt. "They weren't supposed to be seen by anyone. I should've just tossed them like I meant to but I was stupid and kept them."

"Then why were they stamped? Besides, I wanted you to find love. How is that wrong?"

"Love? How did you know?"

Hattie smirked. "I doubt Marty is a cousin or uncle and you used your good pink stationery!"

Mildred muttered something, trying to keep her voice low.

"I didn't hear you, Millie. What'd you say?"

"*Marty doesn't even know that I exist!*"

Hattie giggled. "He does now. So open it already."

"I can't open it! What if he thinks I'm crazy? When I wrote the letters, part of me felt like he could hear the words and he would, I don't know, magically appear and take me away from here." She groaned and hung her head.

"Come on, Mil, just open it."

The white envelope contained either a stroke to add to the painting of Mildred's woes or, just maybe, it could be something she couldn't prepare for. She grabbed the envelope with fingers that barely registered the feel of the expensive paper and peeled the rest of the top open. The folded letter inside smelled a little bit like gasoline and some of the ink bled through where Marty must've held the pen down too long in thought.

"I can't. You read it, Hattie." Her friend delicately took the letter from her shaking hand and cleared her throat.

"Dear Mildred..."

Thank you for the letters. I've never received this much mail from someone all at once, much less someone I've never met before. I am touched by your kind words regarding my mission to help those less fortunate. You seem like a compassionate person from your letters and if your offer of wanting to help me still stands, I'd be interested in talking to you when I arrive in Bresford on the seventh. More people need to be compassionate like you. Our world would be a better place, as you said.

Aside from admiring my charity work, you shared often about your desire to run away and begin a new life. Please trust that I can relate to your agony on many points. There is a world outside bigger than Bresford and bigger than Seattle. I hope you get to see it someday.

On to another topic: you speak as if you know me from my picture and I was hoping that you would've enclosed a picture for me. Would you please mail me a picture so I can put a face to the name?

Yours truly,
Marty Townsend

P.S. If you don't send a picture before I arrive in Bresford, I'll just have to find you.

The whole time that Hattie read, Mildred drained her shake dry without tasting the chilled sweetness. Hattie looked up from the letter, her mouth widening into a toothy grin.

"What does this mean? I didn't scare him away? Or is he making fun of me as a big joke?" Her mind couldn't decide on one possibility over the other. She might as well have written to

Amelia Earhart asking to accompany her on one of her famous flights. If Amelia said yes, at least she wouldn't have felt this embarrassed.

"No, Millie! He wants your picture and he wants to meet you! Those are good things, silly!" Hattie reached across the table and squeezed Mildred's clammy hand.

"What am I going to do? What if he thinks I'm like you, blonde and fashionable?" Mildred growled and slapped her hand to her forehead. "Maybe he is such a kind-hearted person that he wrote me a letter out of pity."

"My opinion says that he doesn't think that and why would someone who is doing this noble thing take the time to make fun of you? It just doesn't make sense." Mildred peered into her best friend's confident face. She wondered how someone so pretty believe that someone as plain as Mildred could honestly catch the eye of Marty Townsend.

Maybe Hattie was the crazy one.

CHAPTER FOUR

THE TANGY SCENT OF fresh paint filled Dominic's warehouse. Much to his chagrin, he had his volunteers stop working on his election banners and turn their focus on the banner for Marty Townsend's arrival in a few days. He had no doubts that the altruistic act of giving donations to Marty would certainly boost his popularity in Bresford. He was already Citizen of the Year 1931 and being elected as mayor would only add to the laurels he already wore.

The boyish pilot's dream caught his attention over the radio a month ago, a simple ad played between songs. If he hadn't been listening closer, Dominic could've misheard the snappy announcer and thought he was peddling the latest instant baking mix.

"Pilot Marty Townsend is calling his fellow Washingtonians

for help. Yes, he means you! Gather donations of clothes, canned food, books and toys, blankets and medicine...anything that you don't need! Marty will personally fly to your town and bring your donations to those in need during this financial crisis. Contact us at KCC radio for information and you could be a hero of the Depression!"

Dominic normally tuned out commercials, but the name mentioned by the announcer rang a big, loud bell. *Townsend, Townsend.* He recalled reading an article in the newspaper nearly three months ago about Gerald Townsend of Townsend Timber up north in Seattle. While most everyone suffered during the economic downward spiral, some more than others, Gerald Townsend had reporters chronicle his purchase of a new log truck. Dominic dug ferociously in the stack of newspapers in a corner of his office and halfway through the stack, he found the edition he was looking for. Standing next to Gerald was a younger clean-shaven version of him and sure enough, the caption confirmed Dominic's curiosity: *"Gerald Townsend with his son and heir to the family logging business, Martin Townsend, posing proudly by Townsend Timber's latest acquisition, a 1932 Hayes-Anderson truck."*

Dominic dialed the radio station, wrote down the phone number the receptionist provided and soon was connected with Marty himself. The young man sounded surprised that someone actually responded to his ad and that he wanted to help with donations. Apparently, Marty learned that there weren't many people who wanted to part with any extra possessions they had laying around, so he had given up hope that anybody would be willing to cooperate. His schedule was wide open, so he and Dominic settled on May seventh for his glorious arrival, just a little over a month away. To sweeten the pot, Dominic promised some advertising in the newspaper within the next few days and a small degree of fanfare, donuts and coffee included. He even spent some of his own funds printing little squares of paper to hand out to his customers. If they could spend money on the latest Parisian-style hat, he was sure they could easily part with other belongings. When he couldn't get the word out, he knew he could count on Vidalia.

Vidalia. She was the reason why he made the phone call in the first place.

His stylish, strong and elegant Vidalia was in need of a husband of substance. None of the fellows she took a fancy to could give her what she deserved. He was disgusted by people these days. The Depression seemed to lower everyone's standards when it came to finding a spouse, making promises to be happy while agreeing to be as poor, if not poorer. Vidalia was not going to have the same fate as the other girls in Bresford. It was known throughout town that she was essentially royalty. Everyone wanted Vidalia to marry their eligible son, nephew, cousin and grandson. As she was taught, Vidalia acted meek and flattered, finding out pertinent details without raising any suspicions. It was Dominic that had the final say in potential beaus. About every time she brought back stories of some young man working for the railroad or working their way up at a car dealership, Dominic would laugh. That was all she needed to know. However, Marty Townsend, pilot he may be to everyone else, would be an ideal match for his green-eyed Vidalia.

"I need you to do something for me, my darling," Dominic told Vidalia over dinner the day he got Marty's promise to fly to Bresford.

"What is it? Do I need to work the counter tomorrow?" she asked, boredom in her voice. By now, she learned to do whatever her father asked, whether she wanted to or not.

"Why so glum? If you achieve what I've lined up for you, I pray you'll never have to work another day in your life." He gently took his daughter's smooth hand in his own. "How would you like to marry an heir to a timber fortune?" Dominic slid a photo of Marty in front of her. "Does being the future queen of Townsend Timber sound like something you want to be?"

At once, Vidalia's face lit up. The gorgeous man in the picture looked like he'd make a fine husband, especially if her father approved, and of course, having a vault of money didn't hurt his chances in the current economy.

"You think I can do this? You really do? What makes you sure he'll fall in love with me?" Uncertainty now shadowed her original burst of excitement over the prospect.

Her father smiled warmly. "Out of all the girls in Bresford, you outshine them all. I highly doubt that he's married or even engaged because if he were, he wouldn't be out flying all the time. Someone like Marty Townsend needs a wife like you. Luckily, you have me as your father and when have I ever failed you? Trust me. If he's looking for a wife, you'll be as obvious to him as a lighthouse on a clear night."

"Mrs. Vidalia Townsend. I love the sound of that." Her pout disappeared to reveal a real smile, the biggest that her father had seen in a while. "I'll do it."

Dominic slapped his big hands to rival a thunderclap and guffawed. "That's my girl."

VIDALIA WASN'T WITHOUT CERTAIN freedoms. For the last few years, she's participated in the Bresford Ladies' Aid Society, which was where she was headed with a handful of paper squares promoting the donations event. Meetings were usually at the home of Mrs. Darnella Westrick, president of the group. When she dressed and primped for the meeting, Vidalia hoped that Mildred wouldn't be there.

There was something about Mildred that made her unfashionable to socialize with, although she didn't know what it was exactly. Mildred was quiet and friendly, but it wasn't enough for Vidalia to want to have tea with her. Dominic was never particularly warm towards the Westricks and she followed his example. People like Vidalia couldn't risk their reputation with those as plain and dull as Mildred. Besides, Mildred never seemed interested in socializing with her anyway.

With the final adjustment of her cloche over her light auburn hair, she set out into the April sunshine and walked west on Juniper Street, feeling the stiff leather of her new shoes fight against her feet as she broke them in. One of the little papers threatened to fly away. She quickly stuffed it back into the stack. This project of her father's was that much more important to her now, especially considering her chances of marrying handsomely. It wasn't like his usual undertakings, like his mayoral campaign or a splashy sale at the store. None of those things her father did interested her. But now, she had a prime opportunity to leave Bresford and live in luxury while her father got publicity. They were both getting what they wanted.

At the Westrick home, she knocked with her lacy gloved fist while cradling a package of Belgian chocolates.

The door whooshed open. "Why, Vidalia! Look at you, is that dress new? Of course it is, right?" Darnella seemed extraordinarily perky today. Her makeup was perfect, her peach and red striped dress meticulously ironed. Vidalia also noticed that Mildred's bicycle was gone, a good indicator as to Darnella's happy mood.

"Good afternoon, Mrs. Westrick. Please enjoy these, courtesy of my father." Vidalia handed Darnella the box.

"Look, ladies! Real Belgian chocolates!" The women on the couches and dining room chairs nearly jumped from their seats, only stopping so as to not seem more eager than the woman next to her.

"My father wanted to treat the Ladies' Aid Society in hopes that we would help him with this!" She offered a paper to everyone and blinked expectantly.

With an air of duty, Darnella took it and read aloud. "Citizens of Bresford, donations are needed for charity. Bring your extra clothes, books, toys, canned goods, and even medicines. May seventh at noon, Manchester Fairgrounds. Free donuts and coffee. Get your photograph taken with pilot Marty Townsend!"

The pilot's last name sounded oddly familiar to Darnella, but she couldn't place it. It wasn't exceedingly common like Williams, Smith or Jones. Three of the women in the Ladies' Aid Society had such last names: Irma Smith, Ellie Johnson and Doris Williams.

Ellie Johnson with her blonde bob waved her hand too eagerly, smiling too wide for her face. She was a junior member, newly joined that spring, and her energy showed it. "I read this in the paper recently and immediately thought this would be a perfect project for the society. Wouldn't it be great if we make committees for the donuts, coffee and handing out those cute papers for the pilot coming in?"

"Ellie, leave the delegating to me, dear. You can delegate if you ever become president of the society. You'd have to have these fine women vote for you first, so I would just count on being a member," Darnella quipped. Ellie only looked slightly stung, blinked slowly and placed her focus on the chocolate box. "Ladies, I just decided that this project is going to be our pet for the next three weeks. That doesn't give us much time. We want to show this pilot that Bresford women are the best in the state. Who's ready?"

Several arms shot up. Vidalia raised her hand proudly towards the ceiling.

"Myrtle, you distribute papers at the grocery store. Take Ellie with you. Run some by the post office, too. Doris, you make a decent pot of coffee. Rita, you're the best baker, so you're on the donut committee. Pick some helpers. I'm thinking we should have ten dozen donuts." Rita's eyes grew. It was true that she was renowned in Bresford for her baking skills, but she'd never made that quantity of anything before and she wasn't sure if she could even afford the ingredients necessary. The women began to squabble politely with each other as they built their committees.

Darnella turned and rubbed Vidalia's arm. "I'm so excited because I'm making you a co-chair of this project! Won't that be fabulous?"

Vidalia clapped her hands. "Oh, Mrs. Westrick, this project means so much to me, thank you! I will work hard, I promise you."

"Good for you, Vidalia! I only wish Mildred cared as much as you do about her community, or family, if we're splitting hairs. I haven't the slightest idea what I'm doing wrong with her. She has everything she could want, right?"

Vidalia nodded earnestly, believing it bad luck to talk ill of someone in their own home, but she could feel the dislike she and Darnella shared for Mildred. "As a woman her age, I can say that I only wish I had a mother like you."

Flattered, Darnella touched her cheeks with her fingertips. "Oh, stop. But to be honest, I wish you were my daughter. You and I could do fun things all day long. I can't even get the idea of shopping into Mildred's head. God forgive me for saying this, but I will *not* be surprised if she marries poorly. I could help her find a husband, a decent one, but she won't even let me talk about the weather with her. She's still bitter about me replacing her mother. It's not like I was the one that shot her down." She opened the chocolate box and fished out a caramel that melted like a delicious sin on her tongue.

The opportunity hung in the chocolate-scented air and Vidalia nabbed it. "Mrs. Westrick, may I ask you something?

I'm afraid it will sound very odd."

Darnella swallowed her candy. "Please, ask me anything, anything at all!" She guided Vidalia to some free seats on her burgundy velvet chaise lounge. The young girl's eyes darted about as she gathered her thoughts. "What is it, Vidalia?"

"I need your help with the pilot." She looked around, making sure nobody was eavesdropping.

Darnella was confused. "Are you talking about the pilot that's flying in for donations?"

She nodded. "Yes, that pilot."

"Is something wrong with him?"

Vidalia fidgeted. "Nothing's wrong. I am, well, rather interested in Mr. Townsend and if he is an eligible bachelor like my father believes, I want to get him to fancy me. My father says he's a big catch and since you came from an affluent background, I was hoping you could educate me. That wasn't too impertinent, was it?"

Without any doubts, Darnella was more than intrigued. She was handed a cup of tea and she stirred furiously while she thought over what Vidalia told her. "It's not impertinent, but I don't quite follow you, dear. What makes this pilot a catch? Aren't pilots usually poor fellows with gals in every town they visit or some lowly thing like that? Being a pilot doesn't strike me as the sort of job that makes one an *eligible* bachelor, rather just a plain, old bachelor."

"That's not the case with this pilot." Vidalia leaned in and whispered, "He is the heir to Townsend Timber." She sat back up and sipped at her own cup of tea. "I sound like a girl from a Jane Austen novel, don't I?" It embarrassed her to hear the plan in her words, now fearing that the story would spread across Bresford and she'd become a joke. She peered helplessly into Darnella's studious eyes and silently begged her not to laugh.

Of course Darnella had heard of Townsend Timber, just like

many people hear things from one day to the next. When she lived in Seattle, she and her ex-husband, Paul Riley, used to go to parties hosted occasionally by Townsend Timber. Paul and Darnella were young and newly married, and they considered themselves lucky to get invited, thanks to Paul's connections through his father. When they arrived at a party, the steaks were fat like a dictionary and since it was before Prohibition, the liquor flowed all night long. Every time they attended, Darnella struggled to make acquaintances with the owner's wife, Jeanette. If only she could secure the matriarch's friendship, it guaranteed more invites to their luxurious parties, she was sure of it. Lake houses, sporting, sailing on the Puget Sound; she wanted to be in that circle. Out of the flurry of invites the then-Darnella Riley received, she always accepted the Townsend ones and replied immediately. Her soul ached for those days, the healthy bank account and the security in having a certain status. However, she wasn't married to Paul long enough to make any impact on the Townsends.

It wasn't a month after she'd given birth to Opal that Darnella learned of her husband's infidelity with a secretary at his office and instead of turning a blind eye, she exposed the scandal. The only reputation that seemed to get dragged through the mud from the ordeal was Darnella's, even more so when she decided to leave Seattle with her daughter for a boarding house in a fishing community called Bresford. It was the only place she could afford with what Paul gave her and nobody knew her there. To get by, she started selling hats door-to-door and had little luck with that endeavor. It was true that that's how Darnella met Harvey, who was still adjusting to his life as a widower. Rather than sell hats to pay her meager rent for a bedroom, she chose to remarry and regain some security she once knew. Her reputation wouldn't be as large as the one she had before, but it meant she could live in a whole house.

When she tucked her memories back into their compartments, Darnella was certain of this: while she may never join the ranks of her socialite friends again, she might as well help Vidalia and give her a chance to break into that world.

She really began to think of the direction this was going. If the pilot's last name had been Rockefeller, it didn't necessarily mean he was related to the family fortune, but in this case, Marty Townsend was not only connected, but he was the direct recipient. With one swift motion, Darnella deposited her teacup on a side table, grabbed Vidalia's gloved hands in her own and gave a reassuring squeeze.

"Vidalia, what you told me isn't impertinent or silly in any measure. It's smart, which is why I will do what I can to encourage a match between you and Mr. Townsend. Your charms are clear to see, but a bit of help never hurt. Let's toast to Mr. Townsend, may he make you the prominent lady you were born to be."

When they raised their teacups, Vidalia was already working out which lucky girls would be in the bridal party for her ritzy Seattle wedding.

THE SMELL OF PARISIAN perfume always lifted Darnella's spirits. No slump in the economy could take away the joy a spritz delivered to her naked wrists, the mist seeping through her skin to her soul. If only she could afford to buy a bottle without a care like she did in her first marriage, but she'd have to sacrifice part of her allowance for this luxury.

"Mrs. Westrick, you haven't been in my store for quite some time. Is Mr. Westrick keeping your purse hostage?"

The thick and slightly rough voice cut through the fading cloud of expensive scent. Rubbing her wrists together coyly, Darnella spun around to face Dominic York. He stood at least six feet tall, making Darnella look up into his playful eyes. "My husband knows better than to tell me what I can't buy for myself. I've been through a horrid divorce with a child, so I deserve life's little pleasures."

Dominic gave her a half smile. "Just as long as you get your trinkets from me, I'm a happy man." He pointed to the stack of papers in her gloved hand. "Ah, so I see that the president of the Ladies' Aid Society has approved my request?"

"As a matter of fact, I have. Of course I'm happy to support this venture of yours, Dominic. I think it's lovely that we can help the less fortunate in Seattle." She raised an eyebrow. "Although, in a place as big as Seattle, you'd think there'd be a pool of jobs to choose from. No matter, that won't make our donations any less generous in God's eyes." The flirt in Darnella reached out and touched Dominic's arm. "And Vidalia asked me something very important and I want to make sure her father approves of my presence."

He rearranged a display of oil lamps and blew a film of dust off the crystal-cut bases. "What would my daughter be up to? You don't plan on being a bad influence on her, do you?"

As if she were batting away a bear, she slapped her empty gloves on his arm. "You tease! Quite the opposite, actually. I've been asked to help her cultivate her charms to secure a certain...pilot?" She picked up another perfume bottle and spent too much time admiring it, lusting after it, running her finger through the slinky atomizer tassels. Her eyes followed Dominic's broad back as he retreated behind the glove counter and fussed with some baby blue pairs made of kid leather. "Please tell me, was I wrong to say anything just now?"

After scooting another pair of gloves one inch over, he took a moment and ran his palm over his graying beard that he kept trimmed close to his strong jaw. "Mrs. Westrick, I want you to understand that this isn't intended to be a fleeting romance for my daughter. If she can get Mr. Townsend to enjoy her company while he is here for the donations event, she hopes to have him fall in love with her. I have every confidence in Vidalia that she can make this happen."

Darnella nodded enthusiastically. "I couldn't agree more."

"I refuse to see my daughter marry below her, let alone someone equal to her during these times. The economy is not going to ruin my daughter's future and I will not accept anything less than a proposal from Mr. Townsend. It's that simple."

Words could not be formed on her painted lips. The "pilot meets girl and falls in love" plan was far more serious than she thought when she heard it from Vidalia. Darnella wasn't sure if she was prepared to possibly fail with Dominic watching now. She wasn't even sure if Dominic wanted her to help. At that moment, the bell dinged and in walked Vidalia with a paper cup of ice cream.

"Hi, Daddy." She took a bite and looked up to see that she had interrupted a serious conversation. "Is everything alright?"

The warmest smile spread over Dominic's face, making handsome wrinkles by his eyes. "My sweet, I was just squaring away some details with Mrs. Westrick. I believe she's on board with us."

Vidalia wasn't quick to react. Unsure, she said, "For the donations event?"

"Yes, but she has pledged her help in getting the heir to Townsend Timber to give you the life you deserve, darling. Mrs. Westrick will do what she can to facilitate meetings, put in a good word for you, whatever she sees fit. She'll be working closely with him, which means you'll be, too."

Vidalia and Darnella both straightened up, as if they were soldiers getting their marching orders for battle.

Dominic softened a touch. "Now, ladies, this must stay with the three of us. I don't want others girls getting the idea that this is a game to see who can get the pot of gold. Do I make myself clear?"

"Yes." Darnella swallowed, but it was dry.

"Yes, Daddy."

He nodded in approval and timed the end of the conversation perfectly before retreating to his office. Hattie Kilpatrick walked into the store to resume her shift behind the counter after her daily visit to see Leland. Hattie's eyes widened as she realized who was in the store. Darnella smiled a bit too sweetly at Hattie and made an overly grandiose change in conversation.

"Vidalia, why don't we begin planning the donations event? I'm sure you're brimming with brilliant ideas."

"I'd love to! I'm just honored to be co-chair with you, Mrs. Westrick." The women linked arms and found a table by the window. From behind the counter, Hattie observed them discreetly. Vidalia was nice enough to her when they were in school but Hattie didn't care for how she looked down her nose at Mildred, and for no clear reason. Hattie tried to listen in on parts of their conversation, but it was mostly about donations. Her ears caught the word "Marty" being whispered, followed by giggles. It was just a few days ago that she learned about Marty's significance to her dear friend. Nearby, she found a feather duster and took it for a trip around the glassware, edging a little closer to the two women.

"Whoops!" The duster bumped the edge of a crystal picture frame and Hattie scrambled to catch it. Darnella looked up from her notes and didn't make any sort of face, but Hattie sensed that she was not supposed to be that close to them for fear of listening to their hushed words.

"How is Leland? Has he proposed yet?" Darnella asked, already knowing the answer.

"Well, not yet. I hope to get a proposal soon, but he's so shy. You know how the Burris men can be. Five brothers and they're the shiest people on the planet." Hattie stood there with the frame clutched awkwardly at her chest.

"That's too bad. I honestly thought you would've been long married by now and to someone else with more status. Leland Burris, aside from making malts for a living, comes from a family of alcoholics. Do you want to be married to someone with that kind of pedigree? One drink and that's the end of it. Sweet as he may be, alcohol could turn him into a monster. I'm just looking out for the young women of this town, including Vidalia. You understand that I say this to you with a mother's love, don't you?" Vidalia turned from her note-taking and stared at Hattie.

Embarrassed beyond measure, Hattie gulped back tears. "Yes, ma'am." Mildred was right. Darnella was an expert on delivering those barbs to the most painful places. She took note of how Darnella purposefully excluded her own stepdaughter as one of the girls she meant to protect. Like a dog hiding its tail, she placed the frame back on the shelf and made herself busy at the furthest part of the store, mindlessly cleaning as her tears dropped onto the counter.

Darnella and Vidalia were careful from that point on, speaking loudly about the donut committee and where they would get all the cups for the coffee, where they would have everyone bring donations. Seething, Hattie applied a fresh coat of lipstick and wiped her smudged mascara with a tissue. The ordeal left her feeling uneasy, naturally, but it was almost as if something else was going on. Organizing who was in charge of donuts was definitely not a confidential matter, but the way they talked about Marty was...and Hattie couldn't wait to tell Mildred.

BETWEEN THEIR SCHEDULES, HATTIE couldn't tell Mildred what she knew for at least a week and didn't want to discuss it over the telephone. Since that horrible incident with Darnella, she hadn't heard Marty's name dropped once. She found it especially odd because Dominic's had been named the place to bring donations and Vidalia was constantly buzzing around with her arms full of boxes and bags. That Friday, Hattie couldn't handle the suspense any longer. The door opened and sent the bell dinging, revealing Vidalia yet again. This time, she was toting a bag of worn stuffed animals.

"Hi, Vidalia!" she called from behind the glove counter.

Vidalia's eyes registered alarm at first, but then she relaxed. "Hello, Hattie. What puts you in such a good mood?"

Hattie left the counter and pranced towards her. "I'm just getting excited to see this pilot. What if he's handsome? Do you think he's single?" She lifted her eyebrows expectantly, begging Vidalia to chime in, preferably with some meaty details.

"I'm excited, too. I've never met a pilot before. Didn't you see his picture in the paper?" Vidalia dropped the bag of stuffed animals next to the other donations and wiped her brow.

"Actually, no, I don't read it." Hattie cringed because the answer made her sound more ignorant than she intended. Usually, if something was worth knowing, her well-read father shared the information at the dinner table.

"You're right, though. He is indeed handsome, far more handsome than any of these Bresford boys. Working with Marty should be interesting." She said 'Marty' with a degree of ownership.

Hattie swallowed her tongue at the "Bresford boys" comment, knowing full well that Vidalia referred to Leland when she said that. Her eyes flickered rage, but Vidalia was busy examining her cuticles. "What do you mean you'll be working with him?"

Vidalia chuckled and opened her arms, palms up. "I'm the co-chair of this whole venture. It's quite a big project but I'm feeling confident that it'll be a success. Between helping load up his plane and showing him Bresford, Marty and I will be around each other quite a bit. I plan to make myself indispensable to him."

Hattie clicked her tongue. "It sounds like a hoot. I better let you get back to gathering donations and other important...stuff." She sauntered back to her counter and rearranged some lipstick tubes and mascara boxes. The information she just heard was enough to make her head explode. Out of the corner of her eye, she watched Vidalia walk out of the store with the same smug air she just spoke with.

"Are you staying busy, Miss Kilpatrick?" The voice of her boss cut through her thoughts and caused her to drop three tubes of lipstick. Dumbly, she watched them roll off the counter to the floor. When she stood back up with the tubes, she put on a pained face and groaned. Dominic was taken aback. "Are you ill, Hattie?"

"Mr. York, I didn't feel well this morning, but I didn't want to inconvenience you by not coming in." On cue, she put her palm over her mouth and breathed in heavily. "Don't worry, I can still work."

"I think it's probably wise if you went home, Miss Kilpatrick. I'll find someone else to come in for the rest of the day. Now go, please, before you get sick all over the floor." He made for his office to avoid whatever pestilence he believed Hattie carried.

"I'm very sorry, Mr. York. I'll go straight home," she said weakly. She grabbed her purse strap and hat, making sure to walk out of the store looking like she was near vomiting. Once she was away from the store's windows, Hattie broke into a run as fast her heels allowed.

ALBERT YELLED FROM HIS office window upstairs, "Mildred! I got a call that you have a visitor!" She stopped the hose and looked at him, confused. Visitors never came to the cannery, let alone to see her. He nodded, "You have a visitor! She's outside! Make it quick!"

Any excuse to stop pushing smelly guts around with water was excuse enough and she hung up the hose without hesitating. Outside on the dock stood Hattie, looking as if she had the biggest news of her life.

"Did Leland propose?" she asked, laughing. "Hattie! This is wonderful!"

Her face dropped. "Why do people keep asking that? Anyway, this is something else and it's going to be a problem. Can you get out of work for a moment?"

"I can try. Wait here." Mildred ran back into the warehouse.

Ten minutes later, the girls were seated in the most private booth at Boone's Diner with Hattie being overly aware of the patrons inside. She chose Boone's Diner to meet because it was mostly full of the hard-of-hearing elderly type and felt safe to talk there. The younger crowd tended to congregate at Dream Fountain and exchange gossip or eavesdrop, which is what Hattie wanted to avoid.

"Is everything okay? What happened?"Mildred shifted nervously in her seat.

Hattie peered out of her booth to make sure the grannies a few tables down weren't listening. She leaned in and said almost too quickly, "Vidalia has plans for Marty."

At first, Mildred swore she heard, "Vidalia is planning a party." She wasn't sure why her friend would take her out of work for a half hour to deliver petty news such as this. "What did you say?"

"You heard me, Millie. Vidalia is planning on doing all sorts of things with Marty when he flies in. She mentioned loading up his plane, helping him with who-knows-what and then showing him the town. Those were her words to me less than an hour ago, I swear!"

If it was possible, and it definitely was, Mildred felt more embarrassed than when she found out that Marty read her letters. To find out that Vidalia was going to be involved now, her chances of meeting him were even slimmer than before, if they weren't already nonexistent.

"Also, your stepmother was in the store last week to plan the donations event with Vidalia and I could hear them whispering about him. Before I could hear anything more, and trust me that I tried my hardest to listen, your stepmother turned into this nasty, old witch and she made me cry. I don't have a good feeling about this, Millie. Are you okay?"

Tears pushed their way to the edge of Mildred's lashes and hung there without spilling. Her nose began to burn with the humiliation that threatened to ruin her life as she knew it.

"How could I be such a...such a fool, Hattie? There was no way Marty would ever consider me. Put me next to Vidalia, she'd get chosen every time. I'm done thinking about Marty. When he comes to town, I'm going to hide while Vidalia wins." The tears waited long enough and began to flow uncontrollably onto her sweater.

"Oh, Millie, come on now. It's not like you didn't try. That was very brave of you to write him."

"What's to feel brave about? You mailed them for me. I wrote letters to a man who never knew I was alive, letters that I shouldn't have written because there is no chance that someone like me will *ever* get carried off into a fairytale. That's one thing I thought when I wrote them. How pathetic is that? You should be embarrassed to have me as a friend, you really should."

Just then, the waiter stopped by the table. "What will it be today, ladies?"

"Nothing, thank you," Hattie said.

The waiter, in his thirties and looking a tad miserable, grumbled, "If you must sit, you must order something."

At a time like this, food was the furthest thing from Mildred's mind. Hattie fumbled with the menu and said, "We'll split a slice of the carrot cake I saw in the case, please." He took the menu and trudged off with their order.

"I don't have any money on me, Hattie."

"It's my treat. Now look at me, Millie. This isn't the worst thing that can happen to you. People are out there living in those hobo camps, eating moldy bread and sleeping in boxes. A lot of those people are married, but they'd give that up to live in a house like you. Is this helping?" She frowned, wondering if she was only making her friend feel worse.

Mildred sighed. "You're right, you're more than right. I should be grateful for living in a house where I feel alone, working at a disgusting job, and being destined to be single forever. Don't feel bad, Hattie. You tried to help me when you sent the letters, but clearly, God doesn't see this happening for me. I have to get back to work. I'm sorry." She scooted out of the booth and bent over to hug her friend, then left with her head down.

CHAPTER FIVE

TABITHA TOWNSEND SMILED TOWARDS her second-story window when she heard the rumble of her brother's truck engine warming up before he left for the hangar. She seemed to be the only one who got enjoyment from Marty's hobby. Her mother, Jeanette, did her best to ignore it by now and her father despised it almost as much as he despised the shantytown near his business building in Elliott Bay.

"Mother, Marty's about to leave!" she said and reached over to tap her sleeping mother's arm.

Jeanette stirred in her wingback chair and almost dropped her crocheting. "What, darling? Are you hurting again?" As she stirred a bit more, Jeanette could hear the truck engine rumbling in the driveway. "Must Martin *always* leave us?" She turned her heavy eyes to look upon her fifteen-year-old daughter who was not taking up much space in the bed and looking paler than normal.

"This time it's very important, Mother. Remember that I told Marty to help the people in the shantytown and we came up with this plan? Today he is going to Bresford, which is somewhat south, down by the Columbia River. He said the town is even having a donut social for his arrival!"

"Oh, yes, the plan that involves him flying to a town we've never heard of to bring back used items. It's the same plan that started with you having your brother box up your expensive clothes, toys and books to be sent away without my approval. Yes, if that's the same plan, then I do remember." Jeanette rubbed her face. She swore she felt and looked like she was ninety, the glowing complexion she was so proud of now dull, her eyes revealing how little sleep she got.

With a weak frown, Tabitha murmured, "I didn't need those clothes and tea sets anymore. I'm never getting out of this house."

Jeanette shot out of the chair and locked eyes with her daughter.

"*Yes, you will! Don't tell me you won't! I haven't left your side since you became sick!*" By now, Jeanette's fingers strangled the metal frame at the foot of the hated bed, sterile and cold, unlike the oak four-poster frame that used to be in Tabitha's room. It was too high for her and it was suggested they bring in a hospital bed. She composed herself when she heard footsteps thumping down the hallway. "Now, be a good girl and wish your brother a safe journey."

It wasn't Marty, but Dr. Thomas Ward, the doctor that was hired as soon as Tabitha's leukemia cropped up with a vengeance in February. He smiled and reported, "Martin just finished giving me enough blood to supply Tabby while he is away. I have to say, you're one lucky girl because your brother has some of the healthiest blood I've ever seen. It's so rich and bright, remarkable. Did you raise him on steak alone, Mrs. Townsend?"

She chuckled. "Like father, like son."

Another set of footsteps came down the hall, this time belonging to Marty. "Did somebody mention steak? That sounds wonderful. Who's buying?" Tabitha laughed and reached out her hand to her brother. He took it gently. When he noticed how her skin seemed more translucent today, his heart ached. "Tabby, I gave you some of my best blood this time, so use it well, okay? I made sure Dr. Ward added a big splash of Tabasco sauce to give you some pep."

She giggled. "Okay, that's really enough about me and my silly blood. Tell me about what you're going to do when you get to Bresford." From behind her grown son, Jeanette closed her heavy eyes that felt gritty with exhaustion. Whenever Marty left on a jaunt in his plane, she feared the worst. After a few hours, half a day, or even one whole day, he always returned from wherever he went: Bellingham to see a college friend, Long Beach to bring home fresh razor clams, and Wenatchee to enjoy the Apple Blossom Festival. Each time, Tabitha waited eagerly so he could tell her what he saw, what he ate, who he met. If he crashed and never came home, Jeanette knew deep down that Tabitha would not care to live any longer and surrender her soul. Or, if she mourned and kept on living, Jeanette would have nobody to help her deal with the leukemia. Her husband was immensely busy with the logging business and barely had any time left over for anything else.

Either scenario should ever happen, Jeanette was hopeless. By the time Marty was done describing his pending trip, Jeanette forced a smile and leaned out. Obediently, Marty kissed his mother's cheek, which had lost its softness some time ago.

"Martin, I expect you home soon. No longer than two days.

Your father doesn't like you owning that plane and it makes him even more cross when he thinks about this charity silliness that you're doing. That leaves me to care for your sister and listen to your father, and it's just too much for me. Masterson does what she can, but she's busy with the household chores and cooking."

She ran her aging hands over the shoulders of her son's leather jacket and down his arms. It was hard for her to remember when she first noticed him transform into such a stunning man. With his sturdy shoulders and his coy smile coupled with the playfulness in his eyes, he could turn any woman's heart to a bowlful of jelly. "You should be thinking about learning to run the business. Your father can't manage it forever, we both know this. Besides, everyone expects it of you. And I really think you should reconsider Agnes."

His mother brought up the only topic that he didn't want to hear about. Marty broke away and stared at her incredulously. "No, Mother. Agnes and I aren't going to get married and I'm grateful that I dissolved it when I did."

"That is enough prattle about dissolving engagements. We should be talking about the wedding! Now, I've invited Agnes over for tea and I thought you'd still be here when she arrived, but apparently I'm wrong about that. What shall I tell her now? It's only been three months and she still loves you. You must understand that this is hard for me because I approved so highly of her and your wedding was slated to be the event of the season. Please take her back, Martin, while you still have a chance."

He laughed aloud. Tabitha hung onto every word, as did Dr. Ward before he snuck away to prepare the blood transfusion.

"Tea? You think that having my ex-fiancée over to tea will make me see her in a new light somehow? I'm sorry to disappoint you, but I'm not going to marry Agnes simply because you like her. Make her your new companion, if that's what you want. Now, I can't keep the good citizens of Bresford waiting."

He kissed her cheek again but with cold reception and then went over to kiss his sister.

"Marty, fly safely. I wish I could go with you, too." She wrapped her thin arms around his neck and kissed his forehead. "Thank you for helping me with this. You're the best brother."

"Anytime, Squeak. Alright, I have to fly."

SATURDAY, THE SEVENTH OF MAY. When Mildred awoke, she felt like she could throw up all over her bed and hoped she would if it meant she could stay home. Most of the town was going to be at the Manchester Fairgrounds this afternoon, not only to get free donuts and coffee, but to see the pilot and get photographs with him and his plane. Of course, with Darnella going to represent the Bresford Ladies' Aid Society, she expected her whole family to attend, as well. For once, she even wanted to include Mildred.

"We leave at ten-thirty, everyone! Let's not be late!" Darnella hollered from downstairs. The vanity mirror revealed to Mildred that she was a disheveled nightmare. Hattie's beautifying powers would be challenged by even this.

It's not as if Marty will even notice me if I try, she thought with a shrug. But she did try. Before long, she tamed her tangled hair, pinned a bit in a swirl like she was shown and refreshed her complexion with a dollop of cold cream that Hattie got her from Dominic's. While the cream sat on her face, she went to her closet. It was all completely plain and in solid colors, practical like her mother had been, with the exception of a tame floral print or a bow on the outer edge of the neckline. The winner was a blue dress with lacy lapels, white polka dots and buttons that looked like white peppermints she used to get for Christmas. It was the fanciest dress she owned and wore it once to her graduation from Bresford High last summer. Naturally, Darnella bought it for her with the hopes of adding some life to her stepdaughter's wardrobe. Surely, Vidalia would be wearing something more alluring and the polka dot dress would look ridiculous in comparison. In fact, she was confident that Vidalia could wear the most boring dress in Mildred's closet and still manage to be stunning. With a splash of cool water, she wiped the layer of rich cream from her face and looked in horror at her cosmetics. They would be leaving in ten minutes for the fairgrounds and there was no feasible way she could get all of it onto her face. Foundation, powder, lipstick, mascara....

Lipstick was about all she could manage with the small amount of confidence she had. She put it on as carefully as she could, covering her lips with a thick coat, but it didn't look as good as when Hattie applied it. At once, she knew it was a mistake because it looked like she dipped her lips in a bucket of red paint. Girls like Hattie and Vidalia could wear lipstick and not look like the clown Mildred saw before her. She wiped off the lipstick and settled for her barefaced look.

"Mildred, let's go!" her stepmother shouted. The sound of Darnella's voice awakened the nausea that sometimes reared its head ever since her father remarried. Before Darnella barged into the family with her infant in tow, the voice calling everyone together for community events was always Grace's. For any fairs, bake sales, or traveling circuses, Grace was the kind announcer, her voice sounding like a soft caramel. Darnella's voice, if it was a type of candy, was closest to the salty black licorice coins that her grandfather used to give her as a child that she'd promptly spit out into her little palm once they touched her tongue. The strong taste coated her mouth for what seemed like hours. Still feeling queasy, Mildred trudged down the stairs and feared her stepmother's mandatory once-over.

"Is that the dress you wore to graduation?" Darnella asked in a kind voice, honestly shocked to see her stepdaughter wearing something other than brown.

Mildred looked down to see if it was. "Yes, it is."

"I must say, you look much improved in polka dots! Aren't you glad I bought it for you?"

"Yes, thank you." Mildred followed Opal out the door and plopped herself in the car. In less than three minutes, they were at the Manchester Fairgrounds. Darnella took an eternity over the gravel parking lot to avoid dinging her glossy emerald paint. A few of the society members were already there, pulling bags and boxes from their cars and waddling off to the donation pile. From the corner of her eye, she also saw Vidalia and Dominic bringing their donations collected over the weeks from his store. Vidalia walked with an air of importance, as if she were directly responsible for the entire event.

"Now, everyone, as president of the Ladies' Aid Society, this is a very important day for me. I don't need anyone misbehaving and having it reflect poorly on me. Opal?"

"Yes, Momma?" She didn't look up from the doll she played with on her lap.

"Stay away from the donut table and Mildred?"

"Yes?" she answered.

"I need you to watch Opal for me. With your father at work, I'll be so busy directing people and then when the pilot finally comes in, it will be sheer pandemonium." With that, she got out of the car and made her way to the other society members. They all greeted one another with squeals and hugs. Mildred turned to Opal, who looked just as miserable as she was.

"I don't want to be with you!" she grumped. "And neither does my dolly!"

Mildred sighed. "You're not the only one. Let's go." For the next hour, the two girls wandered the fairgrounds, but not without first sneaking a few donuts for themselves. They sat on the swings on the outskirts of the arena, munched on their donuts and watched as cars pulled in. Most of the people, if they hadn't already donated, came with a box or two of secondhand items. The Bresford High band showed up with instrument cases and clumsily handled loose pages of music that flapped against their chests. They assembled on the stage and warmed up in unison while the afternoon sun glimmered off of their polished flutes and tubas. Mildred pushed herself on the swing and wanted nothing more than to be home in her bed, curled up and invisible.

"Millie!" It was Hattie, waving from across the parking lot in a snappy Kelly green dress. Leland was with her, of course. They were the oddest couple in town and didn't seem to care. Hattie knew she was pretty and dressed well, while Leland was tall and a bit gangly, had big ears and always wore pants that seemed two inches too short. Mildred wondered if it was his gentle eyes and shyness that turned Hattie into mush. He did have the prettiest eyes for a boy in school, but then she was reminded of Marty's eyes in the newspaper photograph. It was no contest for her.

"Hi, Hattie. Hi, Leland," Mildred said quietly. Opal stuck her tongue out at Hattie as payback for yelling at her a few weeks ago.

Hattie thought quickly and said, "Leland, why don't you find someone to talk to for a moment? Aren't any of your baseball buddies around?" He looked confused but complied and found a friend nearby. "Are you okay, Millie? I'm surprised you showed up today." Mildred looked up from the swing with a pained face at her beautiful friend. "Not that you shouldn't come, I didn't intend for it to sound like that."

"It's fine. I'm only here because Darnella made me come so she wouldn't look bad. If not, I'd surely be drawing in peace in my bedroom right now. But since I'm here, I sort of want to see what Marty looks like in person."

"Are you going to introduce yourself?"

"No!" The very thought of walking up to Marty to see the look in his eyes when she revealed that she was the crazy letter-writer made her feel sick again. "Besides, it sounds like Vidalia's first in line. I can't compete with her."

Hattie rolled her made-up eyes. "Who says you can't compete with her?"

"Nobody says it, it's just the truth. Why can't you see it?" Mildred hung her head.

"Would you stop with this sad mood for a moment? I'm making you stand with me and you have no choice. It's almost time for him to arrive! Come on, Mil!" Hattie yanked on her friend's arm until she abandoned the swing. Opal followed without being told and trudged just as much as her stepsister. By now, the band was beginning to repeat the songs in its repertoire. A banner gently caught the summer breeze, saying "Bresford Welcomes You, Marty!" The sweet smell of fresh donuts and cardamom floated on the wind, and the bustle of women organizing donations into groups sounded akin to a bunch of clucking hens.

On the stage stood Dominic, looking regal and commanding in his pressed charcoal suit. Behind him, Vidalia sat primly on a bench and smoothed the skirt of her dress. The top was crisp white with a poppy flower pattern and perfectly puffed sleeves, and going down from her lower bust was a candy apple red pencil skirt. She wore a dapper red hat with a false poppy pinned on the side and white gloves. Mildred was right. Her blue dress with its childish polka dots and lace collar made her look hopelessly frumpy when compared to Vidalia.

"Good afternoon, citizens of Bresford!" Dominic boomed. He wasn't mayor yet but certainly played the part. The current mayor, Howard Klemp, was bedridden at home and his condition didn't seem to be improving. It worked in Dominic's favor, as he was also Citizen of the Year 1931 and most had forgotten about

Mayor Klemp in Dominic's confident presence. The crowd clapped, some cheered. "I am honored to be leading this event during our state's time of need. Is Mrs. Westrick out there? Ah, I see she's busy sorting all of your donations. Could you please come up here, Darnella Westrick?"

From behind boxes, Darnella peeked out and pretended to be shy, but broke into a purposeful stride to the stage. She waved to the crowd like a princess and acted flattered when people clapped.

"This woman has worked tirelessly for this cause and I think it is fair to give her another round of applause." Dominic clapped the loudest.

Opal was bored and not even paying attention to the stage. Two butterflies captured her attention, dancing over the field, slicing at each other and drifting apart, only to slice their wings again and meet in a silent duel. Way up behind the butterflies, Opal spotted a plane, but this one wasn't flying high up like the other ones she usually saw. It was coming straight for them.

"Mildred!" She briskly tugged on the skirt of her stepsister's dress.

"Opal, I'm not getting you another donut. We'll both be in trouble," she hissed.

"Look at the sky!" All at once, everyone around them turned to where Opal was pointing. Sure enough, the plane was flying low and slowly beginning to circle around the field for landing.

"It's him," Mildred said, but her words were inaudible.

Dominic faced the band and shouted, "Keep playing!"

The school kids scrambled for their instruments and waited for the band leader to start them with Sousa's "Stars and Stripes Forever" piece. It wasn't the strongest rendition, but it was patriotic enough for Bresford. Hattie's grip tightened on Mildred's arm as the plane finished circling around and gently descended onto the field, rolling to a stop several yards away. The propellers slowed and the engine plinked as it cooled down. There was no movement right away and everyone stared at the plane for signs of life. Suddenly, with a heavy metallic click, the door opened. A man wearing a leather jacket climbed down and jumped the last two feet to the ground.

It was Marty Townsend. "Hello, Bresford!" he shouted, waving high above his head and smiling to reveal strong teeth. Mildred felt faint. The newspaper clipping betrayed how dashing he actually was and she couldn't handle it. He had brown hair that was wild with waves and his pout was perfect, for lack of a better way to describe it. His eyes were set with a pair of soft eyebrows that attributed a kind look to his face. As for his build, Mildred couldn't even find words.

"Welcome, Mr. Townsend! Come on join us up here to the stage!" said Dominic. The band continued to play as Marty walked up the steps and took his place by the podium. Darnella glanced over, more than approving of what she saw. She glanced back at Vidalia and raised her brows with a smile, then behind Dominic's back, she pointed her finger towards Marty and mouthed "go!"

Back down in the field, Mildred witnessed Vidalia stake her place on stage awfully close to Marty. "That's all I need to see. Can I go now?" Mildred whined. "They'll go out to lunch after this and Vidalia will have a proposal by the end of the day."

Hattie sputtered and clucked, "I bet you money that she won't."

"End of the week, then." She cast her gaze down at her shoes, refusing to watch any more, but she couldn't help but look when Dominic spoke.

"This selfless gentleman before you is the one that is going to take everything we've donated and give it to the needy in Seattle. If Bresford was in need, I know that our fellow

Washingtonians would do exactly what we're doing." Everyone clapped in agreement. "Before I give the stage to Marty, I'm sure Mrs. Darnella Westrick would like to add something?"

Darnella had been waiting for her turn. "As president of the Bresford Ladies' Aid Society, I want to thank everyone for their efforts in bringing us donations. Because of you, we have plenty of blankets, shoes, coats, books and toys. There is enough to keep this poor pilot busy for a week! If you have any additional items, please come speak to me..." she continued on.

Behind Darnella, Mildred could tell that Vidalia was thinking hard and felt her heart sink when Vidalia placed her gloved palm on Marty's arm. She thought she would die not knowing what they were about to say. Hattie's grip tightened on Mildred, also in anguish.

STUNNED BY THE UNEXPECTED touch, Marty turned and looked into the girl's young, heavily painted face and managed a small smile. "Yes?"

"I just wanted to tell you good luck!"

"That's kind of you. What's your name?" asked Marty.

"I'm Dominic York's daughter, Vidalia." She placed a palm on her chest and cocked her head coyly like she practiced.

"It's nice to meet you, Vidalia." Now he had a face for the daughter he heard so much about over the phone. Without saying more, he turned to listen to Darnella until he felt another pat on his arm.

"Yes?"

Vidalia fluttered her lashes and said quietly, "We'll be working together quite a bit, you and me, and I wanted you to know that I'm here to help with anything you might need."

He smiled awkwardly. "Thank you. I'll bet you're...efficient." His comment made her giggle far more than it should have.

*   *   *

MILDRED WANTED TO CRY. There was Vidalia, flirting without shame and making progress. She made it look easy, from her posture while sitting to how she fluttered her eyes and tipped her head inquisitively. If Mildred tried to mimic Vidalia's motions, she was sure she'd get laughs instead of an invitation to dinner.

Darnella was still speaking. "...be sure to make Marty welcome and show him how great our little town is! And here's our guest of honor himself, Marty Townsend!" She clapped and clapped as if she had just introduced the President.

Marty moved to the center of the stage and scanned the crowd that stood in clusters around the arena. "Hello, friends in Bresford! I am deeply grateful to Mr. York for reaching out to me and allowing me the chance to help those in the shantytown. This couldn't happen without you. I expect to fly back to Seattle and return here several times this week, as I see you all have generous hearts. I will probably need help from time to time and there is one girl I believe that is fit for the job..."

Next to him, Vidalia straightened up and smiled expectantly as if she was about to win the crown in a beauty pageant.

"...and that girl is Mildred Westrick!"

Her name echoed over the crowd and a chill flashed down her back. She was sure Marty said her name, but she couldn't believe it one bit. On stage, Dominic and Vidalia stared at each other in masked horror and then they both looked at Darnella who wore the same expression as both of them.

Squinting, Marty looked into the crowd and saw a handful of girls, but was unsure which one could pass for what he thought Mildred looked like. She never sent him a photograph or described herself. "Is Mildred Westrick here today?"

She was certainly there, but now hiding behind Hattie and

doing her best to pry her friend's strong hand from her wrist.

"*Hattie, let go of me!*" she whispered. "*I can't let him see me. It's too embarrassing!*" Reluctantly, Hattie freed her and frowned as Mildred walked backwards from the arena. Opal stayed put and wasn't sure why her stepsister was acting like a loony. People watched her with funny looks and murmured to themselves, some pointing. It was too much for Mildred. She turned and ran towards the cannery, as nobody would be there and hopefully nobody would come looking, either.

AFTER HE CALLED OUT for Mildred from the stage, Marty watched as a girl wearing a blue dress with white polka dots scurried off, heading southwest to whatever was in that part of Bresford. He didn't get a glimpse of her face, but by trying to be sneaky, the girl, who may or may not be Mildred, ended up standing out the most.

Dominic cleared his throat and announced to the crowd, but mainly to Marty, "There are already volunteers assigned to help you in this venture. Everyone in town knows my daughter, Vidalia. She'll be marvelous as your assistant. Now, let's all go over to have some donuts and coffee, generously prepared by our own Bresford Ladies' Aid Society. You can meet Marty and get your picture taken with him for only five cents! Thank you!"

The band resumed playing and Dominic clapped Marty on his back on their way to the covered reception area. Marty still looked around the arena and hoped that some girl would introduce herself as Mildred. None of the girls that accosted him were her, however. They were all too squeaky and bouncy with too much makeup on. When they greeted Marty and heard his voice, most of the girls erupted in giggles and then skittered off with their friends, all the while looking back at him.

"Wait for me!" Vidalia huffed. She pranced across the field while she kept her red hat in place. From behind Marty, she took in his scent of gasoline, soap and clean sweat. If that's what a real man smelled like, she wanted to be a woman more than ever.

Darnella was on her heels and whispered to her, "Don't let him leave your sight."

"You men walk so fast with your long legs. I can barely keep up in these darn heels!" Vidalia finally caught up to Marty and made it a step further. Her sway was sure to grab his attention, especially in her new poppy dress.

Marty chuckled and said, "I don't know how women can walk in those shoes. They look impossible!"

"They're simple, actually. It's all about how you walk in them. Most girls look like a newborn filly in heels, but not me. My father imports the finest shoes from Italy..."

"I'm terribly sorry to interrupt, but do you know who that girl is that ran off?" Marty asked. "She was wearing a blue dress with polka dots."

"I don't know, I didn't see anyone," Vidalia chimed in, almost too quickly.

"Sorry, Marty. There were too many people present for me to notice just one person," said Dominic nonchalantly. "Ah, here we are. Donuts made by our dedicated society women."

Vidalia delicately grabbed a donut with a napkin and offered it to Marty. "Care for one? Can I get you a cup of coffee? How do you take it?" He hesitated for a moment and saw the fear of rejection in Vidalia's eyes. To ease her spirit, he took the donut and ate a small bite. The eyes that were full of fear seconds ago were now watching him hungrily. Awkwardly, he swallowed.

"Miss York, that was delicious. Thank you. I do apologize, but I really need to find Mildred Westrick. Do you know who I can ask that may know about her?" He met blank faces and got nothing. Darnella pretended to be busy with rearranging a stack of donuts and scraping crumbs off the table. "Well, keep up the good work here. I'll be back in a while. Don't worry about me."

"What about the photos with you and the plane? People are expecting it!" Dominic called out.

Nonchalantly, Marty said, "With me, they are postponed until further notice. My plane, however, is free all day. Cheers!" He waved briskly and took the path he hoped would lead him to the girl in the polka dot dress.

CHAPTER SIX

As DISGUSTING AS IT was, the cannery with its fishy stench was reassuring for Mildred, a kind of slimy sanctuary where few dared to venture. She sat on the edge of the dock and dangled hr feet over the side. The fish never let her down from day to day. They were always there by the boatload to greet her, dead or alive. The fish never dashed her hopes, never had the chance to be smitten with someone better. A tear came to her eye and threatened to multiply.

I hate this place, yet here I am, hiding like a coward, she thought. The hot tear splashed into the water below as she looked at her pitiful reflection. She imagined all of the gleeful citizens posing next to Marty and his plane and then Vidalia swooping in with her seductive red dress and alluring looks to use on him like a witch's spell. If anybody in town could have a handsome man like Marty without trying, it would certainly be Vidalia.

The waves lapped against the algae-covered pylons like an aquatic lullaby that Mildred found soothing. In the distance, a train whistle sounded just as sad and miserable as she felt. Normally, she loved the various sounds the trains made as they charged their way through Bresford, feeling comfort in them ever since she was a child, but today it made her loneliness harder to bear. Next to a boat named *My Columbia Miss*, a familiar harbor seal popped its head up from the water. During the day, it waited patiently for scraps to fall into the water rather than work to catch its own fish. Now, it watched Mildred with its bulbous, inky eyes.

"I'm not very good company right now," she said. As if it understood her meaning, the seal slipped back under the surface and swam beneath the dock.

She was determined to stay there at the cannery until Marty flew back to Seattle for the day and hoped he would never think about her again, and likewise. The sooner he was gone, the sooner she could forget that she ever dreamed of them together in her pathetic fairytale. She promised she'd never write to anybody from the newspaper for as long as she lived.

Solid footsteps on the boardwalk broke through the peace. The last thing Mildred wanted was a talk about "rallying again" from Hattie, as if she could rally from anything today. The steps got closer, but fell a tad too heavy to be Hattie, and stopped about five feet away from her.

"Hello, miss. May I ask you a question?"

Her heart jumped up into her throat and wedged itself there, threatening to crawl out and dive into the water beneath her. She couldn't breathe and felt completely frozen to the boardwalk.

"Can you help me find someone?" The man's voice was unfamiliar to her, possibly someone who drove in from Kalama or Ridgefield to see the pilot. She scooted herself up onto the boardwalk and smoothed out her silly polka dot dress that made her feel like she was five-years-old. While she had her back turned to the visitor, she wiped her cheeks free of tear trails. When she faced him, she gasped aloud.

It was Marty Townsend.

He can't be here for me, it's not possible, she thought.

"Can I help you?" she offered nervously. He took another step forward and examined her face with the eyes that spoke to her from the newspaper photograph she memorized weeks ago. His eyes, to Mildred's surprise, weren't full of horror or disgust at the sight of her. They studied her with a sort of lightness, even amusement. She took a half step back and looked at her shoes to avoid the agony of making eye contact again. On cue, her cheeks warmed with a telling blush.

He answered, "Yes. Do you know where I can find Mildred Westrick?"

There was no use in lying at this point. He was here, looking for her, just like she secretly hoped he would but never believed it would actually happen.

"I'm Mildred." She tucked a loose bit of hair behind her ear.

"Mildred Westrick?"

"Yes." She peered up and waited to see some sort of disappointment in his face, for him to turn around and walk away, laughing hysterically all the way back to his plane.

Marty *did* laugh.

"This is fantastic! Nobody could tell me where or who you were. Now that I've found you, I have to say, your letters are very interesting, all five of them. Would you be willing to talk to me about what you wrote? It'll save me lots of paper and postage." He laughed again and resumed studying her, going from her hair to the soft curve of her chin.

She nodded without saying anything, still glued to her spot like a statue.

"Would you want to talk about them now? Or is it not a good time?" he asked, but then he grimaced. "I think I got on Mr. York's bad side by running off, so maybe I should take care of that first."

Her heart was still lodged in her throat and made her thoughts scatter around like unruly kittens. She finally said, "We can talk later, but only if you really mean it."

The same expression of amusement came over his face. "Why wouldn't I mean what I say?"

She took longer than she meant to find the words, feeling nervous heat rising from her sweating neck and scalp. "I'm...I'm not the kind of girl you're probably accustomed to talking to, that's all. Some people may say nice things but don't mean them. I'm used to it and kind of expect it now."

"Let me prove you wrong, Mildred. How about we walk back together?" Suddenly, Marty held out his arm and waited for her to place her hand in the crook. It seemed like years before she made her move. Her hand floated in time before finally resting inside his arm.

During the walk back to the fairgrounds, they didn't talk much. Often, Marty glanced over, taking in her plain yet beautiful face, her chocolate-colored hair and the sweet shyness that turned her cheeks red.

Mildred could see from the corner of her eye that Marty kept looking at her. At this point, her face felt sunburned. When the fairgrounds came into view and she could hear the chatter of the people, Mildred stopped.

"M-Marty?" she asked uneasily.

"Yes?"

She fidgeted for a moment, biting her lip a little too hard in her nervousness. "Maybe I shouldn't show up with you. I think some people might get upset if we do. There is this girl who already detests me and this would make her madder than the devil."

"I've only been in town for less than an hour, but I'm guessing you're talking about Vidalia York?" He laughed at the shocked look on her face. "For your information, I've met all kinds of ladies like Vidalia over the years and they're all identical. Sometimes I don't even notice them."

Mildred was confused. "Why not? Vidalia's pretty like a film star. Everyone says she looks like she could be Bette Davis's sister, plus her father is doing well with his store. And don't forget, she doesn't write a complete stranger a series of embarrassing letters."

He sputtered and flashed a remarkable smile. "This is exactly why I want to talk with you. Your letters made me smile and feel melancholy, similar to what you're doing this very moment. Let me ask you this: do you know who I am?"

She wasn't sure what he meant. "I only know from what I read in that article, which says you're a pilot helping people in the shantytown."

"You're sure, just that article and nothing else?"

"Yes, the one with you standing in front of your airplane."

Marty ran a hand through his helmet-flattened hair. "Then that's who I am, a pilot trying to do some good during these poor times. Speaking of that, I'll need your help loading up my plane for the first trip."

"Help you, in front of everyone? Why?" Nobody else knew about the letters besides Hattie and she was certain that people in Bresford would be more than interested as to why quiet cannery girl Mildred was suddenly friends with Marty. If nobody else wondered, she knew Vidalia would.

He partially suppressed a teasing grin. "Don't you

remember your letters? You wanted to help me and I'm collecting on that offer, Miss Westrick." Mildred's hand slipped from his arm as he moved forward. "What are you doing just standing there? There's work to be done."

"Okay," she said, barely above a whisper and forced her lead feet to move. It was just like in a nightmare. When she was younger, she had terrible dreams about dogs chasing her down the street, except that she couldn't run because her feet were cemented to the pavement. No matter how much she willed her feet to go, they remained planted and the dogs swarmed over her, thrashing her body to pieces.

Slowly, her feet felt less heavy and she was a step behind Marty. He put her arm back through his and walked on, clearly unashamed to be seen with her. Nothing bad happened, but the dream was still real and she couldn't shake the feeling that the dogs from her nightmares waited patiently in the shadows.

A FAINT BAND OF sweat formed on Vidalia's brow between doling out donuts and organizing incoming donations. Half of the crowd left after the ceremony and getting their free donut while the other half waited to get their picture taken with Marty. Opal fell asleep with her doll on a hay bale behind the donut table while Dominic paced, glaring both at Vidalia and Darnella.

"Did either of you know about this?" he hissed when people were out of earshot.

"I didn't think she was capable of speaking to a man besides her father," said Darnella.

"What about you, Vidalia? Doesn't gossip get around Bresford fastest amongst girls your age?" her father asked. She shook her head with vigor.

"Mildred isn't in any social circle that I'm a part of, and even so, I didn't have a single inkling that they knew each other. But what do I do now?" It killed Dominic inside to see his daughter despair.

"Leave that to me. I won't let one girl ruin this chance for you." He wiped the perspiration off his forehead with a handkerchief. "I absolutely refuse."

In the distance, he heard younger voices. Coming across the field was Marty. The pilot had been gone for thirty minutes, but it might as well have been the whole day as far as the event was concerned. As he feared, he saw that Marty found Mildred and she was walking arm-in-arm with him. They made their way to his plane, where he greeted those that were patient enough for him to return. The photographer from *The Bresford Daily* looked only slightly irritated. Marty acted as if he hadn't disappeared and hopped in front of the plane to pose with an elderly couple.

"You ladies stay here and manage things. I'll take care of this mess." Dominic marched off towards the plane and its wayward pilot. "Marty! You're back! I was afraid you got lost in our small town." The elderly couple shuffled off after thanking Marty and shaking hands.

"Mr. York, I give you my deepest apologies again. I did find who I was looking for, as you can see. Do you know Mildred?"

Dominic's and Mildred's eyes met for a few uncomfortable seconds. "Yes, she comes into my store from time to time. How do you two know each other? I wasn't even aware that you knew someone from Bresford when I first spoke to you on the telephone. You should've told me a detail such as that."

The fiery redness came back to Mildred's face. She didn't know where to go and it was too late to hide. If she went over to help with donations, she'd have to deal with her stepmother and Vidalia, who were both intensely watching the conversation. Out of habit, she stared at her shoes and prayed she would disappear. Hattie wasn't here to save her; she was on her own.

Marty smiled. "Actually, I didn't know her. Mildred wrote to me after she saw the article in your paper. She's kindly offered to help with the donations." He noticed Dominic's nostrils flare and a slight clench in his jaw, both signs that something wasn't going according to his plan.

"Has she now? My daughter was already in line to help you, you know. I can't very well tell her that she's been replaced. Sorry, Mildred, but Vidalia is going to be the one helping Marty from here." Dominic said everything with a grandiose smile and something in his voice told Mildred to look up at him. A single tear waited to drop as she saw the rapid calculations behind his eyes, a hunger that she couldn't understand. Clearly, she was not the prime choice or any choice at all. She was nothing.

"Please reconsider, Mr. York. As you can see, there are plenty of donations. Are you sure that Mildred can't help with part of it?" Marty pleaded, being careful not to overstep onto Dominic's bad side, if he hadn't already. "With your daughter being in those fancy high heels, I can't imagine she'd be able to carry much at a time, you see? I'd hate for her to twist an ankle because of me." He looked from Dominic's hardened face to Mildred's. There was no hardness there, only soft features and brown eyes that were far prettier than brown. The color was closer to a cup of fresh coffee with a touch of cream. Her ruddy cheeks were nearly scarlet as she stood before Dominic, silent and ashamed.

"If everyone was allowed to help that wanted to, we'd be overrun with volunteers and not enough jobs. You understand that, don't you, Mildred?" His tone was dripping with condescension.

She absorbed the sting and relented. "You're right, Mr. York. Vidalia is the co-chair of this event, after all. I'm sorry to have interfered. Goodbye, Marty. I wish you much success and have a safe flight." Without waiting, she turned and rushed towards home. As she passed the donut table, she felt Darnella and Vidalia's eyes burning into her back like an ant being roasted under a magnifying glass. This time, Marty wouldn't be able to chase after her. With Dominic and Vidalia's meat hooks into him, there would be no escape. And even if he managed to get away, he was well-educated by now that Mildred was considered low-class and not worth his time.

The tear she held back slipped down, followed by a stream that had no end.

"WE'RE PROCESSING A HUGE delivery, folks! Let's go! Pick up the pace!" Albert shouted from behind the line of workers. The salmon delivery the next day was enormous enough that he offered to run the hose so Mildred could slit fish bellies on the line. The conveyor belt was a bouncing sea of shimmery scales.

For her, the job was the hardest during the first five minutes when she felt like she was a murderer. After about fifty fish was when her guilt tended to fade. She grabbed one and couldn't bring herself to cut into it. Accidentally, Mildred dropped the live salmon on the belt and watched helplessly as it slapped and wriggled all over the dead fish. Its tail slapped a spray of blood into the air, arcing like a rainbow before it landed on Winnie. Shocked to see a live one come down her way, Winnie expertly slit its belly and ripped out the innards in one tug. She turned to see Mildred standing still as if she forgot how to do her job. In the year since Mildred started at Pacific Bounty Cannery, Winnie had never seen her pause, always giving her best effort.

"Wake up!" Winnie shouted over the mechanical whirring and spraying water.

Mildred snapped to and continued slitting fish bellies. "I'm sorry, Winnie! I'm just not myself today!"

Winnie dropped a handful of sloppy innards to the floor. "What's bothering you?"

"Vidalia York is ruining my life!"

Fred raised an eyebrow. "Miss York is your nemesis, eh? I

knew she was in charge of the young women in Bresford, but I didn't know she holds you as a bad egg. How the hell did that ever happen?"

Mildred searched her memory for some a solid answer, one that would explain all of Vidalia's frigid treatment throughout the years. "Honestly, I don't know why we're enemies. I was never good enough to be in her group of friends. She only talked to me at school if we were partners on a project. Outside of that, she never chose to socialize with me. But now..."

"I'm listening, keep going!" Winnie said.

"There's this person, a friend. He and I barely got to know each other before Vidalia and her father put a stop to it."

Still slitting bellies without missing a beat, Fred leaned in. "A man? I didn't know you knew any men besides the codgers here at the cannery. Who is he?"

Mildred caught herself smiling like a fool and scaled back the grin. "He is the pilot bringing donations to Seattle. His name is Marty Townsend. Have you heard of him?"

He laughed. "The cocky pilot? I was there, wasting time to get my picture taken but he was gone, so I just got my picture with the damned plane instead. Grabbed myself a donut, dropped off a bag of my old trousers and went home. Only saw the bastard on stage and then he disappeared."

"He was with me."

Winnie chimed in. "Did he hold your hand? Did he kiss you? Are you going to marry him?"

Fred answered her sharply, "Didn't you hear? Dominic has it in his head that the pilot is intended for his daughter. If you're going to listen in, get all of the information first."

Winnie rolled her eyes in jest. "Like I asked, did he kiss you?"

Overwhelmed, Mildred said, "No, no, no, none of that. But he did hold out his arm so I could walk with him from the cannery."

"You were at the cannery during the ceremony? Why in the world would you be here except to work?" Winnie asked.

The more Mildred talked, the sillier she sounded to herself. "I thought that Vidalia was Marty's, so I ran away."

Fred chuckled. "Running away is for weaklings. Unless you're a weakling, stop it right now. You'll never get what you want by running away."

Winnie countered, "And how do you know this, Fred?"

"Well, I ran away from my wife and three kids in Oregon when I couldn't bring home a paycheck anymore. I send them money but my wife won't have me back for fear of skipping out on them again. Does that answer your question?" Fred's face was flushed and he slit the fish with more vigor.

Mildred spoke up softly, "I'm sorry, Fred. It's just that running is easier than staying and watching things happen without having the power to stop them. Even after Marty found me and tried defending me in front of Dominic and Vidalia, I knew I wasn't going to win."

"All I'm saying is that you need to stop running. Not a day goes by when I don't think of my two boys and my baby girl, although she isn't a baby anymore. She must be twenty now. I thought I was saving them by leaving. I knew the community folks would bring them bread, eggs and milk easier if I wasn't there, but I'm sure Lorna has remarried by now, and better than she did the first time." Fred twitched his mouth and sniffed. "Don't do what I did, Mildred. If you let Vidalia win, then you're no better than me, no better at all."

Mildred quietly yanked out the innards from three fish before she responded. "What can I do at this point? Dominic made it clear that Vidalia was going to help Marty and I can't go back. Vidalia is fancier than I am and once Marty gets to know her, he'll be embarrassed at himself for ever talking to me. I'm the brown bird."

Fred laughed. "You still don't understand, do you?"

She thought she understood every word he said, but apparently she didn't. "What do you mean?"

This time he was more animated and spoke with his hands, swinging fish guts around and narrowly missing his face with them. "Who cares what Dominic says or what his daughter says? If this Marty fellow likes you, then there is nothing they can do about it. Do you see what I'm getting at, Mildred?" She had always thought of Fred as grouchy and miserable, but the warmth radiating from his eyes touched her heart. Weakly, she nodded.

He half-smiled and pointed towards the door with his knife. "So get out of here already."

"I can't just leave my post at the belt, Fred. We're so busy today!" Mildred cried. The wave of salmon hurdling towards them on the belt appeared to have no end.

"Leave your work to me. Go find the pilot and I better not see you back here today. Did you hear me? Go!"

A wave of panic came over her as she took a step back from the line, afraid of the reality of facing Marty again.

"Mildred!"

She spun around, brown eyes wide to see who shouted her name. "Yes, Albert?"

"I heard everything."

Instantly, she begged for mercy. "I'm sorry, Albert. I don't know what I was thinking. I know it's an enormous shipment today and I'll get right back to work!"

"Mildred, leave."

"What? Do you mean that I'm fired?"

Albert laughed. "Not today. Take care of this pilot business. Hurry, before I change my mind!"

With only a moment of hesitation, Mildred fought to remove

her rubber bibs, as if they tried to keep her from leaving, and then made haste for the door.

Fred bellowed after her, "Fly, Brown Bird, fly!"

AT THE MANCHESTER FAIRGROUNDS, Vidalia swapped her heels for sensible shoes earlier in the day so that she could carry bags and boxes without breaking an ankle. She fantasized how romantic it would've been to have Marty swoop in and care for her had she actually broken anything.

After Marty tried convincing her father to let Mildred onto the team and exclude Vidalia on account of her high heels, she bit her lip and wore a pair of white and red Kedettes with a candy-striped wedge heel. Marty would be flying out to Seattle with the first delivery of donations that afternoon and much to her disappointment, they had made little progress towards a relationship. How long it would take, she didn't know, but she assumed that her sweet guile and style would have been more powerful than it was proving.

Today, her ensemble was nothing short of chic for a sleepy river town like Bresford. Highlighting the narrowness of her waist was a pair of navy trousers with a line of six chunky, white buttons going down the side of each pocket. The legs widened towards the knee, which made her look even thinner. She chose a peach blouse with puffed sleeves and matched it with a peach Bakelite bangle. To finish off the look, she tied a sheer white scarf around her neck, ensuring it had the perfect drape.

Even then, none of it seemed to catch Marty's eye beyond a meaningless glance. All he did was sort donations and stuff them into several smaller boxes for the plane. When he did speak, it was only related to the secondhand goods.

"Vidalia?" he asked.

"Yes, Marty?" she answered, ready to serve, ready to be told that she captivated him from the very beginning.

"Would you hand me some hats, please? And if you could, go see if anybody else dropped off more coats."

Hope sank to the bottom of her tiny stomach, but she obliged and handed him some dented bowler hats. "Here you go, Marty."

"Thank you." She didn't understand him at all. As she went off in search of coats, her mind replayed the events from the previous twelve hours for anything she could've done to make herself so invisible to him.

Before dinner last night, she primped and changed into an alluring dress that her father had imported from France. This dress was reserved for special occasions only, like Christmas galas or the theatre in Portland, but last night was special to her. Her father invited Marty to dinner at the conclusion of the day and her heart soared when he accepted. This was when she hoped her father would work his charm and convince Marty to marry her or forever live in regret.

The wine-colored silk gown demurely highlighted her figure and a pair of ruby drop earrings flirted with her shapely bare shoulders. She ditched the poppy hat and piled her hair into glossy curls on top of her head, looking more like the Seattle socialite she wished to become. Her face looked similar to that of Bette Davis, everyone said so, with doe eyes and a nose that would always look youthful. She had a full pout that only needed a touch of lipstick. In short, she felt blessed to be born beautiful.

Perhaps Marty will see tonight that I can be the wife he needs, she told herself. How could she go wrong? She studied the actresses in her *Hollywood* magazine and prayed her evening look would translate to "future Mrs. Townsend."

At the dining room table, Dominic and Marty drank Minnehaha Maids and were engaged in conversation about the living conditions of those in the shantytowns, a topic that did not interest Vidalia at all. The thoughts of living in a paper and board shack and wearing the same clothes day after day made her skin crawl.

She stepped purposefully down the stairs, bejeweled hand on the banister. Her heels clicked delicately on the wood and she imagined herself being introduced at some fancy party as the fiancée of Martin Townsend. At the bottom of the staircase, she paused as her father and Marty turned, both expecting Vidalia in casual clothes, but their eyes betrayed their surprise.

To see his daughter looking this regal, Dominic felt a pang of pride. Marty looked for a few seconds longer, taking in her entire appearance without really hiding it.

"Good evening, Father. Good evening, Mr. Townsend," she greeted breathily, making "Townsend" come off her lips as smoothly as she could, and floated behind Marty's chair.

Immediately, Marty put down his glass and said, "Let me get your chair, Miss York." Gracefully, she eased down into the seat and opened up her napkin over her silken dress.

"Thank you, you're so kind. What did I miss?" she inquired and then took a sip of the cranberry drink her father poured for her.

"Actually, Marty and I were talking about the work he's doing and why. Turns out his little sister put him to the task. Sounds like a good girl. Generosity must run in the family, am I right?" Dominic smiled across the table at him.

Marty shook his head. "I wouldn't say it runs in the family, but for my sister, it is true. She isn't well and I wanted to do this for her."

"Does your wife approve of you flying around Washington like this?" Dominic asked casually. A bit bold, but a valid question, nonetheless.

With an equally casual tone, Marty answered, "I'm not married."

"So you have a fiancée, then?" Vidalia added. If he answered "yes," she swore that she'd faint, as she hadn't thought of that possibility. If so, she would just have to work harder and make Marty change his mind, make him realize that she was the only one in the world for him. Her breath hung suspended in her lungs, not going anywhere until she heard his answer.

"I don't have a fiancée, either." With a rapidly beating heart, Vidalia clung to the words "I'm not married" and "No fiancée" like they were promises meant just for her. They filled her mind with images of wedding gowns covered with lace and pearls, merrily packing her honeymoon suitcase, decorating her baby's nursery with flowery wallpaper. She normally would have devoured at least half of the slab of juicy roast beef on her plate, but her appetite vanished as she mulled over the opportunity before her.

Marty was as good as hers.

Dominic nodded and said, "When you do find that lucky girl, I'm confident you'll choose wisely."

Seeing that there was no better time to run with Marty's fortunate singleness than now, Vidalia leaned over playfully and asked him, "So what's on our agenda tomorrow?"

Marty pretended to contemplate the vast options while he swallowed his bite of buttered dinner roll. "It'll probably be more or less the same, boxing stuff up and then boxing more stuff. I plan on flying back around two o'clock with the first load of donations."

"Good, because I want to show you around town since that is part of my job. I can show the place that serves the best salmon chowder and then we can get a malt at Dream Fountain. And maybe after all of that, you can show me the plane and take me for a ride?"

Take it easy, Vidalia. Don't be too eager and destroy the whole plan, she scolded herself. Finally, she took a few bites from her plate to distract herself.

"If we have time, a plane ride could be possible." He gave Vidalia a warm smile.

"That would be lovely!" she chirped. Her gaze met her father's, his full of optimism. The rest of the night went about the same, with Vidalia trying to act interested in the hobo situation but really showing more interest in Marty's handsome face. When dessert was served, she turned her nose up at the prune whip.

Once I'm Mrs. Townsend, I'll never have to eat prune whip again, she comforted herself. She wondered if Marty and his family dined every night on cream puffs and soufflés of all kinds instead of the purple-brown muck before her. With a degree of shame, she realized that she had never tried a soufflé.

Back to the next day, Vidalia had only been marginally successful by finding three coats to bring to Marty. As she shook them out and slung them over her arm, she tried and tried to figure out what she did wrong last night.

"Why didn't I take smaller bites? Maybe my face looked bored when he and Daddy talked about the hobos?" Those didn't seem like big enough reasons for Marty to act uninterested in her. She knew that the look he gave her when she first entered the dining room was the complete opposite of disinterest. His eyes didn't glance, they *lingered.* No matter, she had a plane ride to look forward to, a smaller space in which she could have his full attention with nothing to dilute her charm.

THE WINE-COLORED DRESS IN all its clingy and shimmery glory, which was completely wrong for a casual in-home supper, acted like a magnet for Marty's eyes. It was similar to how he couldn't stop staring at the bearded lady at the circus, no matter how many other spectacular things were going on in the other rings. The bearded lady, the slinky slip of a dress, both were meant for shameless gawking. If Vidalia was attending a New Year's party in Seattle, she would be dressed perfectly, maybe even underdressed, depending on the caliber of the crowd. Tonight was not Seattle or New Year's, just the seventh of May with nobody to kiss at midnight.

She walked behind his chair, clearly planning on sitting next to him. Lacking some grace, he bounded up and pulled out her chair, which didn't have to come out far at all. Easily, Vidalia was one of the thinnest girls he'd ever seen. Her bony shoulder blades jutted out of the draped back, lacking enough fat to soften their points.

"Thank you, you're so kind. What did I miss?" Vidalia asked earnestly.

The conversation flowed to his family, which was natural when getting to know someone new. Playing his cards close, Marty only said that Tabitha wasn't well and when asked about having a fiancée, there was absolutely no way that he was going to reveal his broken engagement to Agnes Crane.

He knew the game Vidalia was playing all too well, the one where a single girl puts on her best dress and flirts without trying to be a tart. The father of said single girl would then angle the conversation to highlight his daughter and subtly convince an eligible bachelor to choose her.

Growing up and going to swanky parties might seem like pure fun for most, but to Marty, they were merely opportunities for objective character study. The older he got, the more the studies became subjective. Some people covered their ulterior motives with a coating of honey and did all they could to get Marty and his family's money stuck to it. Most of the time, however, people weren't cunning enough and Marty was able to turn conversations on their tail so that they'd be talking about the family dog instead.

Memories flooded forth of Mr. John Attison cornering Marty

at a benefit for the Seattle General Hospital, all but pleading him to meet his daughter, an accomplished pianist with a knack for needlepoint and collages. At a summer party hosted by Townsend Timber for the workers and their families, Marty was the most popular person there besides his father. However, the crowd around father and son varied by two generations. Men with hunched backs and silvery hair kept his father company with talk of treacherous logging roads and losing fingers to chainsaws, while men old enough to be Marty's father competed with one another to advertise their daughter's virtues and education. The mothers were worse. Marty couldn't begin to count the dozens upon dozens of recipes he heard over the years, recipes he'd be lucky enough to taste if he got in their families. It was as if these parents didn't have a daughter at all, but simply a product they were promoting from the Sears & Roebuck catalogue.

This season's eligible ladies, available now!

Choose from the following models: Harriet Attison (redhead), Irma Jean Wallace (blonde), and Victoria Clifton (brunette).

All models are guaranteed to keep a spotless home, perform well in society and bear you handsome & intelligent children! Limited quantities available, order now! We pay postage.

In between Vidalia's questions, Mildred's innocent face was all he could see. She had tried with all of her power to hide her pain as she took Dominic's final word that she wasn't wanted. That was Dominic's move in the game and it was a ruthless one. Marty knew fathers could be protective, his included, but to bestow such bitterness upon Mildred seemed unfair.

"And maybe after all of that, you could show me the plane

and take me for a ride?"

The last thing he wanted to do was to be stuck with Princess Vidalia York in the cockpit. If Mildred couldn't help with the donations, Vidalia wasn't even getting ten feet off the ground. His ambiguous answer of "maybe" seemed to satisfy her.

That night at the quaint Riverside Inn not far from the fairgrounds, Marty couldn't buy sleep if he tried. Thoughts of his poor sister haunted him, the rage in his mother's eyes saying that she hated him for leaving. Sometimes, he would unintentionally picture Tabitha in a casket and he regretted his mind wandering that direction. Immediately, he'd squint hard to make the morbid thought disappear, hard enough until his eyes hurt and left his lashes wet. Then he would remember that Tabitha was the one who wanted him to venture out and do something good. How could he feel guilty when he was making his sister happy?

He hadn't told Tabitha about the letters, however. It was a secret that she didn't need to know, just his alone. From his bag, Marty pulled out the five letters that were still in their petal pink envelopes. Every letter, awkward as they were, brought him joy. Not once did Mildred come across like the frilly society girls back in Seattle. She was innocent, insecure and honest. Best of all, she didn't appear to be anything like Agnes. However, he was afraid he wouldn't get to know more about her beyond that after Dominic was done with her. Spooked kittens were always hard to find.

The next morning at the fairgrounds, Marty labored over boxes of men's hats while Vidalia flitted around to gather items he requested. Despite her fussy outfit, she wasn't a slack worker. Obediently, she sorted through volumes of books, beat old mud out of boot treads, then folded clothes and grouped them by category.

"Vidalia?"

Too quickly, she answered, "Yes, Marty?" When he sent her to look for more coats in the massive donations pile, he noticed the twinkle disappear from her eyes. When she turned her back, he looked up to see her walking with her head held a bit lower.

"Was she expecting a marriage proposal?" he mumbled. Then he realized that Mildred had gone away in the same manner yesterday, head low, eyes betraying the tears about to fall. He sighed, upset that he might not get to see her for the rest of his time in Bresford. It was a small town and he was confident he could find her easily enough, but if she truly didn't want to be found, there was nothing he could do.

Thanks to people like the Yorks, Marty was tired of trying to be won over and wished he had been born poor instead. It used to be flattering, then it simply became irritating. None of the girls had anything special to set them apart from each other. They all wore their hair the same, bought the same dresses and talked about the same hollow things. This wasn't true for Mildred. As quiet as she was, she stood apart and captivated him all the more for it.

"Just my damn luck," he mumbled and tossed a frilly blue hat with fake purple flowers into the box with the other impractical women's hats.

"Marty?"

The voice was hesitant and soft, definitely not the voice of Vidalia. Marty almost didn't hear it with the bombarding thoughts in his head. He turned slowly and saw Mildred before him, blushing and panting.

"Mildred!" This time, his feet were the ones frozen to the ground. "I didn't think I'd see you again after yesterday," he said, smiling and concerned at the same time. "Is everything alright?"

She nodded wordlessly. Her brown eyes searched around her feet, something he noticed about her. Just above a whisper, she said, "I'm sorry."

He was baffled. "What could you possibly have to be sorry for?"

"You called my name and I ran away, then Dominic York belittled me and I ran away yet again."

Marty clicked his tongue three times and said playfully, "You're going to have to make it up to me then."

"Yes, please allow me the chance to do that. I feel so awful."

A smile grew across his face. "Come to Seattle with me." With a bounding leap, he climbed into the cockpit like a monkey climbing a tree. He flipped levers and pushed buttons to bring the plane to sputtering life.

"What, right now? Are you serious?" By the tone of her voice, Marty took it that going to Seattle might as well have been a nonchalant picnic on the moon.

He looked over his shoulder at her as he buckled up boxes into empty seats and winked. "Serious as serious can be, Miss Westrick."

"I can't, Marty! Seattle is so far away and I'd get into a mountain of trouble; don't forget that we barely know each other!" She took a step back and shook her head. "I'm sorry, but I don't think I can."

Marty crawled out of the plane and gave her the blush-inducing look that she first saw on the boardwalk. "You're going to turn me down? Why? Would your father disapprove?" She nodded and looked around like she expected her father was spying on her from afar.

"He most absolutely would. Then Vidalia would make my life miserable for as long as I am in Bresford." Her shoulders fell just enough to make her look even sadder than she already did.

Marty crossed his arms and shrugged. "You won't know how mad they'll get until you actually do it." Like a track star, he leapt forward with grace and placed an arm around Mildred, but felt her push back.

"No! Are you crazy?" The horror on her face looked as if she was dangling over a pit of snakes.

"I'm not as crazy as you're acting right now. You said you wanted to explore in your letters, so let's go explore! Trust me." Under his palms, he suddenly felt her ease up. She was silent for a couple moments, staring at the plane before her.

"You know what I just realized?" Mildred said. She chuckled and shook her head.

"What's that?" Marty said quietly, genuinely wanting to know.

"I *wished* for this to happen, to get plucked out of my everyday existence to do something else. This is exactly what I hoped for and here I am trying to stay in Bresford." When she looked to him, there was a new clarity in her dark eyes, less fear this time. She laughed aloud. "You're absolutely right, Marty. I want to see what else is out there and nobody, not even myself, can keep me from doing just that."

He clapped his hands. "Brava, Miss Westrick, brava!"

Without any resistance this time, she placed her clammy hand in his and followed him to the steps of the 4-passenger plane. "Up you go, watch your head. Buckle up and put the helmet on that's sitting right next to you."

As Mildred fumbled with the buckle in the passenger seat, Marty hopped up the step and took the liberty of putting the helmet over her chestnut hair. He must've been smiling like a fool because Mildred looked at his face and she let out the first silly giggle he heard from her.

"What?" he asked, blue eyes shining.

"I'm the kind of girl that follows rules and does what people ask. Breaking the rules is not something I'm accustomed to," she breathed. "I can't believe I'm doing this." She tapped her fingers on her lap nervously.

"Believe it. Now hold still so I can snug the strap just right." His fingertips slipped by the soft skin on her throat while he cinched the strap of her helmet, making her stiffen and avert her gaze. When he left his touch there, she turned and let her eyes trace the outline of his face.

"*Where are you going? Marty, come back!*"

Marty jumped and banged his head on the ceiling of the cockpit. "Shit! Shit!"

A short distance from the airplane, Vidalia pranced closer with an armful of coats and her mouth gaped open in a painted O. Her steps became faster and huffier.

"Give me one second and we'll be out of here, okay?" Marty said with a tone of panic. Mildred bobbed her head with the weight of the helmet.

He jumped from the step and jogged around the plane, checking propellers and other gadgets as fast as he could manage. Everything looked good, so he climbed up into the pilot's seat.

"*Marty! Wait! Why are you leaving?*" Vidalia screamed over the two engines. "*What about my plane ride?*" She chucked the coats to the ground and balled her fists in front of her stomach.

He opened his window and leaned out to yell, "*Have a wonderful evening, Miss York!*" Ignoring her questions, he put on a charming smile and waved. Normally his smile would have made any girl swoon, but he could see the hellfire behind her eyes and imagined steam blasting out of her ears. With Vidalia sufficiently enraged, he shut his window and readied for takeoff.

WITH A PILE OF COATS strewn before her feet and heat rising to her face, Vidalia couldn't believe how rude Bresford's honored guest was being this very moment. Not only did Marty not seem interested in her as a potential wife, he didn't seem interested in her as a measly acquaintance. All of the boys in Bresford had been interested in Vidalia on different levels at some point in time, whether they knew it or not. Some wanted to be her friend, others tried pursuing her as a girlfriend (but never receiving her father's approval), but none had ignored her like Marty did.

"*What about my plane ride?*" she cried out. Her heart had been set on it since yesterday.

Over the engines, he yelled at her, "*Have a wonderful evening, Miss York!*" and then he had the nerve to smile and wave at her like some chummy pal.

If this was how it was going to be, then she would let him fly away in his noisy tin can and not care if he ever returned to Bresford. He could go back to Seattle and roll around in his logging business money all by his miserable self.

After Marty shut the window to the cockpit, she saw someone sitting in the passenger seat. The passenger looked back at her.

"Who in God's name is that?" she said aloud, but the words drowned in the growling of the engines. The helmet skewed her view of the person slightly, but then she was positive of what she saw.

Brown eyes, brown hair, brown, brown, brown.

Mildred Westrick. Dowdy Mildred Westrick was the reason she wasn't riding in the plane next to Marty. It was the last thing she expected to happen.

"No, no, no! She can't go! I'm the co-chair, not her! Why is this happening? This is all wrong! *Marty!*" she screamed up at his window, but the plane had already started to inch forward and turn, blowing her sheer neck scarf up into her face. She clawed at the scarf smothering her and yanked it off her neck. It took to the air like a bird. The engines whirred faster until they sounded like they were about to explode. She saw too much red to remember much after that.

By the time she unfurled her aching, white-knuckled fists and released her clenched jaw, the plane had long disappeared from sight.

CHAPTER SEVEN

Mildred steadied herself during the bumpy ride in the plane as they sped over the field of Manchester Fairgrounds.

What have I done?, she thought. Seeing the knowing look on Vidalia's face as they motored by made her feel like her fate was sealed, the wake causing damage along the way. The heat from being excited and worried to death collected in her helmet like an oven and made her feel nauseated.

She must've looked several shades of green because Marty said, "You're not going to vomit, are you?"

She shook her head under the heavy helmet. "I think Vidalia saw me. By the time we get back, she'll have told everyone."

"Let her tell people until she's blue in the face," he said. He studied his gauges and pushed the engine a little faster, making the field bumps feel like mountains. "Now hang on, it's going to get a bit rough here!"

He wasn't joking. Mildred screeched when her rear left the seat and slammed back down into it. The whir of the engines became so throaty that everything vibrated to the touch, even her teeth.

"Is this field big enough?" she yelped. Visions of crashing in a fiery mess of metal and bones flashed through her rattling brain. She hadn't even considered Marty's abilities when it came to flying airplanes. For all she knew, he was lucky and pushed the right buttons and pulled the right levers, but if something happened outside of his skills, they'd be as good as gone.

He didn't answer. The intensity in his eyes frightened her as he stared just yards in front of the plane's nose. She stared, too, hoping that her added attention would help guide the plane. The blades of grass whipped by so fast that the field looked like a solid green sheet. It was clear they were running out of field and quickly.

"Here we go!" Marty hollered. With nothing in her experiences to prepare her, Mildred held her breath and felt like she was sinking to the floor as the plane lifted off the ground. Her heart slumped into the pit of her stomach with each lurch and gallop the plane made as it gained altitude.

"Look out your window, Mildred!" Marty said. Without knowing it, Mildred had shut her eyes and clutched the sides of her seat. When she opened them, she wasn't prepared and gasped in wonder.

The tiny homes with miniature cars in the driveways fascinated her, how the trees resembled crowns of broccoli in their green May splendor, how the river had more curves and wispy veins coming off of it than she ever knew. Amazingly, the fear of falling or being that high didn't scare her like she expected. The magic of the shrunken land beneath her left no room in her mind for those thoughts.

The jewel-blue Columbia River below curved softly left, headed west for the Pacific. The other river below, the Cowlitz, was much smaller, just as curvy, but with a north heading.

"Marty, are we really going to Seattle?" For a good chunk of time, Marty had been silent, content to let his guest study the view without interruptions. "I thought you were trying to be funny when you said that."

"Of course we are. Why would I lie to you?" he said. "Even so, I don't have enough fuel to get back to Bresford until I refuel at the hangar tomorrow."

The first time Mildred had stayed overnight away from family was when Grace was still alive and she had been with her grandparents for a droll evening without any toys. She used her shoe as a pretend boat for the rag doll she brought with her. All of the other times had been at Hattie's place where they threw weddings for their dolls, and when they were older, listened to records and exchanged teenage gossip. Back then, she only had to worry about bringing a satchel with a clean change of clothes and her sketchpad.

"But where will I stay? I don't have anything with me." At the risk of sounding like a Victorian prude, she added, "And I don't think it would be proper."

"You don't need to worry about any of that. I'm sure we'll find you something for the evening. Just follow my lead." Marty sounded altogether too casual compared to how she felt inside.

Mildred didn't know where to begin thinking. First, she gets pulled into a plane and next, she is on an overnight trip to Seattle with the man that seemed to magically materialize from the newspaper. It all seemed to be happening so fast, like a glitzy train headed for derailment.

*   *   *

THE DESCENT WAS LESS eventful than the takeoff, getting only a small squeak out of Mildred when the tires skidded to a landing on the runway. When Marty drove the plane to his spot and shut the engine off, he reached over to help her remove the helmet. She sat still and let him. Then he took her hand in his. Her eyes widened and blush rushed to her cheeks.

"You won't regret this experience, Mildred. Don't think about what your father or Vidalia or anyone else will think. Believe me when I say it gets easier with practice."

She leaned her head to one side and used her free hand to rake her hair over to her right shoulder. "I hope you're right. Whatever they are saying this moment can't change the fact that I'm not even in the same town. With that said, what can I do to make myself useful?"

He caught himself smiling and staring at her chocolate-colored eyes, probably for too long, because she had to look away. She smoothed out her pants after pulling her hand out from under his. "Let's get started, shall we?"

Before long, Marty and Mildred unbuckled all of the boxes, one box per seat, and took the first load to his truck parked near the hangar.

"That's yours?" she asked, clearly impressed. She was so used to seeing boring, old farm trucks lumbering down the roads in Bresford, all brown or gray and covered in a multiple layers of dirt, some probably many years old. This truck, a glossy cherry-red Chevrolet, was the fanciest truck she had ever seen. The shiny wheels, domed like bowls, reflected Mildred's image as if they were little fun house mirrors.

"You like it?" Marty loaded his box and took Mildred's, giving it a good push down the bed.

"Like it? It's beautiful."

"Thanks. Just don't scratch the paint and ruin it now."

Mildred giggled. "I wouldn't dare."

Soon, the plane was completely empty and the boxes filled the back of Marty's truck. When he opened the passenger door for Mildred, he would've been lying to himself if he said he wasn't excited. The girl that he never would've met had it not been for her strange letters; the girl that he was afraid, but eager, to see; this girl was real and in his truck, admiring it the same way he did when he first bought it.

The engine gave a satisfying rumble when he turned the key. "Are you ready to see a shantytown?"

"I think so. Isn't it dangerous?" Mildred asked. They drove out of the hangar lot and up the street several blocks. From everything she read, they might as well drive into a back alley in Chicago and say hello to a bunch of rival gangsters squaring off with their guns.

"You'll be perfectly safe with me. I have a contact in there, my friend, Randall; he's a college buddy of mine. When I heard that he and his wife and son had the unfortunate luck of having to relocate to Elliott Bay, I reached out to him. From time to time, I would give him staples, but that's when my sister, Tabitha, told me to go broader. That's how I met you, in a roundabout way."

"So you have a sister? She sounds like she's quite the philanthropist."

He smiled just thinking of Tabitha. "Yes and you'll get to meet her tonight, actually." The truck slowed to a crawl. "Okay, we're here." He crossed the lanes and parked the truck outside the entrance to what looked like a shrunken village. The acreage was spotted with nothing but basic wooden boxes to live in, most with a toothpick of a chimney pipe poking out of the boarded roof. Some of the homes had an additional room and more than one window, but not many. Laundry floated morosely on the evening wind like dingy, pathetic ghosts too tired to haunt anything.

When he got out of the truck, Marty slung a sack over his shoulder and saw trepidation on Mildred's face.

"What's wrong?" she asked. "Are we going to get mugged?"

"Wait right here," he said, and then cupped his hands around his mouth, "Randall Fryar!" A few glum heads turned up from their smoking groups and stared. Others turned back to their prized smokes and couldn't care less about the visitors. Moments later, a boy no older than five ran up to Marty's knees and crashed into him.

"Whoa, Leo! You're fast as lightning, buddy!"

"Did you bring me any candy?" Leo asked. For a young boy, his voice sounded as if he ate gravel and his eyes were wild with hunger. While his face was covered in a layer of grime, his dark blonde hair looked like it had been caught in a windstorm of dust and tree sap. His feet were still a little pudgy like a baby's, but they were bare and calloused. Either he outgrew his shoes or they fell apart. Right then, Marty felt ashamed of his rather expensive boots and the fact that his feet probably weren't nearly as roughed up as Leo's.

"Of course I brought you something, pal. What do you think of these? Huh?" Marty reached into the sack and pulled up a handful of Tootsie Roll Pops, bringing forth a light from within Leo and making his tiny mouth hang open. Any other kid could have access to Tootsie Roll Pops or any variety of candy whenever they wanted for no special occasion at all, but Leo likely hadn't had any candy since Marty's last visit a few weeks ago when he brought mounds of maple peanut treats.

"Can I have some?" he asked just above a whisper.

"Where are your manners, Leo Fryar?" Leo stood straight up as if he were caught red-handed. He turned to face his father, who towered over the little boy with his frame built like a celebrated boxer's. With a gruff hand, Randall turned the boy to face Marty.

"*May* I have some, *please*?" Leo slowly corrected himself. As a reward, Marty handed him a fistful of suckers in their colorful wrappers, which Leo had to cradle in his arms like a pile of pirate's loot. As he started to bolt, Randall savagely grabbed his shoulder, making Leo let out a yelp.

Randall hissed in his son's ear like a viper. "*Go back to your mother without anybody else seeing what you got. And next time you come out without asking, we're going to get thrown out. Understand? Think about that as you suck your goddamn candy!*" Leo scurried back to his shack with his head low and whimpering as he went.

"Was that really necessary? He's just a little kid!" Marty said in Leo's defense. His face was a mixture of shock and disgust.

"Just be quiet and let me explain." Randall whipped off his grubby hat and ran his hand over his wavy, unwashed hair. "The city commissioners are getting stricter about no women or children living here, but I simply can't be apart from Sarah and Leo. There's no way I could live, and you should know that I'm not the only man hiding his family. This one guy, Danny, lives over in the quadrant by the water and it blew my mind when he told me that he's got three kids in his place. Three! How could there possibly be nine acres of men without attachments? I'd rather be dead than send them off to live with family because I failed in the world. The person who dares to separate us is dead, plain and simple."

It was difficult for Marty to see his friend so changed, made remarkably bitter by the circumstances he found himself in. In part, Marty didn't blame him, but Randall had always been a short fuse, even when money was great.

The sunset caught the telling tears rimming Randall's brown-almost-black eyes. "I wish I were you. Things wouldn't be so goddamn hard." Though he was the same age as Marty, a strapping twenty-three, the slump named the "Great Depression" drew out some of Randall's youth and gave him a gaunt face and a bruised ego.

"Don't be so hard on yourself, Randall." Marty grabbed his friend to his chest. "This isn't your fault. Times are tough but you're doing the best you can right now."

Randall, dark-haired and always with a layer of stubble on his broad chin, looked to be on the brink of breaking down or insanity. He pushed out of Marty's arms. "My best? This looks like the best I can do? Thanks for that, Marty, thanks a whole lot. My best and your best look starkly different, if you haven't noticed. I'm living in a shithole box and you arrive in *that* ridiculous chariot," he spat and pointed to the blemish-free truck.

The sting didn't penetrate Marty's good intentions like it was intended to. He felt that if the tables were turned, he might feel the exact same frustration and rage. "That's not what I meant, Randall, please believe me. I just brought some stuff that the people of Bresford donated. Maybe something in those boxes could help you perk up."

Randall seemed to be ignoring Marty now, peering past his head. "Who's that plain thing?"

THE LITTLE BOY LEFT almost as soon as he bumped into Marty's legs and was gifted a handful of candy. Before the kid had a chance to disappear, Mildred presumed it was Randall Fryar that showed up. She rolled down the window and listened as closely as she could. While both men kept their voices relatively low, she could sense the tension between them like a wave of electricity, ready to catch something on fire. When Marty tried hugging Randall and got pushed away, she wrapped her hand around the cool, metal handle.

"...living in a shithole box and you arrive in *that* ridiculous chariot."

Mildred inhaled sharply as Randall motioned towards the truck. Everything about this Randall person was bound tight and she feared that Marty would get the receiving end of whatever was bottled up. As quietly as she could manage, Mildred let herself out of the truck and waited by the front bumper. If anything were to happen, she wanted to be there to help in any capacity.

The sunset cast a tangerine glow over the shantytown, making it appear more peaceful than when they first pulled up. Towards the very back of the property, Mildred saw the last of the day's light dancing on the water. She imagined how primitive, but satisfying, it would feel to have to wash one's blouses and socks in the bay with neighbors, or to gather your day's water and cherish each sip. Darnella complained about the process of washing clothes in her older washing machine, but Mildred would've bet that the women in the shantytown would give anything to have such a modern luxury.

"Who's that plain thing?" The abrupt yet smooth voice shattered Mildred's daydream like a bullet grazing her ear. She instantly saw the disapproving gaze.

"I'm Mildred Westrick," she said, choking back the lump of fear in her throat and holding her chin up a degree higher than normal. It was a new thing she decided to try, doing her best to embolden herself instead of going back in her shell like a turtle. This man didn't know she was shy, had ever been shy, unlike everyone in Bresford.

Randall looked her over from head to toe, but not in admiration. "Let me guess. Are you Marty's newest girlfriend? Was he a gentleman and took you to the pictures and a lobster dinner?" He gave a half-smile that was tinged with a sneer. "You're not like the last girl, that's for sure."

The last girl?, Mildred thought, imagining who she was being compared to.

"Shut up, Fryar. You're being a rude bastard right now and you know it. Mildred has been helping me with the donations," said Marty as he walked over to her. "And she's done a swell job." His wink and smile just now helped to smooth over Randall's odd remarks as they carried boxes from the truck and further into the shantytown.

Randall caught up to Mildred with two boxes in his arms. "Marty's right, you know."

Mildred felt herself bristle. "Isn't he usually right?" she said cheekily, hoping to help put him in his place.

"I am a rude bastard and I am ashamed to admit it, but it's true. This damn slump that I'm stuck in with everyone else here, it tends to turn us into tarnished versions of ourselves. Please don't think I'm totally unworthy of your generosity." Randall's face softened, but barely. "Okay, follow me."

Randall walked ahead, weaving between shacks, and Mildred did her best to keep up with the big box she carried. She then felt a reassuring squeeze on her shoulder. Thankfully it was just Marty.

"Are you alright? I didn't know Randall was going to be that nasty back there," he said quietly.

"No harm done. He hasn't been nastier than my stepmother yet, so I'm fine," she replied. She wanted desperately to ask him about the girl Randall brought up, but didn't have the first idea how without sounding like a prying fool. Were there more girls? Were they smarter or prettier than her? More than that, she wanted to know where she stood with Marty and had even less of an idea of how to ask him that. As they walked side by side through the shacks, she felt the lightning snapping in the small space between them, threatening to overload her pounding heart. If Marty felt like she did, he didn't reveal it. Based on the printed word from her beloved magazines, Hattie once explained to Mildred that boys were renowned for being terrible at revealing how they feel, if they said anything at all, which left girls frustrated and resentful. Mildred could agree to a degree.

Two acres deep into the village, they stopped at a shack made from wooden planks in varying stages of decay with a roof of wavy metal sheets. A crumbly black hole in one of the planks had been plugged with a wad of fabric that appeared to be a sock and tar. The only window, a large and sturdy one taken from an old barn somewhere, had perfect diagonal cracks in two of the four panes.

Then there was the front door.

It was beautiful, painted in an expensive lacquer the color of pressed cranberries. The enormous circular stained glass piece depicted a tree bursting with golden pears, rolling hills in the distance, and a thread of sapphire glass for a river. Delicate white flowers studded a maze of emerald green vines above and below the tree. Affixed beneath the glass artwork was a regal brass knocker shaped like a bull elk. Mildred was confident that the door cost more than any back home on the richer side of Bresford.

"It broke my wife's heart to leave most everything, so I made a point to get our door before we came here. She commissioned it herself for our first home and hated the idea of anyone else putting their grubby hands on it." Randall traced his dirty fingers around the elk, as if he could simply imagine himself out of the slum and back on his groomed street.

"Your wife has wonderful taste," said Mildred quietly. "And I'm sorry, for what it's worth."

"Sorry, sorry, sorry, that's all anyone is when they meet me anymore. I'm sure Hoover is sorry, too, but you don't see him at my doorstep with boxes of donated shit. Let's get the rest and bring it inside before we start getting attention." Mildred followed Marty's lead as she took a mental note to avoid talking to short-fused Randall while they collected the rest of the donations. Marty and Randall made quick work of the remaining boxes, stacking everything inside the shack as tightly as they could without making too much racket. Mildred added some lighter bags next to the tower of boxes. When she stepped back, she tripped on a spindly armchair leg and bumped into the wall directly behind her, making the wall creak from impact. There was barely any room to breathe with all of the furniture inside. What free space she could see, from the rough planks that made up the floor to the cardboard nailed over the walls to keep in the heat, Mildred did her best to not get caught staring.

However, Sarah Fryar saw her looking and said, "I know it's not much, but we find ourselves very comfortable here. It's incredible what you realize you don't need and still get along just fine. I made some tea. How do you take yours?"

"You don't have to make excuses, Sarah. They know we're living in *fucking* poverty!" Randall snapped. Leo looked up from his book, Tootsie Roll Pop in his mouth. Marty tried changing the subject and distracted Randall with mild conversation away from the ladies.

"Randall, please refrain from that language, especially in front of Leo. Well, anyway, here's your tea. I don't have any milk or honey, just sugar, I'm afraid," said Sarah as she handed Mildred a porcelain saucer with a cup of strong black tea. Sarah's round cheeks burned with shame.

"One sugar for me, please, but I don't mind going without. I'm Mildred, by the way," she said. Sarah, black-haired and thick in her stomach, nodded and dug out the small bin of sugar. She delicately plucked one cube and placed it in Mildred's tea.

"Mildred. What a lovely name. I had a great-aunt by the same name and I loved her dearly," Sarah said. She stirred a cube of sugar into her own tea.

"Thank you. And I apologize but you caught me admiring all of your gorgeous furniture. Were they from your previous home?" Mildred noticed that the chairs and bed were made of mahogany, vastly expensive, a sign of wealth. An heirloom long case clock, barely touching the plank ceiling with a quarter inch to spare, presided over them from the corner, its majestic ticking reminding them that no matter where it was housed, seconds and minutes were still ticked away the same.

"As a matter of fact, they were, back when things were better, happier. Back when I never imagined that I'd ever have to beg for eggs to feed my son." Sarah eased into one of the mahogany armchairs and sighed as she gazed upon her beloved marble top credenza that used to house two dozen bottles of wine she had for entertaining. The wine had all been imported from Italy and consumed without worrying about having enough money to import more. Now it stored bags and cans of beans and rice. "When my husband had his accounting business, he got rid of everything we started out with and replaced the furniture in *every* room. Can you believe that? Going from a rickety metal bed to the mahogany one in the next room, I felt like royalty sleeping on that. Randall didn't want to get rid of any of it when we moved to the bay, and I wouldn't want him to."

Mildred had her feet tucked as far under the chair as she could so that she didn't block the foot-wide walkway. The four armchairs, dining table and credenza took up most of the kitchen space and in the living room area, the coffee table and sofa only left a narrow path. In the back part of the shack, she saw that the bed left no space on either side, which meant that Randall and Sarah had to climb or scoot to get in and out of bed.

Darnella would hate to know that these people have better furniture than she does, Mildred thought, amusing herself at the amount of mahogany in the shack. The ornate clock by itself would make Darnella extremely envious.

Suddenly, Sarah asked nervously, "Do you see Randall and Marty?"

Mildred obliged and peeked out the barn window. She could see them talking, surprised to see Marty indulging in a cigarette alongside his friend. For some odd reason, she assumed he didn't smoke. She whispered, "They're just outside visiting. Why?"

Before speaking, Sarah turned around and checked on Leo behind her, who was happily entertaining himself with his truck and car toys on the sofa. Then she leaned in closer to Mildred and said in a hushed voice, "I have been trying and trying without luck to convince Randall to get us moved into my sister's house in Tillamook, down near the coast in Oregon. Ever since my husband lost his business, she's wanted us to live with her and have Randall work on their dairy farm. My brother-in-law has the job lined up for him and it would be good, honest work. It wouldn't be able to get us the life we had before this, but I don't care about any of that. We'd have a real roof over our heads and we'd be able to eat as much fresh beef as we wanted. But he won't go, he won't... *he won't.*" A sizeable tear, followed by more, plopped onto her chest, darkening spots on her dirty blouse.

Mildred lowered her voice just the same. "Your husband couldn't honestly expect you to suffer along with your son, just for the sake of his pride? Is there a stronger argument to convince him?" She thought of her own father, who would do whatever job it took to keep his family fed and clean. How lucky she was in comparison.

Sarah shook her head, secretly relieved to tell someone else her strife other than the fellow women in neighboring shacks that were just as hungry and dirty. "That's just it. No argument is good enough. He feels that moving into my sister's house, a house with running water and electricity, mind you, would make him less of a man. By staying in Seattle and barely accepting anything to keep us from sinking lower, he feels like he is making a point. It's only ever been about his pride. With Leo and a baby on the way…"

"What? You're pregnant now?" Mildred asked, aghast. She chided herself for being frank and softened her tone. "How far along are you?"

Sarah's wary eyes darted about, filling with more tears. "I'm guessing that I'm four months along? What was I thinking? I can't believe I was stupid enough to get pregnant here, especially since women and children aren't allowed in the first place. When it's about the only way I can feel close to Randall and he is sweet to me afterwards…I'm terribly sorry, Mildred. I shouldn't have said that and you probably don't want to hear about our heaping pile of troubles." She wiped her eyes on the sleeve of her blouse.

Just the opposite, Mildred felt like she had been invited to see another side of humanity that she would've missed had she stayed tucked away in safe, boring Bresford. She could see herself now, alone in her room, reading on her bed or maybe talking to Hattie on the phone about Leland. Instead, she found herself drinking tea with a heartbroken woman in a shack a hundred miles from home.

"Sarah, don't apologize. I'm learning that myself. Things will get better, they have to. I just know it." Mildred grabbed Sarah's dainty hand, the unfamiliar touch shocking them both. Sarah's face looked plump and young, with a beautiful scattering of freckles on her cheeks and nose. Her face was that of someone who had lived a hundred years, but didn't give any hints of wrinkle or crease. With an elegant hairstyle, makeup and a proper dress, Sarah could turn heads and probably used to. Now, she was tired and weak, completely defeated.

"I know you mean well by saying that, but I have nothing good to say about my life right now and there's no denying it. It's one sorry thing after another. But I would like to see you again, sometime soon. You lifted my spirits." Sarah offered a genuine smile that revealed a brown tooth on the left side of her mouth. She must've forgotten about it because she quickly pursed her lips and shuffled away with their empty teacups.

Just then, Marty came back in the shack with Randall, ready to leave. Their cigarette smoke wafted in behind them. "Thank you for letting us drop in, Sarah. Mildred and I better get going. Bye, Leo."

"Bye, Marty!" the little boy said from his spot on the sofa. He plugged his mouth with his second sucker. Before they walked out, Mildred felt compelled to give Sarah a hug. To her surprise, Sarah hugged her back with a ferocity Mildred didn't expect. She felt Sarah's growing belly against her own and wondered about the future of the baby inside her.

"Thank you, truly," Sarah whispered in her ear. She squeezed Mildred's hand, as if she was wordlessly asking her to stay longer.

"You're welcome," Mildred replied. Randall stood next to his wife, arms crossed over his chest like a sullen statue and he didn't budge as they left his shack filled with mahogany.

CHAPTER EIGHT

"YOUR FRIEND RANDALL WAS interesting. He was a bit intense for my taste," Mildred said as Marty pulled away from the shantytown. "But Sarah was sweet and I hated to leave. My heart hurts for her and Leo, and I feel guilty for everything I have now."

Marty shook his head. "You can't get caught up in feeling bad. It is just how life is right now and we did a good deed to help. It looked as if Sarah enjoyed your company, too, which is a gift in itself. As far Randall goes, he has always been wound tightly and mad at something."

"So why are you friends? You seem completely different from him." After the question left her lips, she realized that people might have asked the same thing about her and Hattie.

"Back in our college days, we bonded over basketball, football, you name it. His intensity was great in all of the sports we played together and I guess I acclimated to his blunt style of communication. The Crash made him close the doors to his business, but I'm afraid he would've sunk it himself eventually."

"What do you mean?"

"I imagine people wouldn't tolerate working with someone as unhinged and vocal as Randall when they're paying him a hefty fee to do their taxes. He didn't care if he offended his clients by calling them colorful names, that sort of thing." This information made Mildred gasp. "If he lived below his means, he might not have to live in a shack. Unfortunately, he took Sarah and Leo down with him."

"All of that mahogany, it was incredible."

"He was successful, liked for people to see that."

Mildred laughed. "My stepmother likes to put on a show, too. She thinks that people worship her because she wears fancy clothes and drives a new car."

Marty laughed at this. "You'll find many people like that."

She continued, "Did you know that Sarah is expecting a baby?"

Marty was silent at first. "Damn you, Fryar," he whispered. The thought of an innocent baby entering the world in a grubby shack made him hang his head.

By now, it was well past dusk and Mildred was sure that her father and stepmother were furious. Her first instinct was to place a call to Hattie and create an alibi that she was staying the night, but Vidalia witnessed her leaving in the airplane. An alibi couldn't help her at this point. The freedom she was afraid of slowly began to feel like something she deserved, less forbidden. It's not as if she was a little girl that was plucked from her front yard. She was nineteen-years-old, a working woman who agreed to take a plane ride with someone she hardly knew, but trusted and wanted to know better.

"As for dinner tonight, I need to tell you a few things." Marty squeezed the steering wheel and struggled to find the words he wanted.

"Like what?" Mildred asked. This was the first time she saw him act jittery and it made her stomach lurch, like she was going to be awakened from her dream. "Will your family disapprove of me?"

"It's not that...exactly. Remember when I asked you if you read anything else about me besides the article you kept?" Mildred nodded. "Does my name, Townsend, sound familiar to you?"

"I can't say that I know anybody with that last name. Do you know any Westricks?" she asked playfully in return. This made him laugh, but with a nervous edge.

"Well, my family is strongly connected to the logging community. Townsend Timber is rather prominent in Washington."

She was curious. "How prominent?"

Marty clicked his tongue. "Essentially, Townsend Timber dominates the industry. I'm surprised you've never heard of the company before. Usually, people know right away who I am and it changes how they act around me."

"Why would they change how they act?" The thought confused her. She treated everyone in her life the same, regardless of who they were. However, she avoided Darnella and Vidalia if she could, but she didn't think she changed herself for them.

He hesitated. "It's because I'm the heir to it all."

Mildred sat in silence, mulling over his words. She had never met an heir to anything before. In Bresford, the wealthiest girl she knew was Vidalia, or at least that was how she portrayed herself with her Italian shoes and French dresses. Dominic probably had a will set up to give his daughter everything after he was gone, too, which would essentially make her an heiress.

"I'm not trying to change what you think about me. That's not my intention at all, Mildred." Slowly, a band of sweat formed on his brow with each mile he drove the Chevy closer to his home.

"Is that why Dominic and Vidalia acted the way they did? It would make sense if they knew about your fortune. And I cannot believe that my stepmother was helping Vidalia seduce you. No wonder why they were all spitting nails when you stood up for me." She let out a bubbly laugh.

"So you're not put off? Please tell me you're not put off." He clenched his teeth, hoping.

"Put off? Why would I be? Aside from my friend Hattie and some people at the cannery, you're the only person that has taken a genuine interest in me. That's a feat in itself."

"I find that very hard to be true!"

She scoffed at his incredulous claim. "You must be joking! Live one day in my life and you'll see how invisible I am. I'm not crazy, beautiful or wildly social, so it's the easiest thing for me to blend into the background."

"You're wrong."

"Oh?"

"You *are* beautiful. I would've been disappointed if you hid behind layers of makeup and acted like a pigeon-brained girl, to be honest."

"Really?" At that moment, Mildred wished she actually had some powder to cover up the red flush she felt glowing on her face. Marty turned down a lovely street in Queen Anne with massive homes, all with lawns as green and perfect as they could possibly be. At the largest house at the end of the street, he pulled into the driveway and parked in what she presumed was his designated spot.

After shutting off the truck, he whispered, "Shit," and stared blankly at the steering wheel.

"What is it?" she asked. "Are you having second thoughts about bringing me in?" Inside, she kicked herself for offering up the idea that she shouldn't be there, but she couldn't stop thinking it was all too good to be true.

He sighed. "No, it's nothing. I didn't plan to bring you home when I woke up this morning. Just...be prepared for my parents."

"Why do you say that?" *Nobody could be worse than Darnella*, she told herself.

"I don't know how to say it without sounding utterly ridiculous." He fidgeted and she could see him struggling to piece together a sentence. "You see, my parents have rather set preferences of who should be close to the Townsend family. I don't know what they'll say, which worries me a great deal. Just promise that you won't hate me if anything bad happens?" The desperation in his voice and pleading eyes melted her heart.

"Of course I promise, but why would they care who your friends are, as long as they're decent people?"

When he smiled sheepishly, Mildred easily imagined what he looked like as a chubby-cheeked five-year-old trying to convince his mother to let him keep the giant toad he found in the pond. With a smile like that, she was sure he could get whatever his heart yearned for.

"They don't really care who my friends are, necessarily, but...they do care who I fall in love with."

Everything she prayed for and every wish she made finally arrived like a wrapped present on her doorstep. From being searched for at the boardwalk to Marty's lingering touch when he strapped on her helmet, the answer was more than clear. In her mind, the gate flew wide open and he was no longer forbidden to her. Marty leaned the rest of the way across the seat and placed a soft palm on her face. Obediently and willingly, she followed his hand along her jaw to his mouth, tasting the new sensation of his breath and the softness of his lips. His scent, a hint of cologne and sweat, filled her nostrils the same way the bakery at home did in the mornings, the air hung heavily with yeast so thick that she could taste the sweet rolls rising. When she finally opened her eyes, Marty was beaming at her like a drunken fool.

"What?" she asked through her own wide grin, although she couldn't be sure she spoke at all with what felt like her heart leaping with joy into her throat. For a time, she forgot everything around her and the events preceding. Her whole existence in that minute was all about a kiss.

With a wink, he said, "We should probably get inside, get the introductions over with and have some dinner. Ready?"

As they walked up the wide concrete steps, the majestic brick home loomed over Mildred and made her feel two inches tall. This was as close to a castle as she had ever been and wondered if Marty's parents were really the king and queen of Seattle. She followed him inside to the sound of silence except for some distant voices in the middle of the house and some clinking noises from the kitchen.

"Mother? I'm back!" Marty shouted in the foyer. His voice echoed for what seemed like an eternity to Mildred. Up the stairs directly before her, Mildred heard something coming closer, padding softly, but with much enthusiasm, down the hall.

"Marty? Marty, are you really back? Tell me everything!" Then, standing at the top of the stairs was a waif of a girl wrapped in a pink robe, dark half-moons under her eyes and skin almost paler than porcelain. The joy on her face betrayed her unhealthy look. Her eyes, young and twinkly, immediately took in the guest standing next to Marty.

"What on earth are you doing out of bed?" he asked, looking terrified as she attempted to go down a step. He bounded up the stairs, gingerly scooped the girl up and brought her down the rest of the way. "Don't scare me like that."

"Sorry, Marty. Who is your friend?" the girl asked with a sweet curiosity. Marty carefully set her down and made sure she held onto him for balance.

"This is Mildred. Mildred, this is my little sister, Tabitha. Don't be fooled by her adorable face. She's actually a terrible, terrible beast." The thin girl and Mildred both giggled.

Inside, Mildred was shaken by the girl's apparent poor condition but touched by the bond she witnessed between brother and sister. "It's wonderful to meet you, Tabitha. I heard that you're the big heart behind your brother's operation. You must be so proud."

Fifteen-year-old Tabitha came right up to Mildred, standing just a few inches shorter and bore the same unremarkable brown hair color. She reached for Mildred's hand and said, "He does make me proud, and please call me Tabby. I'm so glad Marty brought you because I almost died of boredom! He usually brings me gifts from his adventures, but never a person before! Walk with me to the parlor. Would you like to play checkers and talk about movie stars?"

"MASTERSON! MASTERSON!" JEANETTE CALLED as she rang the bell from her wingback chair in the library. After a day of sitting by Tabitha's bed tending to nosebleeds and dealing with a rage from her husband over some droll logging issue, she simply didn't have the fire in her to get up and fix herself a cup of tea.

"You rang, ma'am?"

Jeanette turned in her chair and sighed at the sight of her handsome yet exasperating son. She should've been glad to see him safely back home but lately it seemed that being perturbed by him elbowed out any other emotion. "About time you decided to return," she snipped. Marty took careful steps into the room. "I hope you enjoyed yourself gathering dirty, old things for the bums. Agnes showed for tea less than ten minutes after you left, which put me in quite an awkward position. She was excited at the thought of seeing you. I didn't tell her about your little mission for fear she'd think you'd gone insane."

Agnes. "Mother, I don't know what to tell you. The engagement is over and it won't be resurrected, for lack of a better word. And yes, I did enjoy myself in Bresford, but there is something else I need to tell you for tonight."

She felt her eyes squint out of habit when preparing to hear bad news. No matter what she did to train herself out of it, the squint couldn't be stopped. The creases that grew from the squint seemed to be ironed onto her otherwise youthful-looking face, allowing her to freely blame those that caused the squint to begin with. "And that 'something else' would be?"

Marty did his best to hide his nervous exhale before speaking. "I brought someone with me, a girl from Bresford. She's remarkably sweet."

Her squint hardened. "A girl? What exactly possessed you to bring her into your airplane? And further, what made you think you could bring her *here* and impose on me in my home? Honestly, Martin, you make stupid, impulsive decisions just like your father." Deep inside, Jeanette knew that she sounded like a sourpuss, the queen of killjoys, but it couldn't be helped. After having her hopes set on Agnes as a daughter-in-law and then having them dashed by her reckless son, it became easier than ever to slide into a bitter mood and stay there.

"Mother, please listen."

"Yes, ma'am, you rang?" Ada Masterson, the family's long-time housekeeper and cook, older and beginning to gray at her temples but still beautiful in the classic sense, peeked into the library and her face warmed at the sight of Marty. She'd been serving the family since Marty was barely a toddler. "Hello, Marty." He nodded respectfully at her.

"Tea, please, Masterson, and hurry," she said in a voice hinting that she was moments away from fainting.

"Yes, ma'am, right away."

Jeanette's pasted-on smile faded after the housekeeper extraordinaire left. "I'm listening, Martin. Continue."

"Her name is Mildred Westrick."

Immediately, she sorted through the calling cards and faces from years of parties, trying to find a connection somewhere: countless girls trying to elbow their way into her circle at galas, mothers doing what they could to promote their daughters. Nothing came up except Joanne Weston, whose father was a head chef at some hotel she couldn't remember the name of.

He continued. "Mildred wrote me a few weeks before I was set to arrive, asking to help and telling me about her life. When we finally met, she was so afraid that she ran away."

Jeanette tried to look less interested than she actually was. "Ran away? Did she not know about you being a Townsend then?" A woman running towards the Townsend fortune was to be expected, but running *away* from it was unheard of.

"She didn't have a clue about my connection until I told her today. I felt she needed to know, but I'm not worried and you shouldn't be, either."

Jeanette drummed her fingers on the arm of her chair, just about the time her tea would arrive. On the dot, Masterson came into the room with a tray. She was kind enough to have a cup on the tray for Marty, as well.

"Dinner will be ready in fifteen minutes, ma'am," said Masterson as she backed out of the room.

"Very good, thank you," Jeanette said. She took a cup of tea and stirred in some sugar and cream. "And where is this meek girl that I'm supposed to feed and house tonight?"

"Tabby is actually feeling well enough and entertaining Mildred with a game of checkers. I'm sure that she has some nightclothes that she can lend to Mildred and Masterson can freshen up a room for her," he explained casually. "I know what you're thinking, Mother. Please don't assume she's like the other girls."

After the first few sips of tea, Jeanette felt mostly human again. "I can't promise anything, Martin. Let's go to dinner, shall we?"

DOWNSTAIRS AT THE OAK dining table, Jeanette sat at the head with Marty and Tabby on each side of her. While it was a regular evening with nothing to celebrate on the calendar, Mildred noticed that Jeanette wore a taupe silk blouse with a delicate emerald necklace draped about her neck with matching earrings. At home in Bresford, a dinner on such a night called for no formality, even if steak was on the menu.

Mildred sat next to Tabby without speaking and tried to stop her feet from fidgeting wildly under the table. Her senses were overwhelmed by the grandeur of the room with its dark paneled walls and shelves lined with fine vases and small, yet detailed, brass sculptures of logging equipment. She wanted to guess that seven of her dining rooms at home could fit easily in one of Mrs. Townsend's. Since she hadn't eaten since breakfast that morning, the smells coming down the hall made her mouth water and she realized that she would've happily eaten a slice of Darnella's disgusting meatloaf, cold and without gravy.

"Your name is Mildred, is that right?" Jeanette finally asked. Mildred's foot wiggled even more as she managed to look upon Marty's regal mother. She was exactly what her stepmother strived to be: polished, classy and respectable. Her heart-shaped face maintained most of its youthful radiance, but signs of age showed at the corners of her eyes, as well as a few telling grays that flowed with the rest of her honey-colored hair, pinned elegantly on the side of her head with a golden comb.

"Yes, ma'am, it is."

Tabby chimed in, "She also goes by 'Millie,' but then she said her best friend is the only person that really calls her that. And then she said—"

"Tabby, please mind your own business," Marty interrupted, knowing full well that his mother was dying to know what Tabby wanted to finish saying. For the first time since being seated at the table, Mildred looked at Marty. Something in his eyes told her that seemingly harmless conversation was to be treated differently tonight.

"Dinner is served," Masterson announced. She carried a hefty platter of salmon filets bathed in a pale yellow cream sauce. Even the lemon slices and sprinkles of dill were done with an artistic touch. As much as Mildred despised most everything about salmon because of her job, she couldn't wait to put a bite in her mouth. Masterson served everyone swiftly with hands that have prepared countless elegant meals. What was once an empty china plate was now filled with a palm-sized portion of fish, buttered peas, wedges of herbed red potato and a roll that was more like a yeasty pillow from heaven.

"This looks delicious. Thank you," Mildred told Masterson. The housekeeper paused for a moment with her basket of rolls and gaping mouth. She wasn't used to hearing appreciation for doing something so routine to her, but she smiled in return.

"You're welcome, miss," Masterson said softly before retreating from the dining room.

In the silence, Mildred felt guilt wash over her. "Mrs. Townsend, I am deeply sorry to impose. I hope I won't be a bother, truly. I'm willing to sleep in the basement or attic so that nobody fusses over me. I can even take care of my own dishes or help the housekeeper with chores."

Jeanette hadn't touched her meal during Mildred's speech, her eyes clearly showing interest in the girl that her son dared to bring home. Tabby picked at her fish and bread. With her illness, her fickle stomach couldn't handle much but Jeanette still insisted she try to eat. Marty sat still and observed his mother as if she was a bomb about to be detonated.

"You look like a polite young woman and I doubt you could be that much of a bother. Please don't think I'm going to mistreat you by placing you in the attic. As for the dishes, that's part of Masterson's job. Please eat before it gets cold." Jeanette lifted a bite of salmon to her mouth, so Mildred did, too.

Marty added, "However, if you break anything, I will have to send you to the dungeon filled with hungry crocodiles." He showed his teeth and made a *chomp-chomp* sound, despite his mother's audible sigh.

"I, for one, am pleased you're here! I hope you don't have to leave soon," Tabby said and put her dainty hand over Mildred's. She beamed so wide that her smile threatened to stretch beyond her thin cheeks. A glimmer of blood appeared in her nose and she was quick enough to stop the flow with her dinner napkin. "Pardon me," she mumbled through the napkin.

"Oh my!" Mildred gasped. "Are you alright?"

Marty jumped out of his chair to aid his sister, but she waved him away. "Please, let me help."

"I'm fine, Marty," Tabby said, but the napkin was getting more saturated by the second.

Jeanette rubbed her forehead and sighed impatiently. "She's been getting nosebleeds all day. Masterson, Tabitha needs a fresh napkin!"

"All day? When did it get this bad?" Marty asked. His face was nothing but knots of worry. Mildred didn't know what to do.

Aside from losing her mother horrifically in the blink of an eye, she had never experienced a malignant disease in her family. Watching Tabby deal with the bleeding was surreal.

"It got this bad the day you left. Imagine that, my son. Maybe it's a sign from God that you shouldn't leave on these little trips," his mother said evenly. Anger lurked under the surface of her tone.

Tabby hid the stained napkin on her lap, the nosebleed having finally subsided. "I'm better now, so let's stop arguing and return to the original conversation. As I was saying, Millie, I hope you can stay more than the evening. Can you?" Masterson silently swooped in and deposited a fresh linen napkin by Tabitha's plate and took the bloodied one.

Mildred answered slowly once she was sure Tabby was over the worst of the nosebleed. "Well, I imagine I'm going back to Bresford tomorrow morning but I would love to become better acquainted. Everyone in Bresford knows everyone else and what is going on. It feels good to escape from that and meet new people."

After a ladylike mouthful of fish, Jeanette set her fork down and folded her hands in her lap. "Mildred, would you tell me a bit about yourself? Martin says that you wrote to him, out of the clear blue sky." She chuckled. "I don't know anyone from Bresford, so naturally I'm intrigued beyond measure. Are you all farmers like I suspect?"

Was Jeanette being sincere about wanting to know more or trying to weed her out like a rogue dandelion? The anxiety she felt in Marty's truck disappeared when Tabby stole her away to play checkers but his mother's questioning to gather intelligence was the moment she dreaded and her anxiety returned threefold. It faced her squarely and there was no clever way she could think of to dodge it. Without fail, her cheeks erupted in a deep rosy shade.

"It's kind of a long story," she began awkwardly. As quickly as she could, she covered her mother and her horrible death on the highway that still remains a mystery, then she spoke about gaining a new mother and sister with Darnella and Opal, how her best friend Hattie is gorgeous like a starlet and then she stopped herself abruptly before mentioning her job at the cannery. The whole time Mildred recounted her life, Jeanette listened, seeming interested enough and nodding at the appropriate times. Marty didn't take his gaze off Mildred.

"What a fascinating story. You mentioned your parents. Are they affluent in any way in Bresford?"

"Mother, that's not important." Marty shook his head. Clearly, his mother didn't want to heed his request and proceeded.

"Of course it is! Please show some understanding, Martin. A few questions won't harm anyone and besides, most people are proud to have connections and mention them before anything else." Jeanette forced a smile and returned her attention to Mildred. "I apologize for my son. He doesn't seem to care about his mother's feelings anymore these days, but as I was saying, is your family important?"

Without summons, tears burned at the edge of Mildred's eyes and she couldn't speak. While she did mention her father and stepmother, she purposefully didn't go into what they all did on a daily basis. Her father sold feed to farmers, her stepmother used to peddle hats and Mildred bloodied her hands with fish. There was no rank in any of that. She made the tears retreat and pushed herself to perk up. "Actually, my father is a shop manager and my stepmother leads the Bresford Ladies Aid Society. She is featured in the newspaper from time to time."

An unimpressed nod from Jeanette confirmed that her last bit of information wasn't good enough.

"Mother, are you quite finished?" Marty asked. Hearing his

melodic voice, despite the edge he just used, reminded Mildred that she was here for him, not anybody else. However, Tabby was proving herself to be sweet as cream and she hoped to gain a friend in her.

"I believe so. Are you enjoying your meal, Mildred?" Jeanette smiled warmly at her as she raised her crystal glass, as if to toast herself for a successful interrogation.

"MY BIRTHDAY IS NEXT WEEK and I really want to have a party. My mother would say no without hesitating, but I think my father would allow it since I'm not going to be around much longer. If I have a party, can you come?" Tabby asked Mildred, who sat in Jeanette's chair next to the hospital bed. After dinner, Marty helped his sister wash up, change into nightclothes and get her into bed. After he handed Mildred one of Tabby's nightgowns, he left the two girls to talk while he went in search of Masterson for coffee.

"What do you mean you won't be around?" Mildred asked. She could see that Tabby wasn't a picture of health and her bed was designed for patients in hospitals, but that didn't necessarily mean she was going to die. It wouldn't be right for someone her age.

Tabitha shrugged nonchalantly. "It's leukemia. I got sick with it earlier this year in February. Marty helps and gives me a whole bucketful of blood every week, but that only makes me feel better for a little bit. So, will you come to my party?"

So many things happened that day that Mildred had a difficult time absorbing anything more. Aside from the crazy plane ride business, she was now in a dying girl's nightgown and about to go to bed in a house that was more like a palace, and she was being invited to return to the same dying girl's birthday party.

Mildred couldn't help but smile at Tabby's genuine

kindness. "I'd love to celebrate your birthday more than anything, but I have to see what happens when I go back home tomorrow."

"What do you mean?" asked Tabby. Despite her dark circles on her young face, her eyes were as intense as any Mildred had ever seen. While she claimed to be dying, this sweet girl was more concerned about her new friend's gossip than the state of her fragile health.

"I didn't exactly tell my father or stepmother that I was going with your brother to deliver the donations. It was a surprise to me in a way, but I don't really do anything exciting or against the rules, until today, I guess."

Tabby's mouth dropped open and she smiled devilishly. "Aren't they going to think you're scandalous now? I wish I could be scandalous at least once in my life."

"Who is scandalous?"

Both girls looked towards the door to see Marty peeking in the room. He pulled up a chair to join the girly chat with his cup of coffee. Tabby studied their shared glances and smiles before asking in a calculated tone, "Marty, tell me how you met each other."

Not the embarrassing letter story again, thought Mildred. She dreaded telling it or hearing it, but for Tabby, she'd make the sacrifice to entertain her.

"You see, little sister, I went to the circus and there was this tightrope walker doing all sorts of tricks without falling. I couldn't take my eyes off her. The tightrope walker was Mildred! I couldn't believe it! The back flips she could do astonished me!"

"And let me guess, you were selling popcorn and cigarettes?" Tabby added.

He snorted. "Wrong! I was the bearded woman!" They all laughed heartily, almost close to tears, until a husky voice broke into the room from the hall.

"Martin, come to my office immediately." Mildred didn't see who it was but she knew that the fun was over for the night based on the looks she saw on their faces.

With all seriousness, Marty whispered, "It's probably best to go to bed now. I'll see you in the morning." He obeyed the deep voice and left the room.

CHAPTER NINE

Back in the plane the next morning, Mildred was anxious to know what happened last night and whose voice beckoned Marty from all the fun in Tabby's room. There had been the prim dinner with Marty's mother and her pointed questions, but the evening vastly improved after that and she didn't want it to stop. The gruff voice ruined it all, that threatening tone telling her that whoever owned it was in charge of everything. Even at breakfast, when things usually started fresh between people, the tension remained. It was only Jeanette, Marty and Mildred at the dining table for breakfast, and even Jeanette seemed uneasy in her own home. Tabby's strength was low, so she took her breakfast in her room. As much as Mildred wanted to enjoy the creamy eggs, sausage and sourdough toast, she felt like an unwelcomed guest and barely tasted her meal.

Over the roar of the engines, Marty said, "I'm sorry if my mother said anything to make you feel uncomfortable. I was being selfish by bringing you and I knew she would do what she did." He failed to mention who was responsible for putting a halt to their evening, but she didn't want to force it from him.

"I'm sure she was just trying to protect you from a poor girl like me. Don't worry, Marty. I'm used to not being good enough for anybody." She shrugged as she watched the snaky river far below as they got closer to Bresford.

"You shouldn't tell yourself that, Mildred. Those people that make you feel that way are the ones who aren't good enough. They're cowards who are incapable of being happy for anyone, let alone themselves. You're better than them."

Mildred sat up straighter and played the words in her mind again and again. "I've never thought of it that way."

"You're good enough for me and I want to keep seeing you, if you'll let me."

Mildred looked at Marty, perplexed but pleased. Just yesterday, they shared a simple kiss that stirred her soul and the dream didn't end when she closed her eyes that night in the lofty guest bedroom. And now here he was, practically begging to be around her. Not many people begged to be around Mildred Westrick, but perhaps Marty was just as different from everyone else as she was.

"Yes, I'd like that. When can we see each other again?"

"WHERE HAVE YOU BEEN? Do you have any idea what you've done by running off?"

Just as Mildred expected, Darnella had a full round of ammunition to fire at her as soon as she walked through the front door. She reminded herself of what Marty said to her in the plane, which seemed to act like a shield when Darnella cornered her into an armchair.

"Your father is furious! You've made me look like a bad mother, with you flitting off here and there! And poor Vidalia..." Darnella looked shaken in her dark orange dress as she sat across from her stepdaughter, searching the room for an answer to the insanity presented before her. "Did you even think of anyone besides yourself when you threw yourself at Marty? How could you be so selfish? Vidalia was intended for him, not you!"

The people that make you feel that way are the ones who aren't good enough. The words Marty said reverberated, fanning the little fire inside her. She studied her stepmother's painted face and mustered enough bravery to look her straight in the eye. While she didn't know what she wanted to accomplish by it, she was satisfied when she noticed something change with Darnella's face. Her nostrils flared, her pupils dilated and her lips pursed into a thin red line.

Darnella was scared.

Without looking away, Mildred raised her chin triumphantly. "He kissed me."

"*He did not!*" Darnella protested and pointed an accusatory finger at Mildred. "You're lying and you know it!" Her right eye flickered.

"I'm *not* lying! Why can't you believe that someone like him can love me? You, Vidalia and her father, all of you didn't pay me any mind until Marty showed up. Everyone was fine with how things were as long as I was hidden from the world!" She stood up and looked squarely at her stepmother and declared, "I'm not hiding anymore."

Darnella turned a shade of green. "That letter, I should've opened it but I went against my better judgment. I thought I could trust you. I'll give it time, however. I highly doubt the Townsends would even consider a connection to a girl that works in a cannery. Now I must run. Opal, come along!" She smoothed her skirt and placed her rust-colored cap at the perfect angle over her hair, then eyed Mildred from a safe distance. "You'd be wise to stay away from Marty Townsend. He may have kissed you, but he would never marry you."

Opal wandered into the room, clueless to the conversation and took her mother's impatient hand. With that, Darnella was gone and sped out of the driveway in her emerald sedan.

Mildred stood still, her knuckles white from making fists, and felt vomit rising steadily in her throat.

ON THE OTHER SIDE of town, Marty walked into Dominic's in search of the man himself. Mildred convinced him to let her deal with her family and wanted to go back to work, but they promised to see each other soon. When the bell jingled on the door of Dominic's, Hattie looked up from wiping fingerprints off the display cases and dropped her rag. She hadn't heard from Mildred in over a day and had been worried sick.

She rushed over to Marty and said quietly, "Hello, I'm Hattie Kilpatrick. We haven't formally met, but Mildred is my best friend. I heard she disappeared with you. Is that true?" Nervously, she twisted her hands together.

Marty obliged the friend that Mildred described to his mother as the one who looked like a starlet and agreed that she was fairly accurate. "Nobody disappeared. She was perfectly safe with me. If you're looking for her, she is back at work."

"Oh, that's good! I was beside myself with worry."

"Do you know where I can find Dominic?" Hattie nodded and pointed towards the back of the store.

A brass plate that read *Dominic York, Owner* was affixed on the door of the office. He knocked quickly and a voice boomed from inside. "Come in!"

Marty entered the room and saw not only Dominic, but

Vidalia, too. He braced himself for the fury he saw her unleash as he flew off yesterday, certain that she saved some of it to deliver in person. Instead, she smiled as if she hadn't been jilted at all.

"Marty! Welcome back!" Vidalia said cheerily.

Does Dominic not know what happened? Marty thought. He was there to discuss the progress of the donations, but instead, he stood confused in the doorway.

Dominic sighed deeply. "Are you here to tell me what in the hell Mildred Westrick was doing in your airplane?" He spit out Mildred's name.

There it was.

"Mr. York, if I may, it's up to me who gets in my plane, now isn't it?"

Dominic smiled sweetly, which looked out of place on him. "Marty, please close the door." He waited for Marty to obey. "Thank you. And to answer your question, I fully comprehend that you're the owner of your airplane and that you're a grown man who is capable of making his own decisions. I respect that. What I don't understand is how you are allowing someone like Harvey Westrick's daughter to blind you. My daughter is far more appropriate for you than Mildred, yet you can't see this."

He couldn't believe what he was hearing and his face said just that.

Dominic spoke up before Marty had a chance. "Vidalia saw everything. Don't try to deny it."

"I won't deny it. I invited Mildred to accompany me and help with the donations. And I *am* blinded by her. Her shyness, the way she smiles..."

"That's enough, please. I don't tolerate Harvey or his daughter, never have. Nothing bothers me more than to see someone have something they don't deserve." Dominic locked eyes with Marty and jutted out his lower jaw.

Marty didn't know if he should laugh or feel panic. "And I suppose you wanted me to fall in love with your daughter? Is that why you contacted me, when you realized that I'm from the Townsend Timber family?" Dominic narrowed his eyes and chose to remain silent.

Vidalia inhaled sharply and made her eyes as doe-like as possible when she looked up at him. "Why didn't you want me?"

"I'll see myself out. Good day to you both." Marty could feel Vidalia's eyes on his back as he fled the office and then Hattie's when he left the store.

"First my damn father and now this bullshit," he mumbled to himself on the way back to his airplane.

Gerald Townsend, his father, was the one who requested his son's presence in his office last night. In the darkened room, Marty could see that his father was seated in his leather chair and had two glasses of bourbon on the massive desk before him, despite that Prohibition was alive and well.

"Your mother tells me you brought a friend home. Let me guess: she isn't Agnes Crane.". Gerald spoke slowly, condescending.

"Enough about Agnes, Father. I keep telling Mother that it's over but she won't listen. I would at least think you'd trust me." Marty eyeballed the smooth bourbon that called his name but he didn't want to go for it. Gerald swirled the liquor and studied his son who looked just like him in his younger days: a strong brow, a mouth to drive a woman mad and a defined jaw that could've been designed by the gods.

He slung his drink back and gave himself another healthy pour. These days, it took about four drinks for him to begin feeling good. "Martin, while I can't say much about this girl I haven't met, I don't see why you can't just settle with Agnes. You two were engaged, for God's sake, and then you had the bright idea to break it off. Tell me, what was so wrong about her? Was she too rich and beautiful?"

Marty couldn't tell him why. His own mother didn't even know. Tabby was the only other person that knew and she wouldn't say a word. Just the idea that he had ever proposed to Agnes made him queasy.

Gerald waited impatiently for an answer but didn't get one. "You've nothing to say? Very well, then. So tell me about this other girl. Was her name Winifred?"

"Her name is Mildred. She's the total opposite of Agnes."

Gerald swallowed some bourbon and had a wet smile. "Wonderful. So she's poor, stupid and ugly? She must be a good lay if nothing else recommends her."

Marty balled his hands into fists, ready to knock the glass clean out of his father's grip. "She's not any of that!" he snarled.

His father let out a semi-drunk laugh. "Easy, boy! I'm not trying to be nasty. Be a good sport."

"If you must know, she's a sweet sort of girl and isn't obsessed with herself or money."

"How disgustingly refreshing. Does she live under a rock and have no idea about the economy?" When Gerald laughed into his glass, it amplified the drunken state he was getting himself into.

"Just because she doesn't worship money doesn't make her less than us, Father."

"Listen to me, Martin. There are two types of people that aren't about money: people that have enough of it to not worry, like us, and the people who are as poor as dirt and no longer give a shit, like her."

"You would be pleased with Mildred if you gave her a chance. Just leave it for now and focus on your bourbon." Marty plucked his glass off the desk and tossed it back like his father. With alcohol having a bad reputation these days, he made a point to savor each sensation. The bourbon was warming, smooth and expensive. He held his glass out for a refill. Gerald chuckled and obliged.

"That's my boy."

EVER SINCE HE MARRIED Darnella five years ago, Harvey Westrick found himself behind the counter at Farnsworth Farm & Feed, waiting on customers and assisting the aging Mr. Farnsworth with managing the business. Harvey was clean shaven and his dark, wavy hair was slicked back, completely unlike his appearance when he was with Grace. Back then, she appreciated a little stubble on his face and he didn't even own a single tin of pomade. It was a newer idea for him to dress nicely and work one job compared to his days as a filthy mechanic working several side jobs. Grace stretched his hard-earned pennies with ease and even if a week was tighter than she planned, she simply added more water to soup and used less butter on their bread. Sometimes, Harvey was paid in cash, but he mainly bartered his services. He'd bring home filets of fish caught that morning, cuts of beef and jars of honey, hand-knit socks, empty canning jars and many kinds of books, all of which Grace was pleased to utilize. One friend even lent them the use of a family cottage in Long Beach for a weekend after Harvey painted their whole house. They talked about that weekend at the coast for years.

Harvey remembered Grace's chocolate-colored curls dancing on the ocean breeze. Her hair and soft face even smelled like the ocean when he embraced her often those two days. He gazed with starry eyes at his beautiful wife as she walked the beach barefoot, glancing back at him and saying how much she loved him. Mildred, about two-years-old at the time, toddled after her mother. She was mesmerized by the sensation of sand on her baby skin and erupted in giggles as sandpipers zipped around a few feet ahead of her.

"Excuse me? Harvey?"

The sand, surf and Grace's face dissipated into the ivory foam he remembered seeing roll along the beach until it became nothing. Harvey felt a twinge of panic when he finally opened his eyes and didn't find himself in Long Beach, but behind the counter at work. In front of him stood Irma Smith's wrinkled husband, Wayne, dressed in his standard plaid shirt and thick overalls. He came in daily for random things for his farm and was usually pleasant to deal with.

"I'm sorry, Wayne, you caught me in the middle of daydreaming. Do you ever do that?" Harvey apologized while ringing up the shovel, some chain and bird seed.

"A little, sometimes when I'm milking the cows. Might I ask what you were daydreaming about? You looked awfully happy, whatever it was."

"You remember Grace, don't you?" Saying her name aloud was oddly difficult, as if it was sacred.

Wayne's wrinkles moved as he smiled. "Of course I do. What a beauty she was. She used to come over and crochet with Irma and she'd bring Mildred. Such a sweet woman you had there. Did you know that I had Mildred help me milk cows once? She squealed like a funny little thing when she touched an udder, but she got the hang of it and was so proud to drink a glass of that milk."

Harvey chuckled at the memory. "Grace told me that ages ago and I hate to admit that I forgot all about it."

"It's a shame about Grace. She was too young to be taken up to our Lord that soon, and in such a way, just horrible." Wayne looked as if he might cry. "Have you heard anything about the Highway Shooter?"

That's what Grace's murderer had been dubbed shortly after news of it broke. For a few months, Harvey thought of nobody else besides his dead wife and the Highway Shooter. If he could avenge Grace, he would do it faster than a heartbeat. Instead, he stopped living. The Bresford Ladies Aid Society, led by Irma back then, volunteered to bring meals and wash laundry for him and Mildred. At fourteen, Mildred was capable of helping but she couldn't do anything that reminded her of her mother without breaking down into a sobbing mess. The Highway Shooter took everything from them and for no reason anybody could find.

"Well, Wayne, I guess there hasn't been any news on him since it happened five years ago. Nobody reported the vehicle, nothing. I guess that's where it will stay for all eternity." The familiar panic crept up Harvey's body, ready to remind him how that day felt in every raw aspect. He pushed it back down by thinking of his second wife, Darnella.

"How is Mildred, by the way? I hear she keeps busy at the cannery but I also heard from Irma that she is now an item with that pilot fellow from Seattle."

Mildred catching the eyes of the "pilot fellow" was the hottest gossip in Bresford since Dream Fountain showcased an ice cream sundae topped with candied salmon. In the two weeks since Mildred returned from her surprise overnight stay in Seattle, she carried herself differently, like someone who was no longer living in the shadows.

Harvey bobbed his head a bit and shrugged. "Mildred is fine, but she's not the same since she met Marty. She's not blue all the time, she's..."

"Happy?" Wayne smiled.

"Yes. She's happy, alright." Harvey handed Wayne his purchase and waved him out the door.

Mildred is happy, he thought. *But for how long?*

It had been made public that Marty was from wealth and destined to inherit even more of it from his father, that he wasn't just some cocky pilot with good looks. Why Marty selected

Mildred to romance over someone affluent from his own circle, Harvey hadn't a clue. Mildred Westrick was from a lower-class working family, pure and simple. It didn't mean she wasn't worthy of him, but when it came down to the finer details, hope chests filled with quilts and silverware took second place to piles of family money. Lower-class girls married lower-class boys and brought their hope chests with them. In addition to this, Harvey had to deal with the tension between his wife and Mildred. Apparently, Dominic York had every intention of setting up Vidalia with Marty since he first arrived in Bresford, according to Darnella. Somehow, she was enlisted as a matchmaker to help make this happen, which didn't surprise him. His wife was itching for some semblance of the society she left after her divorce and if being a busybody satisfied her, then he was happy for her. The fact that it was a York she was dealing with made him feel ill.

Dominic York always tried to nab the best for himself, always. For the longest time, Grace had the ability to turn Dominic's head without doing anything on her part. If Grace shopped at his store, he'd try to give her discounts and compliments intended to make her blush, but each time, she politely declined his offer and paid full price. As for the compliments, she only thanked him politely but never flirted in return. This knowledge always hung in the air between Dominic and Harvey whenever they met in public. Not for one second did Harvey doubt Grace's fidelity, but it was Dominic that he couldn't trust. His daughter was just like him, willing to step on people to get where she wanted to be.

The simmer in Harvey's mind cranked up to a rolling boil after his conversation with Wayne. Dominic York could make life miserable for those that crossed him, including Mildred. He might be the jolly shop owner to most everyone else in Bresford, but to Harvey, he was a jealous bully. Vidalia wasn't any better.

Harvey shouted towards the back of the store, "Hey, Mr. Farnsworth, I need to take a break but I'll be right back!" A grumble of approval came from the back office. Harvey whipped off his apron to go in search of his daughter.

IN A MOMENT OF generosity, Albert let Mildred take a break when her father showed up to speak to her. Together, they walked to Boone's Diner and found a booth by the window. Even sitting across the table from Mildred, Harvey noticed that a light seemed to shine from within her. Before Marty, she was glum and made herself barely noticeable.

"Can I get you coffee? Lunch? Pie? The cook made apple walnut pie with last year's apples he spiced and canned. Does that interest you?" asked the waitress. She was a short white-haired lady with a slight gap in her front teeth named Bonnie and had been a waitress at the diner for as long as Harvey could remember. Her apron was in need of a serious washing, but so was most of the restaurant. Boone's Diner was nothing like The Orchard, but at least the food was comforting and delicious.

Harvey beamed at Bonnie. "Coffee with cream for me and we'll both take a slice of that apple walnut pie."

"A la mode? Made the ice cream fresh this morning myself," she offered with a mischievous voice and a wink.

He clicked his tongue. "Absolutely, Miss Bonnie! I believe it's the only way to eat pie." The waitress chuckled and brought back two slices of pie with vanilla ice cream. It wasn't Mildred's favorite kind, but it still tasted good. Her favorite pie was also her mother's favorite. In the summer, Grace made blackberry custard pie that the three of them would eat for breakfast if it hadn't all disappeared after the dinner the from night before.

"Thanks for the pie, Dad. What did you need to talk to me about?" She took a ladylike bite and tried not to drop ice cream off her spoon and chuckled at her clumsiness.

Harvey compared his only daughter with the image of his late wife that was still vivid in his mind, Mildred being so much like her in personality and looks, even down to the way she sneezed. Mildred wasn't going to be in the movies for her appearance anytime soon but she was a different kind of beautiful that lasted longer than any starlet's. It hurt his heart to know that Grace would never physically see their daughter try to navigate her life like parents should. Mildred's sweet spirit, exactly like her mother's, made her sensitive to everyone around her and that much easier to wound. That's what worried Harvey the most with what he was about to say.

"So...when are you going to see Marty next?" he asked as casually as he could. He met Marty shortly after Mildred's late return from Seattle and he couldn't say anything bad about him yet. Marty explained himself right away, coming across as upstanding and responsible, and Harvey felt assured that nothing immoral happened. In addition to that, he was courteous and witty which Harvey felt were both good traits. Since then, Marty had picked up Mildred twice for a day flight and delivered her home by the promised time. Once was to the Washington coast and the other was to a country fair in Oregon to see a rodeo. Each time she returned, she glowed more and she never quit smiling.

"You don't remember? Marty's picking me up tomorrow morning for his little sister's birthday party. I doubt it will be an overnight trip again, but like Marty told you, I have a room to stay in down the hall from his sister and it's quite proper." Mildred even sounded like a different person to Harvey.

"I want to talk to you about that." He paused for a moment, thinking of the best way to say it. "Now that we all know where Marty comes from, money and all, I am worried that he might lose interest in you after a while. He's not like us small town folk, Mildred. We've had to work hard for every quarter to buy shoes for our feet and meat for the table but he gets a mountain of money without breaking a sweat. His family, I guarantee you, will want a girl from the same background for him. I just don't want my precious daughter to get hurt when it happens."

Mildred stared at her pie. Her breathing became deeper and deeper as she avoided her father's face. "I do make him happy, Dad. We're still learning about each other, but it's like we've been friends for a hundred years. He knows I'm not persuaded by money and he likes me all the better for it, trust me," she explained with a shaky voice.

"Your stepmother and I care about you..."

Mildred hissed, "Darnella does *not* care about me. Why would you say that? She was trying to help Vidalia win Marty, so this whole situation has her spitting mad at me. Also, you didn't hear the awful things Darnella said to me." Her eyes looked wild.

Harvey shook his head. "I can't imagine that your stepmother would purposefully say things to hurt you." He took a bite of pie.

"You've changed so much since Mom died. You would've laughed at someone like Darnella if Mom was still alive, called her desperate and pathetic with her demands for fancy clothes, jewelry and that car! Now you do whatever she says, buy her whatever she thinks she needs. Admit it that you just needed a new wife and you didn't care who it was."

The conversation was going downhill fast. "Don't talk about your stepmother that way, Mildred. You can't comprehend what I went through with losing your mother. What did you expect me to do? Live alone the rest of my life?"

Her lips trembled and tears emerged, her wet eyes begging for mercy. "You...you had me, Dad." Bonnie and some patrons glanced worriedly over at their table.

He sighed. "People change, Mildred. Marty will change and

I'd bet you money that you'll change, too."

Mildred narrowed her eyes. "I'll never change who I am for someone, especially Marty."

"Marty may be nice and fun now, but he'll realize that he's different from you, from all of us. He'll soon tire of Bresford, the people in it, and stay in Seattle where he belongs. It's just how the world works."

Only a few bites were taken out of each piece of pie and the ice cream melted into mournful puddles. Harvey stood up, plunked a nickel on the table and left the restaurant with Mildred trying her hardest not to cry in front of everyone.

CHAPTER TEN

"Hello, Marty. Please come in," Darnella said warmly, clearly surprised to see Marty at her doorstep at nine o'clock in the morning. He took long, rejuvenating breaths, a sign of him having walked the mile or so. The Manchester Fairgrounds served as the temporary place to park his plane when he visited and he didn't mind walking. Darnella hungrily eyed his strong shoulders through his suede jacket and averted her gaze to the dusty light fixture on the ceiling when he turned around.

"Is Mildred ready to go?" he asked politely.

Too quickly, Darnella answered, "I wouldn't know. I'm not her mother." She tried to recover by saying, "What I mean is that she is just so...independent...since she's met you. I can hardly keep track of her."

Marty half-smiled and turned to study the dozens of portraits of Opal on the wall. She had to have had a dozen sessions in her first year of life, barely looking any different from one month to the next. Several were of Darnella in luxurious gowns and jewels, two of them being from her two weddings. In the pictures where she was clearly much wealthier, her ex-husband was carefully cut out. Only a few existed of Mildred for the last nineteen years and none of them were done in a studio.

"So, tell me, Marty, is it true that you're taking Mildred to your sister's birthday party? Please extend my best wishes to her."

Marty turned from the portraits. "Thank you, I will."

She sat on the arm of the chaise lounge and said with a tone of longing for her gilded past, "I used to attend those parties your father put on ages ago, back when I was Darnella Riley. He sure did know how to entertain, kept opening wine bottles all night, never let the band stop. I loved dancing with my husband—my ex-husband, I mean. Does the name Paul Riley mean anything to you?"

"I'm sorry but I don't think I've ever heard of him." He honestly had never heard of Paul Riley, but if he did, he doubted that he would feel generous enough to tell her.

Darnella scrunched up her face. "Don't be sorry. He was a rascal, took away my lifestyle, left me with a child and reduced me to...well, never mind. Seattle is behind me now, but I bet it has quite grown up since I left." She ventured by saying, "Vidalia has never been to Seattle. It would be such a treat if you took her one of these days."

Marty's half-smile turned into a full-face smile. "I'm perfectly content taking Mildred with me. Vidalia is a bit, how do I say it...young. Maybe it would be best if she went with her father."

Darnella pursed her lips so tightly that they looked like a

single red line. "Please don't punish Vidalia for her passion, Mr. Townsend. She deserves a second chance, just like we all do. It would sadden me if you think being a bore is a sign of maturity."

"What are you implying exactly, Mrs. Westrick?" He cocked his head to the side and lost his smile completely.

Darnella laughed and put a nervous hand at her collarbone, her finger fiddling with her necklace. Her cheeks reddened beneath her layer of makeup. "I wasn't implying a thing! Don't be silly!" Without waiting for a response, she turned on her heel and disappeared into the kitchen.

Just as Darnella left, Mildred came downstairs with a wrapped gift in her arms. She looked chic in a lightweight short-sleeved striped sweater tucked into a long skirt, both of which she proudly ordered a few weeks ago from Sears & Roebuck. The five dollars it cost was more than she wanted to spend on an ensemble, but it felt good to buy something new other than socks. Hattie forced her to borrow a pair of blue and white Oxford heels that tied the outfit together perfectly. When she came to get the shoes, Hattie was nearly shaking with excitement for Mildred's second trip to Seattle. Of course Hattie took the chance to give Mildred another session on how to style her hair before she let her go. Obediently, Mildred replicated Hattie's steps and achieved a somewhat perfect result.

"Marty!" She sat the gift down and rushed into his arms. "I missed you." As badly as she wanted to kiss him, she restrained them both so Darnella would have less ammunition if she dared to spy. His embrace meant the world to her, especially after her father insinuated that she wasn't good enough for him yesterday. Mildred had made peace with how Darnella, Dominic and Vidalia felt about her and Marty, but her father's position on them was a shock to her world.

"I missed you, too. Are you ready to go?"

"Yes, but give me one moment." Mildred peeked into the

kitchen. "Bye, Darnella. I might be getting back late tonight, so don't worry about waiting up for me." It might have been shallow and probably was, but Mildred couldn't help but remind her stepmother that Mildred Westrick was in the spot that she and Dominic wanted Vidalia so badly to be in. After Mildred's return from her first overnight in Seattle, it didn't take long for Darnella's curiosity to get the better of her. She quizzed her about the layout of the home, the type of décor in each room, what type of food was served, and most importantly, did she ask Mrs. Townsend if she remembered Mrs. Paul Riley. Mildred obliged and said everything she could remember. Unfortunately, she didn't bother to ask Marty's mother about someone she might not even recall. Darnella seemed down about it, but perked up when Mildred described the outfit Mrs. Townsend wore to breakfast.

"Have a swell time," her stepmother sighed without looking up from her *Redbook* magazine. When Mildred left the kitchen, she added a hop in her step to get out of the house that much faster.

"Are you sure you don't mind walking to the plane?" asked Marty.

"I'll be fine, better than fine. Let's go before someone else ruins my day."

"What do you mean about someone ruining your day?" Marty asked.

Mildred breezed by him, anxious to leave. "I'll tell you later. I don't want to think about it right now."

THE RED CHEVROLET PULLED into the family driveway at the Townsend's. The weather was perfect with a slight breeze on this twenty-eighth of May, but Mildred hesitated to feel excited like she wanted to.

"Is everything alright?" Marty asked. She was quiet on the

plane, thinking about her father's words, over and over and over again. Finally, she divulged everything to Marty in the privacy of his truck.

He sighed with angst and said, "Why should he think I would get bored with you and cast you aside? That's ridiculous!"

"It's because I work at a cannery and wasn't brought up wealthy, that's why. I tried so hard not to cry when he said I'm not good enough for you, but I cried anyway. What if he is right in the end?"

"Don't even think that way. About the cannery, though..." he began softly.

Mildred snapped before she could catch herself. "What *about* the cannery? Is it because I might smell like salmon on a daily basis or that nobody would ever dream of wanting someone who works in a cannery? It doesn't seem to bother you!"

Marty cast his eyes downward. "It's not that. I just don't want anybody to judge you for it. For now, how about you don't mention that you work in a cannery? That will spare us both a lot of questions."

A low, frustrated growl left Mildred, something she had never really done in front of anyone besides Opal. "Are you supporting me or my father? If you're on his side, then I might as well take a train back home and save you the headache." She turned away from him as tears fell.

Marty's face looked as if he just ran over a puppy. "Oh, Mildred, please don't cry! It's my fault! I'm a complete idiot. It's just that I just don't want my parents to needle you for it when it doesn't make one shred of difference to me. Let them get to know you." With strong hands, he pulled Mildred into his side and let her rest her head on his shoulder.

With her jacket sleeve, she wiped her eyes and damp nose, followed by a few pitiful sniffles. "I'm sorry. I promise I won't mention the cannery to your parents or anyone. It's not who I am, it's just what I do for now."

"There you have it! Now, let's go inside and eat a big slice of cake with the whole lot of them." He squeezed her to his ribs again and kissed her forehead, leaving his lips on her skin for a lingering moment. There was something about a forehead kiss that Mildred discovered that she loved, even craved. While she enjoyed being kissed on the lips, a kiss to the forehead was tender in a way that other kisses weren't. Instantly, felt safe, special, adored. Out of curiosity, she wondered if Leland gave Hattie forehead kisses. Marty opened her door, took her hand, and led her up the wide, white steps to the house. Inside the foyer, maids took their coats. Others walked around with trays carrying flutes of sparkling lemonade with frozen strawberries floating on top like plump, red buoys.

Marty took two flutes and laughed. "Tabby's favorite! She would drink lemonade all day if she could." He held his flute to Mildred's lips for a sip and her eyes lit up with joy as she tasted it.

"That is amazing, so delicious, just like everything else I've ever had in this house!" Decidedly in a better mood, Mildred allowed herself to be towed into the drawing room by Marty's warm and confident hand. In her striped sweater with its snappy white collar, flattering skirt and Oxford pumps, Mildred felt insanely fashionable...that was, until she entered the room and didn't take a further step. Most of the women were in slinky silk gowns or smart pantsuits, even at three o'clock in the afternoon. A fair amount wore decorative hats that couldn't even be purchased at Dominic's. They were dressed, in Mildred's opinion, for a restaurant far superior to The Orchard. The 'insanely fashionable' confidence she had dwindled into nothing. She might as well have come to the party in her favorite Scottish plaid nightgown that had belonged to her mother, patched up at the shoulder seam with blue thread. She would've felt the same level of embarrassment in either outfit.

"Is something bothering you? You just stopped walking," he whispered. Hattie taught Mildred that boys cared little for female fashion and that their input on such things didn't really matter, that they would always lie to make the girl feel better.

Defying her friend's advice in her head, Mildred asked anyway. "Are my clothes unsuitable for this party? I feel like I'm the wearing the plainest clothes in the whole room. I don't even have any jewelry on!" She blushed when Marty looked her over at her request.

"You look fine, Mildred. It's the other women that aren't dressed suitably, in my opinion. It's my sister's sixteenth birthday, not a royal wedding. See the woman in the gray dress talking to my mother? Look what's around her neck. It's absolutely hideous and out of place." Mildred looked as he leaned his face closer to hers. He whispered, "Who in their right mind wears a fox scarf on such a warm day? Just look at the poor, dead thing. It looks like it desperately wants to drink some lemonade from her glass. Do foxes even like lemonade?" Indeed, the fluffy red fox scarf rested in such a manner that the fox's snout was an inch from dipping into the woman's drink.

They erupted in giggles, immediately catching his mother's attention. Jeanette, looking regal in a navy chiffon dress with a wide lace neck, murmured something to Fox Scarf Lady and sashayed over to greet them. Despite Marty having knocked the fancy dresses in the room in favor of Mildred's outfit, she couldn't help but gawk at the expensive lace collar on his mother's dress. It was so delicate that it looked like it could unravel with the slightest snag.

"Hello, Mrs. Townsend. Thank you for having me to Tabby's birthday," Mildred said. She resisted the urge to curtsy.

"Welcome, Mildred. Please call me Jeanette," she said. This time, she seemed to be warmer towards her and gave her a genuine smile. "Your outfit is...cute. Martin, why don't you get Mildred a plate? Masterson made all of your sister's favorites." He obeyed his mother and went away in search of food. Jeanette placed a hand on Mildred's forearm and said lowly, "Forgive me for acting somewhat less than pleasant the first time we met a few weeks ago. Martin hardly tells me a thing, so I'm just itching to know all about the two of you. I'm under a lot of pressure, you see, with Tabitha's illness and my husband's company. Plus with Martin's wild ambitions and bringing you home for an impromptu visit that bordered on impropriety...it is a lot to absorb for a person who is at the end of her rope. Please forgive me." The scent of alcohol was on her breath.

"I understand perfectly, Mrs. Townsend, I mean Jeanette, sorry. It must be so much to juggle all of those things."

"*Juggle*. That's a clever word for it; makes me sound like I belong in the circus." Even though Jeanette seemed to be on friendlier terms with Mildred, she was looking beyond her shoulder at someone else that just arrived and excused herself by saying, "Sorry to be rude, but there is someone very important that I must talk to. Enjoy yourself." Luckily, just as Jeanette sauntered off, Marty showed up with a porcelain dish filled with small bites.

"Oh, good, I'm starved," she groaned. "Where do I even start?" For a prominent girl's sixteenth birthday, Ada Masterson and her kitchen crew prepared Tabitha's favorite meals with such degree of presentation that they were a shame to devour. They served small ramekins of creamy macaroni and cheese topped with toasted bread crumbs and chopped parsley, soft white bread with thin slices of boiled egg, toasted baguette slices smothered in warm Welsh rarebit sauce, tender venison sausage balls and pastry cups filled with crab salad. Marty explained that he purchased the crab fresh that morning from the Pike Place Market, caught off the frigid waters of Alaska just a few days before. He made her laugh when he put his two hands side-by-side in front of his face to show her literally how big the crabs were. When she took bites of each item on her loaded plate, she got lost in a world of flavor. There were no words to describe the beauty of what her tongue tasted. The Orchard's chef could learn a thing or two from Ada Masterson.

When she finished scraping the remains of the cheese sauce from the ramekin, Mildred remembered with horror that she hadn't even seen the guest of honor yet. The gift sitting at her feet stared up at her.

"Marty, where is your sister at in this huge room? I hope she doesn't think I lied about coming to the party after I promised her I would," Mildred said sheepishly. She scrambled to pick up the gift and looked where Marty pointed. Off in the corner, on a sofa lined with cushy pillows, sat Tabitha, surrounded by guests that made her laugh and bring color to her pale cheeks.

"Right over there. She'll be ecstatic," Marty said. She scampered off with the gift. He chuckled and nibbled on another venison sausage ball, not hearing the light *click-click-click* of high heels coming from behind.

"Who was that adorable creature? My curiosity hasn't been this piqued in some time. I daresay, she looks a tad provincial, even for you, Martin," said a slick female voice. Standing next to him, with a flute filled with what was probably not sparkling lemonade, was a tall and poised woman with her dark hair in tight waves close to her face. Her lips were painted with her signature shade of midnight plum, a color that made her olive skin glow. Those same lips begged for him as they did before.

This woman who stood uncomfortably close, close enough that Marty could smell champagne on her breath, was Agnes Crane.

CHAPTER ELEVEN

"OH, MILLIE, YOU DID come to my party!" Tabby cried out. She tried to stand up on her own to hug Mildred and pushed on the arm of the sofa with every bit of strength she had, but it wasn't quite enough. Her friends all put their hands around Tabby in case she fell but doing nothing more to support her otherwise. Mildred rushed forward, swiftly placing her arm around Tabby's back. She felt all of eighty pounds resting against her and heard her stifle a pained moan.

"You didn't have to get up just for me. I was coming over to hug you. Why don't you rest?" She helped Tabby readjust herself on the sofa and flared out her rose-colored skirt like a bridal veil. Despite the warmth of the day, Tabby wore a thick lacy sweater the same color as her skirt. The other girls stared with weak smiles at Mildred like she was a foreigner they didn't trust. She instantly felt self-conscious and shabby in her new outfit in front of them. Tabby noticed and intervened.

"Millie, these were my best schoolmates before I got sick." She rattled off their names and pointed, "This is Henrietta, Beatrice and Jane! Beatrice is the smartest one out of all of us and I used to copy her work in school, but now that I'm bedridden, I have to use my own brain for my lessons with a supremely boring tutor. Henrietta is great at making curtains and Jane, well, she's our Jane."

Jane, a blonde girl with a dusting of copper freckles on the bridge of her pert nose, said, "Tabby, aren't you going to say how you know your friend? Is *she* your boring tutor?"

Henrietta, with wild coils of auburn hair and a squash-like nose, piped in, "Or is she a new maid in your house? Did she have to vacuum this room and scrub the toilets before the party? I better go inspect and make sure there aren't any rings!"

The schoolmates laughed wildly as if they cracked the most hysterical jokes of all time. The volcano inside Mildred failed to erupt like she wanted it to, not giving her the words to say to the cheeky snobs. Here she was, thinking she was done getting hurt by peoples' words by getting away from Bresford, but she was now the butt of a joke made by girls she didn't even know. Her mouth hung open and she scrunched her face, not even sure how to respond to such a display of rudeness.

Tabby, however, looked like she was the one about to erupt. "Stop it, the three of you! That's not even close to being funny. Masterson never lets rings begin in our toilets, unlike at *your* house, Henrietta."

Henrietta stopped laughing and gasped with shame, for it was the truth. Jane whined, "We were just joking, Tabby. Aren't we allowed to make some jokes on your birthday?"

In a clear gesture of camaraderie, Tabby stretched out her hand and placed it on Mildred's arm, then said to them in a nonchalant tone, "You all know my brother, right?" All at once, the girls giggled and tried not to blush. They all admired Marty, more or less imagining themselves as his virgin bride on the way to a life of bliss.

"Of course we know him. You're so lucky to have such a handsome brother, Tabby," Beatrice gushed. Blonde like Jane but her complexion free of freckles, she smoothed out her glossy waves, as if Marty was looking at her.

Tabby continued, "Millie, why don't you tell the girls how we became friends?"

She looked at Tabby and noticed a devilish sparkle in her eyes. "Well, about three weeks ago, I met Tabby when her brother brought me here in his airplane. Tabby was kind enough to lend me a nightgown and make me feel welcome."

Stupefied, Henrietta asked, "Why would you be in Marty's airplane?"

Mildred smiled coyly. "We're seeing each other."

The three girls exchanged bewildered glances. They took a good, studious look at Mildred and at Tabby's dashing older brother talking to a slender woman in the crowd. Amazingly enough, Henrietta, Beatrice and Jane decided to clamp their mouths shut and take a keen interest in their glasses of loganberry punch.

Mildred tried not to giggle at Tabby's style of justice. "Anyway, here's your gift. It's not much but I thought you might enjoy it. I ordered it special, just for you." She deposited the lightweight gift into Tabby's frail hands.

"Shall I open it now?" Tabby asked, grinning and hugging the box to her chest.

"If you want to, I guess," Mildred answered. Given the price of the clothes worn in the room as an indication of what the people could afford as a birthday gift, she was afraid her little present bought with cannery wages would pale in comparison to

anything else that sat wrapped by the sofa. Delicately, Tabby
tore the striped paper, revealing an apple green letter writing set
with a bold, black 'T' monogrammed on almost everything. Her
face lit up as she dug through the box of paper, envelopes and
two green pens.

"Look! The notepad has my name on it!" She showed her
friends the thick notepad with the words '*From the desk of
Tabby Townsend*' printed on the top of each page. In unison,
they admired the gift and exclaimed how they all wish they had
one just like it. She held out her arms to hug Mildred as tightly
as she could. "Thank you so much. I can't wait to use it!"

"You must be feeling good today," Mildred commented,
feeling the heartiness of her embrace.

"Dr. Ward asked Marty to give more blood this morning,
something of a boost so I could handle today's excitement. I just
hope Marty gave me something else other than blood as a
birthday present."

Mildred didn't have fond memories of her sixteenth birthday
with her mother dead and Darnella in the family for two years.
Part of her hoped that her father would do something special
despite her saying she didn't want anything. She longed to be
surprised by him taking them all to The Orchard and ordering
her a slice of decadent chocolate cake while the waiters sang her
the birthday song, but he took her seriously. He didn't get her a
gift and he even worked late that day at the feed store. Only
Hattie acknowledged her friend's birthday and celebrated with a
slice of coconut cake from Boone's Diner and a set of jeweled
hairpins.

Suddenly, Tabby didn't look as happy as she was a minute
ago. "What is *she* doing here?" she growled. Beatrice, Henrietta
and Jane looked for a few seconds and lost interest, getting up to
follow each other to the punch bowl.

"Who are you talking about?" Mildred asked.

Tabby propped herself up to get a better look. She gritted her teeth from the effort and in who she saw. "I didn't even invite that...that *snake!*" Mildred searched the crowd for the unwanted guest, even though she didn't know which woman she was looking for. Tabby grumbled and then relaxed back into the pillows. The excitement exhausted her, the powder on her face doing little to veil her dark circles. "About time he got rid of her."

"What? Who were you looking for? I'm dying to know."

Tabby patted the free seat next to her, something that Mildred loved, to be wanted. When she sat down, Tabby whispered, "I can't say who it is but it's someone we don't want meddling in our family affairs. I'm under strict orders not to reveal any details. It's best you don't meet her. She's an absolute witch."

Just then, Marty rushed up, trying not to look peeved, and reached out for his sister's hand, on which he planted a kiss. "I wish you the happiest of birthdays to the dearest and squeakiest of all Squeaks."

"Squeak?" Mildred asked through an amused smile.

Tabby chuckled. "My nickname is Squeak. You tell her why, Marty."

He also chuckled, the way one does before repeating a family story. "The way it goes, I was seven when Tabby was born and when she was just a few days old, she made these awful squeaks instead of crying like a baby should. These squeaks echoed down the hallway and kept me from sleeping. Mother says I ran into her room and demanded that Father fix the squeak on the baby or else I wouldn't eat breakfast."

"And then what happened?" Mildred inquired.

"I couldn't hold out any longer, so Masterson fixed me a plate of eggs while Tabitha kept squeaking around the clock." The thought of a little Marty in pajamas, missing his first tooth or two and making such demands made Mildred giggle with delight.

"Millie?" Tabby asked after she finished laughing herself.

"Yes?"

"Might I bother you to get me some punch and a few things for me to nibble on?"

"I'd be more than happy to. I'll be right back," she said.

"Millie?" Tabby asked again.

She spun on her heel. "Is there something else, Tabby?"

"I also need five minutes with my brother, so please take your time." She held out her bony hands to emphasize that Mildred needn't run back.

"Of course." With that, Mildred went in search of what Tabby asked for, doing her best not to rush, as much as she wanted to learn what was being said. She glanced back at them as she looped her finger through the handle of an etched glass punch cup and wondered if this had to do with the woman Tabby didn't invite.

A LITTLE SPLASH OF whiskey didn't improve the taste of the loganberry punch but it mellowed Gerald's nerves, which seemed to get frayed more frequently as of late. His daughter, Tabby, asked him for a party for her sixteenth birthday and he didn't hesitate to have Masterson throw it together, despite complaints from Jeanette that she was afraid a party would do more harm than good regarding their daughter's current state of health.

"If my Tabby wants a party, I'm going to throw her a damn party. Just have Dr. Ward get some extra blood from Marty to bolster her for the day. It's as simple as that!"

"She's not a Ford, Gerald! You can't just change her tires and pour in fresh oil!" Jeanette had yelled.

When Tabby got sick in February, just after his son proposed to Agnes, Gerald could only focus on two things: the timber business and his daughter getting well. He didn't have enough energy to have a third focus, which would've been his wife, but securing the best doctor and treatments took her place. Marty was self-sufficient enough, properly engaged, but was a little distracted by flying about and gathering things for his hobo friend in Elliott Bay. However, he didn't beg for his father's attention to begin with and slid under his detection most days.

Gerald had been keeping an eye on Marty's company earlier, his fiancée or ex-fiancée, he couldn't make up his mind as to which. Jeanette invited her to come to the party and she eagerly snapped up the chance to join. Agnes planted herself strongly to the floor, standing like a deep-rooted evergreen as she talked to his son. She commanded Marty's attention and clearly had the reins on him. She took after her business-minded father, to be sure. Between cups of spiked punch, he heard his son raise his voice to Agnes and looked over to see the commotion. He assumed they were working on reestablishing their engagement. Not too long after the spat, Agnes disappeared from his sight. Long ago, when he courted Jeanette, he remembered that their courtship wasn't a waltz through the meadow, either, but yet he was happily married twenty-five years later.

To his left, he saw an unfamiliar girl dipping the ladle into the punch bowl. When she looked over at him, she caught a peek at the flask mostly hidden in his large hand. He quickly concealed it in an inner pocket of his formal jacket and winked at her. After years of parties and forcing his brain to recognize the faces that belonged to the ever-expanding list of names, he failed to place her anywhere. She was pretty in a way that separated her from the droves of other girls, with sweet brown eyes that turned downward, eyes that invited you to tell her anything and know that she could be trusted.

He floundered a moment and stepped closer to her. "I'm sorry to stare, but I couldn't help but wonder who you are. Are you a schoolmate of Tabby's or the daughter of someone here that I haven't met yet?"

The girl's gentle eyes widened, surprised that he wanted to talk to her. She said nervously, "I'm here with Marty but I'm also friends with Tabby."

"And what would your name be?" He took a sip of his spiked punch.

"Mildred."

"As in 'Mildred Westrick,' I presume?" He sipped his punch again and forced a smile. Here he was, admiring this young newcomer when she was standing in the place that was meant for Agnes Crane. He wanted so badly to strangle Marty for wrecking his relationship with Agnes. It was common knowledge throughout Seattle that Marty and Agnes were going to be married in June. It couldn't have been a better match because Townsend Timber and Crane Development planned to combine their companies and become the dynamic duo of logging and construction in Washington State. Some wondered if it was an arranged marriage, given the pending merger, but they told those that asked that the two met by chance. If there had been the option to arrange his son's marriage, Gerald would've certainly picked Agnes for him. Gerald still wasn't satisfied by the excuse "We weren't meant for each other" to explain the split.

"Yes, that's right. What's your name?" She asked sweetly and sincerely, clearly oblivious that the man she conversed with was the most important person in the room and probably even more oblivious to the conflicted role she played in the whole situation she was plunked in the middle of.

"There you are, Mildred! Tabby's ready for her punch now," said Marty. He placed his hands on her shoulders in an effort to steer her away from his father.

"I didn't catch that gentleman's name," she said. She broke free of Marty's hands and walked back. "Sorry, I didn't mean to be rude. What is your name, since you got mine?"

Gerald was definitely amused by this sweet girl trying to pretend that she wasn't afraid deep inside. She wasn't the kind of girl Marty usually went for, meek like a church mouse, but then again, Gerald remembered being in his twenties and feeling like there was plenty of time to sample the varieties of women that graced the sidewalks of Seattle.

"Mr. Gerald Townsend, miss."

"You're Marty's father, then? It's lovely to meet you and thank you for having me," she said warmly. Marty placed a hand on her shoulder. The look Gerald got from his son had many meanings, with the strongest message being, *Don't you dare ruin this for me*. The only problem with that look was the fact that he had to give the look in the first place. With Agnes, he wouldn't even have to worry.

"My pleasure, young lady," Gerald said to her. He downed the last swallow of his whiskey punch, watching his son walk away with a girl of no real importance, a girl that wouldn't last.

WHEN HE WAS FINALLY allowed to rest and breathe easily, Marty dove into the piece of birthday cake Mildred handed him. A strong craving cropped up for a glass of calming bourbon, but that would have to wait. It was supposed to be a simple party but it quickly turned into a dangerous game of chess, maneuvering people around the room to avoid being captured and destroyed.

When Agnes sidled up to Marty, chilled champagne in hand, she acted like she had every right to be there, as if she were still his fiancée. To answer her question of "Who is that adorable creature?" that was followed by her calling Mildred "provincial," he had to think for a moment because she was truly the last person he expected to see at his sister's party.

"She is none of your business," he managed. He didn't want

to speak too much, just enough to make his point. When he looked over at her to see how she took his reply, he couldn't help but marvel at how he hated someone so stunning, a woman he asked to marry with his whole, bleeding heart, begging her to be his wife and to give him children. The midnight plum lipstick brought out the golden color in her skin, her strong and dark brows perfectly shaped above hazel eyes that flashed green. What he used to love most about her face was the peculiar shape of her nose, the bridge long and straight with the slightest curve at the tip. Before he could stop himself, he recalled the many times he kissed the tip of her nose, how she smelled like the perfume he bought her, how her eyelashes tickled his chin when she would kiss his neck. His hand ached with the phantom sensation of her trim waist in his grasp, but to stop the thoughts that would surely follow, he forced himself to think of watching Dewey, his beloved Labrador from his childhood, being shot in the head by his father when the poor dog got sick and didn't recover in a timely manner. His nose burned at the terrible memory, but it kept racy thoughts at bay.

"I have to disagree with you, my love. You're still my business, my future husband, which in turn entitles me to know who she is and why she came with you," she shot back. From the corner of his eye, he noticed her bring the champagne flute to her lips, the golden elixir rushing into her mouth. He tried to keep his eyes on Mildred, who was having a lovely time chatting with Tabitha and some of her schoolmates, but Agnes was doing her best to make him look at her. She won.

"What do you want?" he asked as politely as he could. He held back from making a sarcastic comment regarding the reason he broke away, not wanting to risk someone hearing and starting rumors.

"Martin, I just want you. You were having a bad day and you weren't thinking clearly when you broke our engagement.

Can't you please reconsider?"

"Not thinking clearly? Were you not there in my father's study when I...*when I caught you?*" He was having trouble moderating his tone with each second he still found himself talking to her.

Agnes lifted her chin ever so slightly and whispered, "Yes, I was in your father's study, but you never gave me the chance to explain why. Shall I tell you now in front of everyone at the risk of implicating myself to show you how serious I am?"

"*No!*" Some surrounding partygoers looked at Marty curiously. Even Gerald looked over but returned to his own conversation, but it was Tabitha's gaze that chilled Marty's blood. His sister's face was crestfallen at the sight of Agnes and he saw her lips move, which was followed by Mildred looking about the room. He needed to get rid of Agnes and fast.

Marty shuddered with the effort it took to lower his voice. "There is no good reason why you did what you did. Crane Development and Townsend Timber would never break bread at the same table again if I exposed you. I love my family's legacy too much to let you destroy it."

Agnes was flippant. "Destroy it? Please stop being so dramatic, Martin. It's not an attractive trait to possess for a man like you."

"How did you even get invited to my sister's birthday?" He gestured around the whole room and to her flute pinched in her fingers.

"Your mother sent me the invitation just the other day, telling me that you'd be here instead of flying around. She's such a dear, but I wanted to see you, especially after you left before I came for tea that one day weeks ago. At least your mother still thinks we can mend our relationship, pick up where we left off and plan our wedding. That is, we can resume once you return your little country friend home for good."

A strained laugh escaped his lips. "Are you *fucking* delusional?" he hissed. His eyes caught the glimmer of her one carat engagement ring. "Why do you still wear that? There will never be a wedding for us, ever. You wrecked any trust I had. If my parents knew what you did..."

"What was so wrong about it? You tell me here and now. We were going to combine everything with my father's business and Townsend Timber, become one of the greatest partnerships in this region. Your sweet Granny Fran would've understood and I knew she'd give me her blessing. Don't the Townsends, including future Townsend wives, deserve the best?"

He couldn't believe his ears that burned red with fury. Grandmother Frances, or lovingly called Granny Fran by her grandchildren, passed away during the last week of February after a long bout of influenza. At a Christmas party in 1931, Marty met Agnes after one too many glasses of bourbon. It didn't take him long to come around to proposing, presenting Agnes with a $290 engagement ring on St. Valentine's Day. The ornate one carat ring passed her approval and she accepted, duly rewarding him with endless kisses.

A week later, Tabitha was diagnosed with the leukemia that rocked the Townsend family and soon little else mattered, including engagements. Granny Fran and Tabitha had become the center of the family, both being quarantined and fussed over day and night. In that whole time from Christmas to her death, Grandmother Frances only met Agnes once, when the family believed that she was rallying and they all hoped that she would live to see the grand wedding that June. Marty wanted nothing more than Granny Fran's blessing, for her to be proud of his choice of bride. In that visit, however, Granny Fran thought Agnes was Tabitha and that her son, Gerald, was her dead husband. When her fever returned with unpredicted force, the doctor and nurses ushered the visitors out. Three days later, on a snowy Thursday morning, Mrs. Frances Roberta Fielding Townsend passed away in her sleep.

"First of all, my grandmother didn't even know you. She thought you were my sister, so you have no right to call her Granny Fran. Even if she did know you, she would never have given you her blessing had she found out what you were like." He pointed to the door. "You need to see yourself out."

Agnes didn't look hurt. If anything, her hazel eyes became greener as she accepted the challenge before her. "I see it will take more work to make you change your mind. Until I see you next time, my sweet, delicious Martin." As if their engagement hadn't gone up in flames, she reached for his bicep and squeezed tenderly. On her way out, she placed her hand on Jeanette's arm and talked with her a moment. Jeanette appeared to be saddened to learn that Agnes was leaving so soon, but believed whatever she was told and gave her a delicate hug. Before Agnes left, she looked over towards Marty's guest with a dagger stare, then blew Marty a kiss, allowing him another glance at the ring he doubt he'd ever get back.

With Agnes gone and taking a moment to gather his wits, he noticed that his inebriated father was talking to Mildred and he panicked at what he might be saying. He started for them and swooped in behind Mildred, who seemed slightly irritated that he interrupted. Once they were back safely by Tabitha, his head felt like it was spinning.

Enough had happened for one party, in his opinion.

With the birthday song sung, gifts torn open and white cake with raspberry filling passed around, the party was well on its way to being finished. Marty wondered if it was a mistake to bring Mildred, not for anything she did, but it was clear that his mess with Agnes wasn't over. There were a few narrow misses and it could've turned into a disaster had the two women been introduced. His parents behaved themselves, although Marty was confident that they had intentionally invited Agnes in order for Marty to compare the two women and see that the clear choice was with the heiress to Crane Development.

Then again, he had to remember that the truth behind the end of their engagement was still concealed from his parents and that was how he and Tabitha wanted it to stay. If his parents found out why there wouldn't be a Mrs. Agnes Townsend, the effects would go beyond the family and Marty wasn't sure what sort of damage would come from the wake. The wake could be small or it could create the sort of scandal to make Seattle buzz for weeks.

He studied Mildred lovingly as she chatted with Tabitha over some of the gifts she received, like her first tube of lipstick that Jeanette wouldn't let her put on just yet and an intricate ceramic vase in the shape of a mermaid that held a conch to place flowers in. Luckily, Mildred had no knowledge of Agnes. If she did find out somehow, it would only raise questions or worse, turn her away from him. He placed a reassuring hand on her back, her body only inches away from his, making him feel like this was still real and wonderful. Mildred wasn't from any mold the other girls came from and he dwelled on the thought of how lucky he was that things were falling into place, slowly but favorably.

But then he recalled the audacity of Dominic and Vidalia, Darnella and his father...all people who tried to dominate the direction of his life and the varied reactions they offered when he challenged them. He could handle those people but it was Mildred he wanted to protect. Agnes, he knew, would be the jagged piece that would fall where she didn't belong and ruin the entire puzzle.

CHAPTER TWELVE

"LOOK AT ALL OF this uneaten cake! This happens every year. A hundred people come over but we still have enough cake for an army." Tabitha gestured to the laden table with fat slices of cake sitting on gold-rimmed plates. Marty sat next to his sister, enjoying his third piece. The last of the guests left only moments before, wishing Tabitha a year of better health. Napkins and gold-plated dessert forks littered every flat surface, punch cups empty except for the sticky loganberry juice drying inside. A crooked tower of plates offered bits of bread with dried egg slices, spots of congealed fat from the venison sausage balls, and there were dozens of ramekins that needed soaking to remove the hardened cheese sauce. Masterson entered the room and groaned at the hours of work ahead of her.

Mildred sparked. "Marty, should we bring some cake to

Randall and his family? I'd love to spend some more time with Sarah, if you think it's possible."

Through a mouthful of cake, he said, "Fantastic idea! Leo would love that."

"Take all of it, please, or Marty's not going to stop!" He rolled his eyes jokingly at his sister but was finally finished getting his fill of cake. Masterson swooped and grabbed his plate to add to the others she piled up.

Mildred filled a large tin with eight slices. The icing flowers looked somewhat deformed despite the delicate touch she used to slide them in. As she arranged the slices, she couldn't help but feel as if she were dreaming. Here she was, in this grand house of a prevalent family, casually handling cake when only three weeks ago, she barely had a life. She might've been more blessed than others in the world, but having a place to live, food to eat and clothes to wear meant little to her without having someone notice her out of everyone else. Now she was finally beginning the life she wanted, icing on her hands and all.

"Are we ready with that cake, Mildred?" Marty asked. She loved that he called her by her real name, not a nickname or pet name that she felt sounded false. Hattie was the only person who could get away with calling her "Millie" and she wasn't sure why, but it sounded right coming from her. Mildred wasn't the most beautiful name her mother could've picked, she agreed, but Marty wasn't going to make it sound better just because he wanted to. She pushed the lid onto the tin and licked a sweet icing petal off her thumb.

"Ready!" Mildred opened her arms and enveloped Tabitha in them, the newly sixteen-year-old feeling about as thick as a broomstick. "Happy birthday, dear Tabby, and I hope to see you soon."

Tabitha swung her thin arms around Mildred's neck and kissed her cheek. "I love that we're friends and please visit the next chance you have. We can do something, just you and me! I'll convince Mother."

Mildred's heart felt like it could overflow that moment, to be needed so fiercely. It was a sensation she could definitely get accustomed to.

"Happy birthday, Squeak! I love you," Marty said as he kissed his sister. Just then, Mildred noticed how tired Tabitha really was. Her skin looked translucent next to Marty's tan forearms and neck, the dark circles under her eyes bluer than before.

"I love you, too, Marty." Her smile, however, was still radiant as she waved goodbye.

Mildred followed right behind Marty to his truck and cradled the tin of cake on her lap all the way to Elliott Bay. When they arrived, Marty didn't call out for Randall like before, presumably because they didn't have donations to haul into the camp. As Mildred walked alongside Marty, she felt eyes on her and dared to look, only to see nothing besides covered windows. She thought she saw a curtain flutter, but decided she was making herself see things.

The ornate door to the Fryar shack loomed ahead and Mildred felt her heart jump at the opportunity to chat with Sarah. While she wasn't keen on being around Randall and his rudeness again, she knew that Marty would keep him at bay as best he could.

Marty knocked softly and said, "Randall, are you home? It's Marty." From inside, they heard some shuffling and sniffling. Mildred wondered if they were sleeping, but it was too late in the day for a nap and too early to go to bed.

After a minute, the door opened but only wide enough to reveal Leo's face. His eyes were puffy and a trail of mucus ran down to his upper lip.

"Leo, is everything alright?" Mildred asked, even though

clearly it was not. She slowly stooped down, setting the tin at her feet, and took the bottom of his shirt to wipe his slimy nose clean. Then she pulled him close to her and to her surprise, he didn't fight his way out of her embrace. He looked into each of their faces and appeared as if he might cry again. His chin wrinkled and a glimmer of fresh snot peeked from his nostrils. Marty also knelt and placed a hand on his shoulder.

"What's wrong, buddy?" Marty asked gently. He glanced into the darkened shack. The windows were covered by cuts of material that used to be blankets and sheets. "Are you home by yourself?"

Leo shook his head and whispered, "Mama's home. We both got in trouble."

Marty and Mildred looked at each other, unsure of what he meant. "Where is she? Is she sleeping?" he asked.
He wiggled away from Mildred and groggily wiped his eyes. "No. She's on the floor."

Marty bolted into the shack with Mildred right on his heels to find Sarah writhing on her right side next to the credenza, holding her face with both hands and crying without sound. Bits of bread and thick chunks of glass were scattered about the room like confetti.

"Oh, God," Mildred moaned and rushed to her side. "Sarah! What happened?" Timidly, Mildred put her hands on Sarah's shaking ones, only to make her shriek and cover her face even tighter. Leo came over to his mother and sat in the curve of her lap and stomach with the tin in his hands. He appeared to be numb by the whole scene despite his own tear-stained face. With dirty fingers, he pried the lid off and his sorrow melted away instantly.

"Mama, they brought us cake!" Marty and Mildred watched in horrified silence as Leo grabbed a square of cake and held it to his mother's mouth, as if to revive her. Her body softened and she dropped her hands to her chest. Her reddened eyes widened at the sight of the in the cake in her son's tiny hand before her. A thick trail of blood was in the early stages of clotting from her nose and her gums. Without looking over at Marty or Mildred, Sarah nodded to her son and they took fistfuls of cake straight from the tin. They ate one luscious slice after the other as if they never tasted cake before, consuming it faster than they could chew, moaning and eyes closed. Both of them had streaks of icing on their cheeks and in between their fingers. When he was done, Leo licked his hands like a lost kitten that just got a warm bowl of milk, content with his indulgent meal.

"Sarah?" Mildred said. When Sarah's eyes locked with hers, it made Mildred feel like an intruder, a witness to something she should have never seen, pain too private. With a smooth wipe of her finger, Sarah cleaned a swathe of icing by her mouth and licked it from her finger as if nothing strange had just happened. The river of blood from her nose began to trickle as she sat up and a piece of glass clattered to the floor that had apparently been buried in her black hair.

"What the hell happened? Did Randall do this?" Marty asked, incredulous as he motioned at the disaster around them.

"I know what you're thinking," said Sarah smoothly.

Marty reached down and helped her into one of the grand chairs. "Sarah, you have to explain this to me. You're acting like this is normal!"

"You'd better go before he gets back." She raised her chin up defiantly.

"Not until you tell us what happened," Mildred said firmly. "Why is there glass and bread everywhere? And why are you bleeding?" Quickly, Sarah dabbed her nose with a nearby towel. Her eyes darted about, her composure crumbling like a tower of blocks Leo used to build before he smacked them down without mercy. Mildred took the towel from Sarah, dipped it in a jug of water, and gently cleaned her face free of sweat, tears and blood.

"I...I can't say...it would only make it worse. You don't understand until you have nothing," she said, trembling. Mildred went in search of a blanket and halfway across the small room, something cracked and felt slimy under her feet. She looked down in disgust at the shells of several eggs, the yolks and albumen sucking at the bottom of her shoe.

"Let me clean this mess for you," Mildred offered when she brought a blanket back for Sarah.

"Please leave it, Mildred. Now if I tell you, will you both leave and pretend that it never happened?"

Shaking his head, Marty said, "I've known Randall for a long time and he is one of my closest friends. But he if did this, I need to meet with him and he's not going to like it." A wild fear and tears filled Sarah's eyes.

"No! You can't let him know. I don't know when he is going to be back and if you're here when he returns, Lord knows what he'd do then." She now freely sobbed into the blanket.

Mildred was out of her depth by many fathoms, but she knew how Sarah felt on a small level, forever trapped and afraid. "Please tell us, Sarah. We want to help you and Leo."

Sarah slowly lifted her face, her face a mess of tears and blood. "Fine. I'll tell but remember that I warned you." Her eyes searched the ceiling of the shack for where to begin and she rubbed the bump of her stomach where her next child grew. "Randall had always been regarded as a gruff sort of man, can't say that I've ever seen a real smile on his face. Once we had to close the accounting business and leave the house, his moods kept getting worse and worse. The money ran out shortly after that, so he had to stoop to waiting in lines with other men. That's why he hated taking those donations from you, Marty. It killed him inside, I could just tell." Leo crawled onto his mother's lap, just enough room for him around her belly.

With a deep breath, she continued, "But when he'd bring a bag of crackers and cold soup home for us, he'd smell so strongly of whiskey or bourbon that I knew he was up to something. This happened almost daily. The food he'd bring back was always half-eaten by him or cold, barely enough to split between me and Leo. Then he started to get home later and later, his mood either being terrible or even violent."

"Violent?" Marty spat.

Sarah's eyes spilled fresh tears. "Yes. It's a miracle I'm still carrying a baby…"

"Shit," Marty whispered.

"So I'm trying to clean this place one morning to keep my mind off things and I come across a small leather coin purse that I felt through a hole in one of the wall boards. It wasn't mine and I'd never seen it before, so I opened it up. Inside were rolls of dollar bills and change, enough for me to properly feed my son and myself for once. Randall wouldn't be home until dusk, so I did what I had to. I went to the market with less than a dollar to get bread, eggs and a jug of milk. That's all. When we got home, Randall was already back."

Her shoulders began to shake and she melted into sobs again. Leo sat quietly as his mother wrapped her arms around his little body. Mildred could easily tell that Marty was seeing red by the expression on his face.

"And then what?" he prompted.

Sarah choked out the words. "Someone told him I was at the market! And what does he do? He rips the bag out of my arms and goes through it, tearing up perfectly good bread like he was trying to feed the birds. Then he pulled out the jug of milk and eggs. He said, 'How did you afford all of this?' I was honest and told him about the coin purse I found and said I barely used a dollar for everything. I said I needed to feed our son because he wasn't doing the job. That must have set him off because he took the eggs and threw them on the ground at my feet."

"But that doesn't explain how you ended up with a bloody nose on the ground," Marty said. His hands were curled into fists of iron.

"Leo was wailing. At the market, I had told him I was going to make scrambled eggs on toast, something he hasn't had since we lost the house. It was like I was frozen, I couldn't even breathe. Randall comes up to my face, close enough that I could tell that what he had been drinking wasn't cheap. It was quality liquor like we used to buy, so I knew he was going somewhere to get his fix. His eyes had this crazy look in them and right then, I feared for my life. He must've known because he whispered, 'Leave this house again and I'll fucking kill you.' So I looked at Leo and he's eating the chunks of bread off the floor and I feel sicker than I've ever felt before. I tell my husband...I tell him..."

Mildred didn't realize that tears of her own dangled on her lashes, her heart breaking in two. "What did you say?"

"I told him that I hated the sight of him and I was sorry I ever married such a pathetic excuse for a man! Know what he does? He grabbed the milk jug and hit me square in the face with it. I not only heard my nose crack, but I wouldn't be surprised if I end up losing teeth. It felt like I fell for days and I don't remember much else except feeling glass raining down on me and the back of my dress getting soaked. He must've thrown the milk jug right by my head and Lord knows he wanted to aim directly at it. That's the last I remember. It's like I've been sleeping for years."

"Go get a bag packed now. You and Leo cannot stay here!" Marty demanded. Veins protruded from his neck and his nostrils flared like a wild horse.

"But I have to stay! Where would I even go?" Sarah cried.

"What about your sister in Tillamook? She wanted you to live with her family, did she not?" Mildred asked. Sarah nodded dumbly and sniffled.

"Yes, but that was so Randall could work on the farm. Besides, I don't have any money to go anywhere because Randall took the coin purse after he hit me. I'm stuck here." Her head hung like a wilted rhododendron. "I can't leave my husband. That would be beyond scandalous."

Marty grumbled. "And hitting you in the face with a glass jug isn't? Forget Randall and pack your belongings like I said. Both of you are leaving with me today. Just trust me, Sarah."

"But, my sister isn't expecting us and I don't—"

"Damn it, Sarah! Stop talking and pack some clothes!" Marty snapped. Wordlessly, Sarah finally climbed out of the chair and grabbed the largest bag she had from underneath the bed. She tossed in blouses, stockings, dresses and a pair of shoes. For Leo, she packed an array of outfits and a few toys of his choosing, including his bear, Hugo. In the small space left in the bag, she stuffed favorite books inside until it almost couldn't fasten. Without warning, she stripped off her dress that was stained with blood and starting to smell of soured milk, revealing a dingy slip underneath with holes forming in the frayed lace on the back. From the tiny closet, she put on a cornflower blue dress, a traveling coat and a hat. She beckoned her son and put him in a clean change of clothes, as well.

"Ready?" Marty asked, this time using a softer voice.

Sarah, looking tired and shabby, barely nodded. "Let's go before I change my mind. Come, Leo." At the doorway, she turned and looked at everything she was about to leave behind. All of her gorgeous furniture, the antique silverware and tea service set from her grandmother, the clock in the corner ticking its goodbye, Sarah knowing that none of it could go with her. Then she laid her eyes on the wedding portrait atop her beloved credenza. Sarah was grinning like a fool and Randall managed a half-smile. All the years she spent supporting him as his wife, it went up in smoke over milk, bread and eggs. She wriggled her gold wedding band free from her finger and placed it next to the portrait. Then there was the stained glass door. For a moment, she couldn't breathe. She commissioned the work of art herself after her honeymoon, something unique and beautiful for their new home. She closed the door for the final time and forced herself not to look back.

Marty took her heavy bag and Mildred hoisted Leo onto her hip, both of them escorting Sarah to the Chevy without trying to draw attention to themselves. Mildred's heart threatened to either pound through her ribs or jump out of her throat. After hearing the awful story, she felt stupid and childish for hating her life before Marty. While her life at home wasn't the happiest, it didn't compare at all to Sarah's turmoil. With a grunt, Marty tossed the bag in the bed of the truck and rushed everyone inside the cab. He didn't even wait for Mildred to close the door before ramming the truck into gear.

"What about Daddy?" Leo asked. Mildred saw that Sarah was an inch away from bawling again.

"Daddy isn't coming with us," she answered softly. Leo frowned and sniffled.

"I'm sorry we won't be able to see each other very often," said Mildred. "I only have one friend back home and I was hoping to expand my social circle a bit with you."

Sarah looked shocked. "Someone as nice as you only has one friend? I don't understand. I would see at least six friends daily when we had our house. We'd go out for luncheons, teas, shopping, take a train just because we could. But those friends forgot about me when I had to relocate to the bay."

"How could they? You're a splendid person from what I've seen."

A shy smile blossomed on Sarah's face. "That means so much to me. You really only need one or two people to rely on because the others will disappear the second you need them. I thought I could count on my husband, but clearly he's like the rest, the selfish bastard." She dabbed her nose with an expensive hanky she fished from her coat pocket. It looked as if she hadn't used it since she fell into poverty.

Marty pulled into a spot near the bus depot and unloaded the bag. It took Mildred a moment to coax Leo out of the truck but he relented when Marty flashed a lollipop he had stashed. When he scampered off his mother's lap, Sarah just sat there, staring at the ticket booth.

"I never would've guessed in a thousand years that my life would end up like this."
Mildred sat down next to her. "I could say the same thing about me."

"Marty is a tender soul and I'm pleased he found someone like you. Just whatever happens, don't let others get you down or drive you away."

She chuckled. "I have plenty of experience with people trying that."

Sarah placed her hand over Mildred's and said, "This isn't Bresford. The people in Marty's circle are different. They may be kind to you, but it will always be about money. I've been on both sides now and it's painfully clear. Just promise to be careful."

"I will." Inside, Mildred's confidence shook as she mulled over Sarah's warning. There was a reason she never told people she worked in a cannery, but she never thought why. Was she embarrassed by the nature or her job or was the occupation not up to snuff for people like the Townsends and it was better to not claim to do anything at all?

"Mama!" Leo called out from atop Marty's shoulders. The little boy happily munched on a ham and cheese sandwich from the lunch counter nearby. He held one out for Sarah and she snatched it like a frog going for a fly. When she finished her last bite, Marty discreetly deposited a roll of dollar bills into her hand for food and two tickets for the Greyhound bus that was expected within the next five minutes. When Sarah tried to offer the money and tickets back, he placed them in her hand again and curled her fingers so they wouldn't flutter away.

"Please tell me how much I owe you. I mean it, Marty."

"Not a single thing. Just knowing you are safe is enough. I'll deal with Randall when the time is right, don't worry. Just keep this little devil out of trouble." He knelt down to the boy's level and pulled him close. "Be good for your mother, okay?"

"Okay. Can you get me candy?"

"Leo, Marty has done enough for us," Sarah chastised. Leo giggled like mad as Marty tickled his ribs before he broke loose. Behind them, a sleek silver bus rolled to a stop. The people outside gathered their bags and hats for the impending journey, some kissing loved ones goodbye and others looking as if they would rather be doing anything else than be on a bus.

Mildred and Sarah looked at each other for what felt like hours. Her heart bled for the poor girl and she wrapped her arms around her. She felt the curve of Sarah's belly touch hers from under her thick coat. "Safe travels and I hope you enjoy your new life in Tillamook."

"I've had enough of Seattle to last me a lifetime and I miss my sister more than anything. You both saved us, I hope you know that. I'll be praying to God that we meet again soon." Sarah kissed Mildred's cheek and winked. The thrill of a new adventure played across her face, a feeling Mildred was glad to say she knew. Marty gave the bag to the porter along with a good tip and stood with Mildred as they saw them off. Leo waved so fast that his little hand was a blur.

"I better get you home before your father and stepmother send a search party," he joked.

"As much as I hate to go back home, I know you're right."
They got in Marty's truck and started for the hangar. The bus
hissed and lurched before it pulled away, forever taking Sarah
and Leo Fryar out of the shack and away from Randall.

CHAPTER THIRTEEN

"CARE FOR ANOTHER ROUND of scotch, sir?" The glass of Cutty Sark was dangerously low for the second time and Randall was in no position to decline a third. Besides, he wasn't buying. He raised the glass to his lips, drained it dry, and scooted it forward for a refill. He enjoyed this bar especially since public drinking was illegal these days. Getting inside the place wasn't easy, however. One had to know someone that could vouch for them or have a good enough reputation alone, and luckily, Randall knew someone. Nestled in the back of Foster & Sons Hardware, the bar was safely hidden behind a secret door hung with rakes and a variety of shovels.

"Much obliged, Pete," Randall grumbled at the bartender.

"Will it be on the same ticket as last time?"

"You bet." Pete nodded and filled the glass with more

golden scotch without spilling a drop. Randall loved the feeling of a fresh drink, the top always tasting better than the bottom. Technically, he could've paid for the drinks, but nobody needed to know about the leather coin purse in his coat. The money wasn't for alcohol or even food since he would bring soup and bread home most afternoons. Somehow Sarah found the money and used it to buy a few groceries, but that wasn't the part that made him furious. Sarah risked being seen and getting all of them evicted from the shantytown. She increased the odds of being caught, especially with noisy Leo in tow. Fortunately, the person who sighted them and reported to Randall also lived in the shantytown with his wife. Randall didn't even know the woman's name or what she looked like, which was how secretive he wished they were. He knew he went too far when he threatened to kill her, but that's what flew out of his mouth in his moment of rage. If only he could tell her what his big idea was and make her understand, but he couldn't, not until it was ready.

The money was intended for an apartment. He already knew that he would bring Sarah and Leo to the Glen Eden, had even shook hands on getting the corner apartment on the third floor if it was still vacant when he had enough money. The name sounded fancier than the actual building, but it was on a respectable street in Queen Anne and anything was better than the disgusting shack they currently called home. He couldn't wait to see the look on his wife's face when he would announce their moving plans. All of the furniture would come, too, of course. In his mind, he arranged everything perfectly and there was even a nook for the clock. As for the stained glass door, it would just become an odd thing in the apartment that would be great for conversations at dinner parties. As for the source of the money, that was a bigger secret.

"Pete, make me a Pink Lady, if you will."

Pete and Randall looked at the woman that sat daintily at the bar. She looked sharp in a black skirt with a robin's egg blue blouse embroidered with black flowers. Her black hat sat at a stylish angle, partially covering her face.

"Right away, Miss Crane." He shuffled off to make the girly drink she always requested. Randall stiffened and took shallow breaths until Agnes was given her frothy ruby drink. She bit the candied cherry off the garnish pick and licked her lips.

"Hello, Randall. Did you pretend I wasn't here? We've only been meeting at the same time for the last few weeks."

His jaw tightened. "I knew you were there, Agnes. I was just being considerate and letting you get settled with your cocktail."

"How thoughtful of you. So, do you have any news for me?" She stirred her drink without looking at him.

News. The reason they met and the reason Randall squirreled away cash. The topic of the news, however, determined how much money he got based on how valuable Agnes deemed it.

"It was hard to find anything last week, but I do know that he is home for his sister's birthday."

To his surprise, Agnes growled. "Yes, I know. I was there!"

"How did you know?"

She rolled her eyes. "I *was* engaged to Marty for a time, remember? You should because you were at the engagement party and Marty wanted you to be a groomsman."

"Will this affect my cut?" he asked, hating how it left his lips like a whine.

"Of course it will, idiot. Why would I pay you for something I knew about, let alone attended myself? I need to know places he is going to be, who he is with, anything that I don't already know." She sucked down a mouthful of her Pink Lady. Randall noticed the imprint of her plum lipstick on the rim of the glass.

"Do you have anything worth telling?"

Randall tried to recall what he was going to say to her, a morsel believable enough to satisfy her curiosity. He hated to lie but then he had to imagine the apartment at the Glen Eden with a proper toilet, how much his wife and son would enjoy luxurious baths and furnace heat. It was Agnes who sought him out in the first place to be an informant and he wasn't in a place to turn down a source of income. He was minding his own business in a soup kitchen line on when Agnes spotted him and had her driver pull over. The men around him started whispering and nudging each other, speculating a hundred different ideas of why Randall was so special that a fancy car would stop for him. They speculated even more when he had the audacity to leave his post on clam chowder day and got in the car.

The trouble with Agnes's proposal to pay him to give her dirt on Marty was that Randall saw him once a week and it wasn't like they gabbed about their social lives like a couple of women. If he didn't give her any details, she didn't pay him. It was as simple as that.

He pretended to remember his information and said, "I caught wind that Marty might be at the horse races on Saturday, overhead one of our college chums talking about it at a diner the other day. I think it might be a reunion type of deal, but of course I wouldn't be invited because I don't measure up to shit anymore." Believable enough, yet his offerings were tricky to follow up on, just as he designed them to be.

She screwed up her face and took a sip of her drink. "What about that girl, Mildred? Would she be with him?"

"I suppose so, if he's seeing her. Probably introduce her to the guys." Randall didn't give a single damn about female rivalries, but he could tell that what he said boiled Agnes's blood. He felt lucky that Sarah wasn't a scornful and jealous woman. It saved him from lots of trouble, from what he could see.

"That bastard. He used to take me to the races. We'd sit in a private box and sip on iced tea, and then he'd take me out for a fancy lunch afterwards. Sometimes we would spend the night at the lake house..." She tilted her head as she fondly recalled the memory.

Randall neared the bottom of his drink and eyeballed how many sips he had left. "Remind me why you have a burning desire to know all of this again?"

Agnes was close to draining her drink dry, as well. "I was never done with him and I need to get him back. Mildred is a small obstacle to me. I'll send her crying back to Bremerton."

"She's from Bresford."

"Bresford, wherever she comes from, and I promise you that. Her charm may have a hold on him for now, but it won't last forever and when he's tired of her, he'll come running to me with open arms." The look on her face was pure confidence.

"Why don't you just hire a private detective? You'd get more information than what I can give you." *And the information would at least be true*, he thought.

"I already did. Morris Welch came highly recommended by a girlfriend of mine who suspected her husband was sneaking around. Lo and behold, Detective Welch gave her the solid proof she needed in a week. We met just yesterday, but I have a good feeling."

Randall knitted his brow. His face felt warm from the scotch. "So why would you even bother talking to me in a place like this?"

She shrugged. "When I saw you in line waiting for a meal, I felt sorry for you. You know Marty and who he associates with already, so I told myself to help you and myself out in one fell swoop. We both win a little." She slid a few dollar bills to him, which he quickly pocketed. "And besides, Pete makes a mean Pink Lady. Call me if you get any other leads."

"On that note, I suggest you try the races. Thanks for the drinks, Agnes." He felt her prickle as she walked by but it didn't matter to him. She couldn't do anything to him that wouldn't make him hate life more than he already did. He got paid for running a fool's errand and that was all that mattered, as long as he wasn't the fool in the end.

Randall stumbled home, trying to control the stumbling as much as possible. Even though Seattle forces didn't seem to crack down on alcohol like other cities, there were still consequences if one was caught. If he was arrested, he didn't know what would happen to Sarah and Leo. The closer he got to the shack, the tighter he held onto the leather purse. There were a few more dollars inside that gave his family a better chance at having a good life again. Leo barely remembered the house he was born in, but Randall had vivid recollections of the cakes and casseroles brought in by family and friends, the dishes looking inviting on the wide kitchen counters. Marty had been there the day of Leo's birth and even provided fine cigars from Gerald. Those were the types of memories Randall wanted more of, especially with his second child on the way.

The shack looked darker than normal or his eyes were getting worse. Typically, he would be able to make out faint candlelight through the drawn curtains. He wondered if Sarah enforced an early bedtime for herself and Leo after what happened that afternoon. Quietly, he opened the door and listened for his family's breathing, the rustle of sheets. While he couldn't hear anything, he also noticed that the shack was as cold as an ice block. He fumbled for the oil lamp and lit it to reveal an empty bed.

"Where did they go?" he panicked. He swung open the doors to the mahogany wardrobe and noticed that several of Sarah's dresses were missing, as well as her everyday shoes and traveling coat. As for Leo, his coat and half of his tops and pants were also missing. The little toy box had been ransacked and Hugo, his son's bear, was nowhere to be found and guaranteed to be with Leo. On the credenza, something glinted in the light of the oil lamp. He didn't even need to pick it up to know that it was Sarah's wedding ring.

He was sure now. His wife and son left him.

For the first time in his adult life, Randall sobbed.

OVER THE NEXT WEEK, life seemed to flow without any unexpected twists. The innocent attraction between Marty and Mildred grew more serious with each kiss and embrace. At Pacific Bounty Cannery, Mildred still danced, but it wasn't with a stranger whose face she couldn't see, but with Marty. They hadn't danced yet, but her imagination told her it would be divine when they did. Work wasn't the numbing task it used to be, either. Albert barked less and Winnie, Gladys and Fred loved Mildred's new attitude, and they even joined in her dancing from time to time. As far as her home life was concerned, Darnella and Opal gave her a wide berth and Harvey didn't say much at all if they spoke. Even Dominic and Vidalia seemed to fade away for the moment, as if Bresford had never welcomed someone named Marty Townsend.

"You are like a whole new woman," Hattie breathed when she and Mildred finally had a chance to sit down and enjoy a vanilla milkshake together at Dream Fountain. "You just seem incredibly radiant and you're finally not keeping your head down like you used to."

"I *feel* like a whole new woman. Is this how you felt when boys started noticing you?" Mildred asked. Of course she knew that Hattie had always been Hattie, confident and gorgeous.

Hattie contemplated the question earnestly. "I'm not sure, but I do know that I wasn't a late bloomer like you!" Mildred feigned laughter and rolled her eyes. "Actually, I have something to tell you, Millie."

"What? What is it? Not bad news, please. I don't think I can handle it." She dropped her hands in her lap.

"Quite the opposite! Look, look, look!" Hattie flung out her left hand and on it was a modest engagement ring that managed to sparkle like a little star. "Leland proposed! I know, I know, he was slower than a snail's pace but will you just look at it? I'm going to be married, Millie!"

Mildred squeezed her dear friend's hands in her own. "Hattie, I am beyond thrilled for you! You and Leland are going to be so happy."

Behind the counter, Leland beamed and blushed as he scooped ice cream into metal cups. For once, Mildred didn't feel like she was a moping outsider observing other people enjoying the different stages of love. Now that she was loved by a man she claimed as her own, she was part of an exclusive club and it felt incredible.

A club that Vidalia wasn't part of, she thought smugly.

"Will you be my maid of honor?" Hattie asked.

Mildred's mouth dropped open and she squealed. "Of course I will! You have so much planning to do, but knowing you, it's already done," she teased.

"Not really, actually. Leland never talked marriage with me except for the fact that he wanted to marry me someday, but beyond that, I've only dreamt of it and talked to you."

Mildred took a pull of her milkshake through the straw. "Do you know when you want the wedding?"

"Sometime towards the middle of July, I think. We don't want to wait forever. Mrs. Leland Burris. I love how it sounds!"

"I'm so happy for you!"

Hattie giggled. "Just think, pretty soon it will be your turn!" Mildred felt herself blush. Even though she and Marty were definitely a couple and she had her first kiss weeks ago, she hadn't really dreamed about marriage the way she used to. She had wanted for so long to find somebody and now that she was living it, she didn't want to waste time thinking about anything else.

"Do you only ever think about weddings, Hattie?" she joked.

"No. I think about makeup and dresses, and don't forget shoes." She took one last sip. "Well, I better get back to Dominic's, but not before I say goodbye to my future husband." Hattie skipped to the counter and talked to Leland for moment, then walked with Mildred outside, linking arms.

"You know, Millie, you really have changed, but in the best way. I don't know anybody as sweet as you and you deserve the best. We should all go out with Marty soon. What do you think?"

"Actually, he is driving down today for a few hours to see me. I could talk to him about it." She hugged her newly engaged friend and said, "Until we meet again, my fair bride!"

WHEN MARTY ASKED WHERE they should celebrate the engagement, Mildred was quick to answer.

"We should go to The Orchard, most definitely!" It was as if she knew what he planned to ask her. It was three o'clock and he wanted to pick her up from work. Since he didn't know what restaurants were good outside of Seattle, he relied on Mildred's recommendations.

"Be sure to wear this when we go." Marty hinted at Mildred's waders and thick knit cap. "I think it should be the next big trend, don't you?"

Mildred made a face and laughed as they rumbled through town. "Never. I should get cleaned up and find something nice to wear that doesn't smell like fish. Could you please stop at Dominic's on the way?"

When Mildred burst into the store and told Hattie the news,

her friend's breathing quickened. "The Orchard? Are you sure? I'm not sure Leland can afford that right now," she whispered as she glanced at her simple engagement ring.

Mildred leaned in closer, making her waders squeak against the counter. "Marty offered to pay for everyone, rather, he insisted! He wants to celebrate properly. Come to my house at five o'clock. Please?" Mildred begged.

"Miss Kilpatrick, shouldn't you be working?" Dominic showed up as quiet as a shadow and took a few moments to pointedly look over Mildred. "Miss Westrick, please allow my employee to do her job."

"I'm sorry, Mr. York," said Mildred, backing away from the counter. She winked and held up five fingers, mouthing to Hattie, "Five o'clock." Hattie barely nodded and got back to her task of restocking the gloves.

After she left, Mildred knew Dominic looked out the window and watched her get into Marty's red truck, giggling and not seeming to have a care in the world.

A MINUTE BEFORE FIVE, Leland and Hattie rolled into the Westrick's driveway.

"Millie, your friends are here!" Opal yelled from the living room window. The girl turned around and blushed at Marty, who was sitting on the couch patiently waiting for Mildred to finish getting ready.

"You are a regular Paul Revere, aren't you?" Marty chuckled.

Opal shrugged her shoulders. "Momma says that Millie is getting an attitude with you. I don't know what that means, but she says it a lot."

"Really? Well, maybe that's a good thing," he said. Not a moment too soon, Leland knocked on the door and Harvey came from the kitchen to let them in.

"If it isn't Leland Burris himself! I heard you proposed. Congratulations, son!" Harvey said as he reached out to shake his hand.

"Thank you, Mr. Westrick."

From behind Leland, Hattie poked out her head. "Hi, Mr. Westrick. Is Mildred ready?"

He feigned excitement. "Ah yes, the big dinner date! Mildred meets Mr. Seattle and all of a sudden she is going places. New trucks, planes, you name it. What's next? Taking a cruise liner to Europe?" Leland looked confused. Harvey gestured to Marty on the couch to illustrate his point.

Marty grimaced at being called "Mr. Seattle." He got up and briskly shook Leland's hand, too. "Hello, Leland. I'm Mr. Seattle." At that, Harvey was slow to laugh.

"Sorry I took so long, everyone. My hair put up quite the fight." Mildred stopped on the stairs and smoothed the fabric over her stomach. When they all turned to look at her, they wore the same expression.

"What?" she asked. "Do I look bad?"

"Millie!" Hattie breathed. "It's clear you've been paying attention to my teachings. Your makeup is amazing! This dress, those shoes!" She came over to admire Mildred wearing a striped dress of navy, pink and white, laying softly in a layer of chiffon over a silky slip. Her velvet navy heels matched the sapphire stone comb holding back her hair that was freshly curled.

"Isn't that a bit much for The Orchard?" her father asked. Immediately, Mildred felt the corners of her eyes get moist with tears, but she smiled widely, biting her lip in embarrassment before remembering that she was wearing lipstick. She didn't know how to respond to her father's comment, suddenly feeling ridiculous all dressed up in front of him. Thankfully, Marty wasn't speechless.

"She could wear that anywhere, Mr. Westrick." He held out his hand to Mildred and escorted her past her father. In his most genteel voice, Marty said, "Have yourself a wonderful evening."

"Thanks," was all Harvey could say. From inside, he watched as his only daughter with Grace smiled as she carefully got into Marty's truck, looking so much like she did at nineteen. He felt a hand on his shoulder.

Darnella peeked through the curtain as Leland and Marty drove their vehicles down the road. She scoffed. From the darkened side room, she had pretended to have a headache and heard everything.

"She is getting such an attitude with that boy."

IT WAS JUST AS she remembered it. The Orchard admittedly looked less like a palace and more like a regular restaurant, but the chairs still gleamed with gold paint and the napkins were folded into teepees. Ruby red lilies stood tall in crystal vases.

"Oh my..." she whispered. Her velvet heels clicked on the marble floor as they were taken to their table for four. The one thing Mildred didn't remember was the cost of everything. As a twelve-year-old girl, she was more concerned about feeling like a queen in the gold chair and not how much her food would cost her father. Her eyes ran down the menu.

"Marty, this is too much. I wouldn't have suggested this place if I had known," she whispered to him.

He covered her hand with his own and whispered back, "I'd take you to the most expensive place in the world and it would still be okay. Get whatever you wish." The waiter came back with the starter course of chilled shrimp cocktail for everyone that Marty ordered when they first walked in, as well as flutes of sparkling lavender lemonade. Mildred had never tried shrimp in cocktail sauce before and was unsure of it. When Marty coaxed her to have one, she was glad he did. The tender flavor of the shrimp and the zesty sauce was a pure revelation.

"I could eat this everyday!" she said, dousing another shrimp in sauce. Hattie and Leland both nodded as they both went for another shrimp. Just as the shrimp ran out, two servers came out with gilded plates full of steaming food.

"Your spaghetti and meatball dinner, miss," said the server as he placed a bowl piled high with pasta, artfully dotted with the most plump meatballs in creation. As elegant as she appeared on the outside, Mildred wanted nothing more than to scoop up the delicious dish with her hands and eat until she felt her stomach was about to burst. As for Leland and Hattie, they ordered roast veal and prime rib, which they promptly cut in half and shared with each other, and Marty ordered a steaming pot of meaty crab legs covered in prickles. At first, Leland and Hattie tried to order the cheapest items on the menu but Marty caught on and said they couldn't pick anything less than thirty cents. The waiter came by to top off the flutes of lemonade.

"Let us toast to the newly engaged couple, Leland and Hattie!" Marty said, raising his flute. Mildred beamed as they all clinked glasses together and drank the sweet, bubbly concoction. Other neighboring tables clapped and raised their flutes for them, too. Hattie, looking more regal than usual in a velvet wine-colored dress with a large velvet flower at the collar, blushed and was about to cry.

"Thank you, Marty. We appreciate it," said Leland. The next moment, the romance turned into talk about sports between the men as they ate.

Hattie giggled and said quietly to Mildred, "Don't you feel like a movie star? I cannot believe how lucky you are."

"Sometimes I still feel like I'm dreaming and I have this fear that it will all go away." She cringed after she let the words leave her mouth.

"Don't say that! You'll make it come true that way. Let's enjoy this fantastic evening and not worry about anything." Hattie took a bite of veal and rolled her eyes. "I'm not sure how I can go back to Boone's Diner after this, honestly."

"My feelings exactly," Mildred said. She took her first bite of meatball and felt like she was instantly transported to heaven. Her meal tasted better than she imagined when she was left behind at home with her can of cold pork and beans.

"Mildred?" She heard her name and slowly came out of her food reverie.

"Yes?" she asked with pasta still in her mouth.

It was Marty, looking amused. Leland and Hattie were nuzzling each other and whispering, clearly enjoying themselves. Marty asked, "Would you want to go to a party with me? It's in a week and I hope it's not short notice. Townsend Timber is celebrating its fiftieth anniversary this Saturday, the eleventh of June, and my father wants to put on a huge shindig at the office."

She only hesitated because she had to swallow. "Of course I would. That sounds like fun!"

"Good. I was worried that I might have to find a different date." Marty winked at Mildred, making her giggle.

Hattie leaned over. "See? Like I said, you are a lucky girl, Millie."

"Are your dancing skills up to par?" Marty asked as he cracked crab legs and dipped the meat into a cup of drawn butter.

"My what? Dancing skills?" She rested her fork on her bowl, wondering if she heard the word 'dancing.'

Leland, usually quiet, started laughing. "I've never seen Mildred dance, but from what I hear, she does some dancing at the cannery!"

Everyone laughed then. Mildred made a face and said,

"Who told you? Let me guess. Was it Fred?"

"Yep! He comes to Dream Fountain and gets root beer floats from me after work. A few weeks ago, he told me that you tried out some Charleston steps and hosed everyone down and hit him in the head. Is that true?"

Marty was now laughing into his napkin. "Please tell me that it's true!"

Mildred lifted her chin and pretended to be snobby. "If you must know, yes, it's true!" They all laughed and continued to laugh all through the dessert of strawberry shortcake and vanilla ice cream, slices of gooey butter cake and caramel custard. They would've had coffee if they had room to spare. After Marty paid for the check and they left the elegance of The Orchard, Hattie squeezed Mildred's arm.

"Don't worry, Millie. I'll help you learn how to dance."

"How did you know I was going to ask you?" said Mildred.

Hattie smiled. "Trust me, I know."

Mildred sighed, her heart overflowing with happiness for her life that very moment. "Thank God." They waved goodbye as they parted ways, getting into vehicles with full bellies. Mildred loved riding in Marty's truck and hearing the motor work as he stepped on the gas to get on the highway back to Bresford. Something about the evening made her more comfortable. Perhaps it was that she shared it with her best friend, someone who could see that she wasn't making up a story about her romance. Hattie would be the first to call her out and tonight, she did nothing of the sort. When Marty toasted to their engagement, she was touched and she could tell that both Leland and Hattie felt the same.

Too soon they arrived in Bresford, rolling down the dark road past the riverfront businesses, Dream Fountain and Dominic's. When Marty turned onto Juniper Street, Mildred fought the urge to crank the steering wheel to the right and avoid her home altogether. She just wanted to go to Seattle with him.

"I'm looking forward to taking you to the party. You'll be the prettiest one there, no contest. I'll make sure of it." He squeezed her hand.

"What do you mean?" she asked. She already knew what dress she would wear and it was nothing like the cotton sweater ensemble she naively wore to Tabby's party. For the past few weeks, Mildred had her eye on a party dress in the Sears & Roebuck catalogue. On a whim, she sent money and was waiting for it to arrive any day.

"You'll see. It wouldn't be a surprise if I told you, would it?"

She smiled the kind of smile that made her eyes almost disappear, just like her mother's. "I guess I just have to find out, won't I?"

"That's my girl. I'll pick you up Saturday morning, okay?" He leaned in, dangerously close to her face. "Now do I get a kiss for everything?"

"You don't have to ask, you know." Mildred slowly touched her lips to his, familiar yet still such a new sensation that made her heart thump wildly inside her chest. She knew they both wanted more than those few kisses, by the way he breathed and the way she couldn't breathe.

"I'll see you Saturday," he whispered, then gave her one more kiss.

"Bye." Reluctantly, she got out of the truck and waved from the front step as he started his long drive back to Seattle.

CHAPTER FOURTEEN

WITH THE DONATIONS EVENT mostly forgotten, Dominic was ready to get his mayoral campaign underway again. Mayor Klemp, still bedridden, was the center of tuberculosis rumors that floated around town and since he remained quarantined, it was guaranteed to be an easy win for Dominic.

"How does this look, Father?" Vidalia held out a poster she made for a pie social scheduled to be held at the Bresford Nazarene Church on Friday. It hadn't been planned for very long and wasn't advertised well because of the whole ordeal of getting Marty to fly in. With that over, it was time to show the people of Bresford that he wanted to be their mayor and nothing shouted 'Vote for Dominic York' like free dessert.

"It's perfect, just like you, my sweet. Don't forget to have the Ladies Aid Society spread this around. The more support, the better!" he said. She nodded and skipped off to make more before the meeting at Darnella Westrick's. If there were no mentions of Marty's romance with Mildred, his daughter was as happy as he could hope. However, if Vidalia saw Marty's truck or the once-invisible Mildred walking around like she owned Bresford, he could tell her blood turned to lava, something she picked up from him. It ate him alive knowing that he couldn't fix the situation just yet and he wasn't exactly sure he could. That thought reminded him that he needed to make a dreaded call and retreated to his office. He never locked the door but for this call, he did.

After he dialed and waited to be connected to the number he was given, a rough voice on the other end sounded testy. "Who is this?"

Dominic didn't flinch at hardly anything, but he felt himself shudder. "It's Dominic York. I'm sorry I haven't called in a while."

The man laughed once and then coughed like he'd been smoking. "You're damn right you're sorry. I've been waiting. Lucky for you, I'm mostly a patient man. So can you tell me why I haven't gotten anything?"

"Lee, I can explain."

"You know my fucking name. Use it!"

He flinched again and started slowly, feeling stupid that he forgot. "Lee *Carroll*, please let me explain. I've been busy with some events in town and you know I'm running for mayor and that takes money and time—"

"You're full of shit, York. None of that matters to me. What matters is the whereabouts of your payment." Based on the muffled sounds coming through the receiver, Lee Carroll hacked into a handkerchief.

Dominic held the phone away until the hacking stopped and he said, "I was just saying that I've been sidetracked and I don't...I don't quite have a shipment ready." He grimaced so hard that his eyes hurt, knowing that he shouldn't have said it and lied instead.

There was a pause on Lee Carroll's end. "Now you're going to have to cut through your little cake of shit and tell me when it's coming or I'll be sending one of my guys to come and take it from your store, personally. You remember my guys, right?" Dominic felt himself pale. Nobody knew of his connection to Lee Carroll and he wasn't about to tell anyone, not even Vidalia.

Lee Carroll, a widow in his fifties and one of the most disgruntled people in Cowlitz County, was relegated to the shantytown along the Columbia River in Kalama after he lost his job shoeing horses to younger and cheaper men who did it with barely the experience that Lee Carroll had. By then, nobody was hiring and definitely not someone his age. Like many others, he lost his home and most everything inside that had become precious over the years. There was nowhere else to go but the river. Lee Carroll quickly became the man in charge. Men twenty and thirty years his junior looked to him for leadership and he felt like he was where he needed to be. Once he and his men learned how to utilize the train that ran along the Columbia River, they quickly established themselves in surrounding towns as men to be feared and respected. Dominic was fairly positive that he wasn't the only person making "payments" to Lee Carroll and his men, which he felt should be called thugs or goons.

How Dominic sold his soul to Lee Carroll in the first place, he vowed to never utter a single word. He kept silent mainly because Lee Carroll, slightly overweight but stronger than a horse in its prime, promised to gut Dominic like a stray cat if he spilled anything to anyone.

"It won't be necessary to send anyone to my store. Just one man by the tracks, like we agreed. What do you want for this shipment?" It varied from month to month. Some shipments required that Dominic buy horse blankets from Harvey at the feed store or fill up several gas cans of fuel.

Lee Carroll answered without hesitating. "Give me tobacco to last a month, more hooch, a pair of size nine boots for me and loads of candy. Butterfinger, chocolate peanuts, and Chick-O-Sticks, get that kind of shit."

Dominic breathed a sigh of relief and figured in his head what inventory he could part with. Aside from the hooch, which was another problem, this was a simple request. "Okay. I'll do it."

"Damn right you'll do it. Meet the train tonight at the usual spot and my guy will collect the payment when it stops." The phone clicked sharply in Dominic's ear but he held it there for a few frozen seconds, praying that this wasn't his reality. While he should've been busying himself with campaign efforts, he left his office to find what Lee Carroll wanted. If he knew how Lee Carroll would have haunted him when he made the deal, he would've refused in a half second. Jealousy had spoken for him, forever cursing him from the moment he and Lee Carroll shook hands five years ago.

BEFORE SHE LEFT TO attend the Bresford Ladies Aid Society meeting, Vidalia primped in front of her vanity mirror. With Marty's sights unfortunately set on Mildred, Vidalia didn't feel the desire to perfect her appearance but she did it anyway. Every time she saw the poppy red outfit she wore when she first met him, all of the feelings rushed back, the feelings of losing to Mildred, being rejected by Marty. Any other man would've gone weak in the knees over Vidalia and her charm. Some days, she tested out her flirting skills on random men, just to keep them honed. Yet they hadn't worked on Marty on several occasions.

"Mildred will lose her grip on him sooner than later. She has no idea what she's doing. Marty needs a woman and you're that woman," Vidalia told her reflection while she finished applying a swirl of blush. As usual, she liked what she saw in her full-length mirror. A dress made of mustard yellow seersucker flattered her silhouette, bringing out the vibrant red tones of her auburn hair. She put on gray shoes with yellow heels and a gray flannel hat, her outfit coordinated to perfection. On her way out, she grabbed the roll of pie social posters and made her way to Juniper Street for the meeting. As usual, Darnella greeted her at the door with overflowing enthusiasm.

"Look at you! What a fashion plate you are, Vidalia!" she said as she ushered her in. Darnella was just as done up in a pink dress with a large bouquet of white and pale blue silk flowers in the center of the neckline. The regular members sat hip to hip on the furniture and munched on gingersnaps that Doris Smith made. Vidalia sat next to Irma, who sipped on her coffee like a dainty bird. Light clapping from Darnella brought the meeting to order.

"Ladies, it's time to buckle down and get this pie social organized. We don't have much time since it's this upcoming Friday! Lord knows we want to support Mr. York and ensure his victory in the election," said Darnella from her chair at the head of the circle. "Vidalia, would you show us the poster?"

Vidalia unfurled a poster that showed off her tidy print and pie drawing. The admiration from the ladies made her swell with pride.

Ellie Johnson piped up, eager as always. "But if Mayor Klemp is done being mayor with his illness and nobody else is running, won't Mr. York win, no matter what we do?" Vidalia rolled her eyes from behind the poster.

"My dear Ellie, if you treasure your place in the Ladies Aid Society, you'll need to learn how to ask better questions." Darnella waited for Ellie to respond but instead, she took a large bite out of a gingersnap cookie. "As I was saying, it's time to start delegating. Does anyone have any famous pies they want to bring?"

Rita visibly averted her eyes after being volunteered to bring ten dozen donuts for the donations event. Her kitchen was nothing but a floury mess for a week and she didn't care if she saw another donut in her life. She, too, stuffed a cookie in her mouth to look otherwise occupied.

"Rita, lovely, talented Rita! Would you bring a few of your famous cranberry fluff pies? There isn't a function in Bresford without them." The others murmured in excitement and Rita had to agree because it was true. She volunteered to make three, but Darnella talked her into making seven.

As Vidalia wrote down the names of who spoke up to bring what kind of pies and how many, she heard footsteps on the stairs behind her. When she turned to see who it was, she regretted it immediately. It was Mildred, but she didn't look like the Mildred she knew from over a month ago. This improved and confident Mildred stood taller, looked people in the face and she even dressed better. Today, she wore a red and white vertical striped skirt and a cream-colored sweater that nipped in her waist, giving her a trimmer figure than Vidalia's yellow dress. She felt a ping of jealousy when her eyes rested on Mildred's shoes, a pair of red and white heels with bright red ribbon laces that made beautifully fat bows. As for her cosmetics, Mildred appeared to have mostly mastered the skills of applying mascara and lipstick and her hair fell in tidy brown waves around her shoulders. Vidalia couldn't deny that Mildred looked incredible.

Their eyes locked for a moment, both of them surprised to see the other.

"Hello, Vidalia," Mildred offered softly.

Vidalia wanted the old, mousy Mildred back more than ever. She was quiet, invisible and in no way a threat to her future, or a threat to anyone, really. She didn't like the new Mildred one bit, even if she did dress a hundred times better.

"Hello," Vidalia said stiffly. "Are you headed to the cannery?" She made sure she said "cannery" with an added sting to be clear that she still looked down on her.

Mildred didn't look hurt the way she wanted her to. Instead, she smiled and looked her in the eye. "Hattie's giving me some dancing lessons. It's going to take a lot of work since I barely know how."

She couldn't stop her burning desire to know more. "What would you ever need dance lessons for?"

In her life, Vidalia had only been to dances at the big summer dance in August and she never went home with star-studded memories from them. The boys she danced with were only eager to touch her hands and waist, too afraid to freely dance and ended up moving like a board in a tight, boring circle. Hattie was an excellent dancer and even Leland, who wasn't the best player on the football team, knew how to twirl his girl around the floor. Everyone enjoyed the summer dance, celebrating the Bresford community together with plenty of delicious food and conversation as the sun set over their precious corner of the Pacific Northwest.

Then Vidalia saw the blush rise to Mildred's full cheeks and sensed that she was hesitating to say why. "Actually, Marty is taking me to a big party in Seattle this weekend and he wants to take me dancing."

Dancing with Marty? Vidalia's nightmare was almost complete and she was at a loss for words. She could only manage a tight smile but her eyes betrayed how she felt and Mildred could see it.

"Well, have fun organizing the pie social," Mildred said before leaving. When she shut the door and took off on her bicycle, Vidalia dropped the poster and ran to the kitchen with

Darnella right behind her. She clutched her stomach and was afraid she would vomit all over the floor.

"Vidalia, dear, I saw everything!"

Hot tears rolled down Vidalia's face. "How could she dangle that in front of me? Marty should be with me! This whole thing, Marty and Mildred, is just a big joke!" The tears turned into streams and darkened spots on her yellow dress. Her face wrinkled into something ugly as she cried into her hands.

"Come here, come here," Darnella whispered. She pulled Vidalia to her and patted her back with light taps. "Remember when I said I'd help you get Marty? It might be harder than we thought but it could still happen."

Vidalia sniffled. "What if I never get him? What can we do?"

"I'm not sure but give it time. Dancing and parties are exciting at first but he'll realize she isn't the kind of girl he needs when their fire dies out. Something will have to happen, it always does." Darnella kissed Vidalia's forehead and said, "Wipe your tears and let's get back in there. We have a pie social to plan!"

DURING THE BICYCLE RIDE over to Hattie's house, Mildred couldn't stop thinking about the stricken look on Vidalia's face. At first, she just showed poorly veiled envy as she scanned her from her curled hair to the chic bows on her shoes, but once Mildred mentioned Marty's name, Vidalia's nostrils flared and her lips pursed ever so slightly.

"Hattie, you should've seen her face. I actually feel sorry for her," Mildred said after she recounted the scene.

Hattie stopped in her tracks on the way to the study where the Gramophone lived. "Excuse me? Why? What is there to feel sorry about, Millie? You are happy, Marty is happy with you and you are friendly to everyone. Vidalia is miserable because she isn't in your shoes. If she was a nicer person, then maybe things would be different. But she's not, so stop dwelling on how she feels because I can guarantee that she doesn't give one hoot about how you feel. If she tries to bother you again, just ignore her."

"You're right. I can't waste another thought on her or feel sorry just because good things are happening to me." Hearing Hattie say it made the act of ignoring Vidalia sound relatively easy. "You're absolutely right."

"You're fine, Millie. It's not your fault that you're one of the sweetest girls in the world. Enough talk about Vidalia. Are you ready to do some dancing?" Hattie asked. The look on Mildred's face made her snort with laughter.

"Ready to make a fool of myself, you mean? I wish I'd taken you up on your invitations to go to dances over the years, I'd at least know a thing or two," Mildred groaned.

Hattie shook her blonde head as she dug through the records. "If you listen to me, you will be marvelous. Just think of how impressed Marty will be."

"Or he'll be horrified!"

Hattie examined her family's collection of records, unsatisfied with what she found until she squealed when she found the one she was looking for. "If you want to do the Charleston, *this* is the song." Hattie sat the shiny record on the Gramophone turntable, placed the needle and cranked the handle enough to get the machine going. The song that crackled to life was none other than "Charleston" by Paul Whiteman and His Orchestra.

"Come here, Millie," Hattie said with the air of a teacher. "Watch my feet. It's all about staying on the toes and swiveling your ankles, okay? Like this: forward-and-a-tap-and-a-back-and-a-tap..." Her skilled feet moved in perfect time to the catchy song, mesmerizing Mildred like a magic trick. "And add some swinging arms!" As if the shuffling feet weren't tricky enough, Hattie shot her arms back and forth by her hips and then swayed them above her head.

"You expect me to learn all of that by Saturday? It's impossible!" Mildred whined. "I'm going to be such an embarrassment!" Being graceful and outgoing like Hattie weren't her strengths, never have been, and she didn't expect to become good enough to fool anyone in such a short amount of time.

"No, it's not impossible, Millie. I'll just show you the footwork with no music." Hattie stopped the turntable and slowed the steps down to a molasses-in-December speed. "See how they meet? Forward and middle tap, back and middle tap, and keep repeating it."

Dutifully, Mildred studied Hattie's swiveling ankles and tapping toes until she felt her feet wanting to make the same motions. She couldn't believe it when she swiveled and tapped her feet at the right points in the dance.

"That's more like it!" Hattie smiled. Mildred balanced her weight on her toes and swung her ankles out and back. At first, she stumbled forward into Hattie several times and apologized, but she kept practicing until she stopped wobbling about like a newborn calf.

An hour later, Mildred couldn't stop moving her feet once she figured out the puzzle that Hattie made look simple. She was even at the point of adding the different arm motions.

"Now let's practice together. I'll be Marty. Give me your hand and put your other hand on my shoulder." Mildred did as she was told and planted her left hand on Hattie's shoulder and her right hand inside Hattie's left. "I'll go forward, which means you'll go backwards, but don't forget to keep moving your feet. Are you ready?"

"I think so," Mildred hesitated. Hattie cued the music and

counted down, leading with confidence that flowed into Mildred. As she got more and more comfortable dancing with a partner, Mildred focused on adding bounce and attitude to her moves. It surprised her how it felt better, freer, when she put everything into the dance and stopped worrying about looking stupid.

"Whoa, Millie! You are doing so well!" Hattie cried. "Now, let's separate and add the side arms on three, alright? Here we go--one, two, three!" The girls broke apart and swung their arms to the left, right and gracefully overhead as if they were in a snazzy club and not at Hattie's house. By the time the song ended, Mildred's brow glinted with beads of sweat. She ripped her shoes off and flung them away from her as if they were bear traps. Both girls collapsed in the matching wingback chairs.

Hattie applauded weakly. "Mille, you were simply wonderful!"

"You think so?" she asked, panting. She found a newspaper nearby to fan her face with.

Hattie nodded, soundly equally exhausted. "I think Marty will be tickled to dance with you. And I am going to want every detail! Now let me go find us some cold Coca-Colas after all of that wild dancing we did."

CHAPTER FIFTEEN

F<small>RIDAY</small>, <small>THE TENTH OF</small> J<small>UNE</small>, promised to be a sunny but somewhat chilly day in Bresford. The pie social at the Nazarene church was on the community calendar, including Mildred's, and it appeared that more than three-quarters of the town's population showed up with an appetite for a good slice of dessert. There were barely enough chairs in the fellowship hall, but people kept filing in. To show thanks, Dominic greeted everyone at the door that came to show support for him.

Mildred wandered around and studied the pies that lined the tables, counting at least fifty tins altogether. To name some of the selections, she saw plenty of apple pie, strawberry rhubarb pie, lemon pie, chocolate satin pie, peach pie, and of course, Rita's cranberry fluff pie. They all looked absolutely tempting and Mildred wished she could cut a slice of each one before everyone else did. While she was physically there, Mildred's mind was with Marty and dreaming about tomorrow's party and the promised dancing. Being in such a good mood helped her ignore Darnella's snippy attitude that morning as she stormed around the house in preparations for the pie social. Yesterday, Darnella's cherry pie failed miserably. Underneath the soggy latticework crust, the cherries floated in a pool of juice that never thickened up. By that time, it was too late for her to make something else and that's when the ranting started. Mildred didn't even recall anything her stepmother said, even though she saw her lips moving and her dark eyes squinting with disapproval over something. Even Opal hid in her room from her mother.

In the crowd, Mildred saw Hattie and Leland sitting together and found an empty seat next to them. Unfortunately, across from Mildred sat Vidalia, who looked equally horrified about it. Flanking Vidalia on each side were girls that Mildred knew vaguely from school, Rebecca Hennell and Katherine Dahl. Neither girl had much to recommend them except their ability to mimic Vidalia and follow her around like ducklings. During her Bresford High School days, Mildred clearly remembered Rebecca and Katherine copying Vidalia's outfits the very next day, everything from the hair and style of hat to the shoes and earrings. A year out of school hadn't changed anything because both girls wore sleeveless blouses and a silk scarf around the neck.

"Mildred Westrick?" asked Rebecca. "From Bresford High, right? I completely forgot about you." Her blue eyes seemed just as empty as they did in school. Mildred felt Hattie put her hand on her knee, letting her know that she was there for her and taking in every syllable.

The old Mildred would've been at a loss for words, but the

Mildred today had to keep herself from laughing. "I'm not surprised you don't remember me, actually. If Vidalia didn't acknowledge me, then you didn't, either. But enough about the past. What are you and Katherine up to these days?"

Both girls giggled and Katherine spoke up first. "We're each married to a twin brother from Ridgefield. They used to play football against Bresford all the time, which is how the two of us met them. They work at The Orchard as servers now, so we get treated to fancy meals all the time."

"You two married the Grant brothers from Ridgefield High?" Leland asked. On most topics, he stayed silent but when his beloved sport of football was brought up, he had no fear of speaking. The girls nodded wildly, Katherine claiming Reggie and Rebecca claiming Joe.

Leland clicked his tongue and whistled. "Joe and Reggie were the dynamic duo on the field, a tough pair to beat whenever Bresford played against them. They were brutal, been knocked down more than once myself by them, but they were real nice guys once the game was over."

Katherine turned back to Mildred and asked out of courtesy, "What are you doing now, Mildred? Are you married yet?"

Immediately, Vidalia chimed in. "She works at Pacific Bounty Cannery." Again, she added a layer of venom to the word and looked Mildred directly in the eyes. Even though Mildred felt the barb, she didn't look away like she would in the past.

"Are you the secretary?" Katherine asked.

"I prepare salmon for processing." Mildred didn't want to elaborate on the gruesome details.

Vidalia felt the need to chime in again. "She guts them and ends up smelling like fish for weeks." Katherine burst with laughter along with Vidalia. Just then, Dominic York's voice silenced everyone from the little box stage against the back wall.

"Welcome to the pie social in support of my goal to become

Bresford's next mayor!" Applause filled the stuffed room. "When it comes time to vote, I'd be more than appreciative if you'd keep me in mind. I've been a Bresford citizen for over twenty years and I would be honored to have a chance to make decisions that would benefit the town and those of us that live within it. Please keep Mayor Klemp in your prayers. God bless you!" His speech was simple and succinct. Once he left the stage to mingle, the people rushed in polite form to make a line on each side of the pie tables. As luck would have it, Mildred was across the table from Vidalia in the line, as well.

Don't waste another thought on her, she chastised herself. Instead, she busied her mind with finding the perfect pie to dig into. Even though she scanned over them earlier, she couldn't decide which one to choose.

"Was Hattie a good dance teacher? She told me you caught on fast!" said Leland from his spot in line. His plate already had two large slices of pie on it and he was scoping out which kind he wanted for his third.

Mildred sensed that Vidalia was eavesdropping on every single word of the conversation. Carefully, she answered, "Hattie flatters me, Leland, but trust that I stumbled and looked silly most of the time."

Vidalia stabbed the lemon meringue in front of her and dug out a slice like it was a stubborn weed in the garden. With exaggerated motions, she slopped it onto her plate and huffed audibly from her nose. Mildred looked up to see that Vidalia was staring straight at her again. The issue could no longer be danced around or ignored like before. "Please tell me why you're mad at me, Vidalia. This has gone on long enough, don't you think?"

"You already know the answer to that, so why bother asking me?" she spat. Her eyes were intensely blue and wild. People in line looked from one girl to the other. Rebecca and Katherine simultaneously placed slender slices of lemon pie on their plates, pretending that the confrontation wasn't happening next to them.

"Is it because of Marty? Believe me when I say that I never thought it would happen." Her appetite for pie suddenly vanished. She was disappointed by it because her heart was set on having a fat piece of the chocolate pie in front of her.

"*Millie...*" Hattie whispered. Mildred could tell that Hattie was chomping at the bit to swoop in and take care of Vidalia for her, but she knew that it was her battle to fight. The only problem, she realized, was that fighting was uncharted territory for her and she didn't know how far it could possibly go.

I guess I'm about to find out, she thought. The lines froze as people quieted down and watched, most of them looking riveted, some frightened.

"You wouldn't have known this, but the letters I wrote were never meant to reach him. Hattie was being kind and thinking of me when she mailed them on my behalf, so even after I found out, I honestly never expected that Marty would write me back. I'm truly sorry if you're upset by how things turned out." Every word she said was carefully selected, true and heartfelt.

Vidalia didn't even bother pursing her lips with restraint this time and showed her gritted teeth like a cornered animal, ready to attack. "You're sorry? Marty was never meant to be yours! My father arranged everything so that Marty would fall in love with me, not someone who works in a stinky cannery!"

Hearing the commotion, Darnella abandoned her duty of handing out forks and rushed over to Vidalia's side, looking back and forth between the two girls. "Ladies, ladies, remember that we are in a church!"

Men and women holding plates of pie moved aside as Dominic parted through them like Moses. "Can someone tell me what is going on here?" He met Mildred's gaze with a loathing stare that chilled her blood.

His daughter pointed a sharp finger at her and yelled, "*She* ruined any chance I had with Marty and she acts like it's nothing!"

Mildred wouldn't stand for being falsely accused. "No, that isn't true. I ran away from him not once, but twice! Yet he still found me! You had plenty of opportunities to win him over, but...he chose me." The throbbing pulse in her ears was more deafening than any Fourth of July firework explosion she'd ever heard.

"Don't you *dare* speak to my daughter that way, Miss Westrick," Dominic barked. "I won't have it, not here, not ever!"

"Mildred, I think you should go home. Wait until your father hears what you started, in a *church*, no less." Darnella shook her head, clearly disappointed in her embarrassment of a stepdaughter. Something bumped Mildred in the hip and she saw it was Hattie's hand. She glanced up at her best friend amid the heavy silence.

"*Forget what I said*," Hattie mouthed, barely whispering. Without her saying it, Mildred knew that Hattie was referring to yesterday's conversation before the dance lesson, to just ignore Vidalia's bullying the next time she poked and prodded.

Vidalia's muscles tightened in her neck and tears brimmed in her blue eyes, the red veins making them look ghoulish. Her voice sounded deeper than before, fueled with the fury she kept bottled up since she was first jilted. "You don't deserve Marty in the slightest, Mildred! Once he realizes how worthless and boring you are, the better!"

The crowd watching the argument gasped in unison. Hattie shrieked the loudest as the insult left Vidalia's lips. Mildred was at a loss for words once again, but not because she couldn't think of anything to say.

Sitting in front of her was a chocolate satin pie made by

Doris Williams, looking scrumptious with mounds of whipped cream and chocolate curls. When Mildred picked up the chilled aluminum tin, she realized that it was heftier than it looked on the table, but it was too late to set it down and back out now.

Time seemed to slow to a crawl as she raised the pie by her ear and gave it a solid shove. Everyone's eyes filled with horror as they watched the airborne dessert, a testament to Doris's whipped cream as it held its shape as it flew sideways. With a satisfying *wumph*, the pie coated Vidalia's entire face. Splotches of chocolate pie landed on Dominic's beard, his lapels and tie. As for Darnella, she sputtered frantically as she wiped pie off of her face and then realized her dress was ruined. Both Rebecca and Katherine waved their gloved hands around when they felt pie in their hair and scarves.

All eyes were on Vidalia, who stood as still as a mannequin in her father's store. The tin slid down and clattered sharply to the floor. Surprisingly, the sturdy crust was still glued to the pie filling, yet another testament to Doris's no-fail crust recipe. Laughter from children punctuated the stillness as blobs of chocolate pie dropped onto Vidalia's shoulders and down the front of her dress. Hands bent into claws, she raked handfuls of pie and crust off her face and blindly flung the dessert to the side. An animalistic shriek flew from her pie-covered lips and resonated throughout the fellowship hall. Some children hid behind their parents while others covered their young ears. It was a shriek so piercing that Mildred swore she felt her heart drop into the pit of her stomach like a rock.

Not particularly curious to find out what would happen if she stayed, Mildred pivoted on her heel and ran out of the church. Both Hattie and Leland rushed after her. Vidalia was not far behind them. Dominic and Darnella formed the rest of the train headed to the exit as others scrambled to peer from the windows. With his long legs, Leland beat the girls to his car and started the engine.

"*You'll regret this, Mildred Westrick!*" Vidalia bellowed from the doorway of the church.

Before she got into the safety of the car, Mildred couldn't help but look back at the damage she caused. The windows were crammed with curious faces, some people looking entertained while others shook their heads. If Vidalia's face wasn't covered in chocolate pie, Mildred was sure it would be as raging red as Dominic's. Darnella's eyes were as squinty as she ever saw them, promising a world of misery.

"Let's get you home, Millie," said Hattie from the front seat. Mildred slumped heavily onto the bench in the back, feeling numb and doomed.

Hattie turned around and exhaled slowly. "When I told you to forget what I said, I had no idea that you'd be throwing pie."

Mildred made a sound, somewhere between a scoff and a grunt. "Vidalia said I was worthless and I couldn't let her get away with it. I had to show her I'm not the same Mildred she could stomp all over. How am I going to crawl out from under this now?" She groaned into her hands while Hattie lovingly patted her knee.

"You're not worthless. Not to me, not to Marty..."

"Not to me, either," said Leland, winking at her in the rearview mirror. As he turned onto Juniper Street, Mildred felt nausea strike her insides. For almost a minute, she hesitated to get out of the running car, but she knew she couldn't stay in it forever.

"Thanks, both of you. Wish me luck because I'm going to need it."

CHAPTER SIXTEEN

Inside Foster & Sons Hardware, Randall finally had news worth giving to Agnes but this time, he wanted a different form of payment. Wearing a deep purple smocked blouse and an indescribably extravagant hat, Agnes sat next to him with her Pink Lady cocktail in hand and appeared to be annoyed.

"Before you tell me that you've already heard this, listen to what I have to say." With Sarah and Leo gone for almost two weeks now, Randall lost his will and appetite to stand in the soup kitchen lines and stuck to a diet that consisted primarily of booze. Tonight, he was already on his fourth glass of Cutty Sark and didn't feel like stopping anytime soon.

Agnes didn't even let him start. "Why should I even believe anything you tell me? I went to the races and none of Marty's college friends were there, let alone Marty himself. There I was, spending a mint to sit next to the boxes by myself like a fool. Something tells me you made that up just so you could get your few dollars from me. I'd stop listening to you if my detective wasn't so slow getting back to me."

He tried to recall the story he fed her. "Agnes, I said that it was a *possibility* that Marty would be at the races, remember? Now aren't you at least a little curious to hear what I have this time?"

She shrugged and used her finger to play with the cherry floating in her glass. "Go on."

"Have you or have you not received an invitation to the Townsend Timber fiftieth anniversary party?"

Agnes raised a groomed eyebrow over her cocktail. "Why does it not surprise me that you'd bring this up?"

"Damn it, Agnes, I asked you to listen to me. Have you or have you not hear about it?"

"Of course I have! Crane Development is only the biggest catch for Townsend Timber to partner with, so we'd be the first people on the list. Let me guess, is Marty bringing his country bumpkin with him?" Agnes rolled her eyes, even though she had been brought up to know how unladylike it was.

"I'm guessing so because I heard through my connections that Marty has plans after the party, that he was making special arrangements." He made sure to stretch out "special arrangements" for effect.

"Where does he plan to go?" Agnes asked, leaning in closer and clearly intrigued now.

Randall tossed back his scotch and signaled to Pete for another. "That's the thing. I need something from you before I can say what I know."

Her eyes searched his scruffy face. "What? Do you need more money?"

"This." Randall plunked a large tin on the counter in front of her. It was essentially empty except for some patches of dried frosting and crumbs inside.

She looked confused as she sipped her drink. "What is this, a tin to store your money in or what?"

"I need to know where my wife and son went. This tin wasn't one of Sarah's and I know it has to be connected to their disappearance. I have a strong suspicion that Marty was involved."

"What? Why would you think that?" she asked incredulously.

Pete delivered Randall's blessed scotch, of which he took a swig before he continued. "When I came back to my place after I met with you last, it was clear that Sarah and Leo left. Suitcases, clothes and his toys were gone. She even left her wedding ring behind. I searched high and low when I found this tin under the credenza. That was the day of Marty's little sister's birthday party, the one you attended."

She nodded. "Yes, I remember."

"Did you eat any of the cake at the party?"

"No. I avoid cake as a rule, but even if I wanted to indulge in a piece, Marty chased me out before I could've had some. Do you think he brought cake in this tin and left it as some kind of calling card?"

"I *know* he did, he had to! Ever since I relocated to Elliott Bay, Marty would bring sandwiches and candy by, and then he started gathering donations for those of us in the shacks. He'd let me and family have first pick every time. It would only make sense that he'd also bring some birthday cake to us."

Agnes looked as if she was seriously considering the facts he presented, mulling all of the possibilities around. "And what if you're right? What would you do then? I still want to marry him, you understand this. If you're only intention is to harm him, I won't help you any further."

Randall clapped his hands once, making it sound more like a boom than a clap. "I *knew* you'd say that! If Marty is indeed the one who ripped apart my family, of course I'd want to kill him, naturally. However, since you still have your heart set on the bastard, I only want to know where to find my wife and son. What about putting your private detective on their case, see what he can dig up?" He had a good idea of where they were, but he had no idea where to start, no money to call around. He spent everything in the leather purse on alcohol since it was clear he wasn't going to be getting an apartment at Glen Eden.

"So you're saying that you wouldn't hurt Marty if my detective finds out he is responsible?" For once, Randall was a step ahead of Agnes and he loved it.

"It wouldn't do you much good to marry him if he's dead, now would it? Don't assume I'm completely without a heart. Marty would live and I'd expect to be monetarily compensated to the tune of five-thousand dollars instead. If it plays out that way, I'd be able to get my family back, start over as a wealthy man. You'd win and I'd win."

Suddenly, Agnes adopted a serious look compared to the skeptical one she had before. "You *did* think this through. I'm impressed, Randall. Say that I do put my detective on the case of your missing wife and son and he finds out where they are. Will you tell me right here, at this very bar, where Marty plans to be after the Townsend Timber party?" She held out her hand to him, smooth and perfectly manicured, ready to settle. They shook over the barter, an unwritten yet binding agreement.

"You've got a deal," Randall said evenly, despite the vast amount of scotch sloshing around in his stomach. Nothing balanced him like a tangible target, especially when the target was the image of his beloved Sarah and Leo.

Agnes waved at Pete for another Pink Lady to celebrate the

enormous step in her plan to become Mrs. Martin Townsend. She had him once and she'd get him again, she was sure of that.

"Now, tell me everything you know."

IT WAS JUNE ELEVENTH, a gorgeous Saturday morning around seven o'clock and Mildred hadn't stayed over in the guest room. After the pie throwing fiasco yesterday, Mildred called Marty that night to pick her up at six o'clock the next morning at Manchester Fairgrounds. When he asked why, she whispered that she couldn't say it over the telephone, but promised to explain on the plane ride up to Seattle. At a quarter to five, Mildred quietly left the house with her navy suitcase and hustled to the fairgrounds on foot. The arena and grandstands were eerie this time of morning, shadows of past events filling the emptiness, echoes of people cheering coming forth from her memory. She waited by the closed concession stand that smelled faintly of popcorn and started when a mother robin fled her nest and flapped by Mildred's head, squawking furiously at her all the way to a perch nearby. Soon, a familiar hum from the sky made her heart jump and sure enough, she spied Marty's plane from afar. The robin still squawked when Mildred ran to meet the plane as it landed. Once Marty had his plane gently riding in the sky, she told him everything without pausing for breath, from Vidalia's taunting to how she regretted throwing sweet Doris Smith's chocolate pie.

"Don't regret it for a minute. You finally did something about her and in front of a lot of people, too. I'm proud of you!" Marty shouted over the roar of the engines. Hearing him say that made Mildred feel slightly justified in what she had done and the gross feeling in her stomach eased. After they landed in Seattle, Mildred fell asleep during the ride to Queen Anne. Gently, Marty woke her and held her hand as she bumbled behind him towards the fenced backyard of the Townsend home.

"Marty! Millie! You're here!" Tabitha was outside and yawned from her pillow-lined lounge chair. She lazily rubbed her eyes and snuggled deeper into her blankets. Next to her chair was an enormous pond filled with all kinds of fish, flicking around just beneath the surface as they pecked at the bugs that danced above them. It was the first time Mildred saw the outdoor space at the Townsend home and she immediately thought of how much her mother would've loved to see what she was seeing right now. Grace Westrick might've been poor as far as money was concerned, but her flowerbeds and shrubs made people wonder when they saw the bursts of color from bleeding hearts in May, lilies in June, and massive hostas that looked more like elephant ears in July. When she could, Grace took clippings from friends or an obliging plant in the park to create starts of her own. Her mother never failed to gasp whenever she saw the little white buds through the glass of water, baby roots promising to give her something beautiful.

"Do what you're born to do, little one," Grace would say, a familiar line she'd tell Mildred. No matter what it was, Grace couldn't help but to give and nurture, whether it was a plant in a Mason jar or her quiet daughter.

Some of Mildred's earliest memories were of her mother's handiwork in the backyard while she played, seeing Monarch butterflies and bees enjoying all of the vivid flowers alongside the hummingbirds, her mother sitting down at her easel to sketch the nature she created.

"You're up early, Squeak," said Marty. "What brings you out here?"

She smiled as her brother kissed her cheek. "I overheard the call and I wanted to be the first to see you when you both arrived. The sunrise was exquisitely pink."

"Good morning, Tabby! You're looking vibrant today." Mildred pranced over and carefully hugged her, then sat where

Tabby patted the pillow next to her and she obligingly plopped down.

"I feel vibrant. It must be the good summer air," Tabby said. From inside the house, Masterson came out with an elegant tea tray and some fresh scones, the steam rising in tempting curls from the towel-lined basket.

"Something to whet your appetite, everyone," said Masterson with a degree of pride. At once, Mildred's mouth began to water and her stomach, which had been grumbling relentlessly since she left her house, now gurgled audibly. As if she could read minds, Masterson handed Mildred English-style black tea in a china cup, sweet and milky, warming her body as she drank.

Marty prepared a scone for Tabby and one for himself. "Mildred, these are the best scones in the entire world, I swear it. Get it before they vanish forever."

"Yes, do try one!" Tabby urged. Her appetite wasn't very large, but she already put in her order for a second scone as she munched on the first. From the basket, Mildred greedily swiped a hot scone and smeared strawberry jam and clotted cream inside. When she took a bite of the fluffy pastry, she was not one bit surprised that it was as scrumptious as everything else she had eaten there so far.

"If my mother was still alive, she would be begging you to share your recipe," Mildred said earnestly. Grace's scone recipe from her own mother yielded decent results, but they were more dense and speckled with raisins.

Masterson placed a hand to her heart. "Bless you. I'm very flattered by that. Thank you, Miss Westrick." She turned to Marty and said in a business-like manner, "You'll find that I've laundered and pressed your favorite suit for tonight's party. Just be sure and get that airplane smell off of you and fix your helmet hair. You know how much your mother would hate that."

"Thanks for the reminder. Where is my mother, by the way? Is she home?" He rubbed his tired face and looked like he could use some strong coffee.

Masterson shook her head. "Your mother has been running errands since dawn, but she did want me to remind you that Dr. Ward will be here at two o'clock this afternoon to withdraw some blood from you for Tabitha."

From his cushioned patio chair, Marty yawned loudly. He took a long sip of tea and said, "Masterson, before my blood draw, would you be able to make us all some of your remarkable eggs Benedict?"

Tabby chimed in. "Make mine without ham, please! My stomach doesn't seem to care for it."

"Put her slice of ham on mine," he said. "Mildred, do you have any preferences?"

Embarrassed, she said quietly, "I've actually never tried eggs Benedict before. What are they?" She could only imagine what sort of dish it could be with the name "Benedict" attached to it.

"Really? You're in for a treat then." He rubbed his palms together, eager for the next course.

Masterson raised an eyebrow. "Are my scones not enough for you three?" It was obvious she was joking.

"I'm a growing boy, what other excuse do I have?" he teased back.

"How can I say no to you?" After she finished laughing, Masterson looked curiously at Mildred. "Excuse me, Miss Westrick, but before I prepare the eggs, did you have a dress that you'd like for me to freshen up for you for tonight?"

"A dress?" Mildred asked dumbly. Her mouth slowly dropped open as the horror struck her. In her haste packing the suitcase last night, she forgot to take down the light blue dress with fluttery sleeves off the hanger that she had in plain sight.

Several weeks ago, Mildred had Hattie help her order a dress from the catalogue and both of them were beyond tickled that it was prettier in person when it arrived. She couldn't wait for Marty to see her wearing such a dress, a dress that made her look more sophisticated, like a woman that was worthy of the approval of people like the Townsends. Even the new white heels resting on the floor under the dress were still there. "It's at home, right where I left it with my shoes. I'm such an idiot." She felt the familiar burn as the heat of blushing crept across her face.

"Why don't you borrow one of my dresses? I have plenty for you to choose from, all colors and fabrics you can imagine," Tabby offered sweetly. Mildred wondered if Tabby noticed that her wardrobe was probably two sizes too small for her, but it was a sweet thought.

"I'd hate to impose. I'm sure they're all very expensive and I'd be afraid of spilling something and ruining one," Mildred answered. Her eyes and nose burned, thinking of the dress she picked especially for tonight hanging in her darkened room, a wasted opportunity. Where would she ever wear such a dress in Bresford?

"I have a better idea," Marty said. He wiggled a finger at Tabby until she giggled. "Squeak, what is that dress shop called, the one Mother always took you to?"

She pointed a finger back at him. "Evette's! She opens at ten and there are some wonderful places for lunch near the shop. I haven't been there since February but it is one of my favorite places in the world. Have you ever heard of Evette's, Millie?"

Again, something else she didn't know about, so she shook her head. Back home, there were three ways to get clothing: Dominic's, catalogue orders and making them by hand. Aside from seeing the limited options at Dominic's, Mildred had never stepped foot inside a proper dress shop before.

Marty clapped and rubbed his hands together. "It's decided then. Mildred, I'm taking you to Evette's. Pick anything you want, absolutely anything."

Inside, Mildred's heart did cartwheels and she no longer felt bad about accidentally leaving her dress behind. "That would be lovely!"

From the lounge chair, Tabby appeared to be sulking.

"What's the matter with you, Squeak?"

She shrugged. "Why can't I go? Aside from the hospital, I haven't left the house in four months."

Masterson had been waiting to see what was to be done with Mildred's dress situation and hadn't left for the kitchen yet. She answered right away. "Tabitha, your mother would be hysterical if she knew you left the house. What happens if you catch something or get a nosebleed in public? There is no way to keep you from getting an infection out there. Your poor body is already going through enough."

Tabitha stirred her tea until it made a tiny whirlpool in her cup. "If I catch something, I catch something. I'd rather have a bit of fun than stay cooped up in here until I die."

"Enough of that talk! That's no way to speak to me or Masterson. Shame on you, Tabby." For the first time, Mildred saw Marty get firm with his little sister.

Plump tears formed in her eyes. "I'm sorry, Marty. Please just take me to town, it's all I want. It kills me when you go off to do something without me. I promise I'll be careful." The pleading got to Mildred and even made her eyes damp.

After a moment of contemplation, Marty grumbled and sighed. "Masterson, go ahead and make the eggs for us. By the time they are ready, I'll have Tabby dressed and her wheelchair loaded in my truck. Looks like I'll be taking *two* girls shopping."

AS THE RED CHEVROLET rumbled down Mercer Street, Tabby

practically bounced in the passenger seat next to Mildred. Despite her leukemia, she was a vision of life.

"I can only imagine what sort of stock Evette is carrying since I got sick," she said, more than excited. "The last thing I got from her was a bridesmaid's dress."

Mildred couldn't help but ask. "Whose wedding did you wear it to?"

After a small pause, Tabitha said, "I never got to wear it, actually. After I got sick, I couldn't do it." There was a long silence after that and Mildred wished someone would say more.

"Here we are, ladies!" Marty parked the truck in front of Evette's and opened the door, helping Tabby and then Mildred. His sister held onto his arm as they walked into the shop. When they entered, a pleasant bell jingled above the door.

"How I miss that bell," said Tabby. "I adore the smell of new dresses!" She inhaled and sighed happily.

From the back, a melodic voice implored, "Is that Tabby Townsend?" A slender, brown-haired woman wearing a cranberry satin dress entered the room. "My God, it *is* Tabby! Come here, my love! It's been too long!"

Tabby let go of her brother's arm and carefully made her way to hug Evette. Mildred watched the two sway back and forth, whispering and near tears. It was clearly more than a dress shop to Tabby. When they were done hugging, both of them wiped their eyes.

"What can I do for you today?" Evette asked as she smoothed out her dress.

"Tonight is my father's company's fiftieth anniversary party and both Miss Westrick and I need exquisite dresses for the occasion," Tabby explained. The shop owner's wide eyes got even wider with glee as she examined Mildred.

"Welcome, Miss Westrick. I'm Evette Landon," she said. She glided over to greet her with heavily jeweled hands. "The

Townsends have been loyal customers for years and I hope to gain your trust, as well. Are you a friend of Tabitha's?"

"Yes. I actually met her through her brother."

Something twinkled in Evette's eyes as she looked at Marty and then Mildred. "I'd heard about this and wondered if this romance was true. But that's enough idle gossip from me. Feel free to roam around, find something that catches your eye. Let me know if I can assist you with anything."

The ornate shop was almost more than Mildred could take in at once, from the plush rose-colored carpet, antique brass racks and bold black and white striped wallpaper. There were bowls of complimentary chocolates sitting around and Mildred helped herself to a piece. The few times she went to Dominic's to look for clothes, any other employee besides Hattie was less than ecstatic to help her shop.

Evette smiled with amusement at Mildred. "You look lost."

"I really don't know where to start. It's my first time in such a lovely place like this."

Evette cocked her head, her pinned hair staying in place. "I don't understand. Are you not from around here?"

Marty broke his silence. "Evette, I want Mildred to be the loveliest woman at the party tonight. Hair, makeup, the works. Would you be able to come by the house and doll up the girls? The party is at seven."

"I'd love to! I'll be by at five with my supplies."

Mildred felt anxious. "Are you sure that you can make ne glamorous like the women in the magazines?" She'd already been to a few gatherings of various sizes, but this Townsend Timber party seemed to be more important than anything else thus far. Being caught in a casual cotton ensemble with only a swipe of mascara in a sea of finery wouldn't happen again. She felt beyond flattered that Marty believed she could be prettier than the seasoned socialites, but wasn't sure she could actually do it.

"Miss Westrick, look at me. Do you think I woke up looking like this?" Evette stood proudly before her.

Mildred did as she was told and looked Evette over. She had already admired her dress, but she noticed the fine details of her makeup, her cheekbones created by a line of dark powder rather than inheriting them naturally, the rosy blush that was blended seamlessly. Her eyelashes were black and bushy, topped with a thick black line that flicked out in a perfect tail that made her eyes look wide. As for her lips, they were the deepest shade of brick red and perfectly symmetrical. The only thing Mildred didn't understand was the thinness of her eyebrows, but it was obvious that Evette knew a thing or two about applying makeup. What capped it off was her stance, her sheer ownership of everything on her body and what she wanted people to think of it all. It worked.

"You look flawless," Mildred breathed.

"Thank you. That means I did my job and I will do the same for you. Now, what do you envision yourself wearing to the grandest party? What would make everyone focus on you? Colors, textures, emotions...it all matters." Evette was definitely more than a regular shop owner. Whatever her customers said, it was clear that she would do what she could to get them the dress that best fit the occasion. It was no different than a famous painter choosing the perfect palette for a masterpiece. Both Tabby and Marty remained silent and watchful as Mildred considered Evette's words.

"I know what I want and it's something I've dreamt about for quite a while now," Mildred said quietly. "But I've never seen it in a catalogue so I don't know if you'd have it."

Evette raised a thin eyebrow. "Try me, love."

"Velvet..." she began softly. "Dark, green velvet. It's sleeveless and the back swoops down just so..." Mildred explained with her hands, feeling silly as she did.

"Give me one moment," Evette said before she disappeared into the racks of dresses. After five minutes, she came back with a black bag draped over her arm. Mildred's heartbeat quickened. For effect, Evette took her manicured fingers and unzipped the bag as slowly as she could, revealing a hint of green. Finally, she took the dress out of the bag and smiled proudly.

"So? How did I do?" Evette asked confidently. Mildred failed to think of words for the dress hanging before her.

"Oh, Millie! It's gorgeous!" Tabby yelped from the French upholstered chair she rested in. The dress was indeed made out of green velvet, a luscious shade of emerald that shimmered as Evette rotated the dress from side to side. Embroidered chandeliers made out of gold thread and sequins added detail to the V-shaped neckline. When Evette turned the dress around, Mildred gasped as she saw the dangerously low swoop of fabric that stopped just above the tailbone. A row of the same golden chandeliers crossed the back to keep it together.

"It's incredible," Mildred whispered. "It's what I envisioned, only better." She approached the dress, fingering the sequins and fine velvet. It struck her in the same way whenever she saw a woman with the same hair, figure and stride as her mother, walking away in a crowd. At the Bresford summer dance a few years back, a woman from out of town, who eerily resembled Grace, was a guest and every time Mildred saw her walk to get punch or a piece of cake, she had to resist the urge to run up and throw her arms around her. She knew her mother was gone from this earth, existing in her memories and dreams, but it didn't stop her from hoping she was real, just like the dress before her.

The dress was now bagged up in her hands, paid in full by Marty. It would be the most expensive thing Mildred had ever worn and he didn't seem to mind the price tag and he even had her pick out a pair of emerald satin heels and a jeweled headband to go with it. Tabby took longer to pick hers, an innocent pale pink dress made of dreamy lighter-than-air layers that floated up with the slightest swish.

Lunch was at a small place nearby called Walter's and they were only open from noon to three every day, but it always had a line going out the door. Mildred ordered the famous tuna fish and chips while Tabby ordered a chopped egg sandwich that would be lighter on her stomach. To prepare for his blood draw that afternoon, Marty ordered a plate of grilled calf liver with bacon and onions on top. It wasn't his favorite, but he knew it was the best dish on the menu for his blood.

At first, Marty wanted to reserve a table inside but Tabby begged to sit outside to feel a breeze. As Tabby sat, egg sandwich untouched, she looked content to just watch people rushing by, going into stores and coming out with a bag or two. She made guesses on the purchases in the bags based on the person carrying them. When she wasn't joking, she let the wind toss her long hair around. Her mother huffed and puffed to get Tabby to have her hair up, but Jeanette always made it too tight and it felt like agony on her daughter's scalp, so she demanded it stay down.

"I've missed all of this. Shopping, restaurants...I'm going to hate to leave it all behind."

Mildred put a hand on Tabby's knee. "What if you get better?" She noticed Marty stopped eating and closed his eyes.

"I haven't gotten better since I first got sick, Millie. My nosebleeds happen all the time, my bones always ache. No matter what my parents do or how much blood Marty gives me, I don't seem to improve." Her tone was factual, as if she was delivering a simple report of the weather.

Marty couldn't handle the death talk any longer. "Squeak, you *will* get better. Sometimes things get worse before treatments take effect. Dr. Ward wouldn't say that for nothing," Marty said. His voice had an edge of desperation. "You always perk up after a batch of my blood, which we'll be doing as soon as we get back. So eat your sandwich because you'll need your strength for the party tonight."

Obediently, Tabby took a dainty bite of her sandwich and stared out at the glimmering water. Marty finished his calf liver, wiped his mouth and winked at Mildred. "We better get back. There's a party to get ready for."

CHAPTER SEVENTEEN

"YES, THANK YOU VERY MUCH for your time. Good day to you." Detective Morris Welch hung up the phone and scribbled some more notes on his case pad for his most persistent client, Miss Agnes Crane. He had seen her type more than any other, a jealous ex-lover wanting to know who her man was currently with and demanding every detail of the relationship as if he could be within two feet of them at all times. The requests were typically ridiculous. *What did they do all weekend? How much did he spend on dinner? How many times does he call her?*

While it was possible to get some of those details, he could never get the extra juicy bits that his female clients usually wanted without hiding under a bed or in a bush outside a window. He could confirm that a woman's husband had indeed holed up in the Baroness Hotel with a redhead named Gloria for a whole weekend and where they ate down the street, and if he was lucky, he could even get the sound of creaking bedsprings if he walked by their hotel room. Sometimes that was all a heartbroken wife needed to hear, but Agnes Crane was willing to throw more money at him to scrape up the finest information he could get.

Her target was what made this particular case difficult. Martin Samuel Townsend was a relatively well-known young man in Seattle due to being part of the Townsend Timber business (and fortune), so that fact alone would make it hard work to get close. From what Detective Welch had gathered already, he was exhausted. He was in his early sixties, tall and slender, with short hair that turned pure white like his father's. He brought years of investigative skills with him to the Seattle area and kept a steady stream of clients. However, he didn't have quite the same stamina he did in his thirties and was more than tempted to retire and spend the rest of his days fishing in the Puget Sound. To his chagrin, Martin Townsend was all over the place and often out of town in his plane, always moving faster than the aging detective could report. Agnes didn't seem too impressed when she realized she had paid him for a full day to hide at the hangar.

Other information he found did please her, especially about the girl Martin was seen with frequently, 19-year-old Miss Mildred Anne Westrick of Bresford. While Mildred was unremarkable on paper and looked like a sweet girl, hardly a typical "other woman," Agnes seemed to get the world's biggest laugh when she learned that Mildred worked at the Pacific Bounty Cannery in her hometown. Aside from the basics, he couldn't get much else scraped together. Martin didn't have a regular job, so his outings were always unpredictable. Some days he'd stop in at the Elliott Bay shantytown, which he couldn't follow him into without looking suspicious, and other days, he'd leave in his plane.

"I pay you to find out where he flies to, not tell me that you watched an empty spot of land. One more failure and we're through," was the last thing Agnes had barked in the phone to him. Detective Welch wished Agnes would quit him so he could stop digging around and get back to less-crazy jealous clients, but she paid well enough above his going rate that he felt compelled to put her case first. The latest request wasn't crazy, however, and didn't have anything to do with Martin Townsend. It was an easy task for him, locating a friend's wife and son. It took less than two hours to get the details he needed with three calls, some where he had to pretend to be a salesman and another, a mistaken relation. In addition to finding out where a Mrs. Sarah Fryar and her son were, Agnes wanted to know exactly *how* they left Seattle.

Detective Welch looked over his cursive notes and couldn't wait to tell Agnes:

The targets, Sarah Fryar and her son, Leo, are currently living in Tillamook, Oregon with the target's sister, Margaret "Maggie" Arthur, and brother-in-law, Boone. The ticket clerk at the bus depot near Elliott Bay recalls that she saw the targets get out of a newer red Chevy with two other people.

She recognized Martin Townsend from newspaper articles and also said a young brown-haired woman was with him in addition to Mrs. Fryar and her son. The targets took the 3:00pm Greyhound bus en route to Tillamook, Oregon.

> *The tickets were paid in cash by Martin Townsend. He also purchased two ham sandwiches and left a very large tip for the porter.*

*   *   *

AMONG THE SEA OF expensive suits and gowns in a venue rented by Townsend Timber, a dapper Marty held Mildred's hand as they walked to his family's table near the front of the room. He was aware of people looking at him but was even more aware that they stole deeper glances at Mildred. They were slack-jawed and couldn't tear their eyes away from her beauty before they dove into gossiping.

While it was the plain girl in the polka dot dress that he first fell in love with, Marty couldn't keep his heart from stomping in his chest when that same woman was a vision before him. Mildred was polished to perfection, from the voluminous waves in her hair and the painted pout on her lips to the new emerald satin shoes on her feet. To his delight, the dress revealed her shape in a seductive way that he'd never seen before. She possessed a slightly narrow waist, rounded hips and a full chest. The only thing missing from her look before they left was the glitz of diamonds. He provided thirty-two carats worth from his mother's collection.

"Marty, I can't! What if I lose them?" Mildred cried as he clipped hefty pieces of jewelry around her neck and wrist. She looped the dangly earrings through her earlobes and gasped at the sheer weight of them. "This is too much, honestly."

"Stop being silly and just admit that you look stunning." He took her hand and spun her around to examine every inch, making her laugh as he spun her again.

"Stunning? I've never felt pretty, let alone stunning. Do you really think so?" she asked. She stood in front of the mirror in the dressing room where Evette was working on Tabitha's hair. With pursed lips, Mildred studied herself and slowly, her lips spread into a satisfied smile.

"Of course I think you're stunning, and not just when you wear a fancy dress, makeup and diamonds." When she turned from the mirror to him, she was still smiling, but it was more than that. Her eyes started to water and her bottom lip trembled.

"Thank you so much, Marty." She hugged him and felt his hands on the bare skin of her back.

When Marty pulled out Mildred's chair for her, he spied nearby tables for anybody from Crane Development. Close to the stage was one of the newer logging trucks loaded with pieces of perfect timber. Balloons floated in clusters everywhere he looked, a jazz band played familiar songs and tempting smells came from platters being carried around by servers, but he didn't see Agnes amongst it all.

"I'm going to get you something to drink. Sit there and look gorgeous," said Marty. On the way to the punch bowl, he was stopped.

"Martin Townsend, the golden boy himself! We were just talking about you!" He cringed when he looked to his right and realized it was none other than George Crane, Agnes's father and president of Crane Development. Next to him was Gerald looking unimpressed with his son.

"Ah-ha, you found me!" Marty joked. George's jovial face turned serious.

"I see you brought a date to the party. She is certainly a beautiful girl, but it's not my Agnes. When will you two get back together? It's times like this that are so awkward, especially when our businesses plan to merge in the near future. She didn't want to come tonight because she is ashamed by the stigma this breakup carries. I was so excited for the wedding and future grandchildren, you know. So excited..." He ran a fat hand over his graying hair and sighed sadly. From the corner of his eye, Marty noticed his father glaring at him as if he was trying to make him explode into flames.

"You see, George, my son is making a habit of shirking responsibilities. Instead of learning to manage the business, he'd rather spend his time flitting around the sky like a bird. Not to mention that he gets women into his plane from who-knows-where. Now he refuses a solid match with Agnes. I really expected more." Gerald took a sip of whatever he was drinking, which was probably bourbon, and cleared his throat. Ever since Marty expressed his disinterest in someday owning Townsend Timber, Gerald had nothing but daggers for him. With Tabitha being sick, it didn't improve his father's mood any.

George looked surprised. "Picking up with strange girls can be risky, Martin. Why go find someone entirely unknown when you and Agnes were so wonderful together? You two would make beautiful children, I just know it."

"I'm sorry you took our parting so hard, Mr. Crane, I really do, but your daughter and I weren't meant to get married. The girl I brought tonight, however, is someone I'm very keen about. If you'll both excuse me, my date would like some punch." He bowed his head in goodbye and walked between the two men.

Ashamed? Agnes Crane is ashamed? Marty didn't believe it for a second, but he couldn't deny that he was relieved that he didn't have to worry about bumping into her for tonight. If Tabitha's birthday party was any indication of how Agnes would act around him after he ended their engagement, he didn't want to expose himself to it again, as well as his naïve Mildred who still appeared to know nothing of his ex-fiancée.

An irritating heaviness rode on Marty's back ever since he caught Agnes in the middle of his father's study, bent over the desk and scribbling in the business checkbook. Granny Fran's funeral reception had been underway in the Townsend home, Masterson doling out tissues and little sandwiches to guests dressed in black, Gerald red-eyed as he shared stories of his mother with friends. With extreme clarity, Marty recalled the solemn stream of people coming to pay their respects to his father and the rest of the Townsends. Some congratulated Marty on his recent engagement to the lovely Agnes Crane, who went missing shortly after the reception started. Groups of people chatted over coffee and it became clear that his future bride wasn't in the parlor. Before Masterson swatted Marty out of her kitchen, she confirmed that Agnes hadn't stepped foot in there and that if he was going to pester her, at least could he take out a fresh carafe of coffee? He did as he was told and after depositing the carafe with the rest of the coffee and tea service, Marty left the parlor.

When he carefully opened the door to Tabitha's room upstairs, he hoped he would find Agnes visiting her out of the goodness of her heart but he only saw his weary mother in the chair, sleeping next to his sister's bed. Tabitha had gotten her first nosebleed that morning and stained the entire front of her nightgown, sending their mother screaming through the house for help. From deep inside the marrow of her bones, pain made her writhe in bed until her sheets were twisted into tight, damp knots. Dr. Ward had given her something that afternoon to lull her into a deep sleep, so Marty left as quietly as he came in and wandered back downstairs.

His father's study was typically not a place he went into, being filled with volumes of history books and mounted deer heads, which Marty always found morbid. There was really nothing of interest in the room except for a tan globe mounted in the center of a sturdy mahogany frame. As a child, he'd sneak in, examine the world and then spin it as fast as he could make it go, vowing to travel to the place his little finger landed on. His father caught him doing this one day, slapped his hand so hard that Marty cried and told him to never touch anything in his study again.

In the dark, he could make out a person near the desk and heard the sound of a pen scratching on thick paper.

Riiiiiiip!

Who would be writing a check in the dark during a funeral reception? The only people authorized to write checks were his parents and Helena, the business secretary. Marty didn't even have permission to touch the company's money, only his own. He just saw Helena in the parlor and his mother was sleeping in Tabitha's room, so that left his father, who wouldn't dare leave his mother's funeral guests. The flick of the lights revealed Agnes, his Agnes, folding the check.

"What are you doing?" he remembered asking in a dumbfounded sort of way. Obviously she just cut a check, but for who and how much? The look on her face was one of horror before she masked it with a condescending smile.

"You caught me, silly. I was going to surprise you." She fluttered the check between her fingers, the overhead lights glinting off her engagement ring.

"Surprise me with what?" Like an idiot, he tried to think of what she had in mind. A new truck? He already had one. Perhaps money for the wedding?

She rolled her eyes playfully. "If I told you, it wouldn't be a surprise, would it?"

His senses finally caught up to him. "Give me the check, Agnes."

"No." Her chin looked sharp as she lifted it up in defiance.

"Give it to me....*now*. You have no business with the Townsend Timber ledger," he demanded. She remained planted to her spot and grabbed the edge of the desk behind her when he stood a foot away. It was easy for him to grab her slender wrist and yank the check free from her fingers.

"Stop it, Martin! You'll ruin the surprise!" she whispered. He turned his back to her and unfolded the check, paling as he read.

Pay to the order of Agnes Crane. $5,000.00.

The handwriting and signature looked like his father's but the ink was fresh, screaming of forgery.

"Five thousand dollars! Holy shit, Agnes! You're wealthy by yourself! Why are you doing this?" In his suit, he suddenly felt like he was standing over a bonfire. Sweat popped up on his brow and the pit of his stomach threatened to drop out like an anchor.

"Keep your voice down, Martin, before someone comes in here," Agnes said calmly when he turned to face her again. He couldn't deny that she looked astonishing in her black crepe dress and plum lipstick. Had he agreed to marry the Devil who was disguised as a mesmerizing woman?

"Why do you need so much money? You could buy a house outright with that. Answer me now," he said softly. His sister was deathly ill and his beloved Granny Fran had just been buried less than five hours ago. This was the last thing he needed to deal with.

"You win. I was going to buy a house looking over Puget Sound for us. Imagine my delight when only last week I found a six bedroom place with a private drive, servant quarters and the most beautiful parlor for entertaining. It would be our home, paid in full, beginning our life together as carefree newlyweds. That's the surprise. Martin? Are you alright?" During the time she explained, Marty stopped listening and only saw her lips moving. For a moment, he actually thought he could faint right there on the antique rug in his father's study.

"It's over."

"I beg your pardon? What do you mean?" She brought her

left hand close to her chest as if to guard the one carat engagement ring from his grasp.

"I can't marry you, not a woman who turns out to be a fucking thief. I almost fell for your act."

She snarled. "A thief? How could I be called a thief if Townsend Timber and Crane Development plan to merge and we are married by then? It would end up being my money, too, one way or another."

"Except that they're not merged yet and the check clearly says 'Townsend Timber' on it with my father's forged signature. You had me fooled, Agnes."

"Martin, please..."

His hands trembled, the check wilted between his clammy fingers. "If word of this ever gets out, it could severely damage both of our families, especially in these hard times. Don't tell anyone if you have any common sense. Get out of my house and out of my life." That was his best offer. It was received with a raised eyebrow as Agnes left the study and the house without another word. Once more, he looked over the ledger. There were endless entries for equipment, payroll and general business expenses, some of the entries in Helena's handwriting but mostly in his father's. He noticed that there was another entry for five-thousand dollars made out to Crane Development above the check Agnes tried writing to her name. The age of the ink in both entries looked the same, fresh and with a similar hand.

No wonder she surrendered the check to him. She was still going to get five-thousand dollars and he couldn't stop her now. If he reported it to his father, the amount of bad blood between Townsend Timber and Crane Development would turn into an ocean.

"Marty? Marty?"

He snapped out of it to see Mildred standing next to him by the punch bowl. How long had he been there, reliving the horrible memories?

"Is everything alright with you? Perhaps you should sit down after the blood draw from earlier," she suggested. "You do look somewhat pale."

"I'm fine, honestly. Here, I got you punch," he said quietly as he offered her the glass. He poured himself a cup and walked back to the table with Mildred, who still looked concerned. "I'm fine, really. I was just trying to remember something, that's all."

"Any luck?"

He half-smiled as they sat. "No. It wasn't important, anyway." Just then, Gerald Townsend took the stage and bowed when the guests applauded.

"I'm proud to announce that Townsend Timber is going strong in its fiftieth year!" he boomed. More applause filled the room. Marty glanced around and noticed people pointing at Mildred and whispering to their partners as they clapped. He had no doubt that some interesting rumors were being birthed that very moment.

"Marty?"

"What is it, Tabby?" He leaned over to hear his sister better and noticed that she looked radiant tonight. It could've been Evette's mastery of makeup but Tabby didn't appear as sickly and she had gone all day without suffering a nosebleed or much bone pain.

"I saw you talking to George Crane. Is anything the matter?" she said lowly, hinting at the forgery incident. Here was Tabitha, incredibly ill from her leukemia and she still had the heart to worry about someone else other than herself. Marty couldn't have asked for a better sister and wished he was the one who was sick instead of her.

"No, everything is fine, I think. Don't worry yourself over it right now. You look gorgeous, by the way." He leaned further and kissed her bony cheek. "I love you, Squeak."

"Tabitha, Martin, both of you hush!" Jeanette hissed. She suddenly spied her diamonds on Mildred and shot Marty a knowing look that told him he'd have to explain himself later, but for now, she'd allow it. The clapping faded and Gerald went on talking for a few minutes about the history of Townsend Timber, honoring key people who made it the thriving lumber business it was today and presenting them with cash awards for years of service. The evening carried on in the same manner, people swirling around from group to group, laughing, reminiscing and eating.

"Want to go somewhere fun?" Marty asked Mildred.

"What do you mean? I'm having a fine time here," Mildred answered.

He scooted his chair closer so his mother wouldn't be able to listen. "This isn't fun compared to what I have in mind."

"Won't we get in trouble, leaving your father's party early?" she said. Currently, Jeanette was occupied with a group of gussied up ladies, all of them dripping in jewels of all colors. One of them was the Fox Scarf Lady from Tabitha's birthday party. If they left, Marty knew his mother wouldn't find out until they were already gone and she wouldn't have any idea where to look.

"Don't worry about what other people think, Mildred. You'll never do anything if you let that stop you every single time. Remember how you felt when you got in the plane the first time?"

She laughed at how it seemed like it happened years ago. "I remember everything. I was scared, thrilled..."

"Just keep doing that over and over. Jump in the plane, forget about the naysayers."

Mildred nodded. "You're absolutely right."

Tabitha looked hurt. "Can I *please* come, too?"

Marty knelt down by his sister and said, "Not tonight,

Squeak. When you're better, Mildred and I will have another big outing with you, okay? You're doing so well, I'd hate for you to overexert yourself. Mother would murder me if I let that happen."

She bent her lips out of shape and shrugged. "Okay. Just tell me what you did later so I can pretend I did something fun. Do you promise, Millie?"

"Of course I will. I'll tell you everything, once I find out what we're actually doing." Mildred laughed and gently hugged Tabitha, who seemed to brighten up at the prospect of getting a good story later. When Mildred stood, Tabitha took her hand in her own and her eyes pleaded for them to reconsider.

Marty planted a big kiss on his sister's forehead. "Be good, Squeak." Without another word to anybody else, he took Mildred's hand in his after Tabitha let go and they made their exit, Marty knowing that they were being watched, that they were being talked about. He couldn't care less.

CHAPTER EIGHTEEN

A$_{\text{LL OF THE FEELINGS}}$ that came with being spontaneous bubbled incessantly inside Mildred ever since she and Marty escaped from the Townsend Timber party. It was hard for her to describe, but it was a combination of fear, giddiness and freedom. Throughout the evening, Mildred felt eyes on her and whenever she looked back, people were deep in conversation while still watching her. She didn't know how Marty could deal with it all the time, but she figured that he was conditioned to receive attention ever since he was young, unlike her. If anything, she was raised in the opposite manner, that it was better to avoid being the focus. Her mother had a definite skill of being loved by everyone while not being the center of attention.

"If my mother could see me now," Mildred sighed in the

truck. "She'd love this dress, your house, your sister, my adventures, everything. I bet if she was still alive, she'd love to take a ride in your airplane."

"Would she now? You don't talk about her much," said Marty.

"It hurts. Almost five years without her and...it just hurts. The older women back home say that time will heal, but I don't believe them." Her nose started to burn, like it always did when she spoke of her mother.

"How did she pass?" His voice was soft, inviting. Amazingly, Mildred kept her composure as she described the Highway Shooter and all the blood spattered inside the cab of the truck, how her death remains an unsolved mystery and that she hopes the person responsible has a ticket straight to Hell for what they did. Marty shook his head.

"This world is getting crazier every year. Given all that, it makes it even more important to live your life, to take risks and..."

"Jump in the plane," she added.

He laughed and said, "Exactly! Good girl, you're learning." For what seemed like an hour, he drove into the night, taking left turns and right turns down alleys and finally ended up in a vacant lot near a creepy warehouse. Above the doors was an enormous cow-shaped sign that read *Elliott Bay Beef Co.* Upon closer inspection as she got out of the truck, Mildred noticed that the warehouse was actually a slaughterhouse and the rancid smell of blood hanging thick in the air proved it.

"Marty? Where are we?" Mildred didn't move from the truck and covered her nose.

"Follow me," he said quietly. His tailored suit, pert bowtie, her dress and jewels, none of it belonged here, but he kept walking towards the rusty green doors. The further he got, the more she felt like something was going to come out and get her, until she finally left the truck and caught up to him, *clip-clop-clip-clopping* across the lot in her satin heels. He took her hand and led her down the side of the building until they came to another green door with the cartoonish face of a smiling cow painted on it. The bushes behind them quivered as a creature scampered off, making Mildred cry out. Instantly, Marty covered her mouth.

"None of that, alright?" he whispered. She nodded her understanding, although she didn't understand at all. While her heart pounded, Marty knocked four times on the metal door and waited, then knocked three times and once more with a thud of a knock. From inside, someone undid a heavy lock and opened the door a crack. A small chain for another lock dangled in the gap.

"Password," said a male voice in a hushed tone.

Marty answered just as quietly. "Porterhouse." Like magic, the man opened up the door and ushered them inside a chilly and dark hallway, locking the door back up. The doorman didn't say another word, but Marty seemed to know what to do. Mildred held onto his hand tighter than ever as she followed him through a frozen maze of gore. The dead fish she worked with at Pacific Bounty Cannery was nothing like being inside the Elliott Bay Beef Company. Dozens of freshly butchered sides of beef, deep red and marbled with white ribbons of fat, hung on meat hooks and left little room to navigate. Once they cleared that area, Marty took her down a narrow metal staircase that Mildred had to go down methodically with her heels. Any faster and she'd lose a shoe or break her ankles. Towards the bottom, Marty reached out and helped her jump the last few steps. They went into a dark room where a single red bulb burned ominously above the door.

"If this is your idea of fun, I'd rather be at your father's party," she hissed. It was so cold that she could see her breath when she spoke. To try and warm up, she rubbed her arms furiously but it didn't help, and through her chattering teeth, she swore she heard thumping.

"Wait until you see this." Just like he did at the entrance, Marty knocked a certain pattern and when the door opened up, an ocean of sound and smells spilled out. The burly man ushered them in and shut the door on their heels.

Colorful noise from laughing people, glasses clinking and jazz filled the space. Marty pulled her into the dark and smoky club that was all movement, music and pure energy. The heat from the dancing bodies knocked away any chill she had.

Her eyes could barely take it all in. "Where are we, Marty?"

"Welcome to The Slaughterhouse, my darling."

"The Slaughterhouse," she said slowly enough to feel the strange words on her tongue. The image on her mind was one of lambs and calves being butchered for chops and steaks, not a shady club tucked away in the heart of Seattle. Marty led her to a table for two that looked like it had been reserved and upon sitting down, it had indeed been set aside for them. All of the surrounding tables were packed with people already sweaty from dancing. Women in skimpy dresses sat on the laps of the men Mildred assumed they came with and looked like they were having the night of their lives, drinking, smoking and laughing. Then she watched as Marty motioned to the server who came over as fast as he could.

"What'll it be, Mr. Townsend?" The male server, close to Marty's age but thicker in the middle, waited for him to respond and he looked at Mildred with a polite smile.

"Bacon-wrapped dates and the best bottle of Clicquot. Korbel is fine, otherwise."

The server bowed. "Yes, sir, right away." He scurried off to the kitchen as if he just got royal orders. Over time, Mildred was quick to observe how people acted around Marty, trying to crowd around him, get his attention, obeying him without question.

She wondered if those same people would still act that way if Marty wasn't an heir to his family's timber money. He didn't tell her much about the money and she didn't feel like it would be appropriate to ask him. It was Marty she wanted to be with, not his fortune. However, that didn't keep her from feeling impressed by what he could do with a little money and the lifestyle he had with it. If it meant wearing a pretty dress and being treated special in a private club, then she was fine with that for tonight.

"What's Clicquot?" she asked above the music. She wondered if it was type of punch that she hadn't heard of before, which wouldn't surprise her.

"It's the best champagne from France," said Marty, winking. "One sip of that and nothing else compares."

"Champagne?" she asked almost too loudly.

Prohibition was ongoing even though people still managed to make or smuggle liquor. In Bresford, the only man that drank openly was old Larry Birch, a retired fisherman that strolled up and down the boardwalk by Pacific Bounty Cannery every single day, smoking his pipe and staring down the river as if he was contemplating taking up fishing again. One morning, Mildred saw Larry taking swigs from a flask as he stood and watched a boat unload salmon. Fred told her it loosened up his knees so he could walk easier. It sounded reasonable to Mildred and she felt that as long as Larry didn't cause any problems, nobody should make a stink about it and throw him in jail. However, she was about to drink in a strange club in a big town where cops weren't as lenient as the people in Bresford. Prohibition wasn't a mere suggestion in Seattle, even for gentle old men like Larry Birch. The thought of going to jail made her ask, "Won't we get in trouble if..." She glanced around the room, "...we are caught drinking alcohol?"

Marty laughed, clearly not worried like she was. "Relax,

Mildred. The Slaughterhouse is a speakeasy, so we're all doing something we shouldn't be right now, but that makes the champagne taste even better."

"So this is what a speakeasy looks like? I guess I pictured them differently, but this is perfect." It all made sense now. What with the scary vacant parking lot, the off-putting stench of cow's blood, the plain door with the red bulb above it, Mildred only thought speakeasies existed in Chicago or New York, but behold, she was sitting in a thriving speakeasy this very moment.

If only Hattie could see me! Or better yet, if Vidalia could see what I was doing, Mildred thought. She felt deliciously catty as she imagined Vidalia's face wrinkled with jealousy just like she did the other day just before it was covered in chocolate pie. The server appeared with a kind of silver bucket that looked like it was sweating and the neck of a green bottle stuck out. He plucked it from the bucket with a white towel and held it before Marty to inspect.

"1923 Clicquot, the oldest vintage I could find, Mr. Townsend." Marty nodded his head, didn't even say a word, and the server swiftly filled two flutes with champagne. He left and returned with the plate of bacon-wrapped dates, then scurried off to tend to other people happily breaking the law.

"I can't believe I'm doing this!" Mildred squealed. "First it was you with your plane, then it was the pie, and now I'm in a speakeasy with champagne!" She took the flute that Marty gave her and she sniffed it. As the bubbles tickled her nose with fervor, her favorite daydream started playing, the daydream that kept her from feeling dead inside when she hosed fish blood off the cannery equipment.

There she was, sitting in a smoky club, wearing a green dress and loads of diamonds and about to taste French champagne. Delicious jazz filled her ears. While she didn't recognize most of the songs, she still loved how it made her sway in her chair. Sometimes at Hattie's, Mildred would listen to muffled and crackly jazz on the Gramophone but it didn't compare at all to what she heard now. The smooth saxophone and the deep, thumping heartbeat-like notes from the bass created an atmosphere unlike any she'd experienced in her life before and she didn't want it to stop.

"Let's make a toast, shall we?" said Marty.

She raised her glass to eye level. "What should we toast to?"

He laughed, almost shyly. "Us. May we continue to have adventures and break the rules together and may you always amaze me..."

"Really? I amaze you?" Growing up, she knew her parents had been proud of her and showed it with affection, but the word "amaze" hadn't been used.

His eyes were soft as he peered deeply into hers. "Absolutely. Mildred, you're not like any other girl I've met in my entire life and I would be a fool to not be intrigued by you."

A blush rose to her cheeks and she giggled self-consciously. "Oh my..."

"To us!" he cheered, loud enough to make others look and raise their glasses along with him.

"To us!" Mildred *tinked* her glass to his and tipped it back. True to what her nose picked up, the golden beverage had flirty notes of green apples and yeast reminiscent of the bread her mother used to bake whenever she made ham hocks and beans.

"Magic. Champagne tastes like magic." She drank deeply and enjoyed the sensation of bubbles popping on the roof of her mouth. The bacon-wrapped dates were another kind of magic alone. Marty kept her flute full while they nibbled on the food to sop up the champagne in their bellies. He stood up and held his hand out to Mildred.

"Come with me." The room quieted as the band finished the

song and geared up for the next. In unison, the women hopped off of the laps they had been warming and took to the floor in a giggling horde. Mildred's hand in Marty's, there was a type of electricity that surged through her body, telling her to follow him without hesitation to the center of the room. It was almost silent as a grave, the air quiet before a massive thunderstorm as couples were poised for their cue.

"Let's Charleston, you wild party people!" the band leader cackled. At once, the band struck up and couples surrounding Marty and Mildred began to move as one. She watched the feet of other women and wondered how they could move so fast and effortlessly. Their shoes were worn, but lived in and comfortable, probably broken in by dancing every night, unlike Mildred's new stiff shoes. The lessons Hattie taught Mildred, the lessons she practiced for hours until she got it right, were locked away in her brain. The panic must've been evident on her face because Marty's grip on her hand and waist became stronger, reassuring her. The other people dancing seemed uninhibited by silly things like inexperience and shyness. After a few steps under Marty's guidance, Mildred felt the rush of champagne loosen up her paralyzed joints. The tingling sensation of the champagne bubbles coursing her veins meant that her body felt life. Marty grinned as she finally moved with him in time to the music.

Forward-and-a-tap-and-a-back-and-a-tap!

"I got it!" she laughed. She couldn't help but watch her green satin shoes swivel, almost as if it were someone else's feet doing the steps. As for Marty, he looked comfortable bopping around, probably a result of lessons he got in the past.

"Show me what you got!" he said and broke away. She was tempted to freeze without having Marty to hold onto, but she dug deep and swung her arms from side to side, just as Hattie taught her. Her feet never stopped moving as she swung her arms low and then flailed her hands above her head. Other girls around her watched and some cheered her on. By some unspoken command, all of the men went to one half of the dance floor and the women grouped on the other half with Mildred.

"They're following you!" Marty laughed. "Keep going!" Behind her, Mildred saw that the ladies, all wearing an array of gorgeous beaded and sequin dresses, were lined up and waiting for her. Never in her life had people looked to her for the next move, for leadership, but tonight, things were different in The Slaughterhouse.

Forward-and-a-tap-and-a-back-and-a-tap!

Like trained dancers on the stage, the women copied Mildred and on the men's side, they followed Marty. When they met in the middle, Mildred fell into Marty's arms and kept dancing without skipping a beat. He spun her around him as the song dwindled to an end and dipped her close to the floor, just like she saw in the pictures. The whole room burst into applause not only for the band, but for Mildred and Marty.

One of the women, who Mildred assumed was a regular here, put her hand on Mildred's arm and said, "You are adorable, doll! Come back again!" She wandered off with her group of fabulous-looking friends to go smoke.

"This is the most fun I've ever had in my life!" Mildred sighed. She still held onto Marty and wiped the sweat that formed on her forehead. "I think I need more champagne."

"The night's still young," he replied casually. The evening progressed in that same pattern: a little dancing, some drinking, more dancing, another bottle of chilled Clicquot uncorked. The band finally played a slow song and everyone paired up on the floor, men pulling their women close, nuzzling and kissing. With her head resting against Marty's chest and his strong hands against her back, Mildred felt at home, safe and wanted. In her dreams, she never imagined herself where she was tonight, never believed she would be anywhere outside of Bresford.

When Marty exhaled, his breath cooled her damp neck and shoulders. His scent was intoxicating, a mixture of fresh sweat and something else that made her inhale deeper.

"We should get going. It's a hair past midnight," he whispered in her ear as they turned in a slow circle. She sighed with delight and rested her sweaty brow on his chest. When the song finally ended, the band rushed to pack their instruments and servers cleared tables. On their way out, Marty motioned to the server behind the bar and he discreetly traded him a handful of cash for a bottle of Korbel since the evening's supply of Clicquot was drunk.

Sitting almost hidden at a corner table, a woman wearing black and drinking Pink Lady cocktails had been watching them all night.

BACK IN THE TRUCK, Mildred wondered if she was at the cusp of being drunk. Her body felt lighter, she laughed easily and things were somewhat hazy, but she didn't feel sick or stumble or have an attack of hiccups. She just had the most fun evening and the champagne helped make it possible. In the driver's seat, Marty acted like he had nothing to drink all night long.

"Will your mother and father be angry with you for leaving the party?" she asked with a hint of a slur.

"Most likely, but we're not going back to the house." He drove the truck in the opposite direction of Queen Anne and towards Elliott Bay. Mildred didn't even ask where they were going, as she normally would have, and hummed the Charleston tune from earlier.

They traveled up a hill to the entrance of a private driveway. Mildred watched with drooping eyes while Marty hustled to open the gate, drive the truck forward a little, run back to close the gate and finally park in a garage. She more or less needed his assistance out of the truck and into the foyer, where she clung to a pillar until he turned on a bank of lights. The house looked like a glorified bungalow but with modern appliances, expensive furniture, and antique rugs. A musty smell permeated the air, a sign that the house hadn't been used in some time. Marty opened a few windows to let in the brisk evening breeze.

"Is that water I hear?" she asked. Before she took another step, she yanked off the satin heels that started cutting into her feet hours ago and tossed them aside. She padded over to the row of enormous windows that spanned the room as Marty slipped off his bowtie, his shoes and rested his suit jacket on the back of a chair. Without a word, he took her by the hand, something she would never tire of, and brought her outside to a covered deck overlooking what appeared to be a giant lake.

Pop! The cork from the bottle of Korbel that Marty took from the club sailed into the trees below. He filled two flutes he got from the kitchen. "Here, madam. Drink up."

"Thank you." She took a sip of the glorious drink that would secretly be her favorite. "What is this place?" Birds of the night called mournfully as they flew over the water, the moonlight casting their shadows upon the gentle waves.

He almost hesitated to answer, as if he were uncomfortable. "This is just my family's house on the Puget Sound, ever since I was a child. We've spent many a summer up here. Across the way is Bainbridge Island. See?" He held his face close to hers as he pointed out geographical bits and how he used to watch migrating pods of orcas just beyond the deck railing. As hard as she tried to listen while she drank, her attention was limited to his eyes, his voice and his mouth.

"...and Tabby and I would wander the trails for hours. Mother would have Masterson fix us a little picnic basket with some of her famous butterscotch cookies. Tabby found an abandoned dory that we pretended was a restaurant..."

The kiss was enough to persuade him to stop talking immediately, to bring Mildred back inside and clumsily walk down the dim hallway without parting and into the bedroom. Little did she care that she was doing something a clearheaded Mildred would be too afraid to even think about, more forbidden than drinking during Prohibition, more daring than escaping in the plane of a man she just met. In her champagne-soaked state, she reached for Marty's shirt and took a few teasing seconds with each button, torturing not only herself, but Marty, as well. She tried not to giggle and bit her lip when she tugged his shirt from his pants, but it resisted. With a solid yank, she finally freed his shirt and let it rumple by his feet.

"My turn," he said, barely whispering. His fingers found the zipper hidden in the lush velvet. He deftly peeled the dress away from her body and added it to the pile on the hardwood floor. His purposeful fingertips on her skin made her gasp as he helped her remove everything else except the diamond jewelry.

"My God, you're beautiful." In a hurry, his pants and striped boxers topped off the pile. Mildred gasped at their unclothed bodies and felt like covering herself, but before she could, he easily scooped her up and carried her to the bed. She couldn't help but laugh nervously as she found herself naked in his arms while still wearing his mother's diamonds. The bed was soft underneath her and she crawled back onto the pillows with Marty mere inches away.

"What are we doing?" she giggled with a hiccup, which made her giggle more. She was certain she was definitely closer to being drunk now after gulping down the champagne on the deck. Instead of answering her, Marty kissed her mouth and she kissed him back, except this time, it wasn't a polite kiss. It was a kiss of hunger.

That night, the eleventh of June in 1932, Mildred Anne

Westrick was no longer the innocent girl she used to be. Everything melded together as they pushed against one another on the bed, tossing the comforter off to the side and saying the other's name between gasps for precious air. The champagne leeched from their sweating bodies during the delicious struggle, their mutual drunkenness heightening each sensation from above and below. Moonlight poured in and illuminated the bedroom and their bodies with a hauntingly gorgeous shade of blue.

Between her fingers, Marty's dark waves felt thick and youthful, hair that was as strong as him. She realized then that she hadn't been bold enough to feel his hair before, too shy to feel anything besides his hand clasped in hers. Under her traveling palms, his naked backside was soft and damp as her fingers followed the contours of his lean muscles while they moved with each thrust. His eyes were bleary with delight as he grunted and pushed faster and harder. Before Mildred thought she couldn't take anymore without screaming, his efforts increased until he let out a powerful moan and buried his face in her neck.

"Mildred...Mildred..." he repeated breathlessly, his breath hot in her loose hair. She was nearly out of breath herself and sweating underneath him. When he rolled to her side, he panted and wiped his brow.

"That was...that was..." Mildred struggled to describe what just they just did.

"Too fantastic for words?" he said. "I couldn't agree more."

She fell into a pit of laughter. "What am I going to tell Hattie? I won't tell her but it's funny that she waited forever for a proposal and isn't even married, yet here I am, a freshly dishonorable woman."

"What are you going to do next, now that you've wasted your virtue on me?" he asked playfully.

"This dishonorable woman is going to get us more

champagne." The high she felt was unlike anything else. She wanted to dance, go swimming, run around the block and top it all with more champagne.

"Bring it in here, darling," Marty said, running his hand down her back as she scooted out of bed. Next to her was a blanket that she wrapped around herself. It wasn't her habit to be naked anywhere before and she found herself to be chilly. Mildred scampered to the kitchen, grabbed their flutes, the half-full bottle and returned to the bedroom. They sipped in silence and stole shy smiles at each other until their glasses and the bottle were woefully empty.

"Come here," he said and exhaled happily. With a tipsy smile, Mildred curled up next to him and laid her head in the cradle of his arm until she was comfortable. She rubbed his side and felt his rib bones under her fingertips, then ran her fingers over the small area of his chest hair.

"Marty, what made you start flying?" It was a question she never asked him, just took as a regular fact. To her surprise, he took a long while to answer.

"My father pressured me for years to learn the timber business and once I graduated from college, he demanded that I be in those trucks every morning, to be on jobs with him cutting down trees."

"And you don't want to? You're the heir, right?" She walked her fingers up and down his chest.

"That's the toughest part about it. One day, he said that I disappointed him because I didn't show interest, so not long after that, I secretly signed up for flying lessons. If I was going to be a disappointment to him, I'd be the biggest disappoint he'd ever seen. Once I became good enough and enjoyed flying, I bought my airplane in hopes of someday leaving Seattle."

She sat up, astonished. "You, the fearless Marty Townsend, wanted to run away?"

"To put it simply, yes."

"What's stopping you? With your money, you could go anywhere you want." Mildred couldn't believe that they both had in common the urge to run away from their lives. Here was Marty, wealthy and confident on the outside, but inside, he was probably just as afraid as she was.

He shrugged. "It wouldn't be that easy for me to leave my life. Part of me wants to be a good son and take over Townsend Timber when my father passes, but there is a bigger part of me that feels trapped by the name and the money connected to it. Then I have Tabby to worry about. I can't leave her, not while she is this sick and depends on me for good blood. God knows that my mother would blame me if something happened to her if I was gone."

"Tabby is lucky to have you. Speaking of your mother, does she even like me? Sometimes I feel like she does and other times, she just tolerates me. I can see it in her eyes." Darnella crossed her mind. Last night after they were all home from the pie social, Mildred worried that Darnella would come at her and shred her apart with her bare hands. What was worse was that her father ignored the scene and read his paper instead of applauding her for giving Vidalia what she deserved. Somewhere inside, Mildred hoped that her father would be awakened from the fog that kept him from seeing what Darnella was like. It was almost as if he didn't hear Darnella berate her for being impudent, that she would have to make excuses for her at society meetings, to carry the burden of having such an embarrassment for a stepdaughter.

"I'm at a loss at what Marty sees in you," Darnella sneered before retreating to her bedroom with a headache, feigned or real, she didn't know. It was then that Mildred locked herself in her room and packed her suitcase in a hurry before crying once again into her pillow.

Marty sighed, troubled. "Don't worry yourself about my mother. Between fretting over my father, Tabby and me and trying to control every facet of our lives, she doesn't know what to think about anybody else right now. To be honest, I don't even think my own mother likes me some days." He got up to put his boxers back on and tossed the comforter over their bodies.

Mildred yawned, deep and loud, and snuggled next to him. "That makes me feel better."

"Good." He also yawned and then nuzzled the back of her neck until she giggled. "We've had a long day, so let's get some sleep." Like an old married couple, they sweetly kissed and it didn't take either of them long to drift off.

CHAPTER NINETEEN

At THREE O'CLOCK IN the morning, the telephone rang from the lake house kitchen and reverberated down the hallway. It rang several times and stopped, then began ringing again.

The ringing pierced through Mildred's luscious sleep. "Marty, aren't you going to answer it?" she asked.

He grumbled, barely awake. "No. It's probably just my mother seeing where I am."

"Don't you want to tell her?" she said earnestly. Mildred sat up and gathered the blanket around her nakedness like a cocoon. "What if she's worried?"

"She'd scald my ear all the way from Queen Anne and guilt me into coming home. If my mother found out about our early departure from the party, it would be pure agony here on out for both of us. I'll wager that she already knows." He rubbed his face and yawned. For a third time, the series of shrill ringing echoed eerily throughout the house.

"Damn it, it's three in the morning! Doesn't she have anything better to do than hunt me down?" he grumped down the hall in his boxers. He picked up the ringing phone and slammed it back into the cradle, then shuffled back to the bedroom. Like a little boy, he jumped onto the bed and wrapped both himself and Mildred in the comforter.

"That's much better. Let's go back to sleep."

"What if it was something important?" she asked.

He made her laugh when buried his face in the crook of her neck. "I doubt it. Anything my mother has to say can wait."

SIX O'CLOCK IN THE morning arrived and that was when the telephone came back to life. The ringing made Marty sit straight up in bed as if he'd been waiting for it.

"What the hell?" he growled. This time he got out of the toasty bed, not waking Mildred, and went at a snail's pace to the kitchen. He hoped it would be Masterson checking in, seeing if he wanted his usual Saturday morning breakfast. For her, he'd consider going back home but after everything that happened last night, he wanted to stretch out his time with Mildred as much as he could, maybe take her out for a luxurious brunch and come back to the lake house for another go in the bedroom before flying her back to Bresford.

"Hello?" he answered nonchalantly and tried not to sound as annoyed as he felt.

"*Martin, where the hell have you been? I've been calling all around Seattle and you're nowhere to be found!*" It was his father sounding the most irate he had heard him get in a long time.

"Everything is fine, Father. I've been at the lake house all evening. You didn't have to go to those lengths looking for me." He knew that his parents would be unhappy with his actions in general, but he didn't expect this sort of fiery reaction. Through the receiver, he could hear voices in the background and someone wailing at the top of their lungs. It sounded like his mother. Then he heard deep sobbing in the telephone and realized it was coming from his father.

"What's wrong? What happened?"

"It's Tabitha. She—oh, God—she passed away last night." Gerald sobbed until he was hysterical. It felt as if a hundred years came and went as Marty heard the words and thought of something to say next.

"Squeak?"

"Come home now, damn it!" The call ended with a jagged bang as his father slammed the phone from Queen Anne.

"God, no, please no, no, no..." he whimpered into his hands. He entered the bedroom and saw that Mildred was still sleeping peacefully. The diamond jewelry must've bothered her in the middle of the night because it was laid out on the nightstand next to her. "Mildred, wake up. Something terrible has happened."

The makeup Evette put on was miraculously in place, but Mildred's hair was a mess of chestnut waves as she stirred. "What's the matter?"

It was his turn to become a blubbery mess, sputtering the beginning of words, shielding his face that was already wet with a stream of tears. "Tabby died!"

"What? That's not possible. She was doing so well yesterday, not even a single nosebleed!" She shook her head in disbelief. "She can't be gone."

He sniffled and wiped his red eyes. "Get dressed. We have to go." Quietly, they put on last night's wrinkled clothes, pocketed the diamonds, closed windows, rinsed out champagne glasses and locked the house. In the truck, they remained silent. At the Townsend home, several vehicles were parked along the curb and people walked to the door with plates of baked goods. When he entered the house, Jeanette wailed and buried her puffy face in her son's chest.

"Martin, your only sister is dead..." she cried. All he could do was pat his mother's back and silently cry along with her.

"I need to go see her, Mother." Jeanette nodded and kissed her son's cheek. He went upstairs with Mildred behind him and peeked into Tabitha's bedroom, as if he was afraid he'd wake her. Dr. Ward worked in the room taking down equipment and tubes, looking as solemn as everyone else. There laid Tabitha in her hospital bed still wearing her new party dress from last night. She must've been too tired or weak to take it off. With the rosy powder blush upon her cheeks and a hint of lipstick, Tabby didn't look dead at all, just sleeping, but her chest failed to rise and fall.

"Squeak..." he whispered. Hot, plump tears spilled down his face without ceasing. "You weren't supposed to do this. You're only sixteen." Mildred placed her gentle hands on his shoulders to try and comfort him.

Dr. Ward came over. "I'm so deeply sorry for your sister, Martin. I did everything I could, I truly did. She was a special girl." It was clear that Dr. Ward took the loss of his patient almost as hard as the family.

Marty shook his hand and said hoarsely, "You were a wonderful doctor. Tabby was lucky to have you." Dr. Ward nodded graciously and left the room with a box of equipment before he had a chance to weep.

"I'll take you to the bus station so you can get home. I'd drive you but I can't leave my family under these circumstances, not now. I hope you understand." He stared at Tabby's face and wished that she was somehow holding her breath as a big joke, that she'd open her eyes right then and yell, "Gotcha!"

"Of course," Mildred agreed.

"I also assume that Tabby's funeral will be next weekend." He cradled his wet face in his hands, more exhausted at that moment than he was after a whole night of dancing and drinking.

"I'll be there," she said quietly.

Marty stood up and looked down at his sister. "I know you can hear me, Squeak. I love you." He placed a delicate kiss on his sister's cold forehead.

"Goodbye, Tabitha. Thank you for being my friend." Mildred smoothed out Tabby's blanket and followed Marty to his truck and before long, she found herself on a Greyhound bus back to Bresford.

"WHO DO YOU THINK you are, young lady? You've embarrassed me beyond compare in front of the whole town and then you have the nerve to disappear?" Darnella's face looked more like a red balloon ready to explode as Mildred crossed the room with her suitcase in hand. She didn't have a chance to change, which meant she paraded around the house in the green velvet dress.

"Vidalia deserved to get that pie in her face and I'm not the only one who thought so. You should've heard the vile things she said to me," snapped Mildred. Her hair was disheveled and her feet hated to be back in the green satin shoes, plus her head started aching shortly after she woke up from all the champagne. All she wanted was quiet to think about Tabby.

"Exactly where did you get a dress like that?" It dawned on Darnella that she hadn't seen the sultry velvet dress before and knew it was more than her stepdaughter could afford. The old Mildred would've answered quietly before leaving to hide in her room, but after being with Marty, she learned that she didn't have to answer anyone if she didn't want to. But she wanted to do more than answer this time. She spun on the heel of her dancing shoes and marched over to Darnella.

"Want to know where I got this dress? Marty bought it and these shoes for me from this incredible shop in Seattle. I even wore thirty-two carats in diamonds. Then we went dancing all night, listened to live jazz and then we made love at his family's lake house." Mildred raised an eyebrow and laughed coyly, "I had the time of my life."

Darnella looked like she was an inch within vomiting all over the floor. "Mildred Westrick, you've sullied your virtue before marriage! What will your father say?"

"He doesn't seem to care about me much these days, if you haven't noticed. Once he made the awful choice to marry you, he became someone I don't recognize. If only you knew how wonderful my mother was, Darnella. My father was happy when she was alive, but with you, he is a ghost of who he used to be."

Her stepmother's painted mouth dropped open in a wide O. "How dare you speak to me like this, you horrendous girl! From now on, you're not going anywhere with Marty, do you hear me? No more dinners, no more dancing, and no more trips to Seattle!"

"You might've gotten your way before I met him, but I don't have to do what you or anybody else tells me. Now if you'll excuse me, I have things to do today." Lifting up the front of her dress with exaggerated ceremony, Mildred sashayed by Darnella towards her room where she changed into a plain dress, sensible shoes and went on her bicycle in search of Hattie to tell her almost everything.

THE SERVER FILLED AGNES'S coffee cup and cleared away her breakfast dishes while she flipped through some typed pages that Detective Welch put together. When the server asked if she needed anything else, she waved him away like he was a gnat hovering around her ear. For once, Agnes was satisfied with Detective Welch's findings.

"I decided to find more about Miss Westrick's connections in Bresford and I came across something quite interesting. I find anomalies all the time, but this one was distinct. I didn't charge you for the extra time I took on it, but the pieces fell together quite nicely once I dug deep enough," Detective Welch explained. "Depending on how far you want to go with this, I'd suggest talking to Mr. Dominic York, a shop owner and mayoral elect in town. This doesn't happen very often, but I believe I found some information that implicates him to a tragedy, plus some other interesting details that may or may not be useful to you."

"What sort of tragedy?" she asked. She desired to meet Detective Welch at a quiet breakfast nook that Saturday morning along the pier to go over the entire case. The countless Pink Lady cocktails she drank last night at The Slaughterhouse made her brain pound relentlessly and the morning sunshine burned her sensitive hazel eyes. After she saw Marty laughing and touching Mildred, both of them looking as happy as two fools could be, she couldn't stop drinking. Then, after they left, she drove by the lake house and felt her heart crack in two when the lights were on inside. The challenge to get him back would be more work than she anticipated, especially if he insisted on having sex with the cannery girl.

"This page has the details, right here." Detective Welch flipped through the packet and tapped the section with a narrow finger. "See? What do you think?"

Hungrily, Agnes read. The tiny print and his tight scrawling made her eyes throb, but what she saw was something that opened up the gate to a fresh arsenal. "This is incredible, Detective. How did you ever manage to put this together?"

He chuckled and puffed his chest out. "After you've been in the business as long as I have, one picks up tricks here and there. It took a while but I found things that were off in these transactions and phone records, coinciding with local events. But it all checks out. Is there anything else I can do for you, Miss Crane?"

Dazzled, she shook her head and extracted a fat envelope from her coat. True to her word, she paid more than double the detective's standard rate for the whole case. "Thank you for everything, Detective Welch. I'll be sure to recommend you."

"My pleasure, Miss Crane. Good luck to you and I hope you find happiness." They shook hands and because Agnes was too busy reading the packet, she didn't notice Detective Welch's look of relief on his face when he walked back to his car, his job finally complete.

The more she kept reading, the less she noticed her raging headache. The business side of her sparked, the calculations started to take shape and multiply but they were still incomplete, missing a link that she couldn't put her thumb on. Who would she call first, where would she go, what would happen? After she did some digging of her own and fleshed out the details, the possibilities would be boundless. Somewhere in the information she got, there was a solid line that would lead her to what she wanted. She stuffed the packet back into the confidential envelope and sighed triumphantly.

"I have a goldmine."

CHAPTER TWENTY

Leland Burris was sweet enough to let Mildred borrow his car when she needed to get to Seattle for Tabitha's funeral. Marty was occupied with his family and it was quicker than taking the bus. While she possessed a valid driver's license, it was rarely used, so Leland took her around an empty parking lot and country roads until he felt that Mildred could safely drive his precious Whippet sedan that he inherited from his late grandfather.

"Take care, Millie. As soon as you're back, we need to discuss bridesmaid gowns. See you tonight!" shouted Hattie as she and Leland waved Mildred off.

For the first few miles outside of Bresford, Mildred sat stiff and nervous, but once she got a feel for the car and the rumble of the steering wheel in her hands, she relaxed and listened to the radio, settling for jazz that transported her back to magical evening she spent at The Slaughterhouse. After a few hours, Highway 99 soon led her to Seattle and with the detailed directions she got from Marty, she successfully parked the Whippet along the street outside of his house. For some reason, it seemed bigger than it did before. While Leland's car was kept in new condition, it still wasn't as nice as all of the other cars along the block. Once inside the Townsend home, it was as quiet as a tomb, no Tabitha to eagerly call for her to play checkers or to sit and chat by the pond.

"Mildred, you made it!" She looked up the stairs to see Marty wearing a somber black suit. His face indicated that he had been sleeping terribly, but he smiled with ease as he wrapped his arms around her, his freshly shaven cheeks smelling of aftershave. "I need a friendly face about now."

"*Martin!*"

He grimaced and yelled back, "Yes, Mother?" Rushing from the study, Jeanette, clad in a chic gray dress and black gloves, fiddled with a black-veiled cap like it was the root of her frustrations. When she looked up and noticed Mildred, she froze.

"My condolences, Mrs. Townsend," Mildred offered quietly as Marty's mother studied her outfit from head to toe. Mildred wore a tasteful black crepe dress with gray stockings and black T-strap heels and had half of her glossy waves pinned up.

"Did you enjoy wearing my diamonds last weekend?" she snipped.

"That's not important right now, Mother, and I've already explained multiple times that it was my idea to lend her your diamonds. Be mad at me, not her," said Marty. Between his exhaustion and his mother, Marty looked as if he aged five years since Mildred saw him last.

"If it means anything, I didn't want to wear them. I've

never worn anything that fine before."

"You don't say," Jeanette said, feigning surprise. It was clear to Mildred that she wasn't a favorite in the Townsend home yet, but she didn't want to let that stop her from being nice. "Martin, be a good son and pin on my hat."

"Yes, Mother." Dutifully, Marty stuck the pin through Jeanette's hair and made sure her hat didn't wobble. As a final touch, she fretted with the black lace veil again until it fell perfectly over her face.

"It's time to go to the church, the last time for my little girl..." Jeanette wept. On the drive to the church, Mildred sat quietly next to Jeanette, while Gerald sat up front with Marty. Even then, Gerald talked business with his son, who didn't seem interested at all.

Tabitha's funeral proceeded as normally as possible. People dressed in black filled the pews, dabbing their eyes during the hymns and as the pastor read from the Bible while Tabitha lay in her casket. Mildred was surprised that she was allowed to sit in the front pew with the Townsends, especially considering the size of the crowd attending. Luckily she was next to Marty, whose hand she took and squeezed. Despite how distraught he was, he took the time to smile and wink at her. From across the room where the first pew curved, Mildred studied the other people there. Some of them she recognized from the Townsend Timber anniversary party, most people she didn't. Sitting next to an older man that had talked to Marty at the party was a tall, slim woman wearing a black skirt and a silky blouse with a pattern that resembled a black and cream backgammon board. Her face was partially hidden by a large bell-shaped hat, but it was easy to tell that she had defined features. What caught Mildred's attention was how frequently Backgammon Girl looked over at her and especially at Marty. As much as she wanted to ask him who the woman was, she knew it wasn't important right now.

"Please rise as we sing 'Amazing Grace.' Sing for our sweet Tabitha! Rejoice in her victory in the Lord!" The pastor raised his arms as the crowd stood and sang the many verses together. Jeanette could barely bring herself to sing beyond the first chorus before she had to sit and cry into her hanky.

"...*how sweet the sound that saved a wretch like me...*" sang Mildred. She took Marty's hand again and smiled up at him. He must've cried without making a sound because his eyes were wet and his nose was almost as red as a strawberry.

It was five years ago that Mildred remembered sitting next to her crying father during Grace's funeral in the small Bresford Lutheran church. Traditionally, the casket would've been open, but because of the gunshot wound in Grace's neck, too much damage had been done and her casket remained sealed. Tabby's burial seemed to go faster than the funeral ceremony. Jeanette wailed and wailed into her hanky and leaned on her husband's shoulder. On the other side of the pit dug out for Tabitha's casket, the Backgammon Girl stood behind a row of people and tried to be discreet about watching them again. It really started to bother Mildred. Who was this nosy woman?

"Squeak..." Marty cried, his voice hoarse. "I'm sorry I couldn't save you." Then, Marty wailed openly. Mildred rubbed his arm and tried to help, but he only cried harder. Backgammon Girl watched him the whole time, not taking her eyes off him as Tabitha's casket was lowered into the ground.

MASTERSON, DRESSED IN A plain black frock, prepared a spread of luncheon items for a select group of about fifty people that came back to the Townsend home. Throughout the room, Marty introduced Mildred to aunts, uncles, cousins and close family friends. Everyone seemed warm towards her and she did her best to pretend that she wasn't a cannery girl from Bresford.

As far as she could tell, nobody knew much about her except that she was seeing Marty.

"Martin, aren't you going to introduce me to your friend?" From nowhere, Backgammon Girl sidled up next to him with a flute of elderberry punch. The look on his face was a mixture of panic and disgust.

"Are you okay?" Mildred asked. "You look ill." He laughed uncomfortably as he looked from Mildred to Backgammon Girl, who stood there expectantly.

"I'm perfectly fine. Um...Mildred, this is Agnes." That's all he seemed willing to say.

"Agnes *Crane*, and you are?" She shot out a firm hand, tan and manicured.

"I'm Mildred Westrick. I have to say that I couldn't help but notice you earlier. You're so beautiful." Mildred felt herself blush after complimenting the gorgeous, yet intimidating, woman with eyes the color of jade. Her dark purple lipstick made her eyes even lighter and her olive skin darker. However, when they shook hands, Mildred felt something wasn't being said.

Agnes chuckled. "You're a doll! At least some people think so. Anyway, how did you meet Martin?"

"Agnes, why don't you leave us alone and go talk to somebody else?" Marty looked pale and clammy.

"Are you sure you're alright?" asked Mildred. His rudeness was certainly uncalled for, she felt.

"Come with me, Mildred." Firmly grabbing her hand, he stormed off and dragged Mildred through the crowd of black, parting through his aunts and uncles, narrowly missing the tea and coffee service table. Mildred looked back, embarrassed by the scene that Marty made, hoping that Agnes wasn't offended but she wasn't where they left her.

"Marty, what's the matter?" she asked once Marty they

stopped in a quiet hallway. The loudest sound there was an old grandfather clock, dutifully telling the time despite the fact there was a funeral reception going on.

"It's nothing. I just don't like Agnes and you shouldn't, either. It'd be best if you stayed away from her."

Mildred let out a little laugh. "You're sounding ridiculous. What did she ever do to you? Please tell me."

He rubbed his face. "Alright, well, Agnes and I were sweet on each other in the past and she hasn't gotten over the fact that I didn't marry her like everyone expected. That's all. Does that suit you?"

At first, Mildred was shocked. She assumed that Agnes was yet another young and beautiful admirer like she'd seen at other parties, but she didn't know he'd actually courted any of them until now. "You were sweet on her? How sweet, exactly?"

For the first time, Marty rolled his eyes at her. "We went out to a few nice restaurants and then I lost interest in her, alright?" He looked at the ceiling, his shoes, towards the hall, but not at her. For a moment, Mildred felt like she might panic and run away like she did when she first met him. Was Agnes another Vidalia, a selfish and vicious woman trying to swoop in and take everything for herself?

Stop being ridiculous. Marty chose you and made it clear he doesn't like Agnes, she heard her common sense telling her.

"You've had a tough week and today couldn't have been easy. Wait—what time is it?" She looked at the grandfather clock that told her it was a quarter past three o'clock. "I have to go before it gets dark. Tomorrow I have to go dress shopping with Hattie and then work Monday. When will I see you again?"

Marty looked physically drained. Even his eyes resembled those of a dead salmon Mildred was too familiar with, glazed and fixated on nothing. "I'm not sure. Once the dust settles around here, I'll try to fly to Bresford and steal you away, just for myself." He warmed up then, bent down and kissed her tenderly.

"Break it up, kids!" Mildred shrieked and wiped her mouth. It was just one of the crotchety uncles on Jeanette's side. After he passed by on his way to the toilet, they both laughed quietly and kissed again.

"Bye, Marty." She hugged him as tightly as she could and left, wishing with everything in her that she could have stayed with him.

MASTERSON CLEARED AWAY YET another gathering's worth of saucers, china cups with waxy lipstick marks, and crumpled linen napkins. After the fifty or so guests made their lengthy goodbyes and exchanged kisses on the cheeks with Jeanette, the house sounded like it was deserted save for the clinking and running water coming from the kitchen. Gerald drank bourbon from his stash in the locked study and Jeanette retreated to her bedroom.

Upstairs in his room, Marty also had some bourbon in glass bottles he swiped from the crate his father kept hidden in the walls of his study. There were five crates just like it and Gerald wouldn't know any went missing for a long while. That's why Marty took three bottles. They sloshed around in his suit jacket when he made it into his room, where he promptly closed the door and sat on his bed. The dark amber liquid tempted him until he couldn't stand it any longer, beckoning him with its siren call. Savagely, he removed the stopper and put the bottle to his mouth. He paused, only to expect Tabby to knock on his door so she could sit on his bed and talk to her big brother, but nobody knocked. Tabby would never again ask him for details about his adventures or need his blood that Dr. Ward took faithfully twice a week. Marty couldn't even count the many pints of blood he gave to Tabby, all for the sake of getting her healthier to get over her leukemia, not succumb to it.

"Why did you leave me, Squeak?" he cried. He let himself melt into crying that turned into sobbing. Nobody was there to hear him, nobody to tell him to stop and move on. Tabby wouldn't respond, *couldn't* respond, and she could never beg him to take her dress shopping at Evette's ever again. His parents were in their own rooms doing whatever they felt like doing, Tabby was asleep in her casket with cold dirt keeping her lid closed for eternity and his sweet Mildred was back in Bresford.

That only left Marty and his bourbon.

"Damn it all, damn it all to Hell." Marty knocked back the first few mouthfuls of the delicious aged liquor and admired the caramel, vanilla and oak flavors as a sober man, ending with a flash of spicy honey along his tongue and throat. The more he drank, the less he noticed the vanilla, caramel and honey. The more he drank, the less his heart screamed with the loss of his baby sister. His palette became accustomed to the warm sting of the bourbon, the once-distinct notes no longer registering. It was now just a long, pleasant burn that needed to be maintained. By now, Marty was towards the bottom of the bottle.

He tried to think of Mildred, his sweet, shy, naïve Mildred, but he couldn't picture her like he wanted to. As hard as he tried, he couldn't conjure the image of her as a vixen with diamonds in her green dress at the speakeasy, but instead, he could only see the Mildred he met first, sitting in her polka dot dress on the boardwalk in Bresford, almost too scared to say who she was. She didn't have gobs of makeup on, didn't have perfect curls in her hair. He loved that polka dot dress and the fact that she ran away from him. It made her worth pursuing.

A knock came at his door. "Yes?" he answered and did his best not to slur.

"Marty? It's Masterson. Can I get you anything before I retire for the evening? How about a nice cup of vanilla milk or hot chocolate? It'll help you sleep. It's been such a long day for us all." The faithful housekeeper and cook had served them since before Tabitha was born and even now she offered him a mug of vanilla milk, one of his favorites from childhood.

"I'm okay without it for tonight, Masterson," he said, almost too loudly.

There was a silent moment, as if she suspected what he was up to. "Are you sure?"

"I'm fine, Masterson. Thank you."

The devoted member to the Townsend family wouldn't stop. "What would you like for breakfast tomorrow morning? Welsh rarebit, eggs Benedict, or how about fritters? I haven't done those in quite some time. I have some apples that are on their way out, or maybe banana bread?" Masterson was doing her best to comfort him in the way she knew how, with scrumptious food, the same way she did since he was a little boy that only ate plain eggs with toast and no butter.

It was hard to decide with the bourbon. His standard breakfast would be the eggs Benedict with crab or shrimp if it was procured that morning, but in his alcohol stupor, he said, "Apple fritters, please."

"Alright, Marty. You'll have some fresh fritters tomorrow morning. Sleep well."

"You, too, Masterson." He heard her feet gently pad down the stairs, most likely to her maid's quarters where he hoped she had her own stash of sherry or brandy to dip into. Masterson never married and never had children, a huge tradeoff she made to be the well-paid and highly respected woman that ran the Townsend household behind the scenes. Jeanette, for all of her jewels and fancy clothes, was the face of the Townsends alongside her husband, but Masterson made their home as cozy and famous as anybody could want. Helena Silman paid the bills and sorted through the mail for several years, but when it came to food and an immaculate household, Masterson was the winner. Marty envisioned the apple fritters frying in oil, juicy and plump. His mother wouldn't even know how to begin making fritters, but then he realized that he wouldn't, either. He tipped the first bottle back and noticed it was almost empty.

There was another knock on his door. "Yes?" He answered hesitantly and hoped it wasn't Masterson to pester him with the breakfast menu again.

"Martin, can I come in?" The voice chilled the liquor heat running through his veins. It was Agnes Crane standing outside of his door, he was sure of it. What could she possibly want? He specifically told her to leave him alone, that he was happy with Mildred.

"Who is it?" he sloppily hollered. The suit he wore started to make him sweat, so he peeled away the jacket and tossed it somewhere behind him, then kicked off his shoes.

"It's me, silly. Let me in." It was definitely Agnes, there was no doubt in his hazy mind. Her smooth, sweet-yet-business voice was unmistakable over the phone, in a crowd, outside his door. Then she knocked again, making it clear she wasn't going away.

"Hold your damn horses," he mumbled as he rolled off the bed. The bourbon had reached his feet and he felt them dragging along the Oriental rug below. When he pulled the door back about a foot, there was Agnes, smiling and looking gorgeous in her slim black skirt with a cream shirt that had odd black streaks in the pattern. Her black bell-shaped hat obscured the upper part of her face.

"Hello, Martin." No witty barbs and hidden agenda were in her voice. In fact, she had the same sweetness that drew him to her at the Christmas party where they first met in 1931. It was understood at that party, hosted by a mutual friend, that the punch was cut with a good amount of liquor and everyone was to drink it at their own risk. After a few glasses of punch, Marty found himself in the brisk December air with other tipsy partygoers enjoying the light snowfall. From across the deck, Marty spied a slender, regal woman wrapped in a fur cape, laughing among a group of men. It was obvious they all wanted her and she led each of them on, but she wasn't their prey. Instead, she was the wolf taking inventory of the sheep surrounding her. Marty made various introductions as he made his way across the deck until he was standing right in front of her. The other men, some of them he recognized from college, left when they realized they lost their chance with the mesmerizing woman when Marty Townsend showed up.

"I'm Marty." He didn't know what to say beyond that.

"You scared off my friends, you know?" She swirled her punch around in the glass. "My name is Agnes, the daughter of George Crane."

"Of Crane Development?" he asked excitedly. He only imagined what his father would think when he told him about meeting the daughter of someone he wanted to partner with for the last few years. Marty and Agnes continued to talk while everyone else went inside to drink more and dance. They didn't seem to care that they were covered in a layer of snow. It was her business mind that he admired and her beauty that he adored, and with the two combined, how could he not fall for her?

"I'm the next in line to Townsend Timber," he said, hoping it didn't sound like a cocky prince trying too hard to entice a princess.

"I've heard of your father's company. What are you suggesting, Marty? That we get married so we can dominate that corner of the industry? You take out all the trees and I build something up. Sounds like a brilliant plan to me." She bit her lip and teased him a flirty smile, which was when he noticed her perfectly pert nose.

He laughed at the thought. "Wouldn't that be incredible? Our family businesses joining together the same time as us? This punch is making me sound idiotic, but still, that would be something." The punch began to sweat from his pores and scalp and he fidgeted around, not feeling too well. Even then, Agnes looked amused.

"Marty Townsend, meet me for lunch after the New Year and let's talk." That was the last thing Agnes said before leaving him in the frosty weather and pouring herself more punch. The audacity, the ferocity of this woman left him speechless. It was that February that Marty proposed to her and a June 1932 wedding was planned. People went to great lengths to design her dress, to find the most talented calligrapher for the invitations and several bids came forward to host this historic union. This same woman was now in his doorway, eyeing the two remaining bottles on the bed.

"Martin, may I come in or are you going to make me stand here?"

He sighed heavily, shuffled back to the bed and mumbled, "You win." Without further prompting, Agnes entered the room, shut the door and sat primly on the desk chair.

"Do you know what today would've been, Marty?" she asked as she took off her hat and let her hair down, running her fingers through dark brown waves while also removing hairpins. He watched her do it and barely remembered her question.

"I don't feel like playing games." He emptied the first bottle and set it down with a clumsy bang on his nightstand. By now, he could feel his brain swimming happily in a sea of numbness. Agnes left the chair and sat as close as she could to him, then put her hand on his. "Today would've been our wedding day. How could you forget such an important detail like that?"

Instead of answering, he opened the second bottle of bourbon and he offered it to her. "Here, take a sip. You need it."

She didn't hesitate and took a strong pull from the bottle and handed it back to Marty. Silently she exhaled as the heat of the liquor coated her throat.

"To answer your question, I forgot that today was our wedding day because I'm not marrying you. If I was sober, I'd toss you out of the damn house myself." Through hazy eyes, there was no doubt that she was a gorgeous woman, but after she stole a ludicrous sum of money right in front of him on the day of his grandmother's funeral, no amount of beauty could hide the fact that Agnes had a black heart.

"There's no need to be such a grump," she said playfully. "What are those?" Her eyes fell on the pink envelopes on his bedside table. Before he could stop her, she swiped them and began to read using a higher-pitched voice. "*It's me, Mildred. This sounds very silly, but you came into my daydream at work today. I can't stop myself from looking at your picture from the paper!*"

"Give those back to me!" he hissed. Agnes danced around and waved the pink letters above her head. He stood up and tried to grab them as they fluttered around.

She giggled. "These are so pathetic that they make me laugh! Are you sure you are right in the head?"

Tired of her coy attitude, he grabbed her wrist to secure the letters and snapped, "Shit, Agnes, is everything just a big joke to you? Leave Mildred out of it. I know what you did and if you're not careful, I'll reveal your scandal and ruin what our fathers have done bringing their businesses together. I don't even care anymore!"

"You wouldn't do it." The confidence she exuded frustrated him.

"And what makes you think you know that?" he barked. Agnes always loved to challenge him and anybody else in her path, but especially him. He let go of her wrist and knocked back more bourbon. Perhaps she'd get less irritating with each ounce he drank.

"It's simple. Too much is at stake with the current economy and you wouldn't want to leave your family or mine in ruins. You may speak a big game sometimes but you're too kindhearted to wreck our families and their fortunes. I know you better than you think, my sweet Martin." Without another word, she began to unbutton her blouse, revealing her smooth, flat stomach and black lace brassiere.

"What are you doing?" he asked, almost sounding afraid. Her cute nose, her fiery green eyes, both made memories flood back in full force. He'd seen Agnes naked on several occasions before. In fact, his first time with a woman was at the lake house with her. The way she moved her body and carried herself as a woman that evening, he didn't know if she'd been with men before him, but even if she had, he realized it only made their experience better. Playfully, she tossed her silk blouse over his face and he breathed in her scent that mixed with the liquor on his breath. Expertly, she wiggled out of her tight skirt and he found it amusing how it stayed upright in a tube shape when she stepped out of it.

Bleary with bourbon, he didn't fight her off like he should have done when she crawled onto the bed and pushed him back into his pillows. As she straddled him, he unsnapped her stocking clips and let them clatter to the floor.

What about Mildred? Stop this right now before you hate yourself, his mind screamed through the booze, but as his fingers felt her taut olive skin, her dainty body warm on his, he became a defenseless prisoner to Agnes's seduction. She grabbed the bottle and helped him take another deep drink, then took one for herself before she turned off the lamp. When she bent over to kiss him, he tasted the bourbon on her wet lips. He kissed the tip of her nose that he used to adore so much and couldn't stop kissing her.

"Indulge me, call me Aggie like you used to," she whispered, guiding Marty's hands to the clasp of her brassiere. Obediently, Marty unsnapped her brassiere after a moment of fumbling, threw it across the room and felt her small breasts, which were smaller than Mildred's.

"Aggie, Aggie..." he moaned.

Agnes put her lips on his ear and said, "You know you want me back, Martin. Show me how much you want me." That was all it took for Marty to roll Agnes in his bed, to completely lose himself in her body on what would've been their wedding night.

CHAPTER TWENTY-ONE

"As president of the Bresford Ladies Aid Society, I want to congratulate our newest mayor, Mr. Dominic York!" Darnella said from the stage at the Manchester Fairgrounds. The high school band played mediocre fanfare while people in the crowd fanned themselves in the June heat. Most everyone in town showed up to support the new mayor, even though he didn't run against anybody else and sadly, Mayor Klemp was now in his final days. Dominic strutted proudly across the stage and looked over his community. In the front row, Vidalia beamed up at him.

"I am honored to be the leader of such a fine, small town with wonderful people in it like you. Thank you for electing me and I will do my utmost to listen to your needs..." The niceties he rehearsed in his office came out easily enough, especially since it didn't frighten him to be in front of people. Mayor Klemp, as jolly as he was, had a voice that wavered whenever he had to speak and often had to repeat his sentences after he butchered them. Dominic never stuttered once. Towards the back of the crowd, he noticed a scruffy sort of man. Either he was tan or dirty, he couldn't tell, but the two men on each side of him had the broad shoulders of young men, taller and wore smug expressions. The man in the middle didn't look smug. Instead, he looked amused.

Lee Carroll was at his inaugural event.

"...as mayor, I will keep the Depression from destroying our beloved town. Thank you for this chance to serve the Bresford community." To generous applause, Dominic exited the stage and went for a mug of coffee. Much like Marty's reception, there were donuts, assorted pies and cookies. Darnella and his daughter were behind the tables to fret over details as part of their society duties, although Vidalia refused to touch the chocolate pies. The coffee wasn't the best but he wasn't about to complain. He had just won the position of mayor, after all.

"Congratulations are in order, I believe, Mr. Mayor, sir." Dominic turned and barely hid his grimace when he set eyes on Lee Carroll. Since their first business agreement five years ago, they have only met in person a few times and each time they had to be face to face, it was typically because Lee Carroll had an issue with Dominic's form of payment. Dominic thought quickly about what he sent last time and swore he delivered exactly what Lee Carroll ordered: boots, hooch, an assortment of candy and tobacco to last a month. He even went a step beyond and stuffed each boot with a pair of wool socks.

"Thank you, but you didn't have to come all the way from Kalama to see me. You should've told me you were coming during your last phone call." Dominic was keenly aware that people were watching him and Lee Carroll and prayed that he wouldn't be embarrassed on his first official day as mayor. Darnella had a hawk's eye on them as she served up pie.

Lee Carroll chuckled, sounding like gravel was stuck in his throat. "I don't have to tell you shit. Let's walk and talk, shall we?" Without a word, the two younger men with Lee Carroll flanked Dominic and started walking out towards the field.

"Please tell me what's going on," Dominic asked calmly. The stink from the man to his left reached his nose and he made a mental note to toss in some bars of soap in the next box.

"Your payment was on the disappointing side, very disappointing." Lee Carroll pulled a pipe out of his coat and got it started, letting out a long puff of smoke. "The tobacco is excellent, I give you that, but we ran out of booze and candy a week early. You'll have to double it up in your next payment."

"Double? I sent the requested amount of hooch and even added extra candy. You never told me that you needed more!" Dominic lost his calm and began to sweat. "I don't know how much longer I can do this!"

"That's what happens when you sell your soul to me to have someone taken out. You got what you wanted while I keep getting what I want. Are you telling me that you want to stop paying me?" Lee Carroll's voice lowered. "The only way to stop making payments is if I tell you to or else I'll have someone cut your lily white throat."

"No, no, no, that's not necessary. Just tell me what you want me to do." Cowardice screamed from his voice and Dominic hated himself for how close he was to tears. Lee Carroll was right, he had sold his soul to him for all eternity and there was no way out of it unless Lee Carroll felt generous enough to free him.

If only Dominic hadn't fallen in love with Grace Westrick.

Even nearly twenty years later, he can remember with a

smile the first time he met her in his shop. The fine dresses and hats didn't interest her and she walked right by the shelves of Parisian perfume as if they weren't there. Any other woman would've at least sniffed the bottles, felt the fabric of the dresses and end up purchasing one or both items. Not Grace Westrick. In a modest brown plaid dress and flat shoes, she walked in unnoticed until her purse strap caught on an iron rack of hats that fell with a mighty crash. Dominic rushed over, furious at first because he thought it was the wild Conover boy who knocked over an oil lamp last week as he was on his way out with fistfuls of candy.

"You little wretch, I'm going to throttle you!" Dominic's breath caught in his throat when he reached the disaster. It wasn't the Conover boy at all, but a woman sitting in a pile of hats. One had even landed on top of her head and the white paper price tag dangled in front of her face. "Are you hurt, ma'am? Let me help you up." She shot out a hand and he took it, noticing how smooth and small it was. When she took off the hat, he felt his breath catch again. There wasn't a single trace of cosmetic on her bright face, her inquisitive and shy eyes free of mascara and her full lips were naturally a shade of raspberry. Her brown hair wasn't styled but instead, fell in loose waves to her shoulders and a single twist of hair was pinned at her temple. The only thing extravagant about her was the gold crucifix necklace around her neck.

"I'm terribly sorry about that, sir," she said. Her voice was small and mousy, like her. Immediately, she bent over and started gathering hats as if they might skitter away in the gust of wind. Dominic picked up the heavy rack and laughed.

"As long as you're not hurt, I'm not worried about anything." He tried looking at her face again, but she kept her gaze on the hats or her shoes. When she looked up, her cheeks were as pink as her lips. "Are you new in town? I don't believe we've met."

Nervously, she tucked some hair behind her ear and she shrugged. "My husband and I moved to Bresford only about a month ago. I just don't get out much like some people, but I'm actually looking for some art supplies." The hair she tucked back fell forward again and when she placed it behind her ear, Dominic noticed a thin gold wedding ring, confirming that she was indeed married.

"What sort of art supplies?" he asked.

"Sketch pads, the kind with thick paper, and some watercolors. I'm also interested in a set of charcoal pencils if you have some." Her eyes brightened as she spoke about something she clearly had a passion for.

He frowned. "I'm afraid I don't stock those items, but I can easily order them for you." A flicker of disappoint crossed her face. "It wouldn't take long, I promise."

"Well, I was hoping to do more drawing today, but I guess it's my own fault I didn't refresh my supplies ahead of time." She nodded and said, "If you could place an order for me, I'd be grateful." He led her to the counter and flipped through a few catalogues until he found what she described.

"Yes, that's it, the pack of charcoal pencils and a few of those sketchpads," she said excitedly. In less than a minute, Dominic had an order form filled out but he needed one last bit of information.

"What's your name and telephone number so I can call you when the shipment arrives?"

"My name is Grace Westrick and my telephone number is 0719."

Dominic finished writing and tapped the order form on the counter. "I'll get this ordered immediately. Anything else you might be looking for?" Grace shook her head. "Well, it was a pleasure to meet you, Miss Westrick." He held out his hand.

"It's *Mrs.* Westrick, actually, and likewise. Thank you for your help." She left without looking at anything else and he watched her walk down the sidewalk to a green Ford truck parked by the meat shop. The Westrick name sounded slightly familiar and he wondered if Grace was married to Harvey Westrick, the man who took miscellaneous repair jobs around town recently.

Over the next few weeks, Dominic couldn't help but feel like a fool in love whenever he saw Grace. When he called her to say that her art supplies arrived, her voice was sweet over the phone. In the store, she had a bounce in her step, her eyes wide and sparkling as he brought her packages to the counter.

"I'll keep these and anything else you need in stock so you can keep coming back to my store," he said playfully.

"This made my day! You are a hero, Mr. York." Grace paid and took her supplies, and then once those ran out, she came back. Sometimes she would even bring in her artwork to show Dominic what it was she did with everything she bought from him.

He loved her, he realized. All of the other women he used to stock things special for, he forgot about them and only had eyes for Grace. It didn't take him long to learn things about her: her husband was indeed Harvey Westrick; she had a one-year-old daughter named Mildred and they lived on Juniper Street.

Over the next thirteen years, Grace frequented Dominic's for her art supplies. Occasionally she would purchase a new pair of gloves, but only if the ones she had were beyond repair. For Harvey's birthday, she'd get him a pocket square or a book. Most visits, she brought Mildred with her. Her sweet nature remained the same as the years passed by, learning to love drawing just like her mother. As the world changed around Bresford, Grace didn't seem to age and no matter what financial or personal struggles she went through, she always had a delicate smile for everyone she met. When Mildred turned fourteen, she slowly blossomed into a younger version of her mother. Her drawing had become such a passion that Grace signed Mildred up for art classes in Longview that she would be attending the following week.

One late morning, Dominic wanted to deliver Grace's art supplies to her house. School was in and there was no sign of the truck, but he knocked until the door opened. His heart jumped at the sight of Grace, who looked shocked to see him.

"Can I help you, Mr. York?" she asked. She saw the packages in his arms. Her new watercolor paints and more charcoal pencils were inside some of them.

His heart wanted to burst. "I love you, Grace, more than anything. You are the only thing on my mind every minute of every single day. I desperately want you."

Fear filled her gentle brown eyes. "I don't know what to say. I'm flattered but..."

"Do you love me?" No woman, not even Vidalia's mother, made him feel soft in the knees like Grace did. "Please tell me you love me."

Her silence weighed like a house on his heart until she finally said, just above a whisper, "I buy art supplies from you. I'm sorry if that made you think something that isn't true. To spare us trouble, I will not speak of this, not even to my husband. Good day, Mr. York."

Before she could shut the door, he reached in and grabbed her by the arm, making her cry out. "Didn't you hear me? I love you, Grace! I love you!"

"Let me go!" she shouted. When he didn't release his grip, she used her other hand and scratched him across the face. She slammed the door so hard that the dried flower wreath bounced off the hook and fell at his feet, the sound of the locks clicking sharply in his ears. The woman he loved had rejected him, refused to be with him and his success over her odd job-taking, mechanic of a husband. Furious, he threw the packages at the door and left, his heart broken into shards like the charcoal pencils.

However, it didn't take him long for his obsession with Grace to turn sour like vinegar, his devotion to stale. If she was stupid enough to reject him, she was too stupid to live. A rage this strong had never consumed him before. Those countless thoughts he spent imagining himself with Grace were replaced by thoughts of how she would disappear. During dinner with his friend, Herman, who ran a store like his in Kalama, Dominic heard him mention a man named Lee Carroll.

"This guy is a mean prick and all you have to do is give him what he wants after the job is done." Herman stopped cutting into his steak and leaned in, saying quietly, "My sister was being bothered by an old beau from school, so I found this Lee Carroll guy through a friend of a friend. I shake hands and Lee Carroll and some of his buddies roughed up my sister's harasser, gave him a nice shiner and a cracked rib or two. The guy left my sister alone and eventually got out of town."

Dominic was more than curious now. "And what did you have to pay? Five dollars, ten dollars?"

Herman laughed. "That's the great part. Lee Carroll named his price and it was very reasonable. For a whole year, I had to give him a box of my finest cigars every month. I barely noticed a change in my books. Oh, and don't call him Lee. If you don't use his whole name, he takes it poorly for some odd reason. It's best to stay on this guy's good side."

From there, Dominic reached out to Lee Carroll and met him after dark down at the tracks in Bresford. Once the train came to a stop, Dominic saw a man jump from one of the boxcars. Based on what Herman said, Dominic was expecting a man in his late thirties, not a portly man with receding hair in his fifties.

"Make this quick, asshole," were Lee Carroll's first words.

"Of course, I apologize. I need you to make someone disappear, if you know what I mean," said Dominic. Under the hard gaze of Lee Carroll, he felt naked and weak, regretting the decision to meet with him almost instantly.

"Disappear as in they end up dead?" Lee Carroll asked casually.

"Well, yes."

"Murder is going to cost you pretty big, I want you to know." Lee Carroll coughed into a handkerchief. "What did this shithead do to piss you off this much? Did he sleep with your wife and shoot your dog?" He laughed at his joke.

"No. A woman I love refused me and now I can't bear the thought of seeing her going around town, wearing that smile she always has on. I offered her the world and she looked at me like I was a monster." As he spoke, Dominic could almost feel the sting of Grace's nails across his face again.

Lee Carroll whistled. "I've seen a lot, heard a lot, but I've never been asked to take out a woman for saying no to a man. This will take me a few minutes to think of the compensation."

Almost too quickly, Dominic said, "I'm working with someone that will supply me with hooch. I'm told it's decent."

"And you own a store?"

"Yes. Dominic's is just a few blocks from here." Lee Carroll chewed on the inside of his cheek and narrowed his eyes at him, calculating and musing.

"Are you sure you can't just pardon this woman?" By the sound of his voice, Dominic wondered if Lee Carroll was going to turn down this potential job. If it had been a man as a target, they probably would have agreed on a form of payment by now.

Dominic shook his head. "I have too much self-respect to be treated that way, by anybody."

"Alright, I'll do it. Any idea where it should be done? Hurry up, though, I have to get back on the train soon." Lee Carroll looked back at the boxcar he jumped from as the train started hissing.

He snapped his fingers. "Grace is taking her daughter to an art class in Longview next week. She drives a green Ford Model T truck. They'll be on Highway 99."

Lee Carroll raised an eyebrow and held out his hand. "Consider it done."

Sure enough, Lee Carroll held up his end of the deal and news of Grace's bloody death on the highway spread through town. Dominic and Vidalia attended her funeral but had to stand towards the back of the church because everyone in Bresford had come to pay their respects. Grace may have been quiet, but it was clear that she affected most of the people of Bresford. Dominic expected to make payments to Lee Carroll for a year like his friend Herman did, but Lee Carroll blew into town and into Dominic's with some guys carrying baseball bats once the payments stopped. Luckily, Vidalia was in school and no customers were in yet.

"A year? Is that what you think that job was worth? You better not be serious, you pompous son of a bitch." Lee Carroll pointed a dirty finger at Dominic and nodded to one of his cohorts, who used his bat to shatter the top row of perfume bottles. Glass flew everywhere and the room became overpowered by the scent of jasmine and sandalwood.

"Please, stop! Those were imported from France!"

"Oh, really? I'm sorry!" Lee Carroll laughed and signaled for his guy to smash another row until the ground looked like it was covered with bits of ice. "You'll be done paying me when I fucking say so! You got that?"

"Yes, yes, I agree," Dominic said shakily.

That was the last time he was face to face with Lee Carroll. But now he was back, asking for more in his next shipment, which meant that he definitely wasn't telling Dominic to stop. Five years of monthly payments, countless gallons of hooch, pounds of candy, tobacco, and anything else Lee Carroll asked for.

Five years and he wanted nothing more than for this disastrous relationship to be over. "Lee Carroll, what can I do to stop sending shipments for good? Name your price and I'll get you money, anything, just so I don't have to do this anymore. I'm begging you."

He appeared to genuinely consider the plea. "Give me two-thousand dollars. You seem like you've had enough of making these shipments and that sort of money would help me out. Do we have a deal?"

Dominic wasn't sure he heard correctly. "Two...two-*thousand* dollars? In this economy? I don't know how soon I could get that together."

Lee Carroll shrugged. "Well, keep the shipments coming until I see that money. Before we go, we're going to need some more tobacco and candy. Go get it."

"Now?" The look Lee Carroll gave him made his blood run cold. "Come with me." They walked the three blocks to his store and gritted his teeth as Lee Carroll loaded up a bag with loose tobacco and one of his guys cleaned out his supply of candy.

"This will do for now. Have a great remainder of the day, Mr. Mayor," Lee Carroll laughed as he saluted Dominic. He and his two men walked back to the train tracks while Dominic returned to the gathering.

"Who was that you were talking to?" Darnella asked worriedly. "I've never seen those men before. Are they from out of town?"

Waving a hand as if to erase what she saw, Dominic grumbled, "Just some hobos looking for a handout, nothing more."

CHAPTER TWENTY-TWO

AGNES HADN'T HAD SLEEP that delicious in months, even with the rummy feeling swirling in her head. Curled up next to Marty, she watched him slumber, his brow smooth one moment and furrowed the next, as if he was having a troublesome dream.

"Marty, wake up," she whispered and kissed his cheek, running her cool palm over his naked chest. He stirred and pulled Agnes closer to him.

"Shit," he grumbled. "Is it morning already? I better take you back to Bresford."

"Bresford!" she screeched, which was enough to make Marty rub his eyes and see that the voice didn't belong to Mildred.

"What the hell, Agnes? What are you doing in my bed? Get

out of here!" He yelled and gave her a solid push away from him.

"Hey, stop it!" she cried, but he didn't stop and instead, he pushed her again until she fell off the bed and onto the rug.

"You jackass, what did you do that for?" she snarled as she tugged her skirt and blouse back on. "We had a lovely night together and you don't even remember?"

"What do you mean? I had quite a bit to drink and didn't even know you were in here. You just proved that you are even more of a lunatic than I thought."

"We made love *twice* last night! Please don't say you can't remember that. It was better than it ever had been for us. Don't you want to have children together?" Her certainty of getting Marty back crumbled when she saw the horrified look on his face.

"Oh, God, what about Mildred? She must never know this happened. If you ever loved me, Agnes, you won't ruin this for me." His eyes pleaded, looking more doe-like and sweeter than normal. Here he was, asking her to leave him alone so he could take up with the cannery girl.

"How dare you ask me that!" In two steps, she was in Marty's face and slapped him with her whole hand. As badly as she wanted to slap him a second time, she restrained herself and put on her shoes.

He was still groggy enough that the slap didn't sting or rattle him. "Don't forget your hat and anything else you might try to leave behind as an excuse to come back." He grabbed her hat and flung it at her. "I mean it, Agnes. Leave me and my family alone from this day on."

She rolled her eyes. "Why must you always be so dramatic? You'll regret not marrying me, Martin."

"What, so you can slap me and steal my family's money? Let me walk you out. Don't talk to anyone," he barked. He grabbed the back of her arm and guided her through side doors and dodged Masterson in a hallway. When they made it outside, he let go of her with a shove. "I never want to see you darken my door again." Without another word, he shut the door and she heard it lock.

Instead of screaming, crying or coming up with something cunning like she desperately wanted to do, she shut her mouth and kept walking down the sidewalk, blinking away the tears that burned her eyes. After a few minutes, Marty started up his truck and burned his tires on the road as he drove in the opposite direction of her. She guessed he was probably going to see his pathetic Mildred. When she was certain that Marty was gone, Agnes turned on her heel and walked back into the Townsend home from another entrance.

She found herself in a familiar room, the study. The desk was anything but tidy. Towers of notepads held notes for meetings, telephone numbers and bids for new jobs. Like last time, multiple checkbooks were scattered on top of the desk, practically begging to be tampered with. When she cut those two checks for five-thousand apiece, she knew that she risked being caught, which is why she pocketed the one check and let Marty rip up the second. The check she made out to Crane Development cleared without issue and she still had the five-thousand waiting to be used. When she told Marty that she had her eye on a house for them, she wasn't lying in the least, but when he went crazy over the idea, she canceled the pending sale the next day and stashed the money instead.

In the dark study, she made herself comfortable in the heavy chair, its expensive leather as soft and sensuous as her favorite pair of kid gloves, her slight frame looking almost childlike in the piece of furniture. Down the hall, she could hear voices stirring, pots clanking in the kitchen, the heaviness of mourning like a wool blanket over the household. Agnes didn't have much time if she wanted to linger in the study. Her eyes rested on the tempting books filled with blank checks, labeled for each different account:

TOWNSEND TIMBER

MR. GERALD R. TOWNSEND

TOWNSEND FAMILY TRUST

In the trust fund book, the latest entry was for Tabitha's casket and other funeral expenses, and the one before that was hefty compensation for Dr. Ward. In Gerald's personal checkbook, Jeanette paid money to have a chaise lounge and an ottoman reupholstered. To be safe, Agnes opened up the Townsend Timber book, which was riddled with daily entries for the business. She picked up Gerald's heavy fountain pen and it felt good in her hand as she scrawled out what she wanted, what she felt she deserved:

PAY TO THE ORDER OF Crane Development in the amount of ten-thousand dollars and 00/100.
MEMO: Equipment repairs, excavator bucket, miscellaneous.

Easily enough, she forged Gerald's signature and ripped out the check. Ten-thousand dollars was a ridiculous amount of money, but the Townsend Timber account could easily float that sum and if she knew Gerald from what her father said, he didn't pay much attention to numbers and only cared if the business ran smoothly and with the best equipment money could buy. Crane Development and Townsend Timber were close to merging, perhaps within the next year or so, and an expense like this wouldn't be farfetched.

However, the money had nothing to do with Townsend Timber or Crane Development. Marty broke her heart and with that sort of money, she would figure something out to make him regret turning her away yet again. Unfortunately for him, she was done trying to persuade him to take her back and the consequences, while still undecided, she felt they would get his attention.

With the check tucked away in her purse, Agnes sashayed into the dining room to see Jeanette and Gerald sitting at the grand table, alone and morose. "Good morning, Mr. and Mrs. Townsend," Agnes said sweetly. "May I join you for breakfast?"

Jeanette's face brightened. "Certainly! Masterson, please come out here!" While Jeanette was now buzzing with excitement, Gerald looked awful and it was clear that he was a wreck over the loss of Tabitha.

Swiftly, Masterson came out of the kitchen and her face dropped ever so slightly at the sight of Agnes. "Yes, ma'am?"

"Please see what Agnes would like for breakfast." Jeanette stirred and sipped her coffee, as if having her son's ex-fiancée at her table was as normal as anything. Masterson looked expectantly at the surprise guest.

"I'll have coffee with one sugar and cream, grapefruit juice, a single soft-boiled egg and some of your delicious hash browned potatoes. I do miss your cooking, Masterson. I hope to partake of it more in the future," Agnes gushed. With a quick bob of her head, Masterson disappeared into her kitchen without saying another word.

Jeanette, looking like she turned eighty overnight, perked up and laced her fingers. "Agnes, are you and Martin back together? Is the wedding back on? Before you answer, I must say, that Mildred girl he brought around was sweet, but I knew nothing about her! She was as shy as a mouse. But if you're back in the family, this is exactly the kind of wonderful news we need right now."

There was a pause before Agnes answered. "Martin is a tough horse to wrangle, is all I can say."

Gerald cleared his throat and seemed to wake from his bourbon stupor. "I don't know what is wrong with Marty. He had a sure thing going with you, Agnes, and then he throws it all away on this girl from Burlington."

"Bresford, actually, and speaking of her, I acquired some rather interesting news about this Miss Westrick." Masterson rushed in and plunked the saucer holding a cup of coffee in front of Agnes and darted back in the kitchen.

Jeanette looked horrified. "I don't know what has gotten into Masterson. Please excuse her. Continue, Agnes." Agnes wiped the spilled coffee with her napkin and sighed with annoyance.

"Well, from what my private investigator told me, Mildred works at Pacific Bounty Cannery!" She let herself fall into a fit of giggles.

"Pacific Bounty Cannery? What does she do there, open the mail and answer the telephone?" Gerald asked. "I don't understand what is so damn funny about that?"

Once her giggling subsided, Agnes said, "She wishes she did that! It gets even better, Gerald. She guts salmon for an hourly wage! Isn't that hilarious?" Jeanette looked stunned but Gerald turned red and his eyes widened with fury.

"What? Are you telling me that my son deliberately chose a girl who handles fish over a woman like you? Has Martin lost his mind completely?" With a growl, Gerald stood up, tossed his napkin down and stormed off to his study, saying, "I thought I was done teaching my boy lessons, but mark me, he isn't done learning."

Jeanette sighed heavily, weary from almost everything. "It is so unfortunate that Martin isn't seeing reason. I knew Mildred wasn't from any proper social circle like you and I but she had an innocence and sweetness about her. But now my husband is all stirred up like a hornet's nest and I can only imagine what will come of it." She sighed again. Masterson appeared just then with Agnes's breakfast. The hash browned potatoes were blackened in some parts and the egg was overcooked. At least the grapefruit juice looked decent.

"May I bring you anything else, Miss Crane?"

Agnes pursed her lips at her imperfect meal. "No, thank you." Once more, Masterson disappeared. The burnt potatoes and rubbery egg were the least of Agnes's issues.

"Tell me, do you have any plans today? This enormous house is too quiet without Tabitha around anymore and I don't know if I'm ready to be alone. Shall we go shopping at Evette's and try lunch at one of the new hotels downtown? I could use the distraction," said Jeanette. She put her soft hand over Agnes's. As much as Agnes wanted to spend the afternoon with Marty's mother in society and be seen with her, the gaps in the report from Detective Welch were suddenly closing up. Now that Marty made it clear as crystal that he was done with her, what she chose to do with the information was no longer of any consequence and she had the money to get anything accomplished.

"I'm sorry, Mrs. Townsend. There are some urgent matters that I realized I need to take care of today. Please excuse me."

"Right now? Are you sure? Shopping and lunch would be my treat, darling," Jeanette implored. Agnes apologized as she pushed her chair back, and then practically ran out of the house and to her car. Her bank wouldn't be open yet, but she didn't need to cash the ten-thousand dollar check immediately. She navigated out of the Queen Anne neighborhood and eventually found her way to Highway 99, heading south for Bresford.

FROM BEHIND HEAVY CURTAINS, Hattie emerged wearing yet another white wedding dress.

"What do you think about this one?" she asked as she twirled once and swung side to side. By this time, Mildred couldn't tell any of them apart and she felt like going cross-eyed with all of the white material. Each one was lovely on its own, especially on Hattie's trim frame, but satin blended in with silk and silk blended in with rayon until it all looked the same. All of the veils tended to look alike, too, all scalloped with different kinds of lace and pearl beads but all achieving the same effect. If Hattie was obsessed with getting proposed to and married, Mildred should've known that finding a dress would be an equally exhausting ordeal. This dress, however, seemed to be made for Hattie's figure.

"It's beautiful, Hattie, honestly!" Before looking for Hattie's dress, the girls scoured the shop for Mildred's maid of honor dress and found it within ten minutes. Hattie was having her two cousins be her bridesmaids and the flower girl was going to be Leland's niece, Ramona, who already had a flower girl dress from another wedding. For Leland, his brother Lyle was his best man and two of his football buddies agreed to be his groomsmen. For Mildred, Hattie chose a slimming rayon dress in the color of applemint with tiered puff sleeves, a tie-back sash and rhinestone trim at the neckline. When Mildred tried it on, she was pleased with how well it fit, as if it was made just for her.

Hattie scrunched her face in the mirror at the wedding dress. "Are you sure you didn't like the last one better? This one is almost too simple."

Mildred popped up out of her chair and rested her chin on Hattie's shoulder. "Sometimes the best option is the simplest one. You look like you should be modeling this dress in a catalogue."

"Really?" Hattie asked as she smoothed out the satin panel over her stomach.

"Yes." She poked around the piles Hattie created. "Now let's just add some white elbow gloves, one of these veils. I adore this lace edge on you most." Hattie stood still while Mildred fixed the pearly beaded crown on her head and fanned out the rest of the veil. Fern's Bridal Shoppe in Ridgefield might not be as elegant Evette's, but the array of gowns and accessories was decent.

"Millie, I see what you mean. My mother will love this!" Hattie's mother sprained her ankle a few days ago while watering her flowers and had to decline the shopping trip, but she trusted Mildred's opinion and even gave them some extra cash to have lunch at The Orchard.

"Have you settled on a dress, miss?" asked the older owner, Fern. She looked like she was in her sixties but walked like a ninety-year-old with a bad back.

Hattie squeezed Mildred's hand and she squeezed it back. "Yes!" Fern smiled and started working on the purchase.

Back behind the curtains, Hattie asked softly, "Mildred, do you see yourself marrying Marty someday? Perhaps having children with him?"

To her own surprise, Mildred didn't answer immediately. Would she marry the man she fell madly in love with by just his photograph in the newspaper, the man who showed her a world outside of Bresford, the man whom she gave her virginity to? Hattie only knew about The Slaughterhouse speakeasy but she didn't know about their passionate evening at the lake house and all of the champagne. As handsome and exciting as Marty was, Mildred didn't want to be the kind of girl who threw everything away on the first man who turned her head, yet she felt like she would do just that.

"Maybe." It struck her as odd that she never pictured herself in a wedding gown and standing next to him for their formal portrait, packing her honeymoon suitcase and thinking of names for her future babies. The entire vision was hazy, as if she wasn't meant to have it at all.

Hattie popped her head out between the curtains. "What do you mean by 'maybe'? Stop kidding yourself, Millie. You haven't been this happy since I've known you." She disappeared back into the dressing room. "It's okay to let yourself be passionate about something."

Mildred allowed herself to smile like a fool. "You're right. These last few months have been the best of my life." Then she felt her smile fade. "I'm just afraid it could be taken away from me and I'll be left with nothing again."

The sound of zippers and grunting came from the dressing room and Hattie finally emerged in her regular clothes, plopped down next to her on the lounge chair and gave her a look that meant she was more than serious.

"What put that idea into your head?"

She shrugged and sighed. "I shouldn't be talking about it because today is about you and finding your dream wedding dress."

"I found it already so you're fine. Keep talking." Mildred wouldn't know what she would do if Hattie wasn't in her life. The look in her pretty friend's eyes made her feel so accepted, even though she and Hattie were completely different from each other.

"There was this girl at Tabitha's funeral, Agnes, and she kept looking at me, but mainly she looked at Marty. She found him at the reception and he acted quite rude and strange and when I asked him about her, he was an inch away from being angry with me." All at once, Mildred felt herself back in the Townsend parlor, wearing her black dress and seeing Masterson hold back tears as she refilled coffee cups. The girl in the backgammon board blouse and her large, stylish hat meant something to Marty, which should explain his snappy attitude but she didn't know exactly how.

Hattie was deep in thought. "What else are you not telling me?"

She felt her cheeks turn red. "Marty said that Agnes used

to be sweet on him and he only took her out for a few dinners. I had a feeling that I wasn't his first girl and I was alright with that possibility, but the way she looked at him and the way he talked to me, it didn't settle well." Her stomach churned, that instinct telling her she should've stayed with Marty after the funeral bubbling up and making her feel regret and confusion all over again.

"Millie, maybe he was just tired and worn out because he lost his sister. I'm sure the last thing he wanted to see was an old girlfriend who he obviously didn't stay with. I bet that she was jealous of you and was trying to stir things up."

She hadn't thought of that. "How do you know these kinds of things?"

"Girls tend to play games and it sounds like this Agnes is the sort of woman to do that. Don't forget Vidalia is cut from the same cloth."

Ever since the pie incident, Mildred avoided Vidalia like the bubonic plague. "What am I going to do?" She buried her face in her hands, but Hattie pushed her chin up and looked her deep in her scared eyes.

"Easy. Don't let them win. Say it for yourself."

Mildred felt silly but obeyed her loyal friend. "Don't let them win."

"Say it again, but with gusto."

"Don't let them win!" Fern jerked her head up from writing the receipt, spooked by Mildred's shouting. With Hattie's support and a new motto to keep close, Mildred felt a little better and would feel total relief once she saw Marty again.

"Good. Now let's pay for my dress and go to lunch. This bride is starving!"

DOWN AT THE WATERFRONT, Marty closed his eyes as he listened to the gentle waves for hours that sounded the same now as they did when he was a boy. A train's whistle traveled over the miles and sounded the same way he felt, lonely but still moving ahead.

Between Tabitha's funeral, his pounding head and learning this morning the horrible thing he did with Agnes, he felt like his entire world was crumbling fast underneath his feet. The only thing he knew would make him get over his feeling of dread was to be with Mildred, whose calm and quiet he found comforting. Today, however, she was helping her friend Hattie to find a wedding dress for her nuptials in July, so he was without much to do except stew in his hate for himself. Randall was no longer someone he considered a friend and he hadn't seen him since before he and Mildred found Sarah horrifically beaten for buying milk and eggs. If Tabitha was still alive, he was sure he'd be in her room playing checkers, learning chess, or even planning his next adventure.

He got back in his truck and headed home, feeling that perhaps his mother might need his company and he would do his best to be a good son and endure any prodding questions she might have. Once inside, Masterson offered him some iced tea and then said quietly, "Your father is in quite a mood this afternoon."

"Over what?" he asked. He wasn't close to his father like some sons were with their fathers, but he knew him well enough that it was either a money issue, he was drunk, or both. Having lost his only daughter would only add fuel to the fire.

Masterson, one woman he felt could tell him anything, remained silent. Her fearful eyes made him worry.

"Please, Masterson, what is going on? You must tell me." Part of him wished he had stayed at his safe spot down at the waterfront, unsure if he could handle anything else other than what already had his brain spinning out of control.

She lowered her voice so much that he had to lean in close

to her face. "Marty, Agnes was here this morning for breakfast. Your mother wanted to take her shopping and out to lunch, but Agnes got up and left without saying another word. I don't know what to make of it."

His blood boiled, his heartbeat thundering now. "Did she happen to mention where she was going?"

"Unfortunately, she didn't but if she had, I would tell you. That's all I know," she said.

"Thank you, Masterson." Beyond the foyer, his father's booming voice barreled down the hallway from his study. As if the Fates timed the argument, Jeanette ran out of the study, crying and red-faced. When she saw her son, she snarled.

"Martin! What are you trying to do to us?" The front of her dress was wet from tears and her cosmetics smudged like charcoal under her eyes.

"I don't understand. What's wrong, Mother?" The instinct to run away tugged at him but he planted his feet.

She feigned laughter. "Ha! Go ask your father what is wrong and he'll give you an earful, son! As for me, I've had my fair share of insanity and I'm going to lay down for the remainder of the day." His mother stormed by him and stomped up the stairs, then ferociously slammed her bedroom door.

When Gerald stepped out of his study and locked eyes with him, Marty felt like he was six-years-old again and getting in trouble for putting garden snakes in Masterson's toilet bowl in the maid's quarter.

"Come here, son," Gerald said, almost snarling himself. He obeyed and walked towards his father. Suddenly, his father reached out and clobbered Marty on the side of his head, sending him stumbling.

"Shit!" Marty covered his ear to try and lessen the ringing but it didn't help.

"You fell for a fish girl, is that right, Martin? Tell me, how is Mildred a better option than Agnes?"

Inside his aching skull, Marty felt his headache swelling like a thunderstorm, as if his brain might pulse out of his ears. "I don't give a shit about Agnes. If you only knew what she did, you'd change your mind."

"I don't care what Agnes did. Her father and I have an agreement and you were supposed to marry her! She's beautiful, rich, and smart and comes from a good family. It was that simple!" Marty ducked as his father postured to hit him again.

"Agnes stole money from us!"

Gerald stopped his fist. "What are you talking about?"

"At Granny Fran's funeral reception, I caught Agnes with a check she wrote to herself for five-thousand dollars from the business account, but I caught her and tore it up. But she made off with another check that. That's why I broke off our engagement. She is a liar and a thief." Marty watched for some light of understanding to enter his father's eyes. Instead, Gerald laughed from his belly.

"Why would you make up something that ridiculous? I needed to hear a good joke today but I didn't expect to hear it from you. If you continue on the path with Mildred, I will be forced to cut you out of the business. If you are smart, you'd choose Agnes and have a life of security and inherit Townsend Timber like we planned all along. What'll it be, son? The choice is an easy one."

Marty was beyond confused. "You hate Mildred because she works at a cannery but you want me to marry Agnes despite what I just told you? You're unbelievable. I guess I have no choice but to defend my decision until the day you die."

He watched as his father's lips curled. "I never took you for a fool. Now all of Seattle will mock the Townsend name, all because you are blind to what matters most!"

Marty dared to laugh. "Just because you married mother

for her fortune doesn't mean I have to do the same. Mildred may not be wealthy, but she is a real person and has some dignity and I'm lucky to have found her."

"You say that until you lose everything and move into a hobo camp, which I can guarantee will happen. And when it does, don't expect me to bail you out." Gerald's iron gaze didn't falter. For a moment, they were silent, but Marty was done with the interrogation.

"Father, you can go straight to Hell in your new logging truck."

"You little prick!" Gerald swung his arm again but Marty caught it, close enough to his father that he smelled bourbon. He easily ducked around him to escape through the hall and out the kitchen door to his truck. The engine was still warm and instantly turned over when Marty fired it up and peeled out of the driveway. It was as if the whole world was going crazy. Nobody made any sense and he and Mildred were the only sane people in it. It was imperative he put as much distance between him and his family for now, which was why he sped across town to the hangar with his sights on Bresford.

CHAPTER TWENTY-THREE

With a satisfying metallic clunk, Dominic locked his office door and turned to his mystery guest who happened to be one of the most beautiful women he'd ever seen. He didn't even know her name yet but when she first entered the store, she breezed by Hattie and her station of gloves and knocked briskly on his office door.

"Dominic York?" she had asked. His newspaper went flying as he wasn't expecting anybody and he shot up when she opened his door. "Are you Dominic York?"

Before he could answer, he noted her outfit with interest. Despite some wrinkles in the silky blouse with odd geometric shapes, she looked polished in a black pencil skirt and a bell-shaped hat that looked like something he would import from France for his inventory. It was clear she wasn't from Bresford, too well-dressed and refined in her mannerisms. Perhaps she was a reporter from the vicinity wanting to interview him on his newly acquired role as mayor, so he smoothed out his suit.

"May I help you, miss?"

"Lock your door."

"Pardon me?"

She sighed impatiently. "I suggest you lock the door and keep your voice down. I have a proposition that I feel you would be highly interested in." He did as he was told and locked his door and returned to his desk.

"Can you tell me your name? Are you a reporter?"

A low chuckle escaped her plum lips. "Do I look like a reporter, Mr. York?"

"I guess not. Forgive me." He grew more uncomfortable by the minute as the woman narrowed her eyes at him.

"Tell me what you know about Mildred Westrick."

Dominic tilted his head to one side, unsure if he heard her correctly. "Did you say Mildred Westrick?"

"Yes."

"May I ask why?"

"Mr. York, I'm going to be the one asking questions and when I'm happy with what you have to say, I am going to pay you for the trouble. Will that loosen your lips?"

If he wasn't already confused from the start, Dominic was now struggling to figure out what this woman was here for. "Pay me? Why?"

The woman, who still hadn't told him her name, raised a groomed eyebrow, a clear sign she was losing patience. "Again, I am going to ask you the questions. How do you know Mildred Westrick?"

There was no way around her and Dominic had nothing

better to do, plus she was easy on the eyes. What harm could come from a few questions, he told himself. "Alright, I'll oblige. Mildred works at the cannery a few blocks over. It's called Pacific Bounty. She is the same age as my daughter but they aren't friends. Her father works at the feed store and her stepmother is president of the Bresford Ladies Aid Society."

"Is she seeing anyone?"

Dominic felt himself prickle. "Yes. In fact, her relationship has been the cause of a lot of strife for my daughter. There is this pilot, Marty Townsend, that flew into town in May and my daughter and I hoped he would court her, but Mildred, by some miracle of God, turned his head and they've been together since. Mildred even had the nerve to throw a pie at my daughter!"

The woman looked amused. "Rest assured that Mildred has caused strife in Seattle, as well."

"What do you mean?" He leaned closer and could smell the woman's expensive perfume. The scent fit her perfectly, for it was exotic, spicy and alluring.

"Did you know that Marty was already engaged to someone else?"

He gasped. "He didn't say anything about that!" He felt sick at the thought of his Vidalia being in love with an engaged man, but to her credit, she had no clue like everyone else.

"I also have some interesting information about you, Mr. York." The tone in her voice was calculated, telling him that she knew she was several moves ahead.

"Information? What could you possibly know about me? I'm a humble store owner and recently became the mayor of this town." When he got up to open the door, she shot out her arm and stopped him.

"Do you know a man by the name of Lee Carroll?" She smiled up at him, her teeth white and pretty. Suddenly, his office felt like a swamp and his breathing came a little quicker.

"No. I've never heard of him."

The woman shrugged her slender shoulders. "I had a feeling you'd say that. Might I be able to ask Grace Westrick if she knows him?"

The very mention of Grace's name made his blood run both cold and hot at the same time and he feared he might pass out on his office floor. "What do you want from me?" he whispered. The woman, for all her beauty and grace, was nothing more than a viper.

"I know that you hired Lee Carroll to murder Grace Westrick and that you are smuggling in hooch. If the wrong people heard this, you can forget about being mayor or owning this store."

The accuracy of the information this woman had frightened him. "How do you know all of this?"

"Money can do wonders if you have enough of it."

He couldn't argue with the truth. She didn't offer how she came about the knowledge and he didn't dare ask. "Is there a point to this, miss?"

For the first time since she barged into his office, she looked around for anybody who might be listening and leaned dangerously close to Dominic. "You need to hire Lee Carroll to rid ourselves of Mildred."

"Are you insane? There's no way I can do that! Lee Carroll has already been taking monthly shipments from me for the last five years and asking him for another favor would ruin me. He would be more than happy to make me as destitute as him, or dead!"

"What would you say if I financed Mildred's disappearance and paid off Lee Carroll for you?" She leaned back, waiting for it to soak in.

For years, Dominic lived with a certain feeling, like a brick house had fallen on him and he couldn't dig himself out. He would be able to toss aside ten bricks and twenty more would fall in their place, never being able to see light, his air close to running out. Lee Carroll was more than an obstacle to him. He was the grim reaper himself, always glad to remind Dominic that he could also disappear just as easily. Then Dominic remembered the horror on Vidalia's face after the pie hit her. Nobody could do that to his daughter and get away unpunished. However, as the new mayor, Dominic felt like he was scrutinized more now than when he was known as a shop owner. Getting caught in the middle of murder arrangement with Lee Carroll would cost him everything.

"Mr. York, do we have a deal?"

"Before I say anything, how much money were you expecting to spend? Lee Carroll isn't cheap." He remembered Lee Carroll quoting him two-thousand dollars to get him to stop haunting him, but Dominic was afraid the woman didn't have that high of a figure in her head and she'd leave his office laughing.

"How does five-thousand dollars sound?"

The bricks that had been keeping him down vanished. "That's—that's excellent. This will solve so many problems. But how do you plan to do this?"

The woman sighed, as if arranging murders were part of her normal routine. "I'll send you the money. You have by the end of July to get it done." She rose to stand and dusted off her skirt.

"Allow me." Dominic also stood and unlocked the door for her. "Hold on, miss. How will I keep in touch with you about all of this?"

"You won't." The woman breezed by him and turned before she left his office. "I'll call you."

"SOMEONE WANTS TO SAY hello! It's Marty the Salmon!" Fred joked as he held a fish up to Mildred's face and made kissing noises. Winnie and Gladys laughed without stopping their hands from gutting the fish before them. "Marry me, Mildred!"

"Fred, get that away from me!" she screeched, but partly in jest. After her shopping and lunch afternoon with Hattie, Mildred had to come straight to the cannery. Albert had been more than kind in letting her take odd times off work to spend it with Marty and hunt for wedding dresses with Hattie. Part of her wondered if Albert was lenient with her because she finally had something exciting in her life. However, when she returned to the conveyor belt, she made sure to work three times as hard to make up for her absence. Gutting salmon didn't bother her so much like it used to because it wasn't the highlight of her day. She had her drawing, which she knew she'd been severely neglecting since she met Marty, but sketching people and scenery didn't hold her interest like he did. It made her curious to think how many things have changed since Marty landed his plane at the Manchester Fairgrounds.

To start, her father had been cool and detached from her since he took her out for pie and warned her that Marty would get bored and return to his life in Seattle. Darnella still looked like she bit into a bad apple any time they had to cross paths. Of course Vidalia and Dominic never bothered to acknowledge her presence, especially after the pie social fiasco. Despite the opposition from her father and stepmother and the rest, Mildred could honestly claim that she was happy.

Marty made her happier than anything else in the world. Even though he acted strange around Agnes, she had forgiven him in her heart. She was meant to see his picture in the paper and write him letters, for Hattie to find and mail them, and for Marty to find her on the boardwalk. Her palm tingled at the memory of feeling Marty's hand when he helped her stand up. What she would give to have Marty surprise her today and take her somewhere fancy for dinner, just because he could.

"Mildred, you have *another* visitor!" Albert hollered from his office. He tossed his hands up, not able to deal with his employee's newfound popularity.

"Fred, I'll be right back, okay?"

The older man laughed. "You can't get out of work that easy, missy! I'll save some fish for you!" Mildred laughed and headed out the back so her waders wouldn't leave wet, bloody footprints through the downstairs office. God certainly had been shining some of His light on Mildred over the last month. She wished to see Marty barely a minute ago and Albert announced that someone was there for her, an instant answer to prayer. When she came to the front, she didn't see a red Chevy or Marty. Instead, Agnes was standing by her car, arms crossed and a smug look on her face. She still wore the same backgammon blouse from Tabitha's funeral reception yesterday, but it had creases.

"Agnes?" Instantly, her heart sank to the pit of her stomach, the sight of Marty's past girlfriend making her feel sick.

"Hello, Mildred. I came to deliver some rather unpleasant news." Agnes walked forward. Even in her wrinkled outfit, she looked a hundred times better compared to Mildred in her rubber waders, flannel shirt and wool stocking cap. Some of Mildred's wavy hair had fallen out from underneath her cap and her face was covered in sweat, making her look even more disheveled.

"Is Marty okay? What happened?" The wave of sickness grew stronger. Images of his Chevy mangled into a pile of metal with his lifeless body hanging out the windshield crossed her mind.

"No need to worry. Marty's fine and in fact, he is more than fine ever since he slept with me last night. I am his fiancée, after all. You didn't know this?"

Rather than turn red like she did for everything else, Mildred felt her face pale and go clammy at the thought. Her hands and legs began to quake, her stomach threatening to drop out of her body. "You and Marty are getting...married? How can I believe you?"

"You are a simple girl from Bresford so I wouldn't expect you to fully understand his reasons, but Marty doesn't want to see you anymore. He doesn't even want to look at you again. When he saw me yesterday, he knew he made a mistake with you." Agnes appeared as if she was enjoying herself far too much.

"Tell me this isn't true! It's not possible!" Mildred cried. Tears ran down her cheeks in waves, her knees felt like they would give out and they did. She was on all fours and didn't have the strength to look up at Agnes. She choked out, "I...loved...him!"

"I don't know how else to say it. He doesn't love you and that's all on the subject." Agnes turned and slid back into her car, acting completely casual about what just happened. Before she drove off, she rolled down her window and said, "My advice to you is to find a husband in your same class. Perhaps you'll marry a fisherman!" Her laugh was callous, ugly. Mildred watched her car disappear around the corner, presumably to go back to Seattle so she could plan her wedding with Marty.

Emptiness and rejection swallowed her whole and she melted into another puddle of tears. She didn't even have the strength to bring herself to her feet. Now she had nobody. Hattie was her best friend, but she was getting married and she would have her own life soon. Mildred was back where she started.

"Mildred? Where are you?" Fred hobbled around the corner. "Mildred! I'm coming!"

"Fred?" she said weakly.

He reached her and knelt by her side. "Who was your visitor? Was it Marty? Did he say something to make you cry?"

She wiped her puffy face, only to make her skin smell like fish. "It was Marty's fiancée, Agnes!" Uttering that hated name made her sob again.

Fred twisted his wrinkled face. "He had a girl on the side? That damn dog! He better never show his face around here or he'll get the wrath of Fred!" He rubbed Mildred's shoulders in a caring, fatherly way and helped her stand up. "Let's go inside and I'll fetch you a nice cup of lemonade."

As she sipped her lemonade in Albert's office, both Fred and Albert shook their heads in disgust.

"What has this world come to? First we have banks collapsing, widespread foreclosures and now this awful thing. How could someone do this to a sweet girl like our Mildred?" Fred tossed his hands up in the air as if Mildred's broken heart was worse than the United State's floundering economy.

"Mildred, if you need to take the rest of the day off to compose yourself, I'll allow it. However, I expect you to report at the usual time tomorrow. How does that sound?" Albert asked from behind his desk.

Sitting quietly in the middle of the room, Mildred barely heard what either of them said. Her brain throbbed from crying and her temples felt like Agnes smashed a hammer against them, followed by trampling her heart into the ground with her expensive heels. Something inside told her that Agnes wasn't to be trusted from the first moment she saw her at the funeral. If only she had stayed with Marty, perhaps Agnes wouldn't have come around like a scavenger.

A light knock on the office door made Mildred look up. Winnie opened the door and said softly, "Pardon me for interrupting, but Marty is here."

"Let me handle this!" Fred growled. He rushed by Winnie.

"Fred, wait!" said Mildred. Her voice was tired and scratchy as she chased after him. For an older man with a slight gimp, he raced down the stairs and outside quicker than Mildred could catch him. He held his arm out when Mildred came behind him, but she went around him.

Before her stood Marty looking like he did every visit, smiling that handsome smile and ready to find an adventure with her.

"What are you doing here?" she demanded and almost to tears again. His smile faded and he looked between her and Fred, clearly confused.

"I'm sorry?"

Her breathing became shaky and thick, her throat tightening until it hurt. "Agnes was here and she told me you two are engaged to be married. *Married!* I gave you everything, Marty!"

He held out his hands. "She was here?"

She clenched at the sight of him. "Yes! She said you slept with her and that you never wanted to see me again!" Tears flowed freely, splattering on her rubber waders.

"None of that's true! Well...I have to explain some of it. Can we talk alone? Please, Mildred? I'm begging you to listen to what I have to say." Every feature of his face looked twisted with guilt.

Fred barked, "You may not! Leave our Mildred alone. She did nothing to deserve such appalling treatment. Go back to Seattle and stay there!" Mildred didn't fight when Fred put his lanky arm around her shoulders.

"Mildred, I have to explain!" Marty took several steps forward, tears visible in his eyes.

"Go back to Agnes! She'll be a perfect wife!" Mildred sneered. "Leave me alone, Marty. Don't ever call me or fly back to Bresford!"

"Please, listen..."

"We've heard enough out of you! Get out of here before the police escort your ass back home!" Fred waved his other arm as if Marty was a pesky cat roaming the neighborhood. "Come on inside, Mildred."

She allowed Fred to steer her back to the warehouse but not before she turned her head. Despite her anger and barely-beating heart, seeing Marty look as awful as she did made her feel like running to him and agreeing to hear everything he had to say. Then she remembered Agnes and the horrible things she spat at her. As much as she loved Marty, she simply couldn't trust him anymore and felt a chill enter her heart.

LYING ON HER BED in the dark that first night, Mildred prayed for life to go back to the way it was before she read the stupid newspaper with Marty's picture in it. Had she never seen it, she would've been just a face in the crowd with no interest in the pilot onstage. Life would go on without knowing what it would be like to dance in speakeasy or fly in an airplane. Vidalia would've failed in the end because Agnes would've traveled from Seattle to stomp her into the dirt just the same. Hattie called several times and stopped by but Mildred wasn't ready to go into every single detail with her best friend, who promised that she would try again the next day. The strangest person that seemed to care was her stepmother.

When Mildred came home puffy-faced and clearly upset shortly after she had seen Marty, Darnella followed her to her room and asked, "What happened?"

Mildred stood there like a lost child and cried, "Marty's engaged!"

"What? How do you mean?" Darnella looked genuinely shocked as she sat at the foot of Mildred's bed. During her moment of need, Mildred felt her stepmother's façade soften and nearly melted when she did the maternal act of rubbing her back while she cried into her pillow. Every word she blubbered, Darnella listened intently. She even managed to make Mildred feel better when she brought her a cup of warm vanilla milk and tucked her damp hair behind her ear.

Darnella's voice was soft, understanding. "Being in love is one of the trickiest things a person can do. My first marriage wasn't the best and I decided to leave it because I didn't want to feel how you do this very moment. If Marty is engaged to this woman, it isn't your place to interfere. You must move on with your life and pray for God to guide you."

Mildred wiped her nose on a hanky. "What about Vidalia? I know she had her hopes pinned on Marty in the beginning. That's why she treated me so horribly."

"Vidalia will be surprised by the news, that is true, but she will also hold her head high and find a better man. She's a tough young woman. Although I won't deny that I hoped Marty would've chosen Vidalia over you, but look what happened." She clicked her tongue. "What a shame."

Mildred ignored the barb. "I'm sorry I haven't been the best stepdaughter, Darnella. My father hasn't even spoken to me much since I started spending time with Marty. What if he is going to stay cross with me forever?"

"Come now, none of that nonsense. Drink your milk and go to bed." Darnella covered her with the floral quilt and turned off the lamp. There was something comforting in Darnella's manner that soothed Mildred and reminded her of her mother. She didn't request the vanilla milk but it was a remedy Grace used for Mildred when she was a little girl. After she drank the entire cup, a sweet heaviness hit Mildred quickly and within ten minutes, she fell into a dreamless slumber.

*   *   *

OVER THE NEXT FEW WEEKS, word swept across Bresford that

Mildred was no longer an item with Marty, which caused almost more gossip than the day she first got in his airplane or hit Vidalia with the pie. Mildred kept her public appearances strictly to the bicycle ride to work and back. For fear of people talking about her, she didn't visit Dream Fountain when she got a craving for a marshmallow milkshake or to Dominic's to visit with Hattie. Even when she was on her bicycle, she'd see women from the Ladies Aid Society or girls from school on the sidewalks stop in mid-conversation and watch as she rode by, which made her pedal harder and her cheeks burn red. Her coworkers at Pacific Bounty Cannery didn't mention Marty and gave her a wide berth. When it came to prepping salmon, Mildred ripped out their innards with a ferocity that even made Fred take a step away from her down the conveyor belt.

When she finally felt ready to tell Hattie the story in her bedroom, her friend wasn't as willing as Darnella to accept it. "That doesn't sound like him! He would've sold his soul to be with you, Millie. I could tell by how he looked at you."

"Hattie, how can I trust him after what he did? Would you welcome Leland back with open arms if you discovered that he was engaged to another woman?"

Her friend looked away. "Well, I'm not sure—"

"See, you'd be devastated, too!"

Hattie continued to fight her side of the battle. "Maybe you should let him talk to you about it before too much time passes. I know he loves you, Millie, and I know that you still love him."

Almost too quickly, Mildred scoffed, "I do not!"

Her friend gave her a knowing look. "Sure. Anyway, are you still going to be my maid of honor? You know that my wedding is in three weeks."

"July sixteenth. I wouldn't miss it, you know that." Mildred was reminded about the superior feeling she had when she first was with Marty, about being part of an exclusive club for couples. Without Marty, she was no longer part of the club and on the outside once more.

"I need someone to catch the bouquet and I don't want anyone else to get it besides you." Hattie balled up a nearby scarf and tossed it behind her, aiming it at Mildred's head.

She unfurled the scarf and chucked it back at Hattie. "I think I need more than a bouquet to help me find love at this point."

"Love works in mysterious ways, my dear Millie." She bent down and kissed her on the forehead without leaving a print of her red lipstick. "I have to run and meet Leland's mother and my mother for a luncheon, but remember what I said. I know that he still loves you."

Mildred rolled her eyes. "I heard you, Hattie. Go enjoy the company of your future mother-in-law and think of me, your miserable maid of honor."

CHAPTER TWENTY-FOUR

Inside the dimly lit bar hidden within Foster & Sons Hardware, Agnes watched Randall Fryar practically inhale his second glass of Cutty Sark while she hadn't even touched her Pink Lady cocktail yet. Since the last time she saw him, he appeared as if he aged twenty years, his unshaven face gray and gaunt and his eyes framed with bags. Instead of waiting in the line at the soup kitchen, it was clear that Randall found solace in liquor and not much else. The sour smell coming from him told Agnes that he didn't care to bathe in the bay, either.

"Randall, I can tell you're having a hard time. Are you sure you want to learn what my detective found out about your wife and son?" She wasn't confident how many more hits he could take, but after the small fortune she paid Detective Welch, she hoped he would be willing to hear what she had to say. He motioned for a refill of his glass.

"My life can't get any shittier. Pile it high or not at all," he grumbled.

"Before I say anything, remember what we talked about?"

He started slowly. "Of course. Either way it goes, I find my family and who is responsible for taking them away from me."

She lowered her voice. "Alright. Randall, your wife and son are living in Tillamook with her sister. My detective found out that their bus fare was paid for..." She paused and leaned in closer, "...by our very own Marty Townsend."

Suddenly with a snarl, Randall slammed his glass on the countertop and covered it with a layer of liquor. "That rat *bastard!*" he yelled, spooking the other patrons.

"Pipe down, Fryar! Want to give this spot away?" Pete barked at him. With a grumpy look, he mopped up the spilled liquor.

"Sorry about that, Pete. I just got some bad news, that's all." Randall ran his hand over his oily hair and exhaled sharply. "Agnes, I don't think I can stop myself from hurting him after hearing this. I know you agreed to pay me five-thousand dollars to leave him alone so that you could get him back, but he had the nerve to take my family away!" He blinked away tears at the thought of going back to his empty shack again and sleeping by himself and the truth he was burdened with.

She hesitated to continue as her own wound was still deep and close to the bone, festering with white hot pain. "The plans have changed."

Randall's voice echoed in his empty glass. "What do you mean?" Behind the counter, Pete was ready with another refill.

"In short, I did what I could to take Marty back but he is still stuck on that girl from Bresford. He had plenty of chances but he's run out." A maniacal giggle left her plum lips. "I'm finished with him."

For the first time that evening, Randall tore his eyes away from his liquor and focused on her face. "What are you getting at, Agnes?"

Underneath the counter, she put an envelope in his hands with cash she got that afternoon. Five-thousand dollars had been mailed to Dominic York as part of their agreement, leaving the other half for Randall. He took the envelope and discreetly thumbed through it, his eyes wide and unbelieving.

"What the hell, Agnes? You're really going to give me this? Are you sure you can part with this kind of cash right now?" His concern touched her but she didn't feel capable of being warm about much lately.

"Of course I'm sure. I wouldn't have given it to you otherwise." She paused for a beat and said lowly, "However, Randall, you must know that there is a condition that goes along with that money."

Randall eyed the thick stack of bills inside the envelope. There was more money in there than he'd ever seen in one spot during his life, even when he was successful. He sighed heavily. "I should've seen that coming from ten miles away. What is it?"

Before she could bring herself to speak, she did the unladylike act of throwing back her drink, which she'd never done before. She'd seen plenty of men throw their heads back with a shot glass of various brown liquors and wondered how it felt. In three large gulps, she drained her pink cocktail and felt the fire coat her throat and trickle into her belly. Randall was riveted by her act and waited for an answer. As she exhaled, her breath was hot between her lips.

"I need you to kill Marty Townsend."

NEVER BEFORE HAD MARTY felt like a hollow, papery cocoon, wanting nothing more than to curl up on his bed and not exist, to wither away and be forgotten. It wasn't only Agnes that made him feel this way, though. While his mother was almost noncommittal about how she felt towards Mildred, his father and Dominic, along with Darnella and Vidalia, somehow got the idea that they had the authority to decide who he could fall in love with. When it was only his father who had a heavy opinion, it didn't seem to matter, but now it felt like a small army worked to tear him away from Mildred. His daily calls to her at home or at the Pacific Bounty Cannery were never returned. The damage had been done and she didn't want to be anywhere around him.

Above him, the ornate tiles of his bedroom ceiling threw eerie dragon-like shadows as the July sun proceeded to set in vivid shades of pink and orange. Masterson failed for over a week to feed him more than a few simple toasted cheese sandwiches. His father's secretary, Helena, who first encountered Mildred's pink letters, even stopped outside his locked door and threatened to bust it open if he didn't give her a sign of life. To satisfy her, he threw a leather shoe at the wall.

"Martin, you're going to turn into a skeleton if you don't let Masterson feed you more than bread and cheese every other day!" Jeanette bellowed. Her voice revealed that she was just as tired as he was, if not more, her soul worn thin and bitter by the punches thrown by Fate and preparing for the next.

"Please leave me alone, Mother!"

"Go make yourself useful at your father's office instead of moping in your room like a child. I've had enough of it." She padded down the hall, presumably to take a nap, which she did more and more frequently since Tabitha passed away.

He exhaled forcefully through his nostrils and contemplated his mother's suggestion. Maybe she was right. Without Mildred, he didn't exactly have anything to occupy his time and his mattress started to sink uncomfortably under his hips.

Within the hour, Marty freshened up and was present at his

father's office downtown. Helena beamed as he walked in and collapsed in the familiar leather chair where he first read Mildred's letters.

"Care to tell me what happened?" she asked. As fast as rumors typically spread in the social circles he was part of, Marty was surprised that she didn't know the whole story already. Perhaps Agnes didn't want it leaking out, either, whichever version she had ready to mislead people with.

"Not today, Helena. I'm sorry."

"Is it about Mildred? Your father only mentioned that she was a sweet kind of girl but not who he expected for you. Why is it that you never brought her down here so that I could meet her?"

This was what he was hoping to avoid, the questioning that drained his energy on a topic that made his heart crack down the middle. "I wish I could tell you, I really do. It hurts too much to talk about it."

"There are three people you can tell everything to: your bartender, your barber and your secretary. Keep that in mind." He could tell that she was trying to make him smile or laugh, but he did neither. Helena resumed her task of sorting through the various sized envelopes and she chuckled as she held one particular envelope up. For a moment, his heart skipped a beat, thinking that maybe Mildred sent him a letter.

"This one's for you, Marty. It's from a girl named Hattie Kilpatrick in Bresford? What did I miss?" Helena raised an eyebrow, getting more and more anxious to know the gossip. Marty jumped out of the chair and took the envelope. It was the pale green, a shade between sea foam, the sky on a spring day and a perfect green apple. With clammy fingers, he fished out the letter and read to himself.

Dear Marty,

By now you are most likely aware that Mildred told me what happened between the two of you. I am writing to tell you that I think there is still hope. I've known Mildred since we were both little girls and she has always been quiet and afraid of almost everything. When she met you, she changed for the better and learned how to be brave and take risks. She was the happiest I've seen her and I know that she still loves you despite her protests, which is why I am offering you a chance to mend things with her. You are cordially invited to my wedding, where Mildred will be my beautiful maid of honor. The invitation is enclosed. I do hope to see you.

Yours truly,
Hattie Kilpatrick (soon-to-be Burris)

Sure enough, the pale green invitation was stuffed snugly into the envelope. It was at a church in the middle of town and he was vaguely familiar with where it was.

"What is it?" Helena pleaded. "Good news, I hope."

His breathing quickened. "Hattie is Mildred's closest friend and she is inviting me to her wedding. Mildred is the maid of honor." The world of women was still a large mystery to him, but he knew that Hattie had Mildred's best interests in mind. Sending him an invitation was a good sign. "It's on July sixteenth."

Helena was at the edge of her seat now. "That's this Saturday, only two days from now. What are you going to do?" She dropped her other mail and waited for him to answer. There was no way that Marty was going to climb into a logging truck today, not with the opportunity he was just granted. He tucked the invitation in his pocket and ran to give Helena a kiss on the cheek.

"Wish me luck, Helena. I'm going to a wedding." With a revitalized zest, he sped home and found a suit for Masterson to press and asked her for a hefty lunch now that his appetite returned.

Masterson obliged and brought him out some beef Wellington that she made for the previous night's dinner. She stood there for a moment, silent, and then said, "I knew Agnes was a liar from the very first moment I met her."

Marty paused over his meal. "What do you mean?"

"I know what she did. I know that she stole money from your family's business."

He scoffed. "How come you didn't feel like you could tell me?"

She placed a hand at her throat, ashamed. "It wasn't my place to say anything, but I regret not acting upon it sooner."

"When did you find out?" He let his beef Wellington get cold.

She shut her eyes, recalling the memory. "When she disappeared into your father's study during your Granny Fran's funeral reception, I was coming out of the kitchen with fresh coffee and I could tell by the way she moved that she was up to no good. Your father was confused one morning and he couldn't remember writing such a large check for equipment maintenance, but he said he must've been drunk when he wrote it and thought nothing more. That was when I knew she tampered with your family's money. Then when she showed up at your poor sister's birthday and funeral with her meat hooks ready for you, it just made me mad as a bull. I knew it was because of Mildred, too." She looked as if she was ready to spit a ball of fire.

Relief washed over him. "If only my parents had your keen

sense of perception. I still have to wonder what Agnes did with the money. She mentioned buying a house as a wedding present but she'd be foolish to follow through with that now."

"She stole enough to buy a house? Good Lord! If it's in her hands, it's the Devil's dirty money. Nothing good will come of it and I highly doubt she is tithing." She pointed to his plate. "Now look, you let your lunch freeze over."

Instead of handing the plate for her to warm up again, he got up, wrapped his arms around Masterson and didn't let her go. While he loved his mother like a good son should, Masterson had been more like a mother to him over the years and his gratitude overflowed in that moment of stillness. His nose tingled and tears soaked into her apron that smelled like flour, vanilla and a hint of fried bacon. "Thank you, Masterson, for everything."

She patted his back. "I'll do what I can to help you win Mildred back. Between the two of us, anything can happen, right? Now let me warm your lunch so you can fatten up and fit into your suit properly."

CHAPTER TWENTY-FIVE

JULY SIXTEENTH ARRIVED AND Mildred found herself at Hattie's house surrounded by the hustle and bustle of people getting ready for the wedding that afternoon. Hattie's cousins bickered about which dress was theirs and how to style their hair while Hattie's mother was clucking away and trying to make everything perfect. In the dark study, Mildred sat and listened to the same record Hattie used to give her dancing lessons with. Images of her doing the Charleston with Marty flashed in her mind. That night was the best she had ever known in her nineteen years of life. It puzzled her how she was able to experience the most incredible love, the kind that made her heart feel like exploding and overflowing at the same time, only to up feeling dead inside. As much as she promised she'd be happy on Hattie's wedding day, it proved to be harder than she imagined.

"Millie?" It was Hattie. She tiptoed into the study, wearing a pink rayon corset, a fresh pair of hose and fuzzy slippers. The corset accentuated her slim figure until it looked like Hattie didn't have a ribcage. Her hair was pinned into golden swirls all over her head and her face was naked. She knelt known and rested her head on Mildred's knee. "Can I help you with something? Please tell me, my darling friend. Today is supposed to be happy."

She sighed. "Happy. What does that word even mean? I want to be happy again but I don't know if I can. I want to be happy for you, for me, and to forget about ever meeting Marty. Today, the pain is unbearable. I should just go back to being the quiet girl who never does anything."

Ever the counselor and best friend, Hattie rubbed Mildred's back in large, slow circles. "You have every reason to feel hurt but it will get better with the passing of time. Maybe you'll be surprised one of these days very soon."

"What do you mean?" Mildred felt dampening her lashes, as they did daily now.

"I guess what I mean is that you won't have this terrible feeling your whole life. Look for good things and who knows what could happen. Now, it's time for you to get dressed and gussied up. You don't want to be late for my wedding!" Hattie winked and left the study to find her frantic mother.

Mildred took the feather-light dress and made her way down the hall where Hattie's cousins were busy getting ready. It was obvious that they were related to Hattie because they both had gorgeous blonde hair, slim figures and large eyes.

The oldest cousin, Rosie, looked away from her mirror at Mildred and gasped. "You're not ready yet? We leave in an hour. Do you need help?" Rosie's younger sister, Marian, growled after she ripped her hose.

"I could always use help," Mildred joked. "I only know a little bit about makeup and hair from Hattie."

"You're lucky because I'm going to do it for you. Put your dress on first and then sit down here." Rosie was Hattie's cousin on her mother's side and was older by a few years, but was just as sweet and motherly. As quickly as she could, Mildred stepped out of her day clothes, put on her shaping undergarments and took care not to rip the soft material of her dress as she wiggled her arms through the fluttery sleeves. Without hesitating, Rosie got to work at curling and pinning Mildred's chestnut hair faster than Hattie ever did.

Fighting to open another box of hose, Marian said, "So, Hattie tells us that you were with Martin Townsend recently? You're a lucky girl to manage that. He is the toast of the town in Seattle when Rosie and I lived up there for a year. His engagement to Agnes Crane was huge news. She is incredibly fashionable but I've heard she has ice in her veins."

Mildred kept her face still as Rosie busied herself with beautifying it. "That's true. Marty and I were close for a time, but now I wouldn't toast him if he was the only man left in the entire world."

Marian stopped fiddling with the box and her mouth dropped open, aghast. "What do you mean?" Even Rosie stopped applying makeup and waited to hear more.

With both enraptured by the gossip, Mildred couldn't help it and shared all of the details. She began with the letters, tossed in The Slaughterhouse, and ended with Marty showing up at the cannery. "Turns out the whole time he was showing me a good time, he was engaged to Agnes! I must've been a fool because I believed that he loved me. I even thought he wanted to marry me someday."

Rosie sputtered. "What a tale! I guess it's those rich and

good-looking ones you have to watch out for. They think they can do whatever they please without consequence. But what a story to have! I wish my love stories that ended were as dramatic as yours."

Mildred tried to erase the images as they appeared, memories of flying above the world, drinking, dancing, and making love until she was out of strength. "Of course my story would have a sad ending."

"Don't think that! Hattie adores you and I'm sure she can dig up one of Leland's cousins or friends for you. All is not lost, you hear me? You're young and beautiful. Just see for yourself in the mirror." With Rosie's touch, Mildred looked just as glamorous as she did on the night of the Townsend Timber party, except that she wasn't weighed down with Jeanette's diamond jewelry.

"Let's get going, girls! We can't be late!" Hattie's mother trilled as she blitzed by the room, clapping along the way. Mildred, Rosie and Marian walked into the foyer and filed into one of the many vehicles in the driveway while Hattie and her father took his car. Leland and his party already left, since all they had to do to get ready was put on their suits and comb back their short hair. When the car pulled out of the driveway, Mildred had a feeling of vindication wash over her as Rosie squeezed her gloved hand. Even Hattie's cousins could see where Marty was in the wrong and Mildred was innocent, a naïve girl fooled by some greasy cad with money to do whatever he pleased.

At the church, Mildred went wherever Hattie's mother directed people. Leland was tucked in a room with his groomsmen so that he wouldn't see his bride before the wedding. Other people were already there to prepare the potluck reception and decorate the wedding cake. Slowly, she began to feel like she did before, alone but content, a promising sign that she wasn't permanently damaged by Marty's engagement. In three hours, Hattie and Leland would be married and she was determined to let herself be happy.

IT WAS TEN O'CLOCK BY the time Marty pulled into the hanger. Rather, he skidded to a stop that left smoking tire marks on the pavement just thirty feet away from his airplane. The wedding was at noon and he had no time to waste. The flight was short in comparison to driving, but if he could find Mildred and beg for forgiveness, he wanted to do it the minute he saw her in hopes of mending their relationship. Marty wanted nothing more than to throttle Agnes for the destruction from her wake. Stealing money was a crime in itself, but hunting down Mildred and ruining her happiness was inexcusable.

Like he did countless times before, he climbed into his plane and fired up the engines, the sputtering and rich fumes all familiar to his senses. It would take several minutes to warm up and each second passed like a hundred years. On the seat next to him, Marty reached for his helmet but when he did, he saw a flicker of movement to the right of the plane, near the hangar building.

"What the hell?" He swore he saw a person, the top of their head from behind a concrete barricade taking an ill-timed peek at him. It didn't appear to be a cat loitering in the hanger or a bird pecking around for insects. A few seconds passed and he saw it again. Someone was clearly studying his plane from behind a concrete barricade. Something in Marty's gut told him to investigate. When he got out, he noticed a cable running from his plane to the barricade. His blood went cold.

Someone had rigged dynamite to his plane.

When he was within ten feet of the barricade, he locked eyes with the person behind it. It was nobody other than Randall Fryar. He barely recognized him, however. Everything about

Randall was sallow and filthy, his eyes crazed like those of someone locked away in an insane asylum.

Marty couldn't believe what he saw. "Randall? What is going on?"

"Get back!" he screamed as he reached for a box. After hesitating for a moment, Marty jumped over the barricade, grabbed Randall and wrestled him to the ground. Given that Randall was considerably lighter since he lost his job and home, it wasn't difficult for Marty to keep him from writhing out of his grasp.

"Let go of me, you filthy piece of shit!" Randall growled, his sour breath entering Marty's nostrils. Randall struggled to reach for the plunger just inches from his fingertips.

"Stop with this insanity! Tell me what is wrong!" Marty's mind swirled like an eddy as he tried to comprehend the fact that his long-time friend was set to destroy him.

"Bullshit! You are a bastard and you deserve to die like one!" With a burst of animalistic strength, Randall shoved Marty off his chest and scrambled for the box, pushing the plunger down that sent the silent signal whizzing through the cable. Before Marty could fully take cover, there was a deafening boom of thunder. Shrapnel of all sizes pelted the barricade with bits of glass and metal. Glass landed in his hair and a door handle whistled by his head. Marty watched in horror as flames engulfed the entire plane and as they reached the fuel tanks, another explosion sent an enormous ball of fire upwards with billows of black smoke. In the distance, sirens pierced the air.

"No, no, no!" Marty yelled. He turned and raised his hand, but resisted the urge to punch Randall. Perhaps he finally lost his mind and he needed help but was too prideful to ask for it. Marty shouted above the roaring fire, "Why? Why, Randall? We were friends!"

Randall sneered. "You took my wife and son away from me,

you son of a bitch!"

Part of Marty could understand Randall's fury over this, but he remembered seeing Sarah helpless and horribly beaten on the floor of her shack, covered in egg shells while Leo acted numb over the whole scene. "I saw what you did to Sarah! I had no choice but to send your family away for their protection—to be safe from you!" Randall lay on his back, his yellowed teeth exposed in a snarl and his skin gray, a mere shadow of the healthy man he once was.

"You think you're just the fucking prince of Seattle, that you can do whatever you want. You're nothing but a golden child, a weasel of man!" Randall hurled a wad of spit that landed on Marty's cheek.

Marty didn't care anymore. He delivered blow after blow to Randall's face until his knuckles came back glistening with blood. He didn't put up much of a fight halfway through, laying there and taking the hits as if he were dead. "When I'm back, you better be gone. If I see you again, you'll regret it." When he began to walk away, Randall laughed weakly.

"You think you're so tough because you're rich, don't you? I bet you'd like to believe this was just my idea to get revenge but you'd be sorely mistaken."

"What are you talking about?" Marty snapped.

Randall's laugh gained strength and turned maniacal. "Where do you think the dynamite came from, the line at the damn soup kitchen?" He laughed again.

Marty froze and thought hard. "Don't tell me it was—"

"Crane Development, courtesy of Agnes Crane! You angered the wrong serpent, buddy. And if I were you, I'd be worried about your little Mildred. Agnes is on the warpath." He sat up and spit out a mouthful of blood.

"Tell me exactly what she plans to do!" Marty bellowed. He climbed back over the barricade and stood over Randall.

"Mildred has done nothing wrong!"

Randall wiped his bleeding nose and appeared amused at the red smear soaking into his dirty sleeve. "I couldn't tell you because I don't know. And after what you did to my family, I can honestly say that I don't even care what happens to Mildred." With a growl, Marty grabbed handfuls of his shirt and stood Randall up on his wobbly legs. It was clear that there wasn't any fight left in his malnourished body. The wail of sirens got closer, leaving little time to escape.

"You were always a prick," Marty said with disdain. He delivered a final punch to Randall's throat and watched as he dropped to the ground in agony. "Farewell, Randall. I pray that you can turn your life around someday, I really do."

On the way to his truck, Marty felt himself choke up when he looked over at the plane that had faithfully served him. It was now just an eerie skeleton, licked down to its metal bones by the unforgiving flames. Debris from the explosion covered his truck. Chips and scratches ruined the once-glossy red paint, but the truck fired up just the same and he peeled out of the hangar towards Bresford.

IT WAS ROSIE'S TURN to walk down the aisle and Marian was next. Each cousin was paired with one of Leland's football buddies from school. Nervously, Mildred drummed her gloved fingers against the handle of her bouquet. She smiled awkwardly at Lyle, Leland's brother and best man, as she had her arm looped through his.

"Millie!" She turned around at hearing her nickname and saw Hattie beckoning her. "Come here for a quick second."

Obediently, Mildred left her spot next to Lyle and rushed to the bride. "Is everything okay?"

"Of course. I just want to make sure you're doing alright."

Mildred smiled patiently. Ever since she learned the

horrible news about Marty having a secret fiancée, Hattie seemed overly careful about her feelings, afraid that her wedding would somehow hurt her.

"I'm fine, Hattie, I really am. Today is about you and Leland, so stop worrying about me." She hugged Hattie and returned to stand by Lyle just moments before it was their turn. The church organist played "Rondeau" beautifully and as Mildred let Lyle lead her down the aisle, she looked at the different faces in the crowd. As usual, it appeared that most of the town showed up. From some people, Mildred got looks of concern, as if she might break into a waterfall of tears right there and from others, she was surprised to see judgment. Had it been any other girl that Marty chose, the union would've made more sense.

Don't worry about what others think about you, Mildred heard Marty say to her. The advice was true then and true now, but it was the fact that it was Marty speaking in her head that shook her. Halfway down the aisle, Mildred saw her family. Harvey looked disappointed in her. He was there merely out of courtesy to Hattie. As for Darnella, she had her red lips pursed and a drawn eyebrow raised as high as it could go. Poor Opal looked like she would die from boredom, sitting next to her mother like a living doll in her fancy dress and curled hair. Mildred tried to look outwardly calm, despite her heart rollicking around in her chest. A few aisles down, Vidalia wore a melancholy expression and Dominic gave her a level stare.

Quickly, Mildred averted her gaze, unsure if she could lock eyes with anybody else and wonder what they were thinking about her. Standing next to the minister, Leland was one of the tallest men she knew and his suit fit like it was a tad too short, as if he grew an inch since he got fitted. At the end of the aisle, Mildred took her place next to the minister. Everyone stood as the bride entered the sanctuary. Hattie floated down the aisle like an elegant cloud, kissed her father and joined hands with her future husband.

As the minister spoke, Mildred dared herself to look out at the crowd again. She recognized a fair amount of the faces and if she didn't, they were most likely Hattie's relatives from out of town. She saw the women from the Bresford Ladies Aid Society, several classmates from her graduating class, teachers, business owners and even her coworkers from Pacific Bounty Cannery. The one face she was afraid to see wasn't there and she was glad for it. She imagined Marty taking Agnes out to The Slaughterhouse to go dancing, drink champagne and end the day with lovemaking at the lake house, just like they did. Perhaps Agnes was choosing a wedding dress or confirming the menu or selecting the silver and china patterns to be used at the reception. Whatever Agnes wanted, Mildred was sure that he would fulfill her every wish. In a way, Mildred regretted that Marty didn't choose Vidalia over her from the beginning. Her heart would've been spared the torture and at least Vidalia knew about short-lived relationships. Dominic more or less ended them for her but she had experience compared to Mildred, regardless.

"I now pronounce you Man and Wife. Leland, you may kiss your lovely bride," said the smiling minister. Leland, being as shy as he was, hesitated to kiss his new wife in public, but Hattie didn't have any issues with that and pulled him down to kiss her. Mildred laughed along with everyone else and clapped. The newlyweds sauntered down the aisle, both beaming like fools.

Hattie's mother stood up and announced, "The cake and potluck reception will be held in the fellowship hall in an hour. Until then, please mingle and make some new friends. Thank you!" Just as quickly, she gathered the wedding party for photographs outside in front of the church. Mildred posed and smiled as genuinely as she could for the formal portrait that would grace Hattie and Leland's home for years to come. When the photographer finished with the wedding party and took the bride and groom for their own pictures, Rosie asked Mildred to join her and Marian for a sneaky cigarette. As much as she loved to be invited by Hattie's kind cousins, Mildred's soul screamed for some time to herself and she politely declined.

For the first time that day, Mildred was relieved to be completely alone. The quietest place she could find was an unoccupied bench swing in the shade of a regal oak tree. With her new wedding shoes, she kicked herself into a slow rhythm and closed her eyes, listening to the voices inside the church, laughing and sharing stories. The familiar whistle of a train in the distance was a soothing sound amid the rustling of the oak tree's leaves in the summer breeze. She didn't fear being alone like she predicted and in fact, she needed it. Without people around her, she could observe the world as much as she pleased.

There is a reason I'm meant to be by myself, she decided. Her mother, in a rare mood of sadness, also wondered why she was alone despite the fact that she was sweet and giving to everyone around her. Mildred remembered her father telling Grace that she wasn't like everyone else, that it was something to be grateful for. If only her mother had been able to know how many people showed up to her funeral, she would've been amazed. There wasn't any space left in the pews and people had to stand in the foyer during the service. If Mildred was anything like her mother, as she hoped, she knew she could survive in this world, even if she was meant to wander around it alone. As long as she had Hattie, she considered herself lucky.

"Mildred?" It wasn't Hattie or either of the cousins who said her name and as she turned in the swing, her heart jumped into her throat. It was Vidalia York. Her stride was hesitant, almost like a dog with its tail tucked between its legs.

"Yes?" she said, even though she didn't have any idea of

what they could talk about. Part of Mildred deeply wanted to apologize for what she did, but as soon as she recalled the awful things that came out of Vidalia's mouth that day, the urge to apologize vanished. Vidalia looked more like a grown woman instead of a teenager in her dress made of dark plum velvet, matching belt and puffed sleeves. Her auburn hair was meticulously curled and pinned up with ornate combs.

She stopped next to the swing and waited to speak again, her eyes searching the ground at her feet. "Can we...can we go for a walk?"

"A walk? With me?" Mildred asked, dumbfounded. She judged her surprise guest's posture and demeanor, determining that she came in peace. "I guess I could. The reception isn't for a whole hour." Mildred stood and left her bouquet on the swing to pick up when she returned.

"Great," Vidalia breathed. "Let's go this way." The two girls walked in silence away from the church and towards the outskirts of Bresford, the area kids simply called "the woods." There were decent trails made by people over the years, trails that snaked under ancient Noble and Douglas firs. The wanderer would soon find that they were far away from the bustle of town, treading down paths made soft by layers of evergreen needles. Mildred kicked a pinecone and watched it skitter away.

"What did you want to talk to me about?" Mildred ventured to ask. Walking in complete silence with the girl who recently had her face covered in chocolate pie was proving to be more awkward with each step.

"I don't want to talk about anything, really. I just needed to get some fresh air and saw you sitting outside." Vidalia hurried her pace, making Mildred work to keep up.

"Is something wrong?" Mildred called from behind Vidalia. By now, she was ready to confess and apologize, anything to get her to stop. She did. Vidalia kept her eyes focused on the ground while talking, something that Mildred had always done. "Mildred, please don't make this complicated. Let's just walk."

Any progress is good progress, Mildred told herself and followed Vidalia further down the path. By now, they were nearing the train tracks. Beyond the rail yard, the Columbia River peeked through the evergreens.

"Should we start to head back? I'm Hattie's maid of honor and I don't want to miss anything," said Mildred, nervousness in her voice.

"Just a little further and then we'll turn around!" Vidalia called back.

"Okay, but just a little! I don't want Hattie to cut the cake or toss her bouquet without me!" Mildred walked faster in hopes that Vidalia would cross her mystery finish line and they'd return to the church. The train sitting still on the tracks not too far from her must've been the one she heard earlier. As she got closer to it, she was tempted to turn back without Vidalia. There was no chance that she'd miss her best friend's wedding memories, all because she was out gallivanting with her enemy.

"Vidalia, I have to return to the church! I'm really sorry, but I have to!" Mildred hollered. Vidalia was almost to the tracks when Mildred decided to turn around. Two grimy men stood several yards behind her, waiting.

"Stay away from me!" They only walked closer. "Vidalia, run!" she shouted, hoping that Vidalia would get to safety. Her gown fluttered as she ran to evade the men, but they easily caught up to her in a few strides.

"You trying to get away from us, little lady?" whispered the man who caught her. His arms were like a vice around her waist and his breath was steamy and sharp in her ear.

"Let go of me!" she begged, but the more she twisted, the stronger his arms clamped her against his body. The other man scooped up her legs and together they carried her into the rail yard. There were others there and when Mildred got a better look, her heart split in half. Vidalia wasn't being held captive at all and her father stood beside her, as well as Agnes Crane. There was also a scruffy older man wearing dirty clothes, someone she'd never seen before.

"What's going on?" she asked nobody in particular. Dominic acted uncomfortable, avoided her eyes, and Vidalia was near tears, but Agnes looked unsympathetic, just as smug as the last time Mildred saw her.

"Hello again, Mildred," said Agnes smoothly, taking slow steps towards her. Her makeup and outfit were perfect, as usual.

"Let's get going!" the older man barked.

Not one to cower, Agnes turned her head and snipped, "I paid you a fortune so I will take however long I want, Lee Carroll." She said 'Lee Carroll' with a thick sneer.

He shrugged. "Alright, but the train isn't going to wait."

"Paid him for what? To kidnap me?" Mildred asked incredulously. "And why are Mr. York and Vidalia here? Are they in on this, too?"

Agnes's eyes flashed with amusement. "You're close. Let me just tell you. Your biggest mistake was falling in love with Martin Townsend. You signed your death warrant the day you mailed him those stupid, silly letters. But there's more."

Mildred couldn't help but to get sucked into Agnes's suspenseful way of talking, how she handed out parts of the story like bits of a chocolate bar instead of giving it away all at once.

"Dominic, why don't you explain to Mildred why you're here? It would be better coming from you." Agnes took a step back to watch whatever was about to unfold.

Meekly, Dominic worked up the courage to speak. It was odd to see such a tall, confident man act like he was only two inches high, almost afraid to talk before Agnes and Lee Carroll, yet he had no problems being gruff with Mildred in the past. "Before I start, Mildred, if I could take any of this back, I would..."

"Make it quick!" Lee Carroll quipped as he tapped his wrist where there wasn't a watch.

Dominic nodded dumbly. Sweat beaded at his temples and he seemed to get a shade paler. "You see, back when you were an infant, I met your mother when she bought art supplies from me and I happened to fall in love with her. It came to the point where I thought about her every single day and when I told her how I felt years later, she rejected me."

A sick, frothy sensation filled Mildred's stomach. "She was a respectable, married woman! How dare you ever tried to make my mother stray!" Her words made Dominic wince.

With the excitement of a child on Christmas morning, Agnes said, "There's more and it took my private detective to put this together. Dominic, tell Mildred how you know Lee Carroll." It was evident that she got pleasure out of this and Mildred wondered what Marty ever saw in her.

"Please, don't make me say it." His eyes glistened.

"If you don't, then I will," she said coolly.

Tears fell down his face and his chin trembled. "Mildred, I know God won't forgive me and I don't expect you to. You see, when your mother broke my heart, this rage consumed me and I felt that she had to pay."

"What did you do to my mother?"

He shut his eyes. "In a moment of weakness, I hired Lee Carroll to murder her. Lee Carroll is the Highway Shooter..."

Lee Carroll grumbled. "That information better not go anywhere outside of here. You paid for it, miss, but if you abuse it, I'll come after you." Agnes looked unmoved by his threat. Vidalia broke down in tears and ran away.

One of the goons asked, "Want me to catch her, boss?"

Lee Carroll shook his head. "If she's smarter than her father, she'll keep quiet. If not, we know where to find her." Dominic begged for mercy until Lee Carroll told him to shut up.

For a moment, everything went quiet in Mildred's head and the people around her became blurry. When her vision returned, her eyes settled on Lee Carroll. The Highway Shooter, after all these years of mystery and pain, was within three feet of her.

"Mildred, I'm so sorry! Please believe me!" Dominic sobbed. In the days, months and years that followed her mother's death, the pit of darkness inside Mildred healed only a little and she knew it would always remain. In her heart, Mildred felt that she'd made peace with the tragedy and that she would be able to handle almost any situation since nothing could be worse than losing her mother. But this revelation unleashed everything she believed was pushed into the depths of her mind, never to resurface again. The scream was clear and painful, echoing through the trees and sending birds fleeing from their branches.

"Shut her up, moron!" Lee Carroll barked at his men. Obediently, one of them yanked out a rag and struggled to wrap it around her face as she jerked her head around. She writhed and kicked out at Lee Carroll, screaming through the rag like a wild animal whose legs were snagged in a trap.

The train let out another mournful whistle, but this time it sounded piercing being that close to it. A heavy, clunky sound of metal against metal came down the tracks like dominoes as the train was about to be underway.

Lee Carroll didn't want to wait any longer. "Get her loaded up, damn it!"

"One moment, gentlemen," Agnes piped up. She sashayed over to Mildred and gave her a smile that was sweeter than honey. Gently, Agnes untied the rag and let it drop to the ground. Mildred would've loved nothing more than to spit in her face. "Since I consider myself a generous person, I want to leave you with a few parting words."

"I don't want to hear anything you have to say!"

Agnes leaned in, her plum-colored lips only an inch away from her ear. "Martin is still in love with you."

Mildred stopped struggling. Those few words lifted her out of her misery just enough to hope. "He is? Where is he? Does he know where I am?"

Again, Agnes smiled too sweetly. "I'm afraid that if our dear Martin tries to leave in his airplane, it won't get off the ground. The odds of you seeing him again are dismal. Take care, Mildred." Just as if she were saying goodbye to girlfriends after brunch, Agnes waved and walked to her car hidden in the trees. The train whistled again, this time with urgency.

Lee Carroll held out his hand to Dominic. "Nice doing business with you, York. You better pray we never meet again!" Dominic refused to shake hands with him and stepped back, but it didn't appear to bother Lee Carroll any. "Let's load up, boys!"

"No! Don't take me!" Mildred dug her heels and only ended up making trenches in the dirt. The men easily lifted her into the boxcar despite her twisting and kicking.

"Put me down!" she grunted. Suddenly, she was airborne and landed on the filthy floor of the boxcar, the skirt of her applemint dress ripping as it caught on a nail. When she sat up, stunned but unharmed, the last thing she saw was Dominic looking wretched as the door rolled shut. The train let out one more mournful whistle before leaving Bresford.

CHAPTER TWENTY-SIX

DESPITE THE SETBACK AT the hangar with Randall, Marty sped the entire way and made decent time to Bresford. As he raced through the quiet streets in town, people shot him dirty looks from the sidewalk. He slammed his brakes when he turned into the church parking lot and skidded to a stop near a car and almost hit it.

An elderly man and his wife paused on the sidewalk. "You need to take better care of your truck, son. Drive the way you do, it'll be a pile of junk in no time." Marty noticed that they were drinking punch. The ceremony must've been over because other people were milling about, chatting and also carrying around glasses of punch. From what Marty knew about weddings, this was the break before the reception began.

"Yes, sir, you're absolutely right." Marty said to the old man as he dashed passed them and into the church. Inside, there were men in suits helping move tables and chairs around. Women in their finest dress set up the potluck line with plates of cookies, pies, gelatin salads and pickled vegetables. Down a hallway, Marty saw two girls in light green dresses bolt into a room followed by a woman who was acting slightly hysterical. He ran their direction and entered the room where they gathered. The women were talking so fast that he couldn't catch a word. Immediately, they stopped and stared at him. They were all blonde and beautiful, including the older woman, and Marty assumed they were all related to Hattie.

"Young man, make yourself useful and go ask my husband where the extra chairs are. I'm dealing with a crisis at the moment," the older woman said curtly. She flapped her hands around in frustration and the other women didn't stop staring at him.

Marty cleared his throat. "I'm sorry, ma'am, but I'm actually looking for the maid of honor, Mildred Westrick. Have you seen her?"

All three of them dropped their mouths in unison. "Fancy that! We have all been looking for her! I'm the mother of the bride and these are her cousins, Rosie and Marian. How do you know Mildred?"

"I'm not sure if she mentioned me, but I'm Marty Townsend."

The oldest cousin, Rosie, scoffed. "You're Marty? Why are you even here?"

Marian added, "To torture Mildred some more? She told us what you did. How could you be engaged to another woman and play such a cruel prank on a girl as sweet as Mildred? She was absolutely miserable until we talked to her."

He was baffled at first. "That's not exactly true but I'm not here to discuss that. I need to find Mildred."

A vision in white rushed into the room, panting and on the verge of tears. It was Hattie and she looked more worked up than her mother and cousins combined. When she saw Marty, relief washed over her face. "You came! Is Millie with you? She vanished right after the ceremony, but now it makes sense. You showed up and she's been talking with you. That's wonderful!"

"I'm actually here to find her and it's urgent," he replied quietly. The others leaned in, curious.

The hope in Hattie's face evaporated and her voice wavered. "Urgent? I can't have my reception without Millie. It wouldn't be the same. Please tell me what's going on, Marty." Tears filled her eyes.

He hesitated to even talk about what he suspected. "I'm afraid that Mildred's in trouble and I have to find her before something awful happens."

"What sort of trouble?" she asked.

He squeezed her gloved hand. "I'm not sure. I will find Mildred. I promise you that. Go enjoy your reception with your husband, okay?" Hattie hugged Marty and nodded silently.

On his way out of the church, he noticed a woman coming from the wooded area far beyond the property. She wore a dark purple dress and kept her face pointed towards the ground. As she got closer, Marty recognized that it was Vidalia and he had the urge to escape before she saw him, but something about her behavior was different. Normally, Vidalia held her head high and strutted around like she owned Bresford. But now, she was distraught, dabbing at her eyes and sniffling.

"Vidalia?" He walked towards her. "What's the matter?"

She covered her face and began to sob. He guided her to the bench swing and offered his handkerchief. There was a bouquet on the bench. Marty picked it up, examined it, and then set it gently on the grass.

"I'm a horrible person, Marty!" she bawled.

"Does it have to do with Mildred?"

She nodded weakly. "My father forced me to lure her to the rail yard. That bouquet you had in your hands belongs to her." Again, she covered her face, ashamed.

"Tell me where she is, Vidalia."

She dabbed the corners of her eyes. "These men planned to take her by train to Kalama. Their leader, some man named Lee, apparently dealt with my father in the past. I never knew about this until today."

"Who is Lee?"

Vidalia choked on her words. "Lee, the man who took Mildred, is also the Highway Shooter."

Marty's stomach soured. He remembered the story Mildred told him about the Highway Shooter, how he blasted her mother's neck apart with a shotgun while she drove Mildred back home from a drawing class. Now Mildred was in his hands.

Vidalia continued. "There was also a woman there named Agnes and she talked about Mildred making mistake by falling in love with you. She also paid off my father's debt and to have Mildred taken. I should've never had her follow me..."

"Agnes was there? Shit. I have to go now!" Randall's foreboding words rang out tinny in his head: *I'd be worried about your little Mildred. Agnes is on the warpath.*

If his ex-fiancée had anything to do with Mildred's fate, he knew she would do whatever it took to make both of them suffer. She almost succeeded by paying Randall to send Marty to his grave in flames. Who knew what was in store for Mildred once her ride on the train ended. He bailed from the swing and Vidalia started round of crying, but he didn't have time to console her. The keys in his pocket caught on some loose thread and wouldn't come out.

"Damn it..." he said under his breath.

"I didn't think I'd see you again, Mr. Seattle." Marty ripped the keys free from the thread and saw Mr. Harvey Westrick watching him as he casually smoked a pipe on the hood of his car.

The idea struck Marty just then. "Mr. Westrick, you have to come with me!"

Harvey laughed. "I don't have to go anywhere with you, especially not after what you did to my daughter. Ever since she met you, she got this attitude and has been too wild. Now she sulks everywhere she goes."

He didn't have a spare second to tell Harvey what really happened. "Mr. Westrick, Mildred needs help. We can't waste anymore time!"

"What are you talking about? She's the maid of honor in this wedding. She's probably doing something with the girls." Harvey clicked his tongue on the roof of his mouth. "Sounds like you've inhaled too much airplane exhaust, if you ask me."

Marty had no choice. "Remember the Highway Shooter, Mr. Westrick?"

The pipe in Harvey's mouth almost fell out. He growled, "Not a damn day goes by that I don't think about that bastard, whoever he is. Of course I remember the Highway Shooter, Marty. What kind of question is that?" He turned away and sniffled.

"Mildred was taken by the Highway Shooter. I don't have time to explain it all but she is on a train headed to Kalama. I'm going to find her, with or without your help." He didn't wait and ran to his truck, but before he could start it up, the passenger door swung open. Harvey jumped into the seat and didn't say a word. Cradled in his arms was a hunting rifle.

*   *   *

THE TRAIN ROCKED HER body with a gentle, relaxing motion that made it hard to stay awake. If she closed her eyes, she could almost imagine that she was on a boat. Instead, she was trapped in a dark boxcar with three dirty men and several crates filled with cans of stewed tomatoes. She looked down at her poor applemint dress, which was now torn in several places and smeared with dirt. Her white shoes were in the same state of ruin.

"So tell me, girly, have you ever been with a man?" Lee Carroll's intense eyes searched her up and down, making her feel almost naked. She had never seen a man his age so unkempt, silvery prickles covering his cheeks and chin like early morning frost. The older, grandfatherly men in Bresford were clean shaven, wore hats and their hair didn't fly around wildly like Lee Carroll's. She pulled her ankles closer to her body and tucked the thin dress under her legs. With nothing more than a glance from Lee Carroll, one of the nameless men approached Mildred and crouched until he was eye-level with her.

"Don't touch me," she hissed. When he ran his fingertips down her arms, Mildred gritted her teeth, ashamed that she was reduced to acting like a dog. His hands wandered down to her legs and pulled the skirt out from under her, his parched skin rough against her stockings. His fingers gripped the soft flesh of her thigh.

"*Don't touch me!*" she shrieked. Mildred yanked off her dirty shoe and bashed the man repeatedly on the side of his head with it. The point of her heel tunneled deep inside his ear, making him howl in pain and snarl like a wolf.

"You stupid bitch!" With one hand over his bleeding ear, he pulled his other hand out from underneath her dress and struck Mildred straight across her face. She was relieved that she made him stop, even if it meant getting a slap that left a buzzing sting.

Between the two of them, she had done more damage and noticed the man was doing his best to not cry.

Lee Carroll was amused and whistled. "Whoa, tie the filly up! She's wild! It'll take a real man to break her!" He and the second man were laughing while the other man fumed in the corner and tended to his wounded ear.

The uninjured goon brought out some rope and grabbed Mildred's wrists, tied them up and did the same with her ankles. "Please just let me go," she pleaded softly.

"Nice try, filly. I saw what you just did with your little girly shoe, turned it into a damn hammer. You're getting tied up," Lee Carroll said, still looking amused.

"I told him not to touch me. What if I promise that I won't tell anybody that you are the Highway Shooter?"

Lee Carroll lit a cigarette and knelt before Mildred. His eyes were strange, with what looked like bits of yellowed gelatin randomly placed, and she could see the beginning of cataracts. When he spoke, he softened his voice. "You know, after all these years, I still remember your mother. I even resisted pulling the trigger because she was so beautiful. I caught myself staring, almost forgot what I was about to do. It was a shame to ruin such a pretty face." Mildred studied him as he smoked and seemed honest about what he said. "You look just like her, actually."

"Are you going to shoot me through the neck, too?" she asked, a touch of boldness in her voice.

He let out a puff of smoke. "I'm not sure yet. Thinking maybe our camp could use a morale boost and what better way to do that than to bring in a harlot?"

The thought of being shamefully naked to dozens of men made her want to throw herself from the train and die upon the rocks. "You'll never get me to become a prostitute."

"You have a good point. Prostitutes get paid. You'll just get passed around like an old book." He and the two men laughed as they lit fresh cigarettes. Luckily, they left Mildred alone for a while, which gave her time to think, to wake herself up from what she hoped was a terrible dream.

If I never wrote Marty, none of this would be happening to me right now, she thought. Those pink letters she naively crafted and then immediately threw away, only to pluck them out of the trash bin and hide in her hat box, brought her to this end. She didn't blame her friend for mailing the letters, only herself. The best things that came of the letters she credited Hattie for, of course. Without Hattie's good intentions, Mildred would've never stepped foot on the sidewalks of Seattle in the first place.

Marty was the first person that made her heart feel like it would skip out of her throat when she thought of him, smelled him, touched him. None of the other boys in Bresford could have that effect and she wasn't sure she could ever dedicate herself to a man who couldn't make her delirious with mutual adoration. Then she remembered the words Agnes left her with, about the fate of both the plane and Marty. There were so many possibilities and with each scenario, Mildred only ended up picturing Marty dead on the ground in a pool of blood. It was too heartbreaking to bear. The *clunkety-clack* of the wheels changed rhythm and a jolt rumbled through the train as it gradually slowed down.

She burst into tears. This was no dream.

"CAN THIS THING GO any faster?" Harvey shouted from the edge of his seat. "Come on, let's go, let's go, *let's go!*"

Marty was already going over seventy miles per hour and the custom engine roared at its maximum capacity. Other trucks would've overheated and given up under these circumstances, but the Chevy, despite being roughened up on the exterior, performed like a champion as it sped up Highway 99 towards Kalama. Log trucks and families out for a relaxed drive honked and yelled at Marty as he wove through them as if they were standing still. He had never pushed his truck to this speed before and even he doubted its endurance.

"Where's the train?" Marty spat as he studied the tracks to the left. From what he pieced together, there wasn't a huge gap in time between Mildred being taken and when he arrived at the church. However, every second thrown away was a second when something horrific could happen to the girl who made him a better person. The image of the grumpy old man nagging him for the dings on his truck and Hattie's mother and cousins henpecking him for what they thought they knew made him bitter. The only person who helped him was Vidalia, oddly enough.

"Just follow the tracks, Marty! There'll be a way to get over soon, trust me!" Within the next mile, Harvey signaled for Marty to slow down to be able to cross the train tracks. When the turn came, Marty cut in front of a drive hauling cattle and almost drove into blackberry bushes.

"Slow down or we'll end up in the ditch!" Harvey yelped. He held the rifle with a death grip and kept his forearm against the headliner to keep from bashing his head against it. Marty only slowed down a degree, causing them to fly clean over the tracks and crash in the gravel on the opposite side. The truck growled, hungry for more, and when Marty navigated further beyond the tracks, the tires suddenly sunk into sand, a clear sign they were nearing the Columbia River.

"We must be close to where Mildred is," Harvey said quietly. "I feel it in my bones."

"Are you sure?" Marty, as confident as he was to navigate Seattle and the skies of the Pacific Northwest, had no grasp of where he was in Kalama. Mildred could be anywhere for all he knew.

Harvey pointed beyond his right. "See over there?"

When Marty squinted and looked through the dancing leaves of the trees, he could make out tan and brown tents along the river. The hair on his arms stood up. In one of those tents had to be Mildred.

FROM HER PLACE WITHIN the grubby tent, Mildred watched a gaggle of children from the hobo camp playing on the dock that bobbled over the river. Their clothes were dingy and tattered but that didn't keep them from carefree play.

"Whoever jumps the furthest is the winner!"

"You always win, Rudy!"

"And whoever makes the biggest splash wins!"

"*Rudy!*"

In the time since she was taken against her will, this was the first moment she felt somewhat safe. If children were having fun galloping around and jumping into the river, how horrible could her fate really be? Perhaps she'd end up a prisoner that would help the other hobo women make meals over fires or wash clothes in the river. If there were fish to be gutted and cleaned, nobody would know better than her. Then she imagined making an escape one dark night and running home to Bresford. Or better yet, she'd run into Marty's arms and never leave.

Rudy, a lanky boy about eleven with nut brown hair, sprinted barefoot down the makeshift dock. Before he climbed up the ladder to what appeared to be a lookout platform, he noticed Mildred in the tent, tied up and exhausted. Her spirit brightened at the thought of being set free by an innocent kid, who she hoped understood the difference between right and wrong. Instead, he continued his climb and at the top of the platform, Rudy executed a perfect cannonball jump that the other kids knew they couldn't beat. They tossed up their arms and grumbled in a chorus. Clearly, they were enjoying life despite the fact that their camp leader had a girl being held prisoner not more than thirty yards away.

When she was first taken off the train, Lee Carroll and his two men gingerly helped her out of the boxcar. Even the man with the throbbing ear was gentler in his manner. Her feet touched the ground and as they did, she felt the odd sensation of sand cascading into her shoes, filter through her stockings and between her toes. It had been ages since she played in the coarse sand along the Columbia River. Memories surfaced of her mother sketching nature scenes while Mildred built houses that were more or less lumpy mounds with doors made from the peeling white shells of butter clams. The shells also made excellent bowls and plates for the house she built for her doll. While her mother sketched, her father would fill a bucket with live butter for dinner. Grace would create a flavorful and creamy clam chowder that was perfect with a bit of crusty bread on a lazy Sunday afternoon.

"Hello, girly!" The sight and sound of Lee Carroll popping into the tent dashed her memories. Obviously there were no clocks hung up anywhere, but she guessed she'd been tied up in the tent for almost an hour.

"Why am I even here?" she asked. "Agnes paid off Dominic's debt and then paid for you to do away with me somehow. Wouldn't it have been easier to just take the money and not bother with getting my blood on your hands?"

Lee Carroll sat on a giant can of baked beans, casually lit a cigarette and took a few deep puffs to get it smoldering. "I may not live in a house or collect a paycheck anymore, but that doesn't mean I'm not a businessman. You were the result of a transaction, pure and simple. If I didn't follow through, it doesn't send a good message."

Outside, the children made hollering noises that sounded

like the cheers and whooping of cowboys and Indians, pretending to ride horses on the sand and down the dock in pursuit of each other. Mildred watched one of the children take an imaginary bullet in the chest and dramatically fall off the dock and into the water, then paddle out to rejoin the game.

"When are you going to kill me?" she asked, cringing.

Through a cloud of cigarette smoke, Lee Carroll just grinned. "That's a lovely dress. I heard the occasion was a wedding."

Mildred fought tears. "I was my best friend's maid of honor."

"There won't be much honor in what I'm going to do you tonight, I'll tell you that much." He winked at her, smashed the cigarette under his shoe and left the tent. Her stomach turned at the thought of being underneath Lee Carroll and feeling him grind his body against hers, taking in his unwashed scent and smoky breath.

The children ran by the tent and a few of the stragglers stopped on their invisible horses to look at Mildred, as if she was an animal in a cage. One girl remained as they others galloped off. She took the opportunity and said, "Can you come here and untie me, please? I need to get home." The girl backed away and looked behind her. "It's okay, I'm not going to tattle."

"Lee Carroll! The prisoner is talking to me!" She shook her head at Mildred before returning to the game with the other kids. It was clear that Mildred couldn't escape if she tried. While her hands were tied behind her back with rope, her ankles had been secured together. The extra rope had been tied around six mortared bricks when she got to the camp. If she was able to stand and hobble away, she'd have to drag the heavy bricks along with her, which would be impossible. When Lee Carroll stomped into the tent, he was fuming.

"Did you talk to the children?" he growled.

Her voice caught in her throat, afraid to answer him. "Yes, I did."

"Try that again and see what happens." In the distance, there was mechanical rumbling and men called out for Lee Carroll. He ducked out of the tent. "What the hell?"

Mildred heard it, too, and she tried to move around and see what was going on, but didn't get far with the bricks. The rumbling got louder, closer, until Mildred felt it in the ground.

"Marty?" It had to be him. His truck had a special motor and it sounded bigger than most trucks. Or perhaps she was fooling herself and it was just someone else from another hobo camp that Lee Carroll didn't recognize. Suddenly, Lee Carroll and his two men from the train rushed into her tent and grabbed her by the arms, dragging the row of bricks behind her.

"You think this is how to stay off my bad side? Who are they?" Lee Carroll shook her and gripped her arm so tight that she cried out. It all happened so fast that she didn't know where to look first. To her right, children stood wide-eyed, their jolly game interrupted. To her left, the women of the group, all in dirty cotton housedresses, looked at Mildred with unveiled contempt. Just a short walk in front of her was a beat up red Chevy with the motor still running.

"How did he they find us?" Lee Carroll growled at her. "Nobody knows where we are!"

"The other girl, Lee Carroll. Perhaps it was her?" offered one of the men.

Lee Carroll nodded slowly. "Ah, yes, York's daughter, the one who ran off crying. Now we'll have to go after them. So can anyone tell me what this truck is doing here?"

Mildred couldn't take her eyes off the Chevy, waiting for the driver and passenger to get out. It resembled Marty's truck, but it appeared to have been through a tornado made of pebbles and dirt because it definitely wasn't shiny and new. The driver's door finally opened and Marty stepped out wearing a suit and wielding a length of pipe.

"Marty!" Mildred screamed as she stood on her tiptoes. Upon seeing him, she was so happy that she could faint. Then passenger door opened and people shrieked when the barrel of a rifle popped out, followed by Harvey.

"Dad!" She had never been this thrilled to see her father before. Watching both of them advance with the rifle and pipe restored hope that she would actually escape. Her mind then wandered to the macabre side of the situation where they were either captured or killed and her knees buckled.

"Stand up, damn it!" Lee Carroll grumbled. "You better get a good look at these men because they won't be upright much longer."

She wailed. "Don't hurt them, please!" Lee Carroll whistled and three of his men, armed with bats, pipes and pistols, met Marty and Harvey. She shut her wet eyes and screamed when she heard a gunshot and two solid *thwacks* of cracking bone. People hollered and rushed to the fallen men, tending to the broken jaw of the one who got the end of Marty's pipe, the other covering his bleeding skull and crying for the third, dead from a bullet to the chest.

Mildred felt Lee Carroll's grip on her arm tighten and she stole a look at him. Veins popped out in his neck and his eyes fluttered with rage.

"Which one of you bastards is the Highway Shooter?" Harvey shouted. Like a wild man robbing a bank, Harvey pointed his rifle at the men, one by one, waiting to see the face of his wife's murderer.

"Dad! He's right here!" She didn't see Lee Carroll's fist fly straight at her mouth, stunned as she tasted blood on her tongue. She shrieked as the white-hot pain set in.

He held his fist in front of her face. "Be quiet or I'll thump you again so hard that your teeth will fall out!"

"Don't you dare hit my daughter!" Harvey pointed his gun at Lee Carroll's head.

"Mildred! We'll get you!" Marty said. His voice was calm and reassuring, but his eyes were ablaze with fury.

"I'd like to see them try," Lee Carroll grumbled. "You're coming with me."

"No, no, no!" she begged. There was nothing she could do as Lee Carroll and his men dragged her to the end of the dock. One of the men cut the rope and freed her wrists and ankles, but he tied the rope around one ankle, leaving her connected to the hefty bricks.

"Mildred!" Harvey screamed. He and Marty parted through the crowd with their weapons brandished and made their way onto the dock after them.

"You shoot me, she goes to the bottom," Lee Carroll said in a conversational tone and pointed to the bricks attached to her ankle. "You best be leaving before I have no choice but to kill you."

Time went fast and so slow, she couldn't describe the odd sensation of it. The ladder was easily fifty feet tall and she could barely breathe as she was forced to climb. Lee Carroll was behind her on the ladder with her bricks and pushed her onto the platform. At the top, she thought of what she needed to do instead of being led around like a sheep before the slaughter. At the top of the platform, the river below suddenly looked more like the ocean, the waves hungry and dark. The wind blew harder and whipped her dress around her legs. Everyone below was small, but she was able to watch as her father ran onto the beach to make his shot. Her heart thumped but she knew she had to do it now.

"He's the Highway Shooter!" she screamed, pointing her arm towards Lee Carroll, hoping her father could see her like a beacon. She watched the years of bottled fury spread across her father's face while he was quick to aim the rifle. She planned to drop onto her belly as soon as he fired to avoid being shot but she felt tugging on the rope around her ankle and looked at Lee Carroll. The bricks were high above his head.

"Have a nice swim, filly!" Lee Carroll laughed, about to toss the bricks over the side. From the beach below, a gunshot rang out and Lee Carroll roared as the bullet sliced a fiery trail through his body. Blood spewed from his chest and he stumbled. Mildred screamed and tried to move as he toppled towards her, dropping the bricks as he collapsed, dead. The bricks fell onto the platform and teetered dangerously on the edge. She was transfixed by the odd way the bricks leaned over the side, almost like a performer on a wire, and willed them to fall back onto the platform.

The bricks scraped noisily as they fell over the side, bringing the rope and Mildred with it. She tried to grasp for anything but she had already fallen halfway down from the top in mere seconds. With a grand splash, the icy water of the Columbia River swallowed her body. When the bricks landed gently on the bottom, she thrashed around as much as she could, struggled to swim upwards but was yanked back down by the rope. With chilled fingers, she tried to work on the knot at her ankle but it had become swollen in the water, impossible to undo.

The skirt of her dress floated about, as if she were an ethereal fairy in a dream. Her breath was tight in her lungs and air bubbled out of her mouth towards the surface. The urge to sleep became strong and she could no longer keep her breath locked up. As her eyes got heavier and heavier, more bubbles of precious air escaped from her lips. Thoughts of Grace came to her and how much she missed her mother over the years. If drowning meant seeing her mother again, she feared it less. She was at peace knowing that her father had come to her rescue.

And seeing Marty for the final time, knowing he still loved her, was the best thing she could've asked for before dying.

The last of her air escaped and water rushed in, choking her and filling her until there was no space left.

IF MILDRED HAD THE strength to keep her eyes open for just a few moments longer, she would've seen Marty swimming towards her. He fumbled with a knife and sawed through the rope attached to the bricks. With a boost off the bottom, Marty kicked with every shred of strength he could muster. His own lungs burned but he fought through it until he broke the surface of the river, greedily swallowing air. He thanked God when his feet landed on the sloped bank, holding Mildred out in front of him. Harvey, who was in the water to his knees, grabbed his daughter from Marty's hands and carried her to the shore. Gingerly, he laid her down and by the looks of her, he felt like he was losing Grace all over again.

"Mildred, it's me! Wake up, please wake up!" Harvey sobbed as he knelt by her side. "Oh God, her lips are turning blue!" He touched her cold mouth and sobbed even harder. Marty swooped in over her body and gently tipped her to the side. Only a little water trickled from her mouth, but she didn't revive.

"Please don't let her die!" Harvey clamped his hands over his head and continued to sob. Firmly, Marty pinched Mildred's nose and placed his lips over her blue ones and breathed into her, once, twice, three times.

There was nothing. He swore her lips turned bluer.

Frantic, Marty couldn't see or hear her breathe and felt fear bubbling up. He bent down once more and breathed into her the same way, patient and steady. He willed his life into her, the precious air he took for granted too often.

Her chest rose, but barely.

Finally, she stirred, fluttered her closed lids, and then grimaced, as if she was about to be violently ill. Mildred was suddenly rocked with convulsions as the water cascaded down her chin in frothy waves. Raggedly, she sputtered and coughed until she expelled it all. Her breathing was haggard and shallow at first, but then it became smoother, calmer. When she breathed without difficulty, Marty sat her up and watched her slowly open her eyes.

"Thank God!" Harvey shouted, practically jumping as he let tears wet his face.

"Mildred, are you alright?" Marty asked. Slowly, her eyes found his and she nodded weakly. Even though the rescue tired his arms, it didn't bother him when he scooped Mildred up and carted her back to the truck. Harvey followed, but not without grabbing his rifle and glancing back at the hobo camp. After he shot and killed Lee Carroll, nobody wanted to be next.

In the truck, Harvey wrapped his jacket around Mildred and couldn't stop smiling. They drove out of the hobo camp and headed back to Bresford at an easy pace this time. Exhausted, Mildred leaned her damp head on Marty's shoulder and sighed.

"I never thought I'd see you again." Her voice cracked.

"Let's get you home," Marty said softly. He placed a kiss on her forehead, her favorite kind. She had been kidnapped and almost died in the river, but Mildred had never been happier in her whole life as she was at that very moment next to Marty. Everything she had experienced in the last few months, the dancing, champagne and seeing more of the world, none of it compared to simply being with him. That was all she really wanted in the end. Weakly, she rested her head on his shoulder and fell into a dreamless sleep.

THE SUMMER DANCE
August 1932

THE MANCHESTER FAIRGROUNDS HAD been magically transformed into a fairyland with strings of electric lights, torches and candles in used canning jars. The decadent smells of chicken and pork ribs roasting over several barbecues filled the summer air and a local farmer brought in a truckload of the juiciest watermelon.

The new president of the Bresford Ladies Aid Society, Ellie Johnson, led with a gentle authority. Vidalia had been nominated and elected as the vice president, a role that she put everything into. Her father no longer owned Dominic's but she was happy to see it under new ownership. Currently, Dominic York resided in the state penitentiary for arranging Grace Westrick's murder and attempting the same end for Mildred.

Darnella Riley-Westrick wasn't even a member of the Bresford Ladies Aid Society anymore. It didn't take long for Harvey's blinders to come off and realize what Darnella had done to him, to his daughter, all for the sake of pleasing Dominic and Vidalia in the war to win Marty. She put up quite a fight trying to change Harvey's mind, promising that she'd change her ways, apologizing up and down to him for offenses real and fabricated, anything to get him to let her stay. For the first time in almost six years, he told her "no." Later that evening, Darnella came into the living room with several suitcases, hat boxes, and her daughter, to announce that they were moving back to her mother's house in Seattle. Always the gentleman, Harvey helped her load up the car, which he let her keep. He knew that he would see her again, only to get her second divorce and his first underway. When she turned off Juniper Street and the taillights disappeared, Harvey let out a heavy sigh and suddenly he needed a nap.

Up north in Seattle, Gerald Townsend finally took the time to go over his books with an accountant. When the accountant confirmed that Agnes had stolen excessive amounts of money from Townsend Timber, Gerald slammed his fist on the desk so hard that the accountant jumped out of his chair. His son had been right all along and they reconciled over brandy. As for Agnes, the law wasn't kind to her. In addition to the forgery and embezzling she was accused of, her involvement with trying to have both Marty and Mildred murdered fell down on her like a building. Needless to say, Townsend Timber severed its merger with Crane Development. Gerald and Jeanette eventually softened towards Mildred after learning to appreciate the fact that she wasn't like the other girls. Mildred impressed Gerald after one afternoon of logging with his crew, where she got dirty, scraped up and didn't complain once. Whenever she was in Seattle, Mildred's time was the source of many small battles between Marty and his mother. Out of all her socialite connections, Jeanette found her new friend in Mildred and wanted to take her shopping as often as Marty could part with her.

Married a little over a month ago, Leland and Hattie Burris spent a week at the Townsend lake house for their honeymoon. While it wasn't the European trip that Hattie always dreamed of, they couldn't deny that their honeymoon was incredible. Marty even arranged for a boat to take them around the Puget Sound for a whole afternoon with a romantic lunch stop in Friday Harbor. When Mildred was home recuperating after nearly drowning, Hattie was the first to rush in to her house and collapse at her side in tears. She took Mildred's hand in her own and kissed it, then presented the bridal bouquet she saved just for her. Now that the wedding was over, all Hattie could talk about was the baby she and Leland were trying for.

A week ago, Mildred received a letter in the mail that had been forwarded to her from Sarah Fryar. Her pregnancy was a good one and she felt healthy again. Leo was putting weight back on and taking school lessons at home when they weren't doing chores around the dairy farm. She mentioned that Marty reached out to her and explained what happened between him and Randall at the hangar. When Mildred first heard about the plane explosion and the plan for Marty to go up in flames with it, she almost felt the need to run to the bathroom to vomit. The very thought of losing Marty again was too much. The beating Marty gave Randall must've lodged some sense into him because he sought help for his anger and drinking. He left the Elliott Bay shantytown and lived with several people trying to improve their situations, from what he wrote to Sarah. She wasn't sure if she'd return to her husband ever again but knowing he was making strides was better than nothing. At the moment, she thoroughly enjoyed working on her sister's farm in Tillamook, especially taking care of the cows and their calves. Mildred laughed when Sarah revealed that she had the honor of naming a calf shortly after she was born, which Sarah promptly called

"Mildred."

The evening was still young and families started showing up in waves and settling in at tables. Ellie gently delegated people around the fairgrounds for last minute set up here and there but in general, her first major event was off to a grand start.

"The band is here!" she squealed when the bluegrass quartet she hired made its way to the stage. It didn't take them long to get warmed up, perfectly tuned and playing music. Several children danced the way children do at gatherings and at the end of each song, girls curtsied and boys took their bows.

Harvey and Mildred rode over to the fairgrounds together. She couldn't be more pleased to have her father back, to have real talks about Grace and anything else that they could think of. Marty was also a hero in Harvey's book and he could do no wrong.

"You look beautiful, just like your mother."

"Thank you, Dad." Harvey kissed her cheek and left to speak with the group of men milling about the baked goods table, which left her to wander around alone for a little while. Tonight, she wore a dress that Jeanette bought her at Evette's a few weeks ago. It was made of peach chiffon that came to her knees and silver sequins adorned the fabric in a cascading pattern that reminded her of stars scattered across the sky. Jeanette also bought her peach shoes to match, despite Mildred's protests that it was too generous. It fell on deaf ears as Jeanette got the shoes and even a matching hat to complete the outfit.

"Good evening, Mildred." When Mildred turned, she smiled at the sight of Vidalia, whom she was pleased to call a dear friend now. Instead of being overly glamorous, Vidalia learned to go for softer looks. She wore a dress of white and sky blue plaid with navy pumps. Mildred still thought she looked incredible, whether she wore that dress or even a potato sack.

"How are you tonight, Vidalia?" she asked earnestly. When Mildred was ready for visitors at home, Vidalia was next in line after Hattie. Each day, she came by with something: a casserole she baked, new stationery and Belgian chocolates from the inventory at Dominic's, or a hat she thought would look better on Mildred than it did on her. One time, Vidalia brought a chocolate silk pie that she had Doris Williams make. When they both stared at the pie and then at each other, they laughed until their voices grew hoarse.

"I'm exceedingly well, especially since I brought my beau. Jack, could you come over here?" A handsome man about their age eyeing a tray of cookies turned around and beamed when Vidalia called his name. "Jack, this is my dear friend, Mildred. Mildred, this is Jack! He is new to Bresford and works at the auto garage nearby."

"How do you do, Mildred?" He jutted his hand out and shook hers firmly, not seeming to be embarrassed by the grease stuck under his fingernails from working on engines.

"Fine, thank you. Welcome to Bresford."

Vidalia cocked her pretty head. "When is Marty coming in?" When she said his name, there was no trace of jealousy or awkwardness.

"I hope he shows up soon. I'm itching to dance." She realized sadly that she hadn't danced with him since their special evening at The Slaughterhouse.

Jack twirled Vidalia. "Speaking of dancing, I'm going to take this little lady out on the floor. It was wonderful to meet you, Miss Mildred." She waved playfully as they joined the other couples that filled the dance floor. The infectious rhythm from the guitar, mandolin, violin and banjo made her foot tap in time and soon she was swaying where she stood.

"You look like you need someone to dance with."

"Marty!" She wrapped her arms around his neck and kissed

him deeply. There was no time wasted as she dragged him to the floor and became one of many dancing couples. For the next few songs, they didn't speak, just danced with big, foolish smiles. The next song was a slower one, a song about love lost and found.

"Remember when you mentioned the summer dance in one of your letters?" Marty asked her.

"I did?" Mildred laughed. "To be honest, I don't remember much of what I wrote in those letters and I try not to remember."

He chuckled. "You said that the summer dance is better than the Fourth of July and Christmas combined. And you always signed 'Sincerely, Mildred' at the end of each one."

She playfully grimaced as he paraphrased parts of what she wrote back to her. "Maybe you should burn the letters. I'm not the same girl who wrote them, far from it. Because of you, I actually experienced things that I never would have before. I can't even imagine going back to where I started."

He kissed her forehead and let his lips linger for a few moments more. "You may not be as afraid of the world as you once were, but you'll always be my sweet Mildred." Marty twirled her a few times until she giggled from dizziness. As the day slipped into the cool of the night, they felt like the only two people in the world. There were others dancing, too, but they didn't notice them and even the music itself seemed to fade away. Gently, he pulled her close to his chest, the place where they both knew she belonged.

The Real Mildred

Sincerely, Mildred came into being in 2009 when I wandered into an antique store in Kalama. I rummaged through old studio portraits and saw one of a plain-looking girl and at the bottom, she had signed "Sincerely, Mildred." Immediately, I thought of what her story was, who she gave her photograph to. That night, I came up with the premise of the story: Mildred is a cannery girl who falls in love with a pilot named Marty. I told my mother the idea and she loved it. After my mother passed away in June 2010, I struggled to even attempt writing for years. It was simply too painful. My sweet husband encouraged me for years to start writing again and I would tell him why I couldn't. Finally, he won and I wrote this book for the next eighteen months, completing it in September 2017 and then revising it for the next few months. You are now holding my most prized project that was meant for my mother to read first. I know now that she wouldn't have wanted me to stop just because she isn't here anymore. This is for my mother, my husband, for my readers, and the real Mildred.

About the Author

Ashley Hayden was born and raised in the Columbia River Valley region in Washington State. She and her husband live on a family farm along the Lewis River with their two mini Aussies. They love to camp in Leavenworth, Washington, the Bavarian-themed town they were married in, as well as spend lazy weekends in Cannon Beach, Oregon. In July 2014, Redbook published Ashley's winning story about the challenges she and her husband faced to get married because of his epilepsy. Ashley is inspired by authors Kathryn Stockett, Geraldine Brooks and Sue Monk Kidd.

93106833R00236

Made in the USA
Columbia, SC
05 April 2018